Intensive Scare Unit

High Hope Farm

Training-Boarding
Equitation

J. S. Borthwick

St. Martin's Paperbacks

Note: Bowmouth College, the town of Bowmouth, the Mary Starbox Memorial Hospital, and the untoward events occurring in these places as well as the persons described therein are entirely fictitious.

INTENSIVE SCARE UNIT

Copyright © 2004 by J. S. Borthwick.

Library of Congress Catalog Card Number: 2003058636

ISBN: 0-312-99552-0
EAN: 80312-99552-2

Printed in the United States of America

St. Martin's Press hardcover edition / February 2004
St. Martin's Paperbacks edition / February 2005

St. Martin's Paperbacks are published by St. Martin's Press, 175 Fifth Avenue, New York, NY 10010.

10 9 8 7 6 5 4 3 2 1

This is for Lois Mills and Joanna Jordan (listed by age) or Joanna Jordan and Lois Mills (listed alphabetically) with love from their outlaw relative, J. S.

Cast of Principal Characters

GENERAL

SARAH DOUGLAS DEANE—Assistant professor of English, Bowmouth College, niece of Julia Clancy

JULIA CLANCY—Owner of High Hope Farm; aunt of Sarah

ALEX MCKENZIE—Physician at Mary Starbox Memorial Hospital, husband of Sarah

PATRICK O'REILLY—Farm manager of High Hope Farm

MRS. ANTHONY DOUGLAS—Mother of Julia, grandmother of Sarah

HOPKINS—Faithful housekeeper to Mrs. Douglas

EMMA LITTLEFIELD—Frequent patient to the ER of Mary Starbox Memorial Hospital

FLORENCE LITTLEFIELD—Sister of Emma

HOSPITAL STAFF

DR. JONATHAN PHILIPS—CEO Mary Starbox Memorial Hospital

DR. EUGENE SANTARO—Cardiologist

DR. MARGIE SOLDIER—Pathologist

HANNAH FINCH—RN

CLAIRE MITCHNER—RN

JERI SCHMIDT—RN; cardiac rehab supervisor

THE REVEREND JOSHUA STEVENSON—Hospital chaplain; rector of St. Paul's-by-the-Sea Episcopal Church

DAVID BERGMAN—Hospital volunteer

STELLA DUGAN—Hospital volunteer

CHRISTIE RIVERS—Hospital volunteer

CARMEN WILSON—Secretary to Dr. Philips

OFFICIALS
JOHNNY CUSZAK—State pathologist
GEORGE FITTS—Sergeant, Maine State Police CID
MIKE LĄAKA—Sheriff's deputy investigator
KATIE WATERS—Deputy sheriff

High Hope Farm

Training-Boarding
Equitation

HEART: 1. The muscular chambered organ that pumps blood from veins into arteries, and thus, in healthy persons, keeps up a flow of blood through the entire circulatory system. 2. The source of one's sensibilities, emotions, and very being. 3. The home of one's deepest and sincerest beliefs. 4. The center of imagination and intellect. 5. the center from which flow moods and inclinations. 6. The wellspring of courage, generosity, and sympathy. SEE ALSO: Heart-ache, Heart-felt, Heart survery.

1

JULIA Clancy was feeling a little on the wobbly side. Not sick, mind you. Nothing unusual for an old bat of seventy-one. I mean, what did she expect? To be able to leap out of bed, hit the floor running, gulp down breakfast, and make it down to the barn by seven at the latest. But climbing out of bed, getting dressed for the day—work boots, khaki trousers, worn cotton shirt—had been turning lately into something of a chore. Get a grip, she told herself, because she had to go down to the barn to help in the feeding and watering twenty-four horses that made up the major part of the population of High Hope Farm.

She looked at her bedside clock. Twenty to eight. Disgraceful. Friday, and so much to do. She heaved herself out of bed and, stumbling over the uneven pine-board floor, barely made it into the bathroom. In this trip she was followed, as always, by her tail-wagging English setters, Tucker and Belle, one of whom had spent the night across the foot of her bed, the other underneath. But even with the shower at full blast—hot and then cold—her exercises—the ritual bending of creaking knees, the rotating of neck and shoulders—did not rouse a spark of vitality. With a major effort she dragged on her clothes, laced her boots, and then, going to the sink to brush her teeth, comb her hair, she found herself staring into the mirror at this old crone, this wrinkled, weathered face of someone's grandmother—which she wasn't unless you counted the dogs and horses. She frowned at the reflection, the dark eyebrows, eyes underlined by shadows, a tight mouth, gray hair the consistency of Brillo. The whole image that reminded certain friends given to frankness of one of those small rough-coated dogs, a terrier, perhaps.

The trouble was that right now she didn't feel in the least like a terrier. For a few minutes she tried to conjure up exactly what kind of dog she did resemble and came to the unhappy conclusion that she felt remarkably un-dog-like. More like a worn-out pack mule. Or how about a lizard? A sloth? The trouble was August. This year, August had been hot and dry, filled with bugs, a variety of biting flies, and broken at intervals by sudden short thunderstorms that did nothing to alleviate the dry cracked fields and pastures.

In this depressed frame of mind, Julia descended the stairs of the old farmhouse and by the time she'd reached the kitchen and put on the teakettle and an egg to boil, she had decided to take steps. Not to the doctor. That would be a drastic move, particularly since her doctor was one Alex McKenzie, the husband of her niece Sarah, and Julia certainly didn't want any temporary infirmity of hers to be chatted up in family circles. Yes, she knew all that talk about the sacrosanct nature of doctor and patient, but she didn't trust her nosy niece not to screw some fragment of information out of Alex.

No, there was something else she had had in mind for some time. She would make a visit to one of those health-food shops that sold thousands of vitamins and herbal remedies. What she needed, she decided, sawing away with a bread knife on a hard loaf of Italian bread, was a jump-start. It would be like pouring high-octane gas into an ancient engine. Give the engine a boost. There would be someone in the shop who would lead her to a magic mix of potions and pills. She ran through a few names she had heard talked about, names like niacin, fish oil, flaxseed, calcium, some multivitamin for the senior citizen, a tablet to lubricate the joints. It just took a little research.

This plan so energized Julia that after a gulp of orange juice and a few bites of her boiled egg, cradling her mug of tea, she walked with almost a sprightly step down the sloping path to her large lower barn, home to most of the farm's equine inhabitants. Arriving at the open door to the stable aisle and feeling that she must exert her managerial powers, she proceeded for the next hour to hector her stable manager, Patrick O'Reilly. This she did, forcing herself to move briskly about while lecturing on subjects as various as the application of poultices, the mixing of hoof-strengthening preparations, and the management of a tendon problem in her regular riding companion, a sixteen-hand bay gelding named Duffie.

Patrick, dressed as usual in a worn blue denim shirt, leather puttees around his legs, his feet encased in tough boots, his square face lined and reddened with wind and age, went about his business, running his hands down this horse's withers, that horse's shoulders and hooves, administrating medications and supplements, nodding when now and then Julia made a particularly emphatic point. Patrick, gray in the service of High Hope Farm and Julia Clancy, keeping his natural Irish dander in hand, had long ago learned to close his ears and get on with his work exactly as he had planned.

But toward the beginning of the second hour Julia found that it was a lot easier to issue orders to Patrick from a sitting position on a bale of hay. Moreover, she found a strange sense of relief in knowing that Duffie's tendonitis would not allow him to be ridden for some time to come. And looking out of the barn door to the path that rose uphill to the farmhouse door, she thought that it looked steeper, farther away than usual.

It was all, she decided, due to having bolted her breakfast because she was late getting up that morning. Now she would go and have a second cup of tea and make some toast. Or oatmeal. Oatmeal was always good for what ailed one. In the words of her ninety-year-old mother, Mrs. Anthony Douglas, oatmeal stood by you. Julia pushed herself into a standing position, reached over to pat the neck of a chestnut mare on crossties who was being brushed by Patrick, and suddenly felt the barn floor heaving ever so slightly, rather like the deck of a ship at sea.

Alarmed, Patrick reached for her arm. "Hey, Mrs. Clancy. Steady, there. Are you all right? You look pale. Shall I walk you back to the house now?"

Julia drew up her five-foot-three self, braced her shoulders, said, "Nonsense, Patrick," in a loud voice and with a firm step marched out of the barn and started up the drive toward the house. Midway up the rising path, bothered by a certain breathlessness becoming second by second more noticeable, she slowed her steps, hoping Patrick wasn't looking. This unpleasant feeling was familiar; she'd experienced it off and on during the past two or three weeks, but now it seemed more assertive. She came to a halt and at the same time became aware that a disagreeable, almost painful, sensation was rising from below her throat, crawling around her neck, her jaw, and, strangely, heading for her ear. I'll take some Tylenol, she thought. Then look into those vitamins. The health-food store. And maybe I'll start . . .

But she never pictured a third remedy. The gravel path rose to meet her and she fell forward, only just managing at the last second to fling out an arm and save herself from a broken nose.

The next thing Julia was aware of was her setter, Tucker, licking her face and Patrick kneeling beside her, a portable phone in one hand. He seemed, she thought in a confused way, to be calling 911 and in an urgent voice asking for the rescue squad.

"No," called Julia, her own voice sounding to her far away, as if it came from a cavern. "Don't call, I'm fine. Just weak. No breakfast. Let me lie here for just a minute. Patrick, you go back to the barn."

But Patrick, always stubborn when such was called for, began giving directions to the farm, describing what had happened. "Mrs. Clancy, she went down just like that. No, she's conscious, she's ordering me not to call but I'm doing it anyway."

All I need, Julia thought crossly to herself as she let her head loll against her bare arm, the arm resting uncomfortably on the

4

sharp stones of the drive, is to be let alone. Nothing wrong. Tom will come and find me and then everything . . . but Tom, oh, yes, Tom Clancy, he'd been dead so long that he wouldn't be coming from so far away and she'd better stay right where she was. Husband Tom, my God, Julia thought, he was another stubborn Irishman, more so than Patrick, and that was going some. Then, slowly, some of the fog cleared, and she thought again, I should eat something. She raised her arm and fumbled in her pocket and came up with a mint lozenge that had been gathering dust in her pocket. Raising her head, she stuffed the mint into her mouth and crunched down. Then, this effort being almost too demanding, she sank back on the ground.

Patrick, alarmed at this action and apparently struck with the idea that Julia might be taking some sort of fatal drug, reached for her arm and found his hand shoved away.

"It's only a mint," she told him in a hoarse voice. "So go away and cancel the rescue squad and start getting the horses out to pasture. That's an order, Patrick. I'm perfectly fine. A little rest, that's what I need. It's one of those little spells you can have when you miss a proper breakfast." But the idea of breakfast, which a few minutes ago had seemed the answer to her discomfort, now, along with the partially chewed mint, caused a cold sweat and rising nausea. And that weird ache along her jaw was back again.

Of course, she knew what had happened. She remembered now. She'd fallen. On the path. On her way up to the house. Probably tripped on something. A stone. One of those cracked places. She would have to have the whole surface redone in the spring. So, she'd gone right down and hit her chest on the hard ground. And her shoulder. Her jaw. No wonder she felt awful. All right, she told herself angrily, get up, get going. You've fallen before. Lots of times, usually off a horse. There was that time last year in New Hampshire when Duffie had refused the in-and-out and over she went. Just like now. Well, it was stupid to be lying here. Falling off a horse was certainly a more serious event than tripping in one's own pathway. Perhaps she should wear her glasses, even going down to the barn. Or up from the barn. Or . . . Oh, damnation! She couldn't think straight. The discomfort, now it was a pain. A genuine pain. She closed her eyes and felt herself sliding down a slope toward a vast dark hole where everything hurt.

The next few minutes were for Julia a series of scrambled events. Somehow Patrick had covered her with a horse blanket. And then the ambulance, a large white box of a vehicle with lights blinking, appeared from nowhere at the top of her driveway. Now someone was talking about oxygen and pushing plastic tubing into her nostrils, hooking the ends over her ears. Then her shirt was opened and patches of something were being stuck all over her chest and shoulders, plastic lines were snapped onto the patches, then a voice said something about coming in right away to someone else somewhere. And then the hand shoved a little round pill under her tongue and a voice ordered her to hold the pill there and let it dissolve. And before she could pull herself together and object to these liberties, she was bundled up like a package ready for parcel post, slid onto a stretcher, had three little orange aspirins poked in her mouth, was ordered to "chew," and was then hoisted into the interior of the vehicle, and they were off.

Just like the movies, Julia thought in a muddled way. Or one of those ER real-time series. But those you watched in the comfort of your living room; now she was the feature attraction riding facing backward so she could see from her head's elevated position on the pillow the back window of the ambulance and there was Route 17 unwinding behind her. But the pills must be doing their work; she felt relaxed. Light in the head, but relaxed. Nothing much mattered, did it? Up and away. Tallyho and View Halloo. Galloping, galloping over the rainbow. No, that was something else. Judy Garland and Toto. Julia had seen the movie twice. All those Munchkins and Bert Lahr in a fake lion suit. She closed her eyes and was about to float into space when the blood-pressure cuff around her arm suddenly blew itself up tight around her arm and then slowly expelled its air.

She took a shallow breath and to clear her head tried to focus on the blurry road disappearing behind her. When she got wherever she was going, which was undoubtedly the hospital, she'd pull herself together and go home. Assert herself. And give Patrick a piece of her mind, calling the ambulance when all she'd done was to have a little "incident." A bit of discomfort and faintness. A senior moment, they called it. Or was that forgetting things? And she had so much to do that morning. A delivery of hay, shavings to pick up, and Angelina about to foal. There was no time to go rushing off to an emergency room. And she certainly hoped she hadn't given one of these first-aid people— EMT's they called them—Alex's name. That's all she needed, Alex and Sarah getting into a tizzy over nothing. Alex being bossy and ordering a million tests. Keeping her overnight. Sarah hovering, talking about taking it easy, reminding her that now she was over seventy.

"Hogwash!" she said loudly, and the man fussing with the blood-pressure cuff gave a jump of surprise.

Sarah Deane, niece of Julia Clancy, unaware that anything was amiss, had by coincidence decided to drop in and take her aunt out for lunch. Sarah had just come from a two-week vacation on Weymouth Island with her husband, Alex. Labor Day stood on the horizon, and Sarah had settled into the business of getting ready for her Bowmouth College's fall English classes: checking on book orders and putting her office into some sort of order. The office was the size of a broom closet, and she was being threatened with an office mate, since, in the words of the department chair, Professor Ellis Humber, ". . . women like to work together." This, Sarah told herself, must not be allowed to happen. Even a newly anointed Ph.D. had a few basic rights, and one was a minimum amount of elbow room. Besides, the female she was threatened with was one Vera Pruczak, from the Drama Department. Good-hearted, but something of a wild woman who shed bits of scripts and reminder notes in every direction. Vera was certainly not someone to share a closet with. Sarah herself was scattered in her habits; two scattered females in a small space were unthinkable.

Therefore, to bolster her courage in confronting her department chairman, a good lunch was needed. With Aunt Julia. First a walk around the farm to admire any new equine additions. Hear about the mare about to foal, listen with sympathy to complaints about hay delivery, the price of fly spray, and the pigheadedness of Patrick. Sarah had heard from the local grapevine, someone who had bumped into her a few days ago at the supermarket, that her aunt had looked a little pale lately. Seemed rather slow in moving. This description of a woman who by late August was very tan—riding outside ensured a bronzed complexion—and one who usually moved with ferocious energy, was faintly alarming.

She looked at her watch. Almost eleven. Plenty of time for a leisurely tour and a covert assessment of Julia's health. Leaving her Irish wolfhound, Patsy, at home with his Kong toy filled with peanut butter, she put on fresh cotton slacks and a blue-and-white-striped shirt, then climbed into her old red Subaru wagon, swung out of Sawmill Road and headed for Julia's High Hope Farm.

Pulling into the lower entrance, Sarah parked by the indoor riding arena. Julia's Ford truck was parked next to the wide side door. Conclusion: Julia was inside giving a lesson. This seemed confirmed by a strange Volvo parked by the line of horse trailers. But entering the riding arena, Sarah was met by a small girl in jodhpurs and helmet and an obviously irritated mother. "Where," demanded the mother, "is Mrs. Clancy? Heather had a lesson at eleven and it's fifteen after. We haven't got all day. Have we, Heather?" To which Heather lowered her eyes and mumbled something that might have been a negative.

Sarah bit her lip, reminded herself that the customer is always right, and promised to find her aunt. "Perhaps an emergency," she suggested. "One of the horses. Colic. It can come on suddenly."

But a search of the upper stable area, the paddocks, the farm-house itself, and the lower fields yielded no one but a student helper mending fences on the cross-country course. This person, one Megan, said it was funny, but no one seemed to be around. Not even Patrick. His car was gone. But Rafe Posner was around, so try him.

Rafe Posner, the assistant stable manager, was discovered out in a far pasture trying to corner the pony Gingersnap. They made a contrast: Rafe thin as a pencil in his loose khakis, his almost-white hair tied in a neat braid down his back, and Gingersnap, a round little rust-colored Shetland, dancing just out of reach.

"Farrier's coming this afternoon," said Rafe, leaping at the pony, grasping Gingersnap by the mane, and slipping a halter over her head. "She's due for a trim, the little devil."

"Aunt Julia," said Sarah, getting to the point. "I can't find her anywhere, and there's a girl named Heather waiting for a lesson."

Rafe shrugged. "I got here an hour ago. No Mrs. Clancy. And no Patrick."

"But Aunt Julia's car is still here."

"So maybe they went off together. Patrick has been wanting her to look at that eight-year-old gelding the Meyersons have. Maybe she forgot the lesson."

"Julia keeps very close tabs on her lessons," said Sarah. "They're her bread and butter."

"Tell you what," said Rafe. "I'll saddle up Gingersnap. I've been giving some of the beginner lessons for Mrs. Clancy, so I might as well take on this Heather kid."

Sarah nodded and turned back toward the farmhouse. Visions of Julia fallen in one of the far pastures began to form in her head. Maybe she'd stubbed her foot, hit her head on a stone. Julia's arthritis could make her stiff and unsure on rough ground. Then, as Sarah reached the gate leading to the first pasture, a black pickup truck spun into the driveway and slammed to a stop. Jane Zimmer, a neighbor of Julia's from nearby Appleyard Farm, was a no-nonsense woman not usually given to automotive excesses.

"Sarah," shouted Jane, "I'm so glad. I've been keeping an eye out for the family. Or Patrick. What's happened?"

Sarah stared. "What do you mean, what's happened?"

"The ambulance. I saw it turn in here around ten this morning. I couldn't come over because the vet was at my place, but I phoned. No answer. All I saw was the Union ambulance come in. I was too far away to tell if they loaded anyone in it. I guessed someone fell off a horse and broke something. Anyway, the ambulance took off at top speed, with Patrick right behind it driving like a bat out of hell."

Sarah didn't wait. Shouting thanks to Jane, she ran to her car, accelerated up the driveway and sped down the road, straight for the town of Bowmouth, Bowmouth College, and the Mary Starbox Memorial Hospital, which occupied the north end of the campus. Horses, horses, she said to herself. Beautiful, graceful, marvelous animals. But sometimes absolutely treacherous. Riding rated up there with motorcycle racing and downhill snowboarding as activities hazardous to your health. It could either be a student tossed to the ground or an injured Aunt Julia. And the idea of five-foot-three Julia falling off that big Duffie was truly frightening. Women of Julia's age, never mind how active and how many calcium tablets they took every day, were likely to have osteoporosis, and if bounced onto the hard ground were apt to crack half the bones in their bodies. Any other possibilities Sarah didn't consider. Alex was her aunt's doctor, gave her a yearly physical, and Julia had never mentioned any serious problems. If there had been, surely Julia would have shared the news; after all, she and Alex were family, weren't they? They did holidays and took trips together. Julia and her long-dead husband, Tom Clancy, had had no children, but a stableful of horses and a clutch of relatives had filled that gap very nicely.

Anyway, Sarah reasoned, as she swung her car into the emergency room parking lot, whatever had happened, to Julia, or to a riding student, it must be horse-connected.

The emergency room was filled to capacity. A veritable mob. When, what seemed hours later, Sarah made it to the information desk, she gave the woman what she considered the one identifying feature of what must be an accident. Who, she asked of the woman—a person obviously stressed by the crowd milling about the waiting room—had been brought into the ER because of a riding accident? This question producing no answer, Sarah pronounced the name, Clancy. Julia Clancy. "She's my aunt."

This information initiated a shuffling of papers interrupted by three telephone calls, much tapping of the computer keyboard, and finally a report that a Julia Clancy could be found in the

Cardiac Examining Unit, that the facility was down through the ER waiting room, out into the hall and to the left.

"Cardiac!" sputtered Sarah. "There must be a mistake. There's nothing wrong with Aunt Julia's heart. But maybe she broke something falling off her horse."

"She is not with orthopedics," said the woman, who was obviously trying to rid herself of Sarah and deal with the next person in line, a man pressing a folded towel over his ear.

"Does my husband know?" Sarah demanded. "Alex McKenzie. He's her doctor."

The woman reexamined the piece of paper. The patient had not claimed a primary-care physician or a cardiologist. Nor any family. So Dr. Rackliff was in charge. At which the woman turned to deal with the man with the ear.

Trying to move fast, Sarah wove her way with difficulty through the crowded ER waiting room. Every chair was filled with the usual depressed collection of family and friends shuffling through dog-eared magazines while at the edges of the walls it was standing room only, with traffic further impeded by yet another arriving family group. Finally free, she got to the hall, turned left as directed and then skidded to a halt. Before she found herself trapped in another waiting area, she had to hunt for someone who knew something. A nurse, a doctor, intern, a physician's assistant. Find out what in hell was going on. And find Patrick, because where was he? Jane said that he had followed the ambulance.

And after a false start or two, nurses in patterned colored and flowered smocks being indistinguishable from volunteer ladies bringing messages, flowers, or pushing wheelchairs, Sarah got an answer. Mrs. Clancy was under observation. Turn to the right, and she'd find Station 6. Cardiac Examining Unit. They were doing another EKG. Dr. Rackliff was with her now. Evaluating her. One of the hospital's cardiologists had been paged. Yes, she could go in and sit quietly. Mrs. Clancy was upset, being a little difficult, and they didn't want her to become excited.

From which description Sarah knew she had tracked down the right Mrs. Clancy. She turned and, following a gurney on which reclined a blanket-covered patient, she made for Station 6. This area turned out to be a wilderness of sheeted alcoves, each apparently occupied by someone in a questionable condition. Hesitating, finding no desk in the vicinity to approach, no nurse or physician-looking person (the stethoscope around the neck appeared to be a possible identifying mark), she peered in at one bedded person, rejected him, and then felt her shoulder taken in a strong grip. Patrick.

"Sarah, thank the Lord. I tried to call you but no answer. It's Mrs. Clancy. They're going over her now. Another EKG and God knows what all. And where in thunder I'm wanting to know is your Alex?"

"I'd like to know too," said Sarah. "But first I'll go in and see her."

"Wait till they finish with this business. All hooked up to a million machines she is and mad as a wet hen. Told them she hadn't a doctor, nor yet a family, as if she was some kind of bag lady off the streets. Doesn't want Alex, nor you yourself, to know there's anything wrong with her. Tried to make me swear not to say a word. Claims it wasn't an attack, but because she forgot to have a good breakfast."

"But what *is* going on?" Sarah demanded. "I mean, is this serious? Aunt Julia never had anything wrong with her heart, did she?"

"Well, if she did, she kept it to herself. But now it'll all be coming out in the wash. After they'd got her settled down, they let me go in and see her and she's denying there's anything wrong with her at all. Stubborn old coot that she is." Here Patrick's voice trembled and Sarah thought she saw a tear welling up in one eye. Patrick had been part of Julia's farm family for over forty years.

"Okay, Patrick. You and I know that Julia can be impossible. I'll find out what's going on and see if someone can page Alex. I'm sure he's in the hospital somewhere. No office hours until this afternoon. Then I'll force myself in on Julia whether she likes it or not."

* * *

Aunt Julia, the head of her bed elevated, attached to a number of leads, wires, tubes, and IV drips, not to mention an automatic blood-pressure machine and other assorted monitors, was trying to take charge. Her steel-gray hair was wild, her glasses askew on her nose, part of one earpiece being caught under the tube delivering oxygen to her nostrils. With one hand she clutched a cotton blanket to her chest, apparently with the intention of concealing her body in its drooping johnny from public view. To one side, checking an overhead monitor, stood a thin nurse dressed in a smock featuring seagulls in flight. She had a sharp-pointed nose and dark hair cut in a businesslike chop. But Julia was not paying attention to the watching nurse because she had just had a view through the partially opened curtain of what was quite possibly a corpse being wheeled by. Everything about the brief appearance proclaimed it a dead body: the shrouded cart filled with a body shape without a visible head, plus the single attendant, head bent to his task, not keeping watch over a live or semi-live patient. The scene lasted for a bare second. Then the cart stopped and there was a mumbled exchange of remarks and even a joke, judging by the resulting chuckles with a couple of physician aides who stood beside the open curtain. But then any further view of interesting objects was blocked by Sarah's entrance.

"Oh, Aunt Julia," Sarah said, ducking under the IV and stepping up to the bed and planting a kiss on her cheek. "How on earth . . ." She didn't finish, looking first at the nurse who stood to one side and nodded. Of the mysterious Dr. Rackliff there was no sign.

"Now, Sarah," said Julia in what was almost her normal bark. "Don't make a scene. I suppose you ran into Patrick and he frightened you. I thought he had more backbone, but the man is in a state. He's the one who needs his blood pressure checked. And just how did you find out?" But before Sarah could answer, Julia went on. "Jane Zimmer, Miss Nosy Parker the village crier. She saw the ambulance and is blabbing it all over town."

Sarah saw a firm voice was needed. "Aunt Julia, listen to me. You have a family. I don't mean your mother because she's ninety and we don't want to scare her. But you, you're my aunt. I'm your niece. And you have a doctor. Alex is his name. He's my husband. We were married on your farm and he's been taking care of you for the last two years. What's all this secrecy about? We care. We love you. You're acting as if you're incognito."

"We were sure she had a family somewhere," said the nurse, reaching for Julia's finger and fitting it between the teeth of a small plastic item. "Satisfactory," she announced. Then, turning back to Sarah: "Your aunt wouldn't tell us a thing. But we need some personal, medical history for the admission work-up."

"What the hospital wants to do is invade my privacy," said Julia. "But all right," she added grudgingly to the nurse, "I suppose it's not your fault. Sarah, I'll need my handbag with my Medicare and insurance card because I suppose I'll have to pay for this visit."

The nurse—Sarah squinted at her ID tag—was a Hannah Finch and obviously someone used to irascible elderly women because she smiled and said she was so glad a family member had turned up.

"And she also has a family doctor," explained Sarah to Nurse Finch. "It's my husband, Dr. McKenzie. She said she wouldn't go to anyone else even if he is sort of a relative. And he's at the hospital this morning. I've asked a nurse to page him." She turned to Julia, who was making negative gestures with her free hand, the other being strapped and punctured for the taking in of IV fluid. "Be quiet, Auntie. Alex would never forgive you if he wasn't called. You chose him and so you're his patient, like it or not."

"Dr. McKenzie," said Hannah Finch, "was on the floor just a while ago. Came in from the ER. He has a patient who won't go to his office, so he meets her there. And Dr. Rackliff has three new admissions besides your aunt, so he'll want to turn Mrs. Clancy over to her regular physician. To someone who knows her."

Sarah smiled at the nurse. "Yes," she said, "we all know Mrs. Clancy."

Mary Starbox
Memorial Hospital

Emergency ➤

2

ALEX McKenzie had a collection of eccentric patients; Julia Clancy was only one of many. This morning a familiar and particularly difficult specimen had turned up in the ER to command his services. She was a tiny five-foot woman of eighty with dyed-black hair, fierce black eyebrows, and a voice that gave out with a high gravelly squawk when she wanted attention. Her name was Emma Littlefield, but due to her repeated visits, sometimes twice a week, she was now referred to by the emergency room staff as frequent flier ER Emma.

Emma had become part of Alex's life one bleak winter morning a year ago. She had arrived at the ER, as she often did, complaining of a great weakness of the knees and unusual dizziness. Faint when she stood up; faint when she sat down. A buzzing in her ears. Cold hands, cold feet. Emma, after waiting restlessly for what she said was hours, had been seen by the resident on duty, who pointed out after a lengthy examination that her blood pressure, her temperature, her pulse, her oxygen levels, her heart rhythm, her reflexes were all within normal range and that the lab work showed nothing out of the way. Since this news repudiated her self-diagnosis, Emma was furious. But then, spying

Alex as he walked in from a hallway, she pointed and demanded him as her physician.

Alex never knew what about his face, his person—perhaps the black hair, the heavy black eyebrows that might resemble some notable figure from Emma's family—had attracted her. But by hook and by crook, by repeated demands and a scene displaying Emma's theatrical powers, plus the pleas of the ER staff and finally the hospital CEO, Alex had somehow found her attached to his patient roster.

But Emma would never go to his office. Made no appointments, just turned up like royalty and demanded his presence. Sometimes he could come; sometimes he couldn't. But she was an old lady, her health, while appearing stable, might well bear watching, so Alex soldiered on with her. Ordered CAT scans, MRIs, X-rays, lab work, GI work-ups, respiratory checkups, EKGs, stress and bone-density tests, all as Emma's constantly changing symptoms seemed to indicate. So far, nothing remarkable had shown up and Emma was often hard put to reappear with a new set of symptoms in the next week or so.

Today, Friday the seventeenth of August, it had been cystitis. A burning bladder. Emma, hunching up in her chair, said she'd been up all night trying to pee. A urinalysis showed white cells, a finding that pleased Emma, and Alex had sent her home with a suitable antibiotic. Turning to leave, his beeper went off and a message ordered him to the emergency room. A family member, one of his patients, was going to be admitted.

Sarah had gone to the entrance of the cardiac ICU units to wait for Alex and also try to persuade Patrick to go back to the farm because that would reassure Julia. Then, seeing her husband approaching, she left Patrick's side. "Alex. Thank God. It's Aunt Julia. She's in there. Along the hall. It's all right. Or maybe it isn't. I don't know if she's in real trouble. Patrick here said she'd been wobbly and then just went down like that." Sarah, looking distraught, began to steer Alex toward the cardiac holding tank.

"Wobbly? Went down? You mean off a horse?" said Alex. "Lord, I suppose she's been thrown off that damn monster, Duffie. It's not serious, is it?"

"Not off a horse. Patrick says she passed right out while walk-ing up the drive from the barn."

"When she passed out," said Patrick, "I called nine-one-one and followed the ambulance. When I saw her in here later, she tried to swear me to secrecy that I wouldn't tell any of you. Told the hospital people she didn't have a family. Nor yet a doctor."

"And," said Sarah, "now she's being monitored and they say she's stable. In fact, she's driving them crazy, wants out."

Alex frowned. "Julia didn't have a cardiac condition that I know of. Gave her a stress test eight months ago along with her regular physical. Passed with flying colors. No changes in her EKGs either."

"If she's been having symptoms," said Sarah, "she certainly was hiding them from us. Though I did hear the other day that she'd been looking tired."

"She never even hinted at anything wrong when I saw her, so maybe there weren't any real symptoms. But this business of no doctor, no family—well, patients like Julia drive me straight up the wall. And I thought Emma Littlefield was the biggest pain for miles around. Well, let's go see her. Who's in charge?"

"Dr. Rackcliff, who would probably love to hand her to you. He's got too much to do."

"As do we all," said Alex grimly. "Okay, Julia and I will have a face-off. No"—as Sarah looked alarmed—"I'll be kindly old Dr. McKenzie just wanting a meaningful little chat."

"Alex," exclaimed Julia as Alex loomed by the partly open curtain, "get me out of this place. They've already wheeled a dead body past me down the aisle and I'm probably next. No one will admit it was dead; I've asked. Me, I'm fine. I just got faint because I missed breakfast, slipped, and hit my chest on the path down to the lower barn. Now everyone's behaving as if I need a heart transplant. There is absolutely nothing wrong with me. Patrick"—Julia indicated the hallway, where Patrick's shoulder and part of his head could be seen—"overreacted, called the ambulance—you know the Irish, always up for a big scene. So now I'm some sort of a prisoner, and God knows what they're dripping into my arm, something called heparin, which is probably made out of rattlesnake venom. Plus stuffing a million nitroglycerin pills into me. And I certainly don't need oxygen. I think they stick these tubes up your nose for looks. To show that they're doing something."

"Julia," said Alex, reaching for her free hand and letting a finger slide over her wrist, "I love you very much, but you are not going anywhere. You are going to have a complete cardiac work-up. Then you and I are going to have a serious discussion about admitting that you actually have a physician. That's me, your concerned primary health-care provider. If you don't behave, Sarah will swear that you're incompetent and I'll drive over to High Hope Farm and personally sell all your horses. Then, after we fix you up in the hospital, we'll have you remanded to an assisted-living facility where, if you behave, you will be allowed to weave place mats and paint lampshades."

"Why, Alex," said Julia, "you remind me of Tom. He could be just as bullheaded as you. Why we ever stayed married is a mystery. Talk about sexual harassment. Sarah, how can you stand the man?"

"Because," said Sarah, smiling at her aunt, "I'm as bullheaded as he is and almost as bullheaded as you are. It's genetic."

Alex and Sarah attended Julia's removal to a room that was apparently rigged for those patients stable enough to make the journey by wheeled stretcher. Julia had been shifted (promoted, perhaps) into something referred casually as "C-SCU" or, more properly, as the Cardiac Skilled Care Unit. But whatever its name, the switch was to a facility somewhat less severe than her curtained alcove in Station 6. This "room"—more properly, an enlarged cell—number 35, into which her aunt was wheeled, hoisted, and rolled onto the bed was an area in which medical business, not cozy ambience, was the sine qua non. The narrow space held a brown vinyl armchair; a bed table; the bed proper, complete with side rails, and over which loomed a number of monitors. Surrounding the bed stood assorted plastic bags of fluid hung on a wheeled object resembling an aluminum clothes rack.

The only mitigating presence was a small framed print of pale purple poppies drooping in a glass bowl that hung by the bathroom door. Appropriate, Sarah thought, as poppies in these surroundings certainly suggested morphine, not gardens.

Room 35 also came equipped with a Clare Mitchner, RN, if her ID card hanging around her neck was to be believed, except that when the photograph was taken, Clare had long hair and bangs. She had a determined chin, but otherwise was about as far in aspect and manner from the redoubtable Nurse Ratchet as was possible. Clare had an oval face, large dark eyes, smooth brown hair caught behind in a tortoiseshell band, and was built on the lines of a successful soccer player. She wore a flowered smock and crinkled cotton trousers, with a yellow ruffled shirt tucked under her chin. She had a wide mouth with a relentlessly cheerful expression even as she dealt with matters pertaining to bowels, catheters, and body fluids in general. She bustled about the small room with pillows, tubes, medication cups, and cheery words, calling Julia "dear" or "hon."

Julia under these ministrations did not melt as other patients might have been expected to do; she stiffened and bristled and responded to questions with gruff monosyllables and a series of harumphs. In fact, Sarah, sitting in the chair by her aunt's bedside, began to wish mightily for something very like Nurse Ratchet. Nurse Ratchet could handle Julia; Julia could deal with Nurse Ratchet. They would both bark at each other and enjoy a nice combative relationship. But Julia, who did not in the least like being called "hon," had to retire from the fray without a shot being fired because you could no more fight with Clare than with a pillow.

Alex said he had to retire early from the field, citing waiting hospital rounds and patients filling his waiting room. But he promised later attendance, saying one of the cardiologists, a Dr. Eugene Santoro, would be in to discuss tomorrow's catherization, a stress test, and other possible scenarios.

"Scenarios," said Julia sharply. "You make it sound like a Western movie. Spit it out and say what you mean."

"We'll look at a medication program. And angioplasty, insertion of a stent, or a bypass, one or several. Whatever's needed. Or none of the above. Just send you home with or without medication. We aren't Nazis. We will explain and show and tell. And your permission is needed for any procedure."

"Permission my foot," said Julia. "You'll probably handcuff me and do what you want. And now," she added, sarcasm dripping, "we have 'procedures.' Not surgery, not being cut open or chopped up or stealing of body parts."

"Of course," said Alex, with tightened lips, "we also have the murder of the hospitalized seventy-one-year-old female patient by her physician. I'm sure any jury would acquit him. It would be called provoked assault."

"Now, Alex," said Sarah, feeling like the tired mother of two teenagers, "cool it. Julia's bark is always worse than her bite."

"That," said Julia, "is because I haven't bitten either of you yet."

"Now, dear," said Clare Mitchner, slipping in from the hall, "it's time for vital signs. If your family would just step outside."

Alex departed but Sarah stayed. Julia let her head fall back on her pillow and turned to Clare. "Tell me about this body," she demanded. "Do you wheel deceased patients around to frighten patients into behaving, or did someone actually die in there this morning?"

"I'm sure I don't know," said Clare in her nurse voice. "But don't trouble yourself, hon. The staff would never do anything to alarm people."

"That's a non-answer if I ever heard one, but I'm not making it up and . . ." began Julia, at which a white-coated lab person appeared, pulled out a rubber tourniquet, and told Julia to make a fist. And Julia, feeling a little light-headed after her medications, subsided. Two against one. Not fair, but what could you do. Where did that nurse say her clothes were? Maybe she could get dressed and just very quietly leave. Sneak away. Out some back doorway, the sort of door undertakers use to remove bodies. She'd find Patrick and have him help her, drive her home."

"Your vein is rolling," said the lab person reproachfully, sliding the syringe out and dabbing at the crook of her elbow.

"That's not all that's going to roll," muttered Julia.

"What?" said the lab person.

"Now that hurt," said Julia as the needle with a sharp prick found its mark. "How long have you been doing this?"

"Twenty-five years," said the lab person, pressing a Band-Aid over the puncture.

Briefly stymied, Julia let herself slide farther down in the bed and closed her eyes.

"That's the ticket, dear," said Clare, patting her shoulder. "Have a little shut-eye and then I'll bring you a snack. Beef broth and cherry Jell-O."

At which Sarah leaned over and kissed her aunt. "We'll go to the cafeteria and grab lunch and see you later. And cool it or you'll have more than a procedure in your future."

Julia didn't answer. Visions of her beloved High Hope Farm had risen before her. Things to be done. Grain to be ordered. The vet to see Duffie. The farrier coming. Afternoon lessons with the school crowd. The dogs fed Horses brought in. The hay supply checked. She opened her eyes the smallest slit and considered the distance to the locker that probably held her clothes. Wait until Nurse Clare departed, grab her things, dress, and slide out into the hall. Find Patrick before Alex and Sarah turned up again. Then out and away.

Except, what about all these damn tubes? The monitors hanging over her head? How could she detach herself, pull off all those leads on her chest, close down the IV, shut down the automatic blood-pressure machine that kept gripping her arm, unhook the oxygen tubes, all this without setting off bells and lights by the nurse's desk? She closed her eyes again. She was a prisoner. A noncooperating prisoner. Oh, hell.

Alex, seeing Dr. Jim Rackcliff—blue scrubs, mask hanging down his neck—coming out of the cafeteria, gave him a wave while Sarah went on in to snag a table.

"Hey," said Dr. Rackcliff, a cheerful sandy-haired man with a bristle mustache. "Glad you turned up, Alex. Mrs. Clancy is all yours. But how did you end up taking care of a relative anyway?"

"Connection by marriage. And she insisted, and when Julia insists, hell, it's easier to give in."

"Well, I haven't finished my notes on her, but it's fairly clear-cut. She'd apparently been hiding symptoms for a while now. Shortness of breath, fatigue, didn't want to hear bad news, so she kept it quiet. Her EKG got my attention. Of course she kept telling me it was because she hadn't had a proper breakfast."

"That's Julia, all right," said Alex. "But thanks for your help, Jim."

"Glad she's your patient. Along with ER Emma. Aren't you the lucky guy to have those two ladies. Me, I've been running around today like hound dog with fleas. One of the residents and a PA called in sick and the ER's a mob scene."

"So I noticed," said Alex, turning to go. Time was running out and chances of lunch were fast disappearing.

But Jim Rackcliff wasn't finished. "Hey, you heard? Weird DOA. Not DOA from the ambulance. In the ER patients' lavatory. Body in a wheelchair neatly parked between the sink and the toilet. Slumped over. Must have been dead all of ten minutes before this guy with a banged-up knee goes limping in to use the john, gives a yell, scares the bejeezus out of everyone for miles around. Never a dull day. Gotta go, the place is really stacked up."

"Hold it," said Alex. "Who? What happened?"

"Don't know. I was with another patient when all hell broke loose. This dead guy—old geezer—he was all bruised up from some fall he must have had. Looks like he went through a blender. Which I suppose is the reason he came into the ER this A.M. On his own two feet, apparently. No one's claimed him yet. No ID on him. Apparently he just walked in and sat down. With that crowd milling around, his name never made it into the system, since the registration desk never got any stats on him. That's all I know. Or want to. Keep it to yourself. Too much gossip in the place. See ya around."

Alex wanted to tell Jim Rackcliff that he was a fine one to talk about gossip, but in the interest of friendship stifled the remark. He caught up with Sarah at a table at the end of the cafeteria and observed that his wife's spinach quiche, judging from the pressure she exerted on her fork, was made largely of rubber.

Sarah looked at him with some concern. The summer tan from two weeks on Weymouth Island hiking and sailing had begun to fade. The black eyebrows, the dark hair emphasized the emerging pallor—the pallor emphasized by his rather rumpled white coat. As for fatigue, Alex had been on call last night and had come home at around three in the morning, and now his long slit-like mouth looked tighter, his dark eyes dangerous, and in general he had the aspect of a pirate whose ship was leaking and whose crew was talking mutiny. Alex in a sunny mood was positively handsome in an invigorating way; now he seemed merely sinister, a poor choice as a companion for a pleasant lunch. Time for diversion, Sarah decided. Not Aunt Julia, an irritant if there ever was one. Something else.

"Man died in the ER," she announced. "In the lavatory, of all places. In a wheelchair. I heard someone talking at the next table. Maybe that's who Aunt Julia saw being wheeled by, the one she thought was a body."

"Don't encourage Aunt Julia in seeing things," said Alex, settling his baked potato with cheese and broccoli in front of him. "Probably this so-called body was someone coming back from the OR. Still under anesthesia."

"With no head showing? No IVs?"

"Sounds like Julia's overworked imagination," said Alex shortly. He had no intention of sharing Jim Rackcliff's recent bit of news, certainly not with his over-interested wife. "People go by on stretchers all the time. This is a hospital."

"Dead people and live people."

"Correct," said Alex. "Only we don't feature the dead ones. They disappear by way of the service elevators to the basement and out the back entrance." He shoved his plate away. "Time's up. I've got patients waiting. But finish your lunch, then take a little time to concentrate on Aunt Julia. On what's coming up for her. She's in for a tough couple of days. Or weeks."

"You mean weeks if it's going to be a bypass affair?"

"Wait for what the angiogram shows. Then we'll meet up with the cardiac people and hear what they suggest. Now, do you think Patrick can manage the farm?"

"Patrick could handle twenty farms. Besides, he's got Rafe Posner to help him with the riding lessons. Now, who do we have to let know?"

"Your Grandmother Douglas, for one. Have you called her?"

"Good God, no," said Sarah, appalled. "I was afraid to. I don't want to scare her. She's over ninety and she's built like . . ." She hesitated, trying for an analogy for her wisp of a grandmother. "Like a butterfly," she finished.

"Make her a monarch butterfly," said Alex. "That butterfly is capable of migrating great distances. Your grandmother may be old, but she's made of tough material and probably can take anything you throw at her."

Sarah nodded. "You may be right. Aunt Julia gets some of her vinegar from her mother. But you know what Grandma Douglas will do, she'll come here with Father What's-His-Name from the Episcopal Church and they'll pray over Julia. Then Grandma will lecture Julia on her slipshod ways and how her god is a four-legged animal with hooves and how she married Tom Clancy, an Irish Roman Catholic."

"I think we can limit visitations," said Alex. "We don't want Julia's blood pressure to go through the roof." He rose and shook his head. "Forget about any stretchers, carts, gurneys going by with headless objects wrapped in sheets. Okay?"

"Of course," said Sarah. "But if you do happen to hear why someone died in the lavatory in a wheelchair, you could share."

"I'll pick up a text on forensic pathology, and you can read up and try for a degree. It ought to keep you out of trouble for a few years. Teaching English obviously isn't holding your interest." And Alex was gone and Sarah, making a face at his departing back, returned to her now cold wedge of spinach quiche.

Then, losing interest in this item, she exchanged it for dessert, the cup of strawberry yogurt with "our famous country-fresh fruit" topping. "Famous?" Sarah asked herself, inspecting what appeared to be three halved strawberries sprinkled with several blueberries on top of the lump of yogurt. Probably another tri-umph from the *Mary Starbox Auxiliary Cookbook*, on sale in the gift shop. But neither the dessert nor the displayed cookbooks could give the cafeteria a homey ambience. You couldn't shake the hospital aura, not even with flowered curtains, bright Formica tabletops, and pictures of mountain vistas, lighthouses, and clip-per ships. The scrub suits in a rainbow of colors, the assorted smocks, jackets, and cotton coats, the ID tags and stethoscopes stuffed in pockets, all these proclaimed "institution" and re-minded Sarah of a benign penal colony. The cafeteria was a pas-sage, not a resting place. A respite from the demands of the workplace. A place for that elderly man over there by the window to explain to his tearful companion—his daughter?—that Mother would not be coming home. For the surgeon, still in paper boo-ties, to draw with his pen on a piece of paper a representation of the mess his patient's liver was in when they finally opened him up. For the nurses, the aides, the technicians to get a quick breather, a fast coffee before they went back to the floor to deal with the likes of Aunt Julia.

Sarah finished her yogurt in a sort of daze. First, back to Julia's room. Then check on the farm. Find Patrick. Where had he got to? Having Patrick in charge of the home front would soothe Julia and keep Patrick from hanging wretchedly outside Julia's door. Then, Alex was right, she had to call her Grand-mother Douglas—with or without Julia's permission. There were some things that had to be done even if the end result would not be agreeable. Sarah had a sudden vision of Grandmother Douglas, leaning on her cane, marching up to Julia's bed and telling her that prayers were being arranged, but that the best thing for her daughter would be to snap out of it and go home and bear what the Lord brings. To put herself into His hands and stop feeling sorry for herself.

This disturbing picture brought Sarah to her feet and sent her out into the hall. She had better warn Julia that there was no force on earth that could prevent her next of kin, Mrs. Anthony Douglas of Bayview Street, Camden, Maine, from grabbing Hop-kins, her longtime female housekeeper-cum-chauffeur, calling out the 1986 Buick, and storming the gates of the hospital.

But for just a moment, disoriented, she hesitated outside the cafeteria. Which way was Julia's room? Oh yes, past the double ER doors and then turn right and down the hall. Sarah put herself into motion and walked directly into Mike Laaka. Mike, Sheriff's Deputy Investigator of Knox County. Mike Laaka, old buddy of Alex's and recent new buddy of Sarah's. Mike who, along with the Maine State Police CID, was the reluctant participant in a past series of untoward incidents involving bodies and the discovery thereof, all happening with Sarah entirely too close to the scene.

"Sarah!" exclaimed Mike. "I might have known."

Sarah pushed herself away from his six-foot-four presence and stared up into the face of a man who with his almost white hair and pale blue eyes resembled some sort of Ice Age Nordic giant.

"So look where you're going," said Mike. And then: "And where *are* you going? Lunch with Alex?"

"Yes, with Alex. And I'm here seeing a friend." Somehow, Sarah didn't want Mike, who knew and admired Julia but sometimes was entirely too blunt and breezy in his off-duty persona, to turn up by her bed when she was feeling—and looking—poorly.

"Yeah," said Mike. "It's what we all do from time to time. Hospitals are sort of a meeting place. Social center."

"You're here in your social capacity?" asked Sarah suspiciously. "Visiting the sick. Bringing flowers and cards."

"Just a routine check. Nothing to bother visitors like you."

Sarah considered. The appearance of Mike in the hospital corridors was not unusual, but when he did turn up it was usually part of an ongoing investigation. A hospitalized suspect. Someone the police needed a statement from. Or, in more serious cases, the need to see how an injured victim was making out, a chat with the local pathologist, checking on the results of an autopsy—persons whose death was not suspicious, but whose activities had attracted the law. In short, Mike's appearance usually meant trouble. Trouble like that wheelchair body in the ER lavatory.

Sarah looked up at Mike, who kept glancing over his shoulder and clearly wanted to be on his way. "That ER thing," she said. "Man in the lavatory. An unattended death and someone's blown a whistle? And you came running. Right?"

Mike frowned. "Sarah, be a good citizen and go away. Go visit your sick friend. I have a job to do. And stay away from the ER. They have enough trouble as it is. Not room to swing a cat."

"I know," said Sarah. "I came in through there. People stacked up like firewood."

"*You* came in by way of the ER? To see this so-called friend of yours? A friend who had an accident?"

Sarah gave in. She decided that Mike, since he was obviously on duty, would be much too busy to bother Julia. "The friend is my Aunt Julia. A heart attack. Or an 'event,' as they keep calling it. She's in for tests, to see how serious it is. In by ambulance, and I chased her down a little while later. She wasn't going to tell anyone. Including Alex."

Mike shook his head. "Sounds like Julia. Well, I am very sorry. There's only one Julia Clancy, so I'd hate to have her go missing. I'd go in and see her but I'm meeting the state police people, actually your old pal, Sergeant George Fitts. The hospital people want us to check on an incident. Something that went on there this A.M."

"Stop being mysterious and talking about 'incidents.' No one here uses real words. I've just told you I've heard about the man in the wheelchair. Unless there's just been another so-called incident. Event. Episode."

"Hold it," said Mike. "If you really came in through the ER this morning, we'll need a statement from you. The case, if it turns into a case, involves checking ER visitors to see if they noticed a particular person."

"That's what I'm talking about. The man in the toilet."

"I didn't say that. So why don't you go and see Julia, hold her hand, give her my love. And then come back to the meeting room beyond the visitors' lounge. Past the chapel. We're setting up for statements there."

"Alex was at the ER today. Grab him, too. That woman, Emma Littlefield. She won't go to his office, only the emergency room. Drives him crazy. But I'll bet she'd make a great witness because she almost lives there."

"We'll try and track down everyone who came in today," said Mike. "And, Sarah, do me a favor. Don't try and figure out what's happening. No one knows yet. Just see if you can remember any of the characters in the waiting room this morning. What they looked like, what they were doing. If you can only remember two people, it'll help."

Which left Sarah staring at Mike's retreating back. In her anxiety over Aunt Julia, Sarah remembered absolutely no one in the waiting room. Not a single face. She frowned, trying to remember. And since nature abhors a vacuum, she soon found images of waiting patients, real or imaginary, crowding into her brain.

Maine State Police
No Admittance

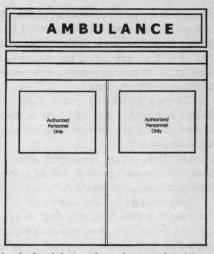

AMBULANCE

Authorized Personnel Only

Authorized Personnel Only

3

EXCEPT for a small clutch of wheelchairs, the volunteers' waiting room was empty. Empty with good reason on this very busy Friday in late August. Hospital visitors and arriving patients thronged the corridors, and many of the latter needed wheelchair delivery, an escort to a lab, to the MRI, the X-ray, day surgery, clinics, and to other feature attractions.

The waiting room itself was a pleasant place where coffee, hot water, tea bags, and biscuits stood at the ready, along with a small refrigerator for cold drinks. These amenities had been provided to encourage volunteers to keep coming and continue their good work. The walls were covered in a flowered wallpaper and hung with prints of hunting spaniels (donated by a dog-loving volunteer). The room also featured two windows giving a view not only of a small grove of birch trees, branching evergreen shrubbery, but newly planted clusters of purple New England asters.

Added to the above items was the sight of arriving cars, and, at a distance, the ER entrance, where assorted town ambulances pulled up, delivered their burdens, and departed. This latter activity kept the volunteers' interest bubbling. Small towns are numerous in the midcoast area of Maine, and the ambulances often carry victims known or even related to the volunteers. The volunteer corps had a median age of sixty-seven and many of them had lived long enough to know most of their town's residents, what ailed them, and which ones were most likely to be toted off to the emergency room.

"There's the Millers' truck. Come right in after the ambulance," one would say. "Old Tom again, I'll bet. Probably his diabetes kicking up. Saw him last week in Camden tucking into chocolate cake."

Or: "Here comes the Union ambulance. I hope it isn't Mrs. Terry next door. She was feeling poorly this morning and her husband was a mite worried."

When things quieted down and the volunteer squad settled for a brief respite from wheeling, escorting, toting messages and flowers, news from the different parts of the hospital would be passed around. Nothing in violation of a patient's privacy, but if the patient was one's next-door neighbor or a cousin, well, word somehow got through. And if a patient being pushed in a wheelchair had a seizure en route to X-ray, the episode and the name of the patient didn't go unreported among the stalwarts of the volunteer brigade. After all, they needed to know what might happen in the pursuit of their duties; had to warn their fellows that a certain patient might suddenly stiffen and tumble out of the chair.

Three of the many Mary Starbox volunteers were varsity players. Holders of the Mary Starbox Gold Pin and chevrons denoting years of service sewn on the sleeves of their smocks and jackets—these garments' varying color depending on the year the volunteer joined up. After all, as one Christie Rivers remarked "I'm not changing my green smock for a blue one just because the gift-shop people wanted blue."

The dean of all volunteers was David Bergman. Seventy-two years young, strong as the proverbial ox, built for felling oaks, he had put in some sixteen years of volunteer work, and if a three-hundred-pound patient needed pushing, well, David was the one for the job. His head was round and bald as a basketball, which it very much resembled; he had a walrus mustache, a smashed nose, tufted eyebrows, the ruddy complexion of a man of the sea, the neck and chest of a weight lifter, a voice that could be mistaken for a bull moose; and if someone tried monkey business, or a patient ran amok on his watch, he could be counted on to deal with the problem. Always on time, David Bergman was willing, ready with a joke, a guffaw, and, in the words of the volunteer coordinator, "a hell of an asset and great for goodwill."

Two other "assets," Stella Dugan and Christie Rivers, had also earned their gold pins, fifteen years each. Stella, seventy-three, was short, built like a root-beer bottle with frizzed red hair (natural but faded), and a soft voice that sometimes moved to a plaintive and anxious squeak. Christie Rivers, sixty-eight her opposite in many ways, was almost five-eleven, lean, with a sharp chin, sharp elbows, and gray hair dragged back into a severe knot. A no-nonsense lady who, it was rumored, had played on some noted field-hockey team during her youth.

These three seniors had another thing in common with one another: each had lost a spouse at this very facility, and because they were the stars of the volunteer corps, it was generally felt by hospital personnel that the three in their bereaved state were setting an example of public service.

Today these three, returned from their lunch and enjoying a brief lull in volunteer demands, were, naturally, rehashing the untoward events in the emergency room.

"It's not just gossiping," said Stella to the others, all seated in full view of an inner glass partition so that they could be summoned by the desk or a passing aide for wheelchair- or some other duty.

"It sure isn't gossip, it's right in our faces," said David, thumping the arm of his chair. "Police. Crawling around like a bunch of maggots. Can't stand 'em. Hospital can't run with a lot of goddamn police underfoot."

"You're a prejudiced old goat," said Christie sharply. "We've got to have them every now and then. Guards have to bring prisoners from the state prison to the hospital and you wouldn't want them cruising around loose."

"But we've never had an army of plainclothes police," Stella pointed out. "Just sometimes one or two in a uniform. But now it's crime scene yellow tape all around the ER lavatory, and people with kits and cameras so I think they're talking a murder. And," she added with a slight trembling of her lower lip. "It's pretty scary because one of us might have been dragged into the lavatory and been finished off."

"Aahh, don't you believe it," said David. "No one wants the likes of us old farts. Might be a grudge thing. Like some guy raped someone's daughter and he was finally nailed in the hospital."

At which interesting point a call came for a wheelchair in room sixty-two, surgical floor, a heavy man with a cast, and David departed.

"I hope," said Christie, "no one's going to ask us questions."

"But we might have seen someone," protested Stella with a little nervous laugh. "We're always around and we go everywhere. I think I know the hospital better than some of the nurses. Besides, as long as it's safe, I sort of like to be in on things."

"Things like homicide?" demanded Christie.

"Well, that does give me chills, but we should know what's going on. After all, the Mary Starbox is our second home. And if there's some maniac running around, we've got to know about it."

"The only maniac around—though that's not the right word—is that Emma. Emma Littlefield. Nutty as a fruitcake. But I don't think she's taken to killing anyone even if she almost lives here."

"And don't block her way into the ER," said Stella.

At which one of the male nurses, Gerry Brock, stuck his head into the door. "You're all on the hot seat," he announced. "One at a time. But Christie first. Go and see the deputy in the meeting room next to the chapel. He's asking questions, so it's your big moment. And tell any other volunteers to stand by when they come back here."

"Lordy," said Christie. "All I need." But she rose, tugged at her faded green smock, straightened the collar of her white blouse, and departed.

Mike Laaka looked up from his notebook and gave a restrained smile. Christie Rivers had been his very strict third-grade teacher, was a friend of his mother's, and a tough old coot if there ever was one. She would probably report to his mother on the interview, and if Mike yammered or mishandled the questions, Christie would pick up on it and perhaps report home. Now everything told Mike to make the interrogation short, to the point, and at all times act like the professional investigator. And in no way to let Christie start making remarks about his grade school performance.

This particular meeting room was long and rather dark, as its two narrow windows looked out into fully leafed bushes. It served usually as a utility space as well as a secondary area for staff conferences and sessions with patients' families. It had been fitted into spaces between the chapel and a larger staff conference room and housed three folding metal tables, now pushed together and taking up the middle of the room. Along the wall ran a number of homeless file cabinets while a collection of mismatched chairs huddled in one corner. An attempt had been made by the Friends of Mary Starbox Hospital to make the room more hospitable, and on the wall spaces between the file cabinets hung a series of framed black-and-white photographs of famous buildings—obviously from someone's attic collection: St. Mark's, the Louvre, Monticello, and Westminster Abbey, all looking out of place. Altogether it was a room with few distractions for an interviewer and his interviewee. Mike sat at the table holding a clipboard; Christie on a straight-backed wooden number.

Christie beat Mike to the punch. "Well, Mike," she said, "I see you've come up in the world. They're letting you ask questions. I am surprised. I never thought you'd end up acting like an executive. I'd have bet on something else. You and that Alex McKenzie, though he's done all right as far as I can see. Settled down. Married. But you haven't. Your mother says you go hopping from one woman to the next."

Mike, to grab control of the conversation, frowned, straightened his shoulders, and tapped his pen on the clipboard.

"Mrs. Rivers. This won't take long, but I haven't time to chat. Much as I'd like to. But we need to hear from those people who

33

were in and out of the ER today. If they saw anything out of the way, and if—"

Christie Rivers interrupted. "In the ER there's always something out of the way. That's why people are there. You know that. Blood and guts. Tossing their cookies. In pain. Worried families. Stretchers being run in from the ambulances. What would be unusual would be someone sitting there smiling and reading a book."

Mike tried again. "This morning, did you see a man with bruises all over? In a chair, in a wheelchair? At any time? Just parked somewhere or being wheeled into the lavatory? Wheeled by someone you might remember? By one of the escort people?"

"I only made it three times to the ER this morning. To pick up a wheelchair, take patients to X-ray. That's it. Nothing else. Just everyday mayhem."

And so it went. Mike worked his way from Christie to Stella. Stella was willing but couldn't seem to remember whom or what she saw. "The place was just packed," she lamented. Mike moved on to other volunteers, then through the ER waiting room family members—as many as could be found; the rest would have to be tracked down through registration and admission records. But all witnesses agreed that the emergency room had been particularly active: ambulances arrived with the regularity of scheduled trains, the walking wounded delivered by a stream of arriving automobiles. No one had seen an elderly man with noticeable bruises around his arms and face being wheeled into the toilet.

Mike now addressed, without much hope of a result, David Bergman, one of the last of the hospital persons connected to ER morning activities—David had been much in demand for some heavy-duty wheelchair assistance.

"Say there's this guy," Mike said. "He's not in a wheelchair, but sitting in the waiting room. Just sitting. Hasn't gone up to the registration desk. Maybe was dropped off by a friend, drove himself. Took a taxi. Anyway, here's a guy in the waiting room looking like he's been in a fight and lost big-time."

And Mike got lucky.

"Yeah. Saw a man all slumped over. Sitting in the corner next to the magazine table," said David.

"Not in a wheelchair?" asked Mike.

"Nope," said David. "Just sitting there. I noticed him because like you said, he looked like he'd gone through a buzz saw. Hands and lower part of his arms all bunged up. Big purple bruises. Black eye, cut over an eyebrow. You know, old people, the least bump it's like they've taken a gang hit. I didn't think that much about it except he sort of reminded me of someone I'd known before. Except who could tell, he was such a mess."

"But no one was taking care of him? No nurse checking him out? Taking him into an exam room?"

"Hey, the place was jumping and this guy, he doesn't act like he's in any real pain. Just sitting there looking like hell but reading a magazine. You'd've thought he was in a barbershop waiting his turn."

"No sign that he was going to pass out?"

"As in drop dead? You never can tell, can you? I mean, people expect someone to die in the ER. One minute reading *Sports Illustrated*, the next, kaput. Anyway, when I went through later on, the guy wasn't around. So what happened? Got himself to the john and went down for the count?"

"That," said Mike, "is what we're trying to find out. Thanks for your help. At least we know the guy—if it's the same one—was alive in the waiting room."

"And catching up on his reading," said David, heaving himself out of the chair, pulling down his blue cotton jacket which, judging from its creases, seemed to have had a rough morning.

"I'm no help to you," said Alex, when he turned up for Mike's interrogation scene. "I had Emma Littlefield and took her off into an examining room for our usual so-called office call. The ER was busting out all over."

"You weren't called to the scene? Pronounced the guy dead?"

"There were two residents, plus three regular ER docs to do the honors. I was out of the whole picture. After Emma, I got beeped to see about Julia Clancy."

"That's it?"

"Except I did run into Jonathan Philips."

"Your high mucky-muck."

"Right. Hospital CEO. A staff doctor recognized the victim even with his banged-up face, so the police called Dr. Jonathan Philips down to the morgue for the formal ID. Turns out the dead man, of all things, is his grandfather, Dr. Henry Dent Philips. Was the CEO—only that wasn't the title—back in the dark ages. And he used to hang around a lot after he supposedly retired."

"You guys are a mile ahead of us," said Mike. "No wallet on the body. Right now we're waiting on a parking-lot check to see if he drove himself here even in his lousy condition. Or, more likely, he was dropped off at the hospital by a taxi."

"He wasn't. Here's the story. Dr. Henry Philips lived alone since his wife died a few months ago. He was eighty-six, according to his grandson—I gather they weren't close. Anyway, Dr. Jonathan called his grandfather's neighbor and was told that old Dr. Philips had called him this A.M. to say he'd fallen down the last five of the cellar stairs last night, was banged up but didn't think he'd broken anything. Felt not too bad, was taking Tylenol but needed a ride to the hospital. Just be dropped off. Didn't want the neighbor to wait for him."

"Hell, take my place. You people know more than the police. So that explains why there wasn't a worried friend hanging around." Mike looked up, waved at a figure walking through the door. "Hey, Sarah. I'll bet you're sitting on some hot information, too. Maybe you wheeled this guy into the lavatory so you could ace us on this."

"Mike, ease off," said Sarah. "I have Aunt Julia on my mind. But listen—Julia, even in the middle of a heart attack, noticed something. She just remembered because I was quizzing her. It happened just after she was wheeled from the ambulance into that ER examining room or alcove or whatever they call it. Those slots with curtains. There was a guy in the next alcove. The curtains were halfway open and there he was. Sitting on a stool. All banged up and bruised. She said he looked like he'd been trampled in a stallion stall. Well, you know Julia. Everything has to do with horses. That's all because right after she saw the man, the curtains were pulled."

"Back up," said Mike. "Julia sees a banged-up guy from her ER examining alcove? He's sitting on a stool? Not on a gurney or on a bed? Or in a wheelchair?"

"On a stool." Alone, I guess, but she didn't say. Or couldn't see, anyway."

"I don't suppose she remembers a wheelchair *near* the guy on the stool?"

"She didn't mention it. But wheelchairs aren't unusual, they wouldn't get her attention. But men kicked by stallions apparently are."

"But then Julia is wheeled off?"

"Later on, when Alex and I were there, she was transferred to a bed in something called Cardiac Skilled Care Unit. Number 35. That's it. Except . . ."

"Except what?" demanded an exasperated Mike Laaka.

"Except she claims that when she was still in that alcove, she saw a gurney go by that might have had a body on it. Probably on its way to the morgue or wherever the hospital keeps its dead bodies. That is, if Julia saw what Julia thinks she saw."

"My God," said Mike, shaking his head. "Wouldn't you know." He looked at Alex. "Can I see Julia? What sort of shape is she in?"

"She seems pretty stable," said Alex, "but check with her cardiology team. They'll be doing an angiogram tomorrow A.M. to see how much damage, if any, she's had.

Twenty minutes later, Mike stood at Julia's bedside. Julia, her hair now combed back, her color improved from its earlier ashen state, welcomed him by waving a spoon.

"Jell-O," she announced. "Like eating blubber. And lukewarm chicken broth. And water. A feast for the gods. And, Mike, if you're here with sympathy, I don't need it. I just want out. They're pretending it's my heart, so I have to go through this catherization foolishness to prove them wrong."

"Julia," said Mike gently, "I need to ask a few questions. Your cardiologist said it was okay." Even with Julia much improved in appearance, Mike was shocked to see her looking so small and frail in the hospital bed, the bed made more formidable by side rails and its overhanging electronic monitors. Julia was a longtime neighbor of his parents' on Tri-County Road, and until today had been a legend for her indomitable approach to life.

"A cardiologist is what I don't need," said Julia crossly. "But it seems I have no choice. Alex is flinging his weight around and Sarah is acting as if I were three years old. Mike, if this is the way people treat you when you're over seventy, I should have stopped at sixty-nine."

"I can distract you," said Mike. "Sarah says you saw someone in the next examining alcove when your curtains were apart and you said he looked as if he'd been kicked by a horse."

"I said he looked as if he'd been trampled by a horse. There's a difference. This man had marks all over. He was in a T-shirt or an undershirt, not a hospital gown, I remember that, and I could see his arms and his neck. Purple and black bruises. But I only had a quick look and then someone pulled the curtains back in place."

"Did he seem all right? Except for the bruising?"

"He didn't seem dead, if that's what you mean. He was sitting on a stool. One of those examining stools doctors use."

"Did he say something? Or call for someone?"

"Not a peep. I didn't pay much attention. Banged-up people are a dime a dozen in this place, so I didn't think he was unusual. Anyway, a nurse came in and began fiddling with my IV, then later I was carted over here to this place."

"But later, after you saw the man," persisted Mike, "you saw something that looked like a body being wheeled by?"

"There's no privacy anywhere," complained Julia. "Even if you're dead." She struggled to a semisitting position and pushed her IV tube to one side and glared at Mike.

Mike struggled with self-control. "So you saw this cart go by. Or a gurney. With someone on it."

"Well, it probably wasn't an Egyptian mummy or a frozen Yeti, so I imagine it was a hospital patient. Deceased, I'd say. No head. And, I'd like to add, that the person doing the pushing didn't have a very caring attitude. You'd think he was pushing groceries. Stopped to chat and joke with someone. But who knows. Maybe it's hospital policy to wheel bodies past patients at intervals so we'll get used to the idea that we may leave feet-first."

"Julia Clancy," said Mike sharply. "I hope you're not starting to feel sorry for yourself. You're a very tough lady and a role model for us all. We could use you in the sheriff's department. And hospitals aren't just hotels with bad food. Bodies do turn up in them."

Julia subsided on her pillow. "Yes, I know, Mike, and I'm acting like grizzly bear, but I just want to get the hell out of here. I'm afraid they're going to tell me I have to have surgery, and here it is the middle of August and I have a foal coming and two horse shows to get ready for."

Mike reached out, and greatly daring, reached for Julia's shoulder and gave it a reassuring pat. "Don't worry. Even if they cut you up, I'll lay money you'll soon be back in the saddle on Duffie and making Patrick's life miserable. I'll stop in later if I have any more questions. Or to bring you a hot fudge sundae."

Julia closed her eyes for a moment, then opened them as Mike reached the door. "Stop in for a social visit," she commanded. "Besides, you owe me one. You owe me an explanation—off the record—of what happened to that man."

Mike grinned. "The *Courier-Gazette* will probably have it on the front page before the police know anything. I suggest you subscribe while you're in here."

The rest of the interrogations of persons and staff in and around the ER during the probable time of Dr. Henry Philip's death brought forth no new information. The man came in, did not register, waited, read a magazine, turned up in an examining alcove sitting on a stool, not wearing a hospital gown, and then apparently died in one of the emergency room lavatories. The lavatory was, as of course, wheelchair-accessible. A wheelchair was in the room. The man was slumped in it. The toilet had not been used. Or it had been and was then flushed. The whole event was, in itself, no great departure from what occasionally went on in crowded emergency rooms.

"You know who this guy was, because I've just found out?" said Mike to Maine State Police CID Sergeant George Fitts as the two men sat over coffee in the Bowmouth Café, a small shingled number opposite the main entrance to the Mary Starbox Hospital.

George Fitts nodded. "The victim is Dr. Henry Dent Philips. He's related to current CEO Dr. Jonathan. Dr. Henry is his grandfather, a general practitioner when the hospital was just starting up. Later he went into hospital management. He arrived here in the car of a neighbor who, at his request, left him off and drove off."

Mike shook his head. "And I thought I'd scooped you on that. Dr. Henry is one of the founding fathers of this place. But hey, how about cause of death? Because if old Doc Henry collapsed in the john because of a heart condition, a stroke or, a head trauma that caught up with him when he went into the lavatory, well, forget it. There's no point in tying up the ER with yellow tape and trying to track down every visitor for the whole morning. Plus a thousand staff people—aides, messengers, docs, nurses, X-ray, lab people."

"Cause of death?" said George slowly, as if he had never heard the expression. George was the kind of policeman who, when he confronted a witness, a suspect, even asked an everyday question of a passing pedestrian, caused an icy finger to trace down the back of the person. But few, when the ordeal of a chat with George was over, could describe the man because he was essentially faceless. A nonperson. No large nose, no dark bristling eyebrows, no mop of black hair, no assertive chin. Just a blank. Steel-blue eyes, rimless spectacles, smooth bald head, thin mouth, and a voice that rarely rose above a metallic click. And underneath this bland facade lurked, as some associates had discovered, a sharp and ironic view of the world.

"Yeah," said Mike, putting down the sticky shreds of a lemon-filled doughnut and rubbing his fingers on his napkin. "You remember cause of death. If it wasn't natural causes, then maybe someone recognized the guy and had it in for him. Though, considering his condition, I wonder if his own mother would have known him. Only David Bergman—the big volunteer—had vibes, said he looked vaguely familiar."

"I haven't finished what I'm trying to tell you," said George, who preferred to be in charge of all details.

"Well, whether it's trauma or homicide, he was alive and able to sit on a stool after he'd left the ER waiting room. This from a star witness, Julia Clancy—"

"Good God," interrupted George, who had stubbed his toe over Julia in the past.

"Ease up," said Mike. "Poor Julia's not to blame. She came in with a heart thing and was wheeled through the ER. Besides, we can't choose our witnesses. And Sarah Deane was around this morning, too. Coming to look for Julia. And Alex was around, taking care of some loopy old dame who just about lives in the place. But nothing much from any of them except Julia saw someone who fitted the description of this banged-guy when she had a quick look into the examining alcove next to hers. There he was sitting on a stool. Later on she saw what might or might not have been a body being wheeled by."

"She has no idea what time she saw the man?"

"No. It was a quick look and then someone pulled the curtains. In her words she lost interest, and besides, she was being bothered by nurses and wasn't playing detective."

"For which we are grateful," said George. "Well, here's what we have. Dr. Henry, even though he was badly bruised, had many contusions, didn't try to register and get seen immediately, although I've heard he wasn't the type to put up with waiting. But even if he had kicked up a fuss, he wouldn't have been given priority because of the severity of other emergencies coming in. Major cases. Two motor vehicle crashes. A cardiac arrest. Child having seizures."

"Yeah," said Mike. "It was quite a scene, I guess. So, back to cause of death? My coffee's getting cold. You know something and I'm waiting."

"Remember, it isn't final, so keep your guesswork to yourself. Johnny Cuszak gave the body a once-over and set the autopsy for tonight. For what it's worth, the facial and body abrasions and most of the bruising occurred well before death. Probably a result of that fall down the cellar stairs."

"What do you mean, 'most of the bruising'?"

"There was more recent bruising. Face and neck were dark blue. Signs of exterior pressure on the neck. Not likely from a stair tumble. That's all Johnny will say, except it looks suggestive."

"You mean someone wheeled the guy into the john, quietly throttled him, walked out and went about his business—whatever his business was?"

"Or her business," said George. "One other matter, although motives don't concern us now. Dr. Henry Philips was a busy man. For the short time I've had to inquire, he annoyed a lot of people. For a few years he was on the board of Northeast Health and they were glad to see the back of him. Retired because of age but liked to keep up with the Mary Starbox Hospital doings, keep the door open."

"And it looks like someone slammed that door," observed Mike, standing up and reaching for his wallet. "Right in his face."

"No," said George, a stickler for facts. "Not in the face. Johnny is thinking someone got his fingers on his carotid sinus and pressed very hard."

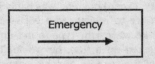

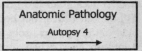

4

JULIA was being settled for the night. Or, to put it in formal terms, attempts were being made by hospital health care providers to settle a difficult patient into something resembling repose. Make her ready for the next act on which the curtains would open early Saturday, August the eighteenth. The angiogram.

Or was it a catherization? Were they the same miserable things? Julia wondered, but not wanting to seem ignorant, had no intention of asking. A pleasant young man, an intern, had visited her room to explain the procedure, but Julia had closed her mind because he looked, with his curly fair hair and healthy color, to be all of thirteen years old, surely not old enough to drive, let alone be allowed loose among adult patients.

This "boy" was followed by a quick visit by the cardiologist, Dr. Eugene Santoro, who would do the so-called "procedure." He was a tall man with high cheekbones, pale blue eyes, and a dark mustache that curled at the ends. He was also noticeably stoop-shouldered, which made Julia wonder about the effect of posture on a physician's hand-eye coordination. She did not take to him. Being in a hospital bed tethered by an IV and other pieces of machinery certainly put one at a disadvantage. An effort would be required for Julia to stay on top of the situation; an effort she didn't feel up to.

"You can call it a procedure," Julia had said to Dr. Santoro as he loomed over her bed. "I gather what you mean is that you plan to dig into my groin with a tube filled with poison and send it into my heart. Then, if you find something blocked up, I'll have another 'procedure' and you'll cut me open like a halibut. I certainly hope you've had plenty of practice doing it. And who is that adolescent who just came in to explain this so-called little affair? He should be skateboarding, not running around with a stethoscope."

Dr. Santoro assured her that angiograms were common affairs, that her anxiety was perfectly normal, that the intern she'd seen was a qualified physician, and they would both be seeing her in the morning. "We'll give you something for a good night's rest," he said. "And make you as comfortable as possible during the procedure." And with a practiced turn and three quick steps, Dr. Santoro was gone.

He was replaced by volunteer Christie Rivers, off duty, just finished with a cafeteria supper. "Julia Clancy! I heard you were here. Thought I'd say hello. You remember me, don't you. I had that chestnut mare, Gilda, in your barn for a summer. We had a little disagreement and I left. Later I gave up riding. Too hazardous at my age."

Julia pulled the top of her johnny up to her neck, a garment with its pattern of tiny flowers that was meant to give the patient a sense of being "at home" in her own bed. But the thing kept getting untied and twisted around her body. Now, aware that she was not at her best, she regarded Christie with a wary eye. Christie, if she remembered correctly, was several years younger than she was, had a temper, and now claimed to have abandoned riding for the ridiculous reason of being "too old." The woman, with the face of a nutcracker, made of sinew, with long bones, could easily have ridden a horse into her nineties.

"Hello," she said reluctantly. "I'm supposed to be resting, but I can talk for a minute or two. So what did you do with Gilda? A nice mare, just coming round. As I think I told you."

"Sold her to someone in New Hampshire," said Christie complacently. "Best thing for all concerned. Well, you certainly chose a busy day to come to the hospital. But I'm sorry you're having trouble."

"Nothing serious," lied Julia. "But this place, never a dull moment. Bodies going by on carts. Policemen sneaking around."

Christie stared. "I've seen the police. Someone is supposed to have died in one of the ER lavatories. Probably of natural causes. A heart attack, maybe. Though I wouldn't know. We volunteer escorts don't gossip about such things."

I'll bet you don't, thought Julia. Aloud she said, "I'm really perfectly fine now, but they're making me have to have an angiogram in the morning."

"I've had one of those," said Christie. "It's not too bad. Putting it on a scale of one to ten."

"The ten being open-heart surgery," Julia put in. "Or being dead."

"Don't be negative," said Christie. "I came out okay. And my husband had three of them. He died here in this hospital, you know. Four arteries bypassed and finally they failed. But you're as strong as one of your horses, Julia Clancy, so I'm not worried. And how is that wonderful Duffie of yours? Plum Duff was his show name, wasn't it?"

Julia began to warm slightly to her visitor. She settled back on her pillow and allowed herself the pleasure of describing Duffie from his days as an awkward yearling who looked like a baby moose to his present handsome condition as a twelve-year-old sixteen-hand bay wonder. Then Christie took her leave, Julia closed her eyes and was just beginning to slip into a doze when Nurse Clare Mitchner stepped into the room carrying a small tray on which sat a plastic cup. "Medications," chirped Clare. "Sleepy-time medications. We want you calm and peaceful all night. And I have some papers for you to sign. So that we have your consent for the procedure."

Julia gave Clare a look of pure dislike and then took the paper and ran a jaundiced eye over the print. "It says I might expect seizures, hemorrhages, blockages, strokes," she said. "And you think I should just smile and sign."

"At the bottom of the sheet," said Clare, pointing.

"But I don't have to? You're not forcing me?" said Julia, clutching her gown to her breast and struggling to sit upright.

"Who's forcing you to do what?" It was Sarah, who had come in behind Clare Mitchner and now bent down to kiss her aunt.

"Now don't go all sloppy on me," said Julia. "It's this angiogram thing. I think Alex and everyone else wants me to just lie here, sign my life away, and let me be wheeled around like a traveling guinea pig."

Sarah pulled over a chair, took the paper, and read it through. "They just want to cover themselves," she said. "It's like the fine print they put in with every prescription. If you believed a third of the stuff, you'd never take a pill. I just had a prescription filled and it went on for paragraphs about possible fits and gastric upset, hives and asthma."

"So I shouldn't sign?"

"Yes, you should. Alex thinks so, too. The angiogram will tell if anything's wrong."

And Julia, mouth turned down, eyes narrowed, signed, and handed the sheet to a pleased Clare Mitchner. "All right, Sarah, I did that just for you. Now have you been over to the farm?"

"All is well. Patrick went home and is in charge. I've called twice. Rafe gave two beginner lessons. Every creature is being fed or grained or walked or put to bed."

"And you haven't seen any more bodies being wheeled down the halls?"

"No," said Sarah. "But I did have to call Grandma Douglas. Your mother, remember. Now don't get upset. She's not coming in. She's going to pray for you. And call Father—what *is* his name?"

"That's Father Joshua Stevenson," said Julia in a weary voice. "A perfectly decent man from all I hear. But I hope Mother isn't thinking of coming to the hospital. It would be too much for her. And for me. Because if she comes she'll bring Father Stevenson and probably acolytes and choir boys and incense."

"Grandma is fine. I saw her last week. And I'll tell her you can have only one visitor and that will be after whatever they decide to do—or not do—about your, your . . ."

"Oh, say it. Heart. What is it anyway about hearts? People can talk about lungs and intestines and rectums and vaginas without flinching, but they always lower their voices and look away when they start in on hearts."

"It's the romance of it all," said Sarah lightly. " 'My heart's in the Highlands a-hunting the deer.' "

"Mother likes to go on about a thing in Genesis that says the 'imagination of a man's heart is evil from his youth.' "

"Now, ladies," interrupted Nurse Mitchner. "Mrs. Clancy has a big day tomorrow and we'll be getting her up early to be prepped."

Julia gave another yank to her hospital gown, pulled the pillow under her neck and fixed Clare Mitchner with a steely eye and intoned:

> *"My heart aches, and a drowsy numbness pains*
> *My sense, as though of hemlock I had drunk,*
> *Or emptied some dull opiate to the drains*
> *One minute past, and Lethe-wards had sunk."*

"Aunt Julia," exclaimed Sarah admiringly, "why, that's Keats."

"I am not," said Julia complacently, "the ignoramus you all think me to be. I had a proper education and learned things like Keats, not like the slop they dish out today in school. And you," she added, turning toward Clare Mitchner, "can start dishing out the hemlock. Good night, Sarah."

It had been decided by the forensic powers in charge of the remains of Dr. Henry Philips that there should be a preliminary examination of his body in the basement morgue of the Mary Starbox Hospital. From there—if foul play, as it appeared, had contributed to his end—his body would be shipped off to Augusta to the forensic facilities there. For now, state pathologist and man-about-town Johnny Cuszak was at the autopsy table, along with the chair of the anatomic pathology department, Dr. Margaret Soldier. George Fitts and Mike Laaka, in gowns and masks and booties, stood by as spectators, along with Alex McKenzie, who had had nothing to do with the whole event, but was present by reason of simple curiosity: His people were involved. Sarah had walked through the ER waiting room and Julia had perhaps noted Henry Phillips, still alive, in the adjacent examining alcove.

"Judging from the bruising," remarked Mike to the others, "this guy took a hell of a fall down those cellar stairs of his. I don't see how he made it to the hospital and just sat there in the waiting room as if he had a sprained thumb. And then somehow got himself to the treatment alcove and onto a stool."

"We ran the body through X-ray," said Johnny. "No bones broken, as far as we can tell. Maybe he was one of those guys who have a high threshold for pain. Or he was in denial. Shock. Who knows. But since he didn't kick up a storm in the waiting room and with all that was going on in the ER, he didn't attract the attention of the triage nurses."

"Get on with it," said George. "We should treat this as a homicide. Correct?"

"And set the ER really on its ear," said Dr. Soldier, a healthy sunburned woman known as Margie. "But then," she finished, "it's good to shake up the ER from time to time."

"The ER is already on its ear," said Johnny. "This will simply stand it on its head. Okay, here's what I see." Pointing with a gloved finger, he indicated the darkened face and head of the former Dr. Henry Philips. "Petechiae, small pinpoint hemorrhages on the head, in the eyes, and probably present—though we don't know yet until we open him—on the internal organs. Judging from the signs of compression around the neck, the man died of asphyxia. You agree, Margie?" he said to Dr. Soldier.

"All the way," said Dr. Soldier with the sort of smile persons meeting her for the first time associated with fashion runways and arty movies and seemed out of place at the autopsy table.

"You mean he was strangled," said Mike. "With a rope? Someone's hands? How in hell was there time for that? One minute he's being seen by Julia sitting on a stool, the next few minutes he's not around, then someone goes into the lavatory and finds him."

"No sign of a rope. Or chain, or tie, scarf, nothing like that," said Johnny. "George's guess was manual compression. I agree. How much time . . . well, that depends. If whoever did the throttling knew what he was doing, got him right under the angle of the jaw and pressed like crazy, it could be over in seconds."

"You mean," said Alex, studying the unpleasing view of the victim's neck, "that here you might have an expert strangler."

"Or a lucky one."

"Or," added Margie Soldier, "you've got an elderly victim in bad shape, unable to fight back, so the job wouldn't be too difficult." Here she spread her small hands and flexed her thumbs.

"Yeah, Margie, you'd make a great strangler," said Johnny. "Anyhow, for now I'm calling it an honest-to-goodness homicide. So we'll get him to Augusta and do a proper job. If we find the guy throttled himself, which is mighty unlikely because as soon as he passes out he'll let go, then we'll leave you people in peace. In the meantime, George, the ball is in your court. You and Mike can set up to make the hospital miserable. Alex, if you and Margie want to drive up to Augusta and see the whole thing to the end, fine. I'll let you both know the time. Now let's bag this fellow and send him on his way."

"What song is that?" said Mike, standing back from the table and unfastening the tabs of his gown. "Something about washing a man right out of your hair."

"*South Pacific,*" said George shortly. "And try and show some respect for a change. Go on back to the ER and tell them what they're in for. Alex, we'll be needing to talk to Julia again. Right now she's about the only witness we've got, maybe the last person to see him alive except, of course, for the murderer. The other big question is, why was Henry Philps in that examining alcove? Who took him there?"

"Maybe he wanted peace and quiet," said Mike.

George, ignoring Mike, returned to Alex. "Let me know what's going on with Julia? Is it going to be surgery? Or do you think we can see her this evening?"

"Wait for the results of the angiogram in the A.M." said Alex. "If it looks like a real blockage, I'm told the surgeon is all set up to take care of it as soon as possible. Maybe Monday A.M. If her cardiologist says okay, you can probably see her after lunch tomorrow. But no heavy stuff, okay?"

"I don't use 'heavy stuff' and especially not with Julia Clancy, for whom I have a great deal of respect," said George, stripping off his gown and picking up a briefcase by the door. "I interrogate possible witnesses in a straightforward way."

"Hah!" said Mike.

"I'm betting on Julia, whatever you do," said Alex.

Julia Clancy in no way resembled the frisky person of Alex's remark. She had had a chat with the anesthesiologist, then had been "settled for the night," as far as someone fastened to leads and tubes and an automatic blood-pressure apparatus can be—the latter being particularly annoying because just as she drifted into an uneasy doze, the damn thing would inflate itself, clamp painfully around her arm and then deflate. The effect of the sedative served by Clare Mitchner, which would, in Clare's words, "make her have pleasant dreams," resulted in fitful episodes of demi-sleep intermixed with dreams of a peculiarly confused nature: horses and barns and floating hospital beds, a body on a toilet, mud slides and bales of hay and an overwhelming sense that something important had been forgotten, that the road she was traveling had been drifted over with snow, was not marked, nor did it lead to anything but a mud-filled pond.

Saturday, with a gray rain-soaked August dawn, came only too early. Julia was roused by the morning shift, a nurse named Tilda Something—Julia couldn't read her ID tag. Tilda approached the bed with a razor and dish of soapy water and spoke briskly of what a nasty day it was outside, but that she and Julia were happily inside and it was time for Julia to be prepped. Then Tilda Something assisted her patient in pulling up her hospital gown and went to work with her razor, making Julia grit her teeth and clutch at her bedclothes. In Tilda's wake a lab person appeared with her tray of glass tubes and stuck Julia where she had not been stuck before, remarked on the poor quality of her veins, and vanished. Then Alex arrived with soothing words before he made rounds of his own patients. Behind came Sarah ready with a kiss, a hand on her aunt's brow.

"You're all acting as if I'm about to have the last rites," complained Julia, brushing Sarah's hand away. "This is all a big fuss about nothing. I expect to be back in the barn by tonight. They can give me some of those nitroglycerin pills in case I feel faint. I will, of course, take it easy for a few days because I'm a perfectly sensible person, and Alex, wipe that smile off your face."

"We'll all think positive thoughts," said Sarah. "One day at a time."

"What I think I need right now," said Julia. "is a double Scotch."

"Time for a buggy ride, Mrs. Clancy," said another relentlessly cheerful voice. A large man in navy-blue scrubs wheeled a gurney into the room, placed it by Julia's bed, let down the rails, and with the able help of Tilda Something, Julia was transferred like an unwilling rag doll to the cart."

"We'll walk along with you," said Alex. "We can recite little proverbs and kind thoughts to meditate on."

"You mean, 'a stitch in time saves nine,' " said Julia, pleased with her own wit. "No scenes, please. But if I don't come back, if someone slips up and puts the tube into the wrong place, my will is in my safe deposit box. Patrick is to have the house he lives in, over by the north pasture, for his lifetime. And Sarah and her bad brother, Tony, my estate."

"Now stop it," said Sarah. "No one is going to slip up. Here you are. . . ."

"If you say 'snug as a bug,' then I will definitely cut you out of my will," said Julia, and with a backward flip of her hand, Julia was pushed through the wide-open doors and was swallowed up in the interior.

"So when do we find out?" asked Sarah as she and Alex walked slowly down the hall.

"Pretty soon. Santoro will beep me in the hospital. And then we'll see what's what."

"I'd hate to think of Julia pale and feeble in a chair sitting on her porch watching someone else exercise Duffie."

"You're as bad as Julia. Remember, you're the one who said one day at a time."

"Or, in this case, two or three hours at a time. Anyway, I've brought my briefcase and I'll just hang out in the lobby."

"What's the news about your Grandmother Douglas?"

"She's in a holding pattern. With the aid of Father Stevenson, who is probably helping Grandma find an appropriate verse in the Bible."

"I'll talk to her myself this afternoon, when we know something," said Alex. He walked off down the hall, and Sarah, toting her overstuffed briefcase, headed for the lobby.

Two hours later, the verdict was in. Alex found Sarah bent over a notebook. She looked up. "I can't concentrate. I keep seeing Julia in a horizontal position. With tubes and monitors."

Alex sat down beside her. "I think you're pretty much on target. They found a fairly large arterial block and don't think a stent will do the trick. So it'll be the bypass route. They're setting it up for Monday. I stopped in her room, where she's being made to stay perfectly still, which she hates."

"Does she know? I mean, about the bypass? Or will there be more than one?"

"I don't know about that. But Julia's being stoical and I'd say furious. At herself. Furious at her body letting her down when, in her words, she has horses to breed and ride and lessons to give."

Sarah grimaced. "Oh dear. I'll go on up to her right now."

"And to brighten up the rest of Julia's day, Santoro and his cardiac buddies have given George Fitts permission for a short interview with her."

"For God's sake, can't they let the poor woman alone?"

"Actually, it isn't a bad idea. It'll take Julia's mind off the coming feature attraction. I think she rather likes the idea of a murder taking place practically at her bedside."

"Julia," said Sarah thoughtfully, "has always been attracted to murder. The kind in books. She reads them all. Murder mysteries that take place in English villages with homicidal vicars and deranged housemaids, plus the gritty American ones with bodies in city streets with syringes sticking out of their foreheads. I'd guess Julia probably knows as much about forensics and police procedure as Johnny Cuszak and Mike and George."

"I don't know if that information cheers me up," said Alex. "But after this morning's interview and the weekend gets finished with, it will be surgery time, and then Julia will be much occupied in getting better. I don't think murder will play much of a part in her recuperation."

Which prediction, as is often the case, was completely off the mark.

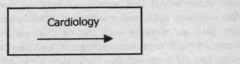

OR 7-First Floor
→

5

SARAH, sitting by Julia's bed that Saturday afternoon, tried to find some words that would bolster—no, not bolster, that was too much to ask—but words that would distract her aunt from her date on Monday with the cardiac surgeon. Julia had been wheeled back from her angiogram, had had bedside conferences with assorted physicians, including Alex, all of whom tried to prepare Julia for the inevitability of going the surgery route.

Now lying flat, denied solid nourishment, submitting to the indignity of a Foley catheter, Julia was under orders not to move a muscle after the angiogram and for six mortal hours to stay perfectly still. Judging from her expression, Sarah thought, she looked like a very small gray-haired and angry gladiator who has just had a bad encounter with a lion in the arena. Well, there was no question about what topic to choose. Horses were the way to go. Therefore, fixing a concerned expression on her face, she asked her aunt her opinion of the quality of hay bought locally. Were her horses thriving on it? What about sour mold? This last nugget Sarah had borrowed from a radio program she had turned on by accident and whose reporter had gone on with great fervor on the disparity between hay bales shipped from other parts of the state and those purchased within the county.

Julia frowned and Sarah felt she had ignited a tiny flame of interest. Even a subject of extraordinary dullness to the average citizen can with effort be made welcome to the right person.

Julia was the right person. Apparently the subject of healthy sweet-smelling hay, bales delivered by a reliable farmer with a truck that wouldn't break down in the middle of the stable yard was a subject close to her heart. A subject that might cause a healthy rise of steam inside the patient.

Julia, immediately more alert, swiveled her head toward Sarah. "You haven't heard anything, have you? Has Patrick called? We were supposed to have a delivery from that new farm in Appleton the day I missed my breakfast."

Sarah wrinkled her brow. "What do you mean, missed your breakfast? Is that the day you had this . . . this attack?"

"I've worked it all out. I was dizzy from lack of food and then tripped over a stone on the way back to the house, which naturally upset my heart. A chain of events. A perfectly good-working cardiac system upset by a stupid fall. Now what have you heard about my hay?"

"Nothing," Sarah assured her. "Patrick hasn't called. I just wanted to know in general. About hay."

"Nothing is more important than good hay. I smell every flake—"

"Flake?"

"Small hay bundle. As you know perfectly well. You've helped with chores. I smell, check for dust, and if I'm the least bit suspicious, out it goes. Straight to the manure pile or compost heap. But why are you suddenly so interested in hay? Are you going to buy a horse or a cow? Or goats? Or simply trying to distract me?"

"No," said a voice behind Sarah. "But I'm here to distract you, Mrs. Clancy." It was Mike Laaka, in tan trousers and a sporty-looking checked cotton shirt. He walked over to her bed, dwarfing the room as he usually did. "You're looking good," he told Julia. "Not like a patient with a tricky heart."

Julia turned on Mike. "I am not 'looking good.' I look like hell. And you always call me Julia, so forget this Mrs. Clancy routine in case you're trying to impress me with how polite you are. I've known you since you aimed your first slingshot at the butt of the horse I was riding and he bolted. And your father and mother are my valued neighbors, whose eggs and vegetables are the best for miles around even if they have a questionable son. And I don't have a tricky heart. Just slightly out of whack because of a fall. Now how are you going to distract me?"

Mike pulled up a chair. "You are a witness to part of this business of a body in the lavatory. Your seeing him in the next-door examining alcove or examining bay or whatever it's called. We want you to think back to your first sighting of this man that you describe as looking battered. Sitting on a stool."

"One of those stools with wheels," put in Julia. "The kind that doctors sit on and whirl around the table when you're lying there trussed up like a turkey."

"Good," said Mike encouragingly. "I didn't know about the wheels."

"I didn't think it mattered," said Julia crossly. "Wheels or no wheels, it was a stool."

"Auntie dear," said Sarah. "Play along with Mike and then he'll leave us in peace."

"Okay, wheels it is," said Mike. "Now you saw this guy sitting. Just sitting. Was he alert? Talking to someone? Crying? Could you see his face? Was he doing anything?"

"Sitting. Just sitting. His hands were folded over his chest. I think. Anyway, I don't think they were hanging down."

"Good. Another detail we need."

"Which I suppose means he wasn't fending off a murderer?" said Julia.

"Possibly," said Mike. "Now who else did you see during that time period?"

"It wasn't a time period. More like half a minute. I had a quick glance. No more."

"Okay," said Mike, the picture of patience. "What and who did you see in that half minute?"

"Whom did you see. 'Whom' is the object of the verb 'see.' "

"Damn it, Julia," said Mike. "You're too healthy to be in here, and so you want to drive me crazy. Okay, 'whom did you see?' "

"I've already told you. Or George Fitts. Someone, anyway. Nurses went by. Doctors, male nurses, female nurses. Aides, I suppose. Maybe lab people, volunteers. Visitors."

"You mean a steady flow?"

"I didn't say that. More like one by one. Or two by two. Like the ark." And here Julia's mouth twitched and Sarah could tell she was enjoying herself.

"Clothes? How do you tell which is which? Or whom is whom?"

Julia allowed herself a larger wrinkle of a smile. "The tall thick ones were probably men, men in scrubs or white coats— or coat and tie, turtleneck and jacket. They're either doctors or physicians' assistants, lab types, or male nurses, I suppose. Or impersonators. The females tend to be shorter and have breast-works, wear scrubs or flowered smocks or white coats. Or they're men in drag. Everyone has an ID tag hanging around their neck. Visitors are usually the ones in home clothes, work clothes, the women carrying handbags."

"You should work for us, Julia," said Mike, grinning. "We need people like you. But you're saying you didn't see a whole gang of people bunched up in your half a minute?"

"You're not listening," said Julia. "I said they went by in ones or twos. Maybe threes. No more."

"Did any of these go into the examining room next to yours? The one with the man sitting on a stool?"

Julia shook her head. "No," she began. And then stopped. "I'm not sure," she added. She closed her eyes and then nodded. "All right. Maybe I did see someone." She smiled and closed her eyes again.

"Damn it, Julia," said Mike for the second time. "Don't torture me."

"I," said Julia, "am being very patient with you even if you don't deserve it. But all right, I saw someone, possibly female. Possibly male. Someone not too tall. Not too short, either. A cotton jacket. Or one of those scrub shirts. Medium blue, I think. It was just a flash. The person must have whisked into the alcove next to me just before the curtains were drawn, and then a lab person turned up next to my bed to suck my blood. And that's it."

"Scrub shirt, not a smock?" Mike asked. "Think. And was it all blue? Or a pattern? ID tag? Color of hair of person? Face?"

"I didn't see the face or the tag. Nor the hair, though I don't think it was blond. Cut short. Or was it? I can't swear. And I don't remember a pattern on the smock or shirt but what I really recall is that banged-up man on the stool first. Just that quick look."

"A wheelchair near the man?" asked Mike.

"As I said before, I didn't notice one. But there are metal carts and chairs and tables being wheeled in every direction—it's like traffic at rush hour. If there was one, it didn't leave an impression. End of interview. Now leave us. Sarah and I were just getting to the bottom of how to choose hay. I think she's going to be keeping goats."

Mike stood up and turned. Then turned back and took Julia's free hand between his own two outsized ones and held it for a minute. "Good luck on all this cardiac business. We can't afford to have you out of action for too long. Think how dull the world would be. And how easy my job." And Mike departed.

Julia looked after him thoughtfully. "Someday I may break down and be really nice to that boy. He works hard and he's good at what he does. Besides, I couldn't live without his family's eggs and fresh tomatoes."

"Don't be too nice all at once, it might upset him," said Sarah. "Mike wouldn't know how to behave."

Julia gave a long sigh, the sort of sigh that began in the bottom of her feet and worked its way through her body, her lungs, and finally, fully grown, blew out of her mouth. "I ought to re-shape my image," she said after a long pause and two lesser exhalations. "I'd hate to expire in the OR and have everyone feel a tremendous sense of relief. Run around giving each other high fives. So maybe I'll try for a kinder, gentler approach."

Saturday and Sunday night passed. Alex and Sarah took turns visiting C-SCU room 35, and reassuring Julia. Cardiologist Eugene Santoro made several visits and tried with pencil, paper, and a chart to explain the minutiae of cardiac surgery and emphasize the improvements made in bypass procedures in the last twenty years.

Beset like Job with "comforters," Julia found herself hard put to maintain her softer approach to the world.

"I keep trying," she told Alex and Sarah, who had arrived at 7:00 A.M. on the Monday morning of surgery. "But someone always turns up to piss me off. I order tea and get prune juice. And those teenagers, the interns and medical students, keep popping in just as I'm going to sleep. They want to practice their gerontology know-how. But I am trying to keep a civil—make that half-civil—tongue in my head. But it's hard. I haven't any personality left."

Sarah grinned at her. "I'm not worried. I think you had enough personality to spare."

"But I feel like someone trying to win the camp-spirit cup by cheating," said Julia. "But I'll try and keep it up. For a little while, anyway."

"That's the idea," said a voice. "I'm Hannah Finch. Remember me? I was on duty in the ER when they brought you in on Friday. And I'll be your nurse until you leave for the OR." Hannah moved toward the bed, the same dark-haired thin, tall, sharp-nosed nurse with bright brown eyes that Julia and Sarah both remembered for the same reason: Finch was a bird and Hannah seemed to favor smocks with a bird motif—today it was chickadees.

"I've a little medication here," said Hannah, approaching with a tray holding a syringe. "To make you relax before your trip. We don't want you anxious or restless."

"Just a drugged traveler going to the guillotine," said Julia.

"What did you just say about kinder and gentler?" asked Alex.

"There's a happy medium," grumbled Julia. "I'm going to give in without a fuss, but I'm allowed to express just a small scrap of irritation."

With which Julia subsided. Alex went off to check on a hospitalized patient, Sarah settled back in the vinyl chair common to all rooms, opened her book, and settled back to rereading *Persuasion* for the umpteenth time. Jane Austen always soothed, and as a plus she would be using it for her Senior English Lit. course in the fall semester.

In the meantime Nurse Hannah moved about, folding gowns, storing bedroom slippers and toilet articles, since Julia would be going to the Cardiac ICU floor after her surgery session. And time dragged—or sped—or ceased to matter—depending on the point of view. For Hannah Finch, time sped; she had much to do in getting her patient ready and her charts brought up-to-date and the details entered into the hospital computer bank. Then she had to prep three other patients and make it out of the hospital in time to catch that new Robert De Niro movie, for which there would be a waiting line.

For Sarah, wanting for her aunt's sake to get the whole affair moving, Julia into surgery and out, time dragged even with *Persuasion* in hand. Maybe *Persuasion* wasn't a good choice; Ann Elliott had such a long history of being pushed about by her family that as a protagonist she sometimes caused her reader to want to kick her. But Sarah persevered.

For Julia, partly drugged, her mind a soft blur, time did not exist. She hovered in a haze at some distance over her bed, and then, with the greatest of ease, paddling her arms in the air, floated out feet-first down the hall, lingered over a water fountain, then light as a feather flew on to the emergency room, back to the examining alcove where she had first been put to bed, and then with the greatest clarity saw a figure wearing a blue-patterned V-necked scrub shirt pushing a wheelchair straight into the next examining bay and disappearing behind the curtains. This vision, although somehow familiar, did not seem disturbing or important, and Julia floated away again and was about to steer herself out the ER door into the ambulance parking area when she was brought to semiconsciousness by hands under her shoulders and the sense that someone was lifting her to a place she did not want to go.

"Up and over," said a cheery voice, and Julia found herself lifted and let down on a cart that had been pushed up next to her bed.

"Ready or not, we're coming," said the same voice, and Julia, half opening her eyes, saw a very large figure in navy-blue scrubs looming over her head.

Julia blinked, shook her head, and forced her eyes wide open. "You may be ready," she said, appalled to hear her voice sounding as if it came from a rusty pipe, "but I'm not ready. I've decided not to go through with this nonsense. I think I'll just go home and get on with things. Evening chores. After all, I have a farm to manage."

At which the large man, blond and ruddy-faced, ready to propel Julia forward, paused—really, Sarah thought as he hesitated, he looks just like the Michelin Tire man. As if he'd been pumped up with too much air.

"Well, you see, Mrs. Clancy," said Nurse Finch, speaking into Julia's left ear, "you've got a date in surgery. And here's Mr. Stonewall—he's a physician's assistant from cardiology—and he's all set to take you down."

"So, Mrs. Clancy," said Mr. Stonewall, "are you ready? I promise you a smooth ride."

"Aunt Julia," began Sarah, bending over her aunt's head. "Everything's all set and—"

"And," said Hannah Finch, "here's Dr. McKenzie coming to walk down with you."

"What I do best," said Alex.

"Alex," said Julia in the same hoarse voice, "I've decided not to. It was a rotten idea. I was talked into it. I need more time to think."

Alex looked down at her. "Say that again, Julia, and look me right in the eye. Because no one's going to force you into cardiac surgery if you've decided against it. But you have a good chance of being patched up as good as new if you do. And if you don't . . . well, I'm depending on what your tests and your cardiologists think and I trust their judgment. They think you should go ahead."

Julia met his eyes and then, after a long moment, dropped her own. "I'm so tired I can't fight. All right, all right. Damn the torpedoes and full speed ahead. What the hell."

"That," said Sarah, "is more like the Julia we know and love."

But Julia had subsided, tightened her mouth, closed her eyes again and began her trip with Alex and Sarah like guards of honor keeping pace with the stretcher—up the hall, down in the elevator, out on the surgical floor, and along another hall. But just as she was about to disappear through the double doors of the cardiac surgery unit, Julia opened her eyes, suddenly more alert, and reached for Sarah's hand. "Take good care of Patrick, he's not so young as he thinks he is. And, tell Alex—oh, there you are Alex—I want to say that I think I did see someone pushing a wheelchair into that alcove room next to mine. A sort of scrub shirt. Or shirt with a V-neck. Bluish, with maybe a pattern. I saw it when I was asleep. As I was flying over the ER. It was like a dream that was real. You know, the room with that banged-up man in it. The one whose body they found sitting next to the toilet."

These words were sufficiently clear that, coming down the hall, a woman in dark green scrubs with a stethoscope draped around her neck and a man in a white lab coat turned their heads for the briefest moment and then went on their way, the words "wheelchair, V-neck shirt, body, toilet" undoubtedly buzzing in their ears.

Sarah just had time to plant a quick kiss on her aunt's forehead before the double doors to the Operating Theater Number 7 swung open and Julia disappeared.

Sarah, left standing uncertainly in the middle of the hall, looked over at Alex. "I feel so useless. What shall I do, wait around here?"

Alex nodded. "Go read for a bit in the surgical waiting room while I try to find Mike and tell him what Julia said about wheelchairs and people in blue V-necked shirts.

"But now Julia's told half the hospital what the killer—if it was the killer—looked like."

"Even if she had whispered, it wouldn't have mattered. It would have leaked out," said Alex. "Human nature is human nature, and the description was very vague. It would fit half of the hospital staff. But I'll pass it along to Mike. Now I've got to see a couple of patients in for observation. Then we can hit the cafeteria for something to eat. I've canceled my afternoon office patients, but it's going to be a long day. We'll have time to kill."

"Nice expression," said Sarah. "But won't Julia's surgery be over when we're eating?"

"No. It's a long procedure. I have my beeper. They'll call when it's over."

"Julia resents the word 'surgery' being replaced by 'procedure.' She said the word could mean cutting toenails or taking out a frontal lobe. I agree with her. It's like calling an undertaker a 'grief comforter.'"

"English teachers," said Alex with a smile, "and persnickety relatives should be kept out of hospitals. The medical vocabulary can cause hypertension."

Mike was still holed up in the meeting (now police-situation) room. He was spending the time between interviews by packing a pile of papers into a briefcase and checking the battery on a tape recorder. His tie was pulled to one side, and even with the air-conditioning going full blast he looked flushed, his light hair damp and his expression one of a man much tried. He waved to Alex, who came in and repeated Julia's possible sighting of a person in a V-necked blue scrub shirt, adding that her remarks had been broadcast to at least two passersby.

Mike listened and grimaced. "Of course everyone around raves about protecting a patient's privacy," he said. "Doesn't make my job any easier. I want them to start talking. I mean this old Dr. Henry Philips hadn't begun to be a patient. I mean he'd just walked into the ER. Maybe he was a wannabe patient but he wasn't registered. I have to keep saying this is a homicide before I can get the time of day out of anyone."

"Yeah," said Alex, "Homicide makes people sit up and take

notice. They can all pretend to fuss about privacy, but give them a hot new tidbit like this and the news will go around like greased lightning. You're right. Mention murder and they'll think it's a legitimate to talk. You'll be hearing more than you want to. I'll bet that by the time Julia's remarks make it back to your ears you'll be told that she saw Lizzie Borden pushing a wheelchair and holding an ax which she brought down on Dr. Henry Philip's head. So get ready. I'm going to meet Sarah in the cafeteria and then we'll wait for Julia to come back from surgery."

Alex's prediction about Julia's remarks was on target. The woman in the dark green scrubs, a neurologist, was an avid reader of mysteries, and after returning to her office engaged in a brief chat with her secretary on the subject of a homicidal someone in their midst. "Someone wearing a V-neck shirt or scrub shirt, maybe with a pattern," said the neurologist, raising her eyebrows suggestively. The man in the lab coat who had walked along with her was not as taken with the description of the person in the V-necked shirt, but, being of a humorous inclination, remarked to his associate in the MRI lab, a Ms. Hengerer, that her blue smock with the V-neck was a provocative garment and that any minute she might find herself hauled up to the police for a good grilling.

These two tiny nuggets of information passed via the secretary and the above Ms. Hengerer, then metastasized into a variety of versions, growing ruffles and flourishes on the way. Thus, by early evening, Mike Laaka had been visited by a number of staff members of the Mary Starbox Memorial Hospital, all of whom wanted him to know that they held patient confidentiality a sacred code, but after all, this was a homicide, wasn't it, and that maybe he'd like to know that just a little while ago some elderly woman on a stretcher being wheeled into the OR had actually seen the killer in action and she had told everyone she'd seen all about it.

Engaged in the important work of discussing the ramifications of Mrs. Clancy's sightings were two members of the hospital volunteer squad plus Clare Mitchner, Julia's cheery nurse from the Cardiac Skilled Care Unit.

These three, gathered before noon in the cafeteria, invigorated by coffee and a plate of cherry-glazed doughnuts, cleared away the question of whether they were engaged in forbidden idle gossip about patients. This was done with a great sense of righteousness by emphasizing the fact that, after all, this was a HOMICIDE, that they all had a citizen's duty TO HELP THE POLICE, as well as to caution one another about the possibilities of encountering a MURDERER just about anywhere in the hospital—halls, hiding in a utility closet, under a patient's bed; who could guess?

"You say Mrs. Clancy actually described someone in a blue shirt," exclaimed Clare. She looked down at her front. "Well, I qualify. I wore a blue smock, or was it a shirt last Friday? Did you say shirt or smock?"

"The whole thing makes me nervous," said Stella. "But I'm glad I was wearing the new blue volunteer smock with no V-neck."

"Shmirt, shmock, what's the difference?" said Christie Rivers. "You'd better go home and burn yours, Clare. I hear that Julia Clancy was on her way to surgery when she announced all this to the whole world. But she must have been pretty drugged by the time she was starting up to surgery."

"I'm sure I don't know," said Clare, shaking her head. "Besides, I never discuss medications."

"All right, so you only discuss murder," said Christie. "But I'll bet she was too out of it to know what she was saying. Anyway, someone told me Mrs. Clancy claimed she saw the wheelchair being wheeled around with this guy in it. The one that was killed."

"Before or after he was killed?" demanded Clare.

"Hey, there," said a deep voice. It was David Bergman, fresh from a second go-round with Mike Laaka, who had wanted another check on persons going to and fro to the emergency room. Now David put a mug of coffee down on the table, reached over for a chair behind him and sank his considerable bulk on the plastic seat. "Listen, you guys, cut out the talk. This Mrs. Clancy story is beginning to sound like one lousy late-night TV show. I mean, like this murderer is going to be pushing a dead body around the ER. Or trying to flush him down the john." David paused, nodded to make his point, and reached for the last doughnut. "These things are the real killers," he said, taking a large bite so that the cherry topping dribbled slightly over his bottom lip.

"The ER Friday morning was something else," said Christie with a note of finality. "Even three wheelchairs with three bodies wouldn't have caused a ripple."

"How many of you have actually seen Mrs. Clancy before she went for the angiogram, because I've never met the woman," said Stella.

"I have," said Clare. "She was one of my patients, but I never talk about my patients."

"Yeah, right," said David. "Sure you don't."

"And I didn't prep her for surgery," said Clare. "So I wasn't there when she was supposed to have said something. She's a nice lady, but a little sharp."

"You mean, not a warm and cuddly granny," said David.

"I don't know a thing about her psyche," said Clare, "but anyone going for cardiac surgery may be forgiven a little bit of confusion. And I hope everything goes well for her. Bypass surgery is no joke."

"Hey," said David again. "I had a quadruple bypass eight years ago and it was hilarious."

And on that note the four brought their attention back to their cooling coffee and the remnants of their killer doughnuts, and Julia Clancy's story faded for the time into the background. After all, they were lingering beyond their usual break; there were patients to push, visitors to direct, flowers to deliver, messages to be taken.

And in surgery, Julia Clancy, out like a light, successfully intubated, had no sense that her sternum was about to be cracked open and her pumping system exposed to the interested view of the cardiac surgical team.

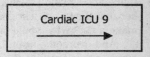

Cardiac ICU 9
→

6

JULIA Clancy, although bodily present in Cardiac Intensive Care Unit number 9 of the Mary Starbox Hospital and watched over by her niece, Sarah Douglas Deane, as well as her nephew-by-marriage, Alexander McKenzie, was in a psychic sense very much elsewhere.

Julia, head spinning, dropped into chasms, over boiling falls, down rushing rivers. She twirled, she tossed, she dangled, and then plunged headfirst into a crackling furnace of yellow and red flames—or were they burning leaves?—a bonfire?—was it October already? Or October last year? But someone had raked the leaves into a pile on her neck and her shoulders and her chest, and if she wasn't careful, didn't get away immediately, she'd be consumed. What did her young riding students say, "You're toast." That was right, she'd be toast. Burned to a crisp. Her hand groped for her chest and she felt someone take hold of her wrist and replace it under something. A sheet, a blanket, a barn door, another pile of leaves?

"Just take it easy, Mrs. Clancy," said a voice. A familiar voice. Who was it? The person burning leaves on her body, the leaves were burning right there on her shoulders and on her chest. What nonsense. People didn't do such things unless they were in one of those terrorist camps. But now it was too much trouble to think, and she didn't want to listen to the person who was telling her that they were just going to take a little blood and could she make a fist? Why would anyone want old blood like hers?

And overcome again by the forces of darkness, Julia drifted away. Away through the long Monday afternoon and evening, through the longer night, and then it was Tuesday morning. Dimly aware that someone was standing close to her, she began to remember. Damnation. She was in this blasted hospital having something done to her that she hadn't wanted done.

"No-good rotten plan," she mumbled. "Not my idea."

"What, Aunt Julia?" said Sarah, leaning over the bed. She and Alex had been watching on and off through the Monday afternoon after Julia, some six hours after surgery, had been wheeled into the Cardiac ICU, swaddled like a mummy and stuck with a million tubes. Sarah had then spent the night curled up on the waiting-room sofa, Alex visiting at irregular intervals. Now it was well past eight on Tuesday morning and the thoughts of both had turned toward something like breakfast washed down by gallons of hot tea and black coffee.

But now, after more indistinct mumbling, and then some mixed-up words about horses and the disposal of manure, Julia subsided, her eyes closed, and her fidgeting hand fell slack.

"That's it, close your eyes and try to rest," said the nurse, the same Hannah Finch who wore smocks with bird designs and who had taken care of Julia before surgery. Now, transferred to Cardiac ICU duty, she hovered over the bed adjusting the drip of the IV. She turned to Sarah. "She's just mixed up in her mind. Surgery, anesthesia does that. I'll be giving her something for pain."

Julia drifted for a few minutes but then became aware that people were talking. Whispering. Making little clicking noises. Scuffing with their shoes. Rustling. And the automatic blood-pressure cuff was inflating itself, gripping her arm like a vise, then slowly deflating. And as it did, Julia twisted to her side and began to retch. And then sank back, exhausted, confused. Struggling with consciousness and nausea, her eyes partly open, her hand plucking at a cluster of tubes entering the side of her neck. Then suddenly, she opened her eyes. Turned her head slightly and saw her visitors. Focused. Then fixed on Sarah and then Alex with the "Clancy eye" and in a thick voice, a voice still hoarse from her throat's encounter with the intubation machinery, recited:

> The best laid schemes o'mice an' men
> Gang aft agley,
> An' lea'e us nought but grief an' pain
> For promis'd joy!

Sarah smiled in relief and Alex grinned. Julia was famed for her sudden recitations of Robert Burns in a heavy if not entirely authentic Scots burr, especially after a flagon or so of her favorite Scotch whisky. And she was a Douglas by birth, with a father born a short distance from Edinburgh.

But to Nurse Hannah Finch, Julia was plainly still befuddled by drugs and speaking in tongues.

"Now, Mrs. Clancy," said Hannah, "you just rest. Don't try to talk. I'm going to give you something for discomfort."

"Discomfort, hah!" said Julia. "Grief an' pain. As I said. Did ye no hear me, ye puir wee nursie."

"Now, Aunt Julia," Sarah began.

But Julia gave the briefest of crooked smiles and shut her eyes.

"It's all right," said Hannah. "Anesthesia does that. Scrambles your thinking. She'll settle down after I give her the Demerol. It's lucky she has the ICU at the end of the hall. Less traffic going by and I'll bet your aunt is someone who likes her privacy. Now why don't you two go out and have a bite to eat. And come back later."

The suggestion was a welcome one, and Sarah and Alex slipped out of the room and began to discuss options for a quick breakfast. "Not the hospital cafeteria," said Alex. "I spend entirely too much time there as it is. Besides, Mike might find us."

Sarah nodded. "Mike has radar if he wants something. So let's not go by that meeting room he's been shacking up in."

"Right," said Alex. "We can cut in behind X-ray, go down to

the basement and leave by one of the delivery doors."

"Down where they take the bodies?" asked Sarah as Alex shoved a heavy door open and they started down the steps, their feet making hollow sounds on the stone-and-metal stairway.

"You can't have bodies being wheeled through the front lobby."

"Because," finished Sarah, "it might discourage patients who are about to register."

Alex strode ahead, turning left, then right, wall after wall, all in a dull beige. Once, a glass door gave out on walls that exploded in color. Murals of seaside scenes complete with large fish and beach umbrellas."

"Look at that!" exclaimed Sarah. "Florida in the basement. But who on earth comes down to see all this? Dead bodies and escaping doctors?"

"Special-use rooms," said Alex. "Cardiac, respiratory rehab, children's playroom. You name it. I think the hospital auxiliary people got hold of some artists. To cheer people up. Now turn left and we'll duck into the parking lot, get into the car and get out of here."

But Mike Laaka was leaning against the hood of Alex's Jeep, a notebook tucked under his arm, his necktie loosened, the sleeves of his blue shirt rolled to the elbows.

"Good morning," said Mike, lifting a hand in greeting.

"Why aren't you back in the hospital doing what you're supposed to be doing?" demanded Sarah.

"We are going to have a two-person meal," said Alex. "Without police help."

"We can be a trio. You can tell me about Julia. How's she making out?"

Nothing disarms so much as a sincere inquiry about an ailing friend, so Sarah and Alex filled in the details, and before they knew it, Mike was in the backseat of the Jeep.

"We'll make it quick," said Mike. "I want a sense of how the hospital—particularly the ER scene—works. You know, 'Emergency Room for Dummies.' Who works there, how long a shift and who's likely to just turn up. And all those volunteers." Mike suddenly gestured toward a road sign indicating the Liberty Diner. "That'll do, won't it? Juice, coffee, and a stack of something."

"You," said Sarah firmly, "were not invited to our little meal. So we'll choose the place, won't we, Alex."

Alex nodded. "We will. And we choose the Liberty Diner. Good chicken sausage, waffles, oatmeal. The works."

"Do I have a vote?" demanded Sarah as Alex swung the car into the parking lot.

"No," said Mike, climbing out of the backseat. "You are just decorative baggage."

Sarah's brain was too numb to rise to the bait verbally and so she contented herself with administering a quick kick to Mike's shin.

They settled themselves in a booth at the far end of the café under a colorful poster showing a handsome windblown youth at the bow of a boat and holding a lobster aloft while the letters below urged citizens to support the Maine fishermen.

"Listen, Mike," said Alex, after the first satisfying swallow of coffee, "I'm no expert on all the hospital setups. I mean, I know generally, but I probably couldn't find a swab or a tongue depressor on some of the floors."

"I don't think," said Sarah, looking up from her bowl of oatmeal, " "that Mike wants blueprints but to know about the people. Different types and jobs."

"There, you see," said Mike. "I thought we might find a use for you. Yes, Alex, start with the ER—the regulars, the patients, and end with the volunteers. How the departments work together, if they do, which I doubt. Just a thumbnail sketch. I'm having trouble getting a grip on all those guys." Here Mike produced a tape recorder from his briefcase and punched a button.

Alex sighed. "You think this is necessary? No, don't answer that. But if I know your boss, Sergeant George Fitts, he's on it already. Has a list of the attendings, the residents, the interns, the PA's—physicians' assistants to you. Nurses, aides, lab people. Med students. But okay, I'll rough in the jobs and the services for you and then you're on your own." With which Alex took Mike on a quick gallop through the hospital staff, the various departments and services, assorted chains of command, the chiefs, the peasants, and the drones.

"Listen," said Mike, turning off the tape recorder, "this is helpful. I'm to fill in the background gaps because George is working full-time on getting a line on the people who came into the ER during the so-called murder period. Most of the ones who came by ambulance were too sick to notice much and were hustled into examining rooms. As you guys say, 'stat.' But here's the real hitch. The other bunch of patients, those who came in to the ER by car or were brought by friends and family. They're the ones who spent quality—no, make that quantity—time in the waiting room. The triage people put ninety percent of those guys on hold. They're the ones who need the magazines and the TV and those little pamphlets about herpes and lung cancer and getting your mammogram. And then there are the waifs and strays who just turn up."

"Where," asked Alex, putting down his fork, which had impaled a piece of his chicken sausage dripping in syrup, "is all this going? What are you trying to say?"

"Mike's trying to say," said Sarah in her role as interpreter for dimwits, "that these people in the ER waiting room are the ones he wants to rely on as witnesses since they spent so much time there."

"Right on," said Mike. "Sarah, you're being positively useful. The problem is, as people keep pointing out, that everybody in the hospital looks the same. You can't tell a physician from the maintenance man. Like someone pushing a vacuum cleaner might not be from housekeeping but a forensic guy from Augusta sucking up bits of DNA. We need to straighten out the cast of characters. Who's playing which part."

"You're saying," Alex said, "that these useful witnesses can only describe people they saw by their hair and eyes and body shape, but not by their uniform. Since nobody wears a uniform anymore." He chewed on a piece of sausage and then shook his head.

"So I can't help you," he added. "I doubt that any one person can identify all the hospital employees. It's a hell of a big place. Ask your ER waiting-room people if they saw a stethoscope hanging around the neck. If they did, well, the person probably isn't a plumber or the dietician. He might actually be involved in something medical. Go by physical appearance. And good luck because anyone can walk into a crowded waiting room and unless they scream or detonate something, no one would stop them."

Sarah stood up suddenly. "So it's hopeless, and now I think we'd better get back to Julia. She should be a little more awake now. Come on, Mike. You've made your point. The hospital is crammed with impostors and clones."

Strangely enough, Julia Clancy, now fairly awake but fretful and generally miserable, was bothered by the same problem as Mike Laaka. She explained this to Sarah, who had pulled up a chair as close as she could to a patient who was encumbered with side rails, tubes, loops, lines, catheters, and overhanging monitors. Alex had settled back in the armchair by the window, a magazine on his lap, but ready when called on with calming remarks or soothing explanations of some arcane piece of medical equipment.

"In my day," complained Julia in those time-honored words, "you could tell who did what by looking at them. You knew who could be trusted." She lifted a limp hand a few inches from the bed and gestured toward the open door, where a figure in a long brown tube dress and with chart under arm, stethoscope around her neck, was passing by.

"Yes, Aunt Julia," said Sarah obediently, forcing herself into an affirmative mode, determined not to contradict a single assumption.

"A nurse in my day," Julia went on, "wore a uniform. A white uniform with a little pin on the pocket or collar so you tell that she'd graduated from something. And a little ruffled starched cap so you could tell that she'd had her training at a real hospital. You didn't confuse her with somebody delivering lunch menus. And doctors wore long white coats and neckties, not flannel shirts and fishing boots. Or long wool dresses with beads clanking around their necks. And interns wore short white jackets and white pants, which told you they didn't know all that much. And medical students wore hand-me-down white jackets and their own trousers, which told everyone, they didn't know a damn thing. And no one ran around in scrub suits unless they were in the operating room. And . . ." Julia's voice trailed off. "And I hate it here," she finished, her voice falling. "I feel like hell. Besides sawing my chest in two, that fool surgeon has broken my shoulder blades."

"Now, Aunt Julia," Sarah began, forgetting her vow only to nod and smile.

But Alex held up a hand, reached over to Julia's call bell. "Time for peace and quiet through the magic of chemistry. Something to take care of those shoulder blades. In a day or so perhaps we can get a massage for you. Ah, here she is."

This as a gray-haired nurse in a black-checked shirt and a pair of green slacks appeared at the door. Alex greeted her, Sarah said, "Oh, good," and Julia huffed with annoyance but then accepted her medication without complaint.

"She wishes you had a nice starched white uniform and a cap with a little black velvet band, and white shoes and stockings," Sarah told the nurse as she and Alex prepared to depart.

"Where's that Hannah Finch?" Julia asked the nurse. "The iron maiden."

"Hannah's off duty. She'll be back tomorrow," said the nurse. "She told me to take extra good care of Mrs. Clancy."

"I'll bet she did," said Julia thickly.

Sarah squinted at the newcomer's plastic ID card that hung from her neck. "You're Tanya. It's good to meet you. And Aunt Julia really doesn't mean what she says."

"I mean every word" came a voice from the bed. "Bypass surgery. That entitles me."

"But only for forty-eight hours postoperative," said Alex. He leaned over, moved a line that entered her neck under the side of her chin and gave her a resounding kiss. "Behave, Julia, or I'll lose my license."

* * *

74

Those who have passed nights as patients in an intensive care unit know that they are not places suitable for repose. Nor rest. Nor tranquillity, peace, and, least of all, sleep. They are, at best, hives of activity. Curtains are pulled back; lights go on; blood is taken (after the tedious business of finding a "good" vein), monitors are noted, hooked and unhooked; heart rate is noted; catheters are examined, urine output measured; IV flow is checked; medications are administered by mouth, by IV, subcutaneously; oxygen levels are recorded; edema is looked for (proddings of legs and feet); fluid intake is encouraged; pain medication is proffered; nurses, interns, residents, physicians' assistants drop by to check on leads and lines and "vital signs," so that the passing night comes to resemble nothing so much as a nocturnal Fourth of July parade.

Of course on Monday, her first night after surgery, Julia had been pretty much out of it. But now, on Tuesday night, she was alternately woozy with medication or restless and fretful. By midnight, Julia had given up any serious idea of having more than twenty minutes of sleep at one time. She had also abandoned the idea of a kinder, gentler approach to the world. All efforts would be directed at finding a semicomfortable position on her bed, hugging a small pillow over her incision so that a small sneeze or cough would not split her sternum into two pieces. Also she must try to avoid entangling herself with all the tubes, keep her oxygen leads hooked around her ears and clamped into her nostrils, and not tangle her left foot in the tube leading to her Foley catheter. And prevent her loose hand from clawing at her aching incision. In short, endurance was all; civility was nothing.

Thus Julia only responded to the passing parade of "caregivers" with a series of grunts, humphs, and growls. Only once, when an aide arriving with fresh water hoped she'd have "a great night's sleep" did Julia's hand, the one unencumbered by IV lines, reach toward her bedside table with the idea of hurling the water glass at her head. But a sharp pain put a stop to the action and Julia subsided with a snarl. And gradually, minute by minute, she slipped into a semisleep; a sleep woven into incoherent images—

or were they hallucinations?—of a flaring of yellow lights, prowling lions, and exploding mountain peaks.

Then she was awake. Groggy but awake. That damn automatic blood-pressure cuff again. Blowing up, squeezing, and letting go. The Cardiac ICU "room,"—actually a glass-fronted cubical with a partly drawn curtain—was in semidarkness so that figures passed by the open door as blurred silhouettes. Somewhere in the hall outside a light blinked. A disembodied voice was paging someone. A Dr. Frankenstein? No, that couldn't be right. Or maybe, Julia thought in a confused way, I've lost all grip on the world and I'm in a movie. I'm a feature attraction, and any minute now someone in a mask and gown is going to come in and attach me to a machine that will . . . will what? Blow me to kingdom come? Give me the brains of a turtle? Transport me to a pink fluffy cloud and serve me a bowl of Jell-O? But with this last thought, a wave of nausea swept over Julia and she closed her eyes again.

And opened them. Someone, yet another someone, was hovering at the door. Someone who no doubt held a syringe or some other object for keeping a patient awake. Julia braced herself. Waited. And then the someone paused at the door, seemed to hesitate, and then on cat's feet (as the poet would have it) padded into the room. Padded as if his shoes had been muffled. Of course, Julia told herself. Some of these people run around not only in gown and mask but with their head in shower caps and their feet encased in paper booties. It was the surgical "look."

But this particular "intruder" did not speak, and Julia in her muddled state wasn't about to initiate a midnight chat. He—or she—simply approached the bed, looked up to check the overhead monitors, then shuffled off into the lavatory and returned with a length of tubing held in a gloved hand. Julia, squinting, could see that the hand was indeed gloved. Nothing unusual in that, she thought. Half the population of those "caregivers" who came in the room was protected against the noxious body fluids and exhalations of the patient. But what about the patients? Julia asked herself, as the figure began fussing with the IV tube. Who's protecting them from injurious hospital staff members? But now this silent shuffler was getting on her nerves. She roused herself.

"What do you want to do?" she asked in a loud whisper. Somehow the darkened room and the late hour made whispering seem appropriate.

The figure paused, hand held on the IV plastic bag. From under the mask came another whisper. "S'okay, dear. Just checking. Your vital signs. Your IV. Go on back to sleep."

"But I'm not asleep. And I can't get to sleep while you're fiddling around," said Julia, still whispering, but louder this time."

"Just relax," said the voice. "Checking your heart rate. Right under your ear."

"Carotid artery," mumbled Julia. "Don't you have one of those finger things with the claws?"

"Not always accurate," said the voice. And a long arm in its gown reached around Julia's neck and gently ran a finger along her throat and settled itself at the angle of her jaw a few inches away from her left ear. The capped head nodded as if pleased.

"I suppose you've found out that I still have a pulse?" said Julia, making no effort to keep sarcasm out of her voice, no longer a whisper.

"Let's get a better read," said the voice, lower now. Almost inaudible. Then, in a single movement, the other arm of the visitor, its gloved hand holding the length of plastic tubing, rose over Julia's head, slipped the tube around her neck, grasped the end with the first hand, gave a savage yank and began twisting the tube tight. And tighter.

And Julia gave a strangled gasp for air, frantically reached into space with her free hand, saw the already darkened room turn darker. Turn black. And disappear.

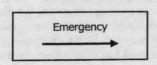

Emergency

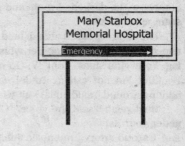

Mary Starbox
Memorial Hospital

Emergency ──────▶

7

NO air. Something pressing down. Squeezing. Throat. Can't breathe. Air. I want air.

Then, suddenly, as if it never happened, the tightness eased. The tube slipped away from around her neck, and Julia was left twisting about on her bed, gulping for air, her throat rattling. Her mouth gaping like a just-landed fish. Her free hand scrabbling at her chest. And at the same time she heard small sounds of someone moving. Moving away, the sound of feet in paper booties shuffling away from the bed. Then someone coming in. Firmer footsteps approaching the bed. Overhead lights—blinding—coming on.

Julia gasped. And gasped. And took three shuddering breaths and someone reached over and took hold of her wrist.

"Mrs. Clancy, Mrs. Clancy," the voice, a woman's voice, said urgently. "Mrs. Clancy, can you hear me? What's wrong?"

But before Julia could dredge up any coherent answer, the room was suddenly crowded. Five people, one pushing a wheeled cart that rattled. Garbled talk of monitors, breathing rates, resuscitation, defibrillation, codes, and then, as the rise and fall of Julia's chest subsided into something like a normal rhythm, the five (three scrub suits and two colored jackets) began to relax slightly and take an inventory of their patient.

Julia struggled to explain. But the more she tried, in a hoarse voice, to describe what seemed like a stealth attack with a length of tubing, the more confused and unreal her story seemed even to her own ears. She couldn't say with any reassuring detail what he/she had looked like, nor exactly what he/she had said. She couldn't describe the sequence of events, or explain in a logical way what had actually happened.

"I think," said a nurse, who had been monitoring her blood pressure, "that you may have been having a dream, a wild dream, and then some saliva went down the wrong way, into your trachea, and you started to choke and cough. Couldn't get your breath and panicked. So all the bells and lights on our monitors at the nurses' station went off. And here we are."

Julia tried again, careful now to keep her voice calm and level—it would never do to come off as an hysterical senior citizen, reacting to a nightmare or worse, having gone completely crackers. "It wasn't my imagination. Even if I couldn't see very well, the person who came in was wearing a gown and a mask and those foot covers. He—or she—or it spoke. Low soft voice, about checking my vital signs. Telling me to relax. Wanted to check the pulse rate at my neck. Then pulled that tubing around my neck. Twisted it. The tubing, I mean. I couldn't breathe. Then whoever it was went away and you and everyone came in."

Julia squinted now and tried to focus on the nurse, because she seemed to be the same person, judging from face and shape, as Clare somebody, the one who had called her honey and dear. So Julia began to explain that she wasn't given to wild imaginings and did not expect to be throttled in a hospital. And look at her neck: wasn't it red and marked?

But Clare, running a quick finger over Julia's neck, a part of her anatomy already disfigured by lines and tubes, just nodded, smiled reassuringly, straightened Julia's pillow, and began to make soothing remarks explaining that vivid and strange dreams were all part of the aftermath of a cardiac surgery package. And then someone began detaching her monitoring leads and fixing new sticky tabs on her shoulders, her breast, under her ribs, and Julia understood that the EKG machinery was about to crank up.

After which came another blood-pressure check, a visit from the lab bloodsucker. Then, last, a knock-out sleeping capsule that Julia, by now shaky and exhausted, accepted gratefully. And in minutes she had passed out and into another series of swirling dreams that made a mere nocturnal strangling seem like an everyday event.

Sarah, arriving at seven-thirty on Wednesday morning, found her aunt asleep. Confronting the nurse at the station—the familiar-looking Tanya, who had cared for her aunt sometime in the last few confused days—she was told that Mrs. Clancy had had a very disturbed night. "You know that after major surgery, the anesthesia, some people stay disoriented for quite a while."

"Aunt Julia was pretty with it last night," said Sarah. "Before I left. She certainly knew where she was."

"Well, possibly," admitted Tanya, "but these things take time. Clare says she was very confused last night, and Hannah Finch tells me the poor woman was talking absolute gibberish yesterday. In some sort of an accent."

Sarah was about to explain about Robert Burns, but Tanya, responding to a light over a cubicle, stood up and moved quickly down the hall.

A sense of great relief washed over Sarah. It was a beautiful day, and since Aunt Julia was, temporarily, at peace, why not grab something for breakfast, a takeout—some juice, tea, a roll—and sit outside at one of those picnic tables the hospital auxiliary had so thoughtfully scattered about the grounds of the hospital. Sarah turned her steps toward the Cardiac ICU exit and then halted. A tall man stood at the nurses' station and in a clear voice was asking for Mrs. Julia Clancy's room.

Before the nurse could answer, Sarah, in the role of the nearest available relative, confronted the man and introduced herself.

The man was an extraordinarily handsome male—tall, brown-eyed, short black hair, high cheekbones, strong mouth, taut skin the color of coffee. In short, some sort of mythic god come down to earth. By way of Tahiti, Western Samoa, or some similar enchanted shore, Sarah thought. He held out his hand and gave his name as Joshua Stevenson—not a name suitable for a deity, but nobody was perfect.

"I'm here to visit Mrs. Clancy," he explained. "I had a call from her mother, Mrs. Anthony Douglas. One of my parishioners. She wanted me to look in. See if I could help in any way, since Mrs. Douglas was told that she shouldn't visit her daughter so soon after surgery. A good decision, since Mrs. Douglas is getting over an upset stomach."

As Joshua Stevenson explained himself in a modulated baritone—the sort of voice any god should have—Sarah saw that under his light denim jacket he wore the circular stiff white collar of an Episcopal priest. Of course, other denominations sported a white collar. Roman Catholics, certainly, and maybe Lutherans. Did Methodists? she wondered.

Sarah came to from these speculations to realize the man had stopped talking and was waiting for an answer.

"I'm sorry," she said, moving her eyes away from his collar. "I was thinking of something else. I wasn't paying attention."

"That happens to me a lot," said Joshua Stevenson. "Especially on Sunday morning. But Mrs. Douglas really thought that some sort of pastoral call might be in order. Or just a friendly visit because Mrs. Douglas didn't think Mrs. Clancy went to church. And I thought, because of the name, Clancy, she might be Catholic. In which case, I suppose she'd rather see her own priest."

Sarah, longing for her breakfast and the morning sun, pulled herself together long enough to say that Aunt Julia wasn't Catholic, although her Irish husband, Thomas Clancy, had been. And that as far as Sarah knew, Aunt Julia didn't go to any church unless it was for a wedding or a funeral. Besides, Sunday mornings on her farm were pretty busy places. Riding lessons, training, horse shows. Things like that."

"So you don't think I should stick my head in and say hello?" persisted Joshua Stevenson.

Sarah considered. He was so handsome. And cheerful. And apparently willing. Who could object to such a person stopping by for a few minutes?

"Wait a bit," said Sarah. "Then give it a try. Aunt Julia had a bad night and is still asleep. And when you go in, well, I wouldn't rush into praying right away. Or talking about the heart attack being the Lord's will. She might chew your head off."

"God, no," said Father Stevenson, appropriately. "It will be low-key. Just a friend of her mother's."

"Which will make her smell a rat right away, if you'll excuse the expression," said Sarah. "But if you know anything about horses or the poems of Robert Burns, it might help."

And Sarah headed for the cafeteria, paid for her takeout breakfast of muffins and tea, and with a sense of stolen pleasure headed for the hospital grounds where, with a copy of *Northanger Abbey* in her handbag—she had finished *Persuasion*—she could enjoy a few moments of reading and the comfort of being outside under an early-morning August sun. It was, she found, possible to get away from the shadow of the hospital itself, which, being a series of concrete rectangles rising up like small factories, offered little joy. However, the expanse of lawn and shrubs on the south side of the building, well away from the packed parking lots, gave visitors and staff a welcome respite from the medical scene.

Thanks to a good sprinkler system, the grounds at the south edge of the hospital complex, even with a dry August, were green. The dark foliage of the azaleas; the rhododendrons, the japonica, the clumps of small annuals, white and purple, circling around the buildings, were well-tended, and a number of benches and picnic tables had been scattered about under trees and by small pathways. Sarah settled happily down at an empty picnic table, opened her cardboard box to two corn muffins, a pat of butter, and a tiny container of blueberry jam. Next to these she placed her paper cup of tea and opened *Northanger Abbey* to the chapter where Mr. Tilney is teasing Catherine Morland when they first meet in Bath. Sarah got happily through two pages—and was joined. Three times over. Joined by the trio of senior and veteran volunteers. Christie Rivers, Stella Dugan, and strong man David Bergman.

Christie Rivers, leading the others, each clutching a container of food and a paper cup of coffee, halted by Sarah's table, claimed her as someone connected with Julia Clancy, and asked if she and her friends could join her.

"I've seen you down the hall going into her room. Julia and I are old acquaintances," said Christie. "I once had a horse in her stable, but we didn't agree on training. Anyway, how *is* she doing? I visited her before surgery and thought she wasn't quite herself."

Sarah swallowed hard. Invasion was at hand, with no escape in sight. She put down her book and smiled. "I'm Sarah Deane, Julia Clancy's niece, and she's coming along pretty well but had a hard night. Won't you . . ." Sarah hesitated, finding the words were refusing to come out.

"Yes, we'd love to join you. You don't mind, do you? You're probably worried and need company. These are my fellow slaves in the volunteer corps." Christie put down her paper cup on the table and settled next to Sarah. "We try to take our break in the fresh air. Been doing it together for years."

"Sort of a club," put in David, sliding into the picnic table across from Christie and banging his larger food container down in front of him.

"Because we all began volunteering at the same time," added Stella Dugan, taking her place. "We got to know each other real well when we did our orientation."

Sarah eyed them and with an effort kept the smile on her face. David, round bald head, gray walrus mustache, bursting out of his jacket; Christie with her lean jaw, clipped hair, and bony hands, like one of those oldtime math teachers who did things to students with a ruler; and Stella Dugan, a hazel-eyed woman of more sympathetic proportions, rounded in a matronly way, her frizzed red hair like a small bush on her head, who exuded a nervous fidgety warmth.

"And," said Christie, as if this put the keystone of their relationship in place, "we three had all lost someone. At this hospital."

"A loved one," said Stella. "My husband. Terry. He had a terrible time, so much pain, and no one seemed to handle it right. It was awful and I almost went crazy."

"It was my dad," said David. He took a bite out of a frosted muffin, chewed and then nodded. "I mean, it was no great surprise. Dad was ninety-one. Died in the ICU. Two days after he'd been brought in. By ambulance." And David took a long draft of coffee and returned to his muffin.

Sarah, trying not to make it obvious, inspected the three. All somewhere in their late sixties, early seventies, she guessed. All friends or at least acquaintances of long standing. Easy in one another's company. Each dressed in their volunteer "uniform" which, as Sarah had begun to realize, was anything but uniform. David who looked like the cartoon of an heroic worker, some sort of Ajax, with hands like shovels, wore the new (new three years ago) regulation-blue, now faded from much washing, his ID card hanging around his neck. Sarah, leaning forward slightly, noticed with interest that David's photograph showed him with a darker mustache than he had at present and concluded that the picture was a considerably earlier version of the man.

The same could be said for the other two ID photographs. Sarah, not as occupied as the others with getting food down her throat, saw that Christie's picture showed that her features were rounder, less chiseled, and that her hair was partly brown instead of the present dark gray. As far as uniforms went, Christie wore the former regulation-green smock, and Stella Dugan the new blue model with the hospital lighthouse logo on a lapel. Stella's ID picture, like that of the others, showed a younger face with darker red hair. But it was hardly diplomatic to remark that none of the present company was properly represented by their hospital photographs.

Sarah considered these contradictions, but how they could be fitted into a murder scenario was beyond her. Just so much trivia, she decided, and returned her attention to her breakfast, sipped her now cooling tea, and listened as the three began to describe their arrival in the volunteer ranks.

"I felt I had to do something," said Stella plaintively. "I mean,

I had to get over the idea that the hospital screwed up with the pain thing. They acted like Terry might get addicted to drugs, and there he was dying right in front of them. Anyway, forget and forgive, I always say. Or at least the church says. And Pastor Hardy, he told me to go out and help out in the world somewhere. And I knew the hospital backward and forward because Terry was in and out like a yo-yo."

Sarah murmured something of a sympathetic nature, and David took up the tale of his dad's dying. His falling out of his hospital bed because someone had forgotten to put up one of the side rails.

"Hell, things like that happen," said David. "They shouldn't, but they do. And Dad was on his way out anyway. So none of us family made a big deal out of it. Hell, just the day before, I lowered his bed rail and walked away, and the nurse chewed me out for it. Tit for tat, I guess it was. Anyway, like Stella here, I knew my way around the hospital, so I decided to volunteer. Since I was retired anyway. I can lift anything and I think they always need someone like me to hoist wheelchairs and stretchers around."

Christie, too, seemed to have a horror story. Her husband had made it clear that he didn't want to be revived if he stopped breathing. Enough was enough and he was shot through with cancer. No hope. The family all agreed. But the order for No Code seemed to have been mislaid and a full-force resuscitation team had come crashing down the hall and done mouth-to-mouth and pounded his chest and zapped him with paddles and injected him until the family rose up and with the help of a resident stopped them in their tracks. It had been a terrible scene, but, as Christie explained, like the others, it was water over the dam. Time to move on. And now she was committed to "making a difference" in the role of a pusher of wheelchairs and taker of messages and flowers.

"The hospital couldn't get along without people like you," observed Sarah, trying to move the conversation away from past distress to present time. "I think it's great to have regular people from the outside world, not part of the medical staff, helping out. Lots of patients, and visitors, too, are a little intimidated by medical types."

"Of course," said Christie, repeating what members of the older generation were forever pointing out, "you can't tell a medical type anymore. Even we get called 'doctor.' Or 'nurse.' Now tell me, exactly how is Julia doing?" She turned to the others. "Julia Clancy told me she was going to have bypass surgery."

"Well, she had it," said Sarah. "And I gather she had a rough night. Awake a lot and having bad dreams. But the first days are always hard."

"Post-op," said Christie knowledgeably, "is never a piece of cake. Especially for bypass. Having your chest carved in two."

Sarah winced and felt a cold knife trace down her sternum.

"That," said Stella, frowning, "isn't a nice way to talk to the patient's niece.

"I'll change the subject," said Christie, "and ask Sarah here if she's been in to see the police yet. They're talking to everyone. Including the volunteers. We've all been asked questions just to make us feel guilty. All about that man, Lord Henry Dent Philips, whose body was found."

"Who?" asked Sarah, puzzled. "What do you mean, 'Lord Henry'?"

"He was called that," explained Stella. "Or Dr. Nosy Parker. Finger in every hospital pie. Caused real trouble. Even after he retired."

"Me," said David Berman, "I don't feel guilty because some cop asks me questions. Wish I could have stopped whatever was happening to Dr. Philips—even if I couldn't stand the bastard. But you can't be everywhere, and I was pushing carts and stretchers from here to kingdom come and I didn't see a thing in the ER. It was in and out, in and out."

"I was in and out of the ER all morning," said Stella with a certain pride. "So they really grilled me. Gave me the shivers."

"Are we forgetting our privacy policy?" said Christie in the voice of a senior instructor.

"Christie, don't go all law and order on us," said David. He flattened his coffee cup, mashed it into the now-empty cardboard box, and stood up. "This is homicide city now. Everyone's into it, and we're not talking about patients or hospital policy. We're talking about this corpse who turned up under our noses. A very important corpse it is. Or was."

"A corpse," added Stella, "who just happens to be one of the hospital VIPs. Or at least he was back in the dark ages. There's even a wing over in orthopedics named after him. He had lots of money and oodles of power and flung both around."

"You're suggesting," said David, "that Dr. Philips, who must have been nearly ninety, did something really bad to the hospital, or to a patient, and then years later he was wiped out?"

"You mean revenge?" said Stella. "Someone biding his time, waiting for that lucky moment, and then one day there he is, all beaten up, sitting in the ER waiting to be murdered."

"Honestly, Stella. That's enough of that," said Christie briskly. "If you add all the people with a grudge against some medical person or place, why, they'd stretch out to the middle of Penobscot Bay."

"It's because hospitals and doctors are about life and death," said Stella. "About things on the edge. That's what I'm saying." Here she gave a tremulous giggle that caused Sarah to give her a quick appraising glance.

"Stop it," said Christie. "It's time to go in. And that detective, Laaka Somebody, said we weren't to go around talking about what happened. Even if we thought we knew something. Which none of us does. This isn't a game or a bad detective novel," she added severely." And to Sarah. "Give Julia my very best. I'll hold off visiting until she's feeling stronger."

And the three cohorts, bearing their takeout boxes, walked off across the lawn.

Sarah looked at her watch. Past nine-thirty. Well, some people certainly had purple imaginations. She could just see Stella curled up with a glass of wine and the latest crime novel held in her lap, shuddering and at the same time savoring the details of sudden assault and violent death. And about that giggle—what did that say about Stella? Never mind, she scolded herself. She didn't have time for idle speculation. She checked her watch. In fact, there was only just time for a quick and necessary walk around the perimeter of the hospital. A gravel path circled the whole complex and at several points gave a distant view of Megunticook Lake and the rising Camden Hills. She jumped to her feet, deposited the remains of her breakfast in the nearby trash container, and took off.

The day having begun fairly, promised more of the same, a breeze was rising, and Sarah's thoughts should have been divided between her Aunt Julia and her upcoming literature classes, but now, due to the evil influence of Stella Dugan and her inappropriate giggle, kept returning in an unruly way not only to Stella, but to the whole business of the "body in the wheelchair." That sounded like a title for one of mystery writer Katherine Hall Page's "Body" books. But how could it have been part of a revenge scheme? Surely killing someone in or around a crowded emergency room showed absolutely no sense. Yes, but murderers often seemed to be lacking this quality. And perhaps Dr. Henry Philips didn't often make himself available for killing. He was a widower, a recluse, too ancient to get around, and then one day there he was in the ER. Unattended. A sitting duck.

But did it mean, Sarah asked herself as she swung around a grove of pine trees and increased her pace, that whoever killed him must work in the ER? No, it could be anyone who worked in the hospital. Or it could have happened by chance. Sarah ran the scenario over in her head.

A visitor, someone taking flowers, buying a gift for a hospitalized friend, or, better, someone taking a family member to the ER for, say, a sprained ankle, a smashed thumb—nothing dire, anyway. This helpful friend, when the injured friend is off being examined, sees the hated Dr. Henry Philips and thinks, Aha! Revenge! Now's my chance. Because Henry looks a little out of it, all bruised and battered. Easy meat. Find a wheelchair—which is easy, since they're all over the place. Arrive in front of Henry, say you're a technician, a nurse, whatever, all assuming Henry doesn't recognize you as a former enemy. Pull the "Doctor will see you now" routine. Help Henry into the wheelchair and, since the place is a madhouse, no one notices. Stick Henry in the alcove, the one next to Julia. Sit him on a stool, wait for a break in the hall traffic, then, wheel Henry into the lavatory. No one would question a battered old man being wheeled to the lavatory. Close lavatory door. Lock it. And then just do it. End of Henry. Revenge accomplished. Leave lavatory. Go about your legitimate business.

So satisfied was Sarah with this script and so forgetful of her resolve not to get herself caught up in the matter of Dr. Philips's demise, that she hardly noticed that she had come full circle and now faced the hospital entrance. Okay, high time to catch up with Julia. She must be awake by now, perhaps had managed a little Jell-O and ginger ale. Could be feeling a bit more human, more like her own self and be ready for action, verbal action anyway. A therapeutic call to Patrick on problems of farm management, perhaps. Or bother Alex about getting her out of the hospital with all possible speed. Sarah would see if she'd like a magazine or a CD player with some favorite Bach or Chopin pieces—Julia was an experienced and energetic piano player, and often when angry seemed to be beating the piano into the ground.

Sarah walked up the slanting hospital entrance (wheelchair-accessible), climbed stairs (healthful exercise), turned left, then right, stopped at the nurses' station of the Cardiac ICU and asked after the well-being of Mrs. Julia Clancy.

The nurse (gray curls, red smock with daisies) gave a small shrug. "Well, she's post-op, you know. Confusion is pretty common. Your aunt had some sort of a nightmare and thinks someone came into her room. We can't seem to change her mind, but we don't want her to stay agitated, so I'm asking the resident for stronger medication. To settle her down."

Sarah got to the point and asked for permission to visit.

"Oh, certainly," said the nurse, who, according to her ID-tag name, was called Margetta. "A visit will do her good. Someone from the real world. Not just another hospital face. And Dr. McKenzie called in and said he'd be stopping in later to say hello."

Julia was at a slightly raised angle, her hair smoothed—by someone else, Sarah decided, since there had been an effort to put a part into the gray tangle.

"Sarah!" exclaimed Julia. "I need you. I need an interpreter. These cretins think I've had hallucinations. That my brain didn't have enough oxygen when I was in surgery. Or the anesthetic got me fuddled."

Sarah pulled over a chair and took her aunt's free hand. "Take it easy," she began.

"Now don't you start. I can't take it easy while everyone's acting like I flew straight out of a loony bin. Listen and don't interrupt." Here Julia's usually indomitable voice turned strangely shaky. "In the middle of the night, when the lights are dim, in came this person. Mask, gown, booties. Tried to strangle me. With a piece of tubing. Right around my neck, like in some sort of horror movie. I couldn't breathe, and if a bunch of people hadn't turned up, I'd be in the morgue right now. What do you think of that?"

"I'm not sure what to think," said Sarah cautiously. "But you must have had a pretty rocky night. The nurse at the desk said—"

"I don't give a good goddamn what the nurse at the desk said. She wasn't there and I was." Julia struggled to raise her head from the pillow and glared at Sarah. "Someone tried to murder me last night and almost got away with it. And the same someone will probably try again tonight."

> Volunteers Waiting Room
> No Smoking

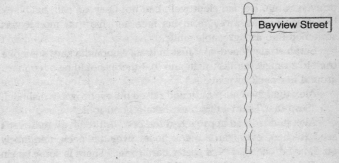

8

JULIA sank back on her pillow and pointed at her throat with a twist of her free hand. It was an imperious gesture that reminded Sarah strongly of royalty instructing a particularly dense lady-in-waiting.

"Don't just stand there," Julia commanded. "Look at my neck. My throat. I can't see it, but I'll bet there's a red line somewhere. Or a long bruise."

Sarah obediently bent over her aunt and tried to make out a distinguishing red mark, but the tubes and lines going in under Julia's chin and into her neck in some complicated configuration had caused a number of dark blotches. Sarah searched her aunt's neck, but it was hard to see whether any red line had been imposed on an already discolored skin.

"What's that long curving tube do that's going into your neck?"

"Never mind the tube," barked Julia. "Concentrate on what we're looking for. Signs of someone strangling me."

Sarah again studied her aunt's neck, her throat, behind her ears.

"You're checking your patient?" said a voice from the door.

Alex. He walked in, complete with white jacket, stethoscope sticking out of his pocket. He looked a lot healthier than did Julia or even Sarah. He had slept well, had not been on call, his black hair was combed away from his face and his thin mouth was stretched into an agreeable smile.

Sarah straightened up. "Just in time. Aunt Julia says someone tried to strangle her last night and that there should be a red mark around her neck to prove it."

Alex tightened his mouth and raised his eyebrows in disbelief.

"Stop that," said Julia. "Just take a good look."

Alex nodded and approached the bed. "All right, all right, let's see." He bent over, ran a quick finger over her neck, and stood up. "Maybe," he said. "It's pretty hard to tell. There is some bruising. But some of that is expected. Are you sure that in the middle of the night you didn't twist around and get your IV caught around your head, your neck? It's been known to happen. And you were having some horrendous nightmare and when you got entangled with the IV tubing, the sense of being throttled added itself to the dream."

Julia opened her mouth to deny this scenario. And then closed it. She remembered her series of dreams—flames and clouds and sunrises, strange people rushing about. And then she eyed the IV pole with its bags of fluid and the long line running into her left wrist. "I suppose," she said slowly, "something like that could have happened. But you see, I heard this person, the feet on the floor. He or she spoke. A low whisper. And wearing a surgery-type costume."

"In dreams," Alex reminded her, "people wear clothes. Uniforms, tiger skins, bikinis. Fig leaves. And since you're in a hospital, dreaming about someone in medical clothes would be natural."

"Alex," said Julia crossly, "the trouble with you is you're too damn logical. I can't argue with someone who just stands his ground and sounds reasonable. But, believe me, I am not off my rocker."

"I think it's the Robert Burns and going 'aft a-gley.'" said Sarah.

Alex grinned. "The nurse down the hall mentioned it. She said that Sarah explained that Julia was reciting Scottish poetry, but that with a name like Clancy she should be doing something Irish."

"Oh, God," groaned Julia, "Save me from little minds. But," she faltered, "did I really recite poetry yesterday? I'm losing my whole sense of time and space."

"It was Robert Burns," said Sarah. "Your favorite. Ode to a . . ."

"A Mouse," finished Julia. "I remember now. 'Wee, sleekit, cowrin, tim'rous beastie/O, what a panic's in thy breastie!' Perfectly appropriate."

"Ah, Mrs. Clancy. Doing your poetry again." It was a nurse, another nurse, Dawn (short blond hair, yellow jacket with maple leaves, Sarah noted). "I've had the resident prescribe something to make you easier. Less anxious."

"I've been anxious with good reason," said Julia, but with not the same assurance as before. Then, unexpectedly obedient, Julia allowed herself to accept two small pills and swallow them without more than a snort of disapproval.

And the nurse was almost immediately replaced by Father Joshua Stevenson in his round collar, denim, and tan khakis. Tall, serene, he smiled at Sarah, nodded to Alex, and then walked over to Julia, extended a hand, introduced himself, apologized for walking in, referred to her mother, Mrs. Anthony Douglas. Her concern over her daughter.

"My mother," Julia said, "is a worry wart. She isn't strong enough to come to the hospital, and," she added firmly, "I'm not strong enough yet to have her. She'll try and have me go through some sort of prayer scene. Sarah, will you go and visit her and calm things down? But don't tell her about my being strangled."

Father Stevenson paused slightly, then stepped over the word "strangled." "Your mother," he said, "is naturally quite anxious, and she knows she shouldn't visit for the first few days. And since she's rather fragile, it makes sense. So I'm here—"

"As a spy," snapped Julia.

And Sarah and Alex tiptoed out.

They came to rest at the end of the corridor—Alex to go on hospital rounds, Sarah to linger until Julia had, it was hoped, made peace with her visitor. Then she had to brace herself for what could not be put off longer: a visit to her formidable Grandmother Douglas.

"Who exactly," demanded Alex, "is the man in the collar?"

Sarah told him, adding, "I think he's the new man at St. Paul's-by-the-Sea because old Father Smythe just retired. If anyone can calm Julia down, I'll put my money on Joshua Stevenson. Sidney Poitier with a little bit of Denzel Washington rolled into one. From some better world. I keep thinking of gods from faraway islands."

"You mean we'll come back and find he's anointed her with some magic potion and she'll be all loving kindness?"

"Actually," said Sarah, "Julia is all loving kindness, but it's awfully well wrapped up in burrs and thistles. But back to topic A. Do you really think Julia was attacked in the middle of the night?"

Alex considered and then shook his head. "If we make light of it, we'll probably find her body hanging from an IV pole in the morning. If we take her seriously, we'll discover it was all a post-operative nightmare."

"So better to take it seriously?" asked Sarah.

"I suppose so. After all, Julia was a witness of sorts, if you can call a five-second glance in the middle of a heart attack being a witness. Whatever the case, the police don't want a witness assaulted in her bed. I'll talk to Mike Laaka this morning."

With that Sarah had to rest content, although more and more she was inclining to the idea of an hallucination. After all, this appeared to be the accepted wisdom on post-surgery patients. This view had been reinforced by a pamphlet on cardiac surgery she'd picked up the night before. This publication had gone on at some length about the vivid and disturbing dreams often visited upon these patients, and Julia certainly seemed to fit the category.

After a quick circuit around the parking lot for exercise, Sarah came back to the hospital and found her aunt alone and drowsy. It was the medication, perhaps, or the effect of having been visited by an Episcopal god. And she looked like nothing so much as an elderly and discarded rag doll, her gray hair now ruffled, her face thinner and drawn, the oxygen tubes hanging from her nostrils giving the strange effect of a woman with a pale mandarin mustache. Sarah felt a sudden rush of sadness. Aunt Julia had been such a fixture in her life, her life and Alex's. Such a sharp and sturdy presence.

Julia opened her eyes halfway. "Sarah," she said. "There you are. Who was that man? Oh, I know he's part of my mother's church team at St. Paul's. But he should be on the stage. In the movies. Television. It seems a shame to waste him on a small congregation in midcoast Maine."

"He's probably under the delusion he's doing God's work," said Sarah dryly.

"I said he could come back," said Julia. "As long as he didn't say it was a pastoral call or ask me to join him in prayer. Just as a visitor. He knows a lot about horses and grew up with a pony. A Welsh pony."

"All the proper credentials," said Sarah, speaking softly because Julia had closed her eyes again. She slipped from the room and made for the visitors' lavatory. A visit to her grandmother called for attention to appearance. Mrs. Anthony Douglas had often castigated the sloppy ways of the younger generations and had barely allowed "casual" to be an accepted term. Sarah opened the door to the ladies' room and turned her attention to repairs. Pull down the sleeves on her blue shirt. Button it up to the next-to-the-top button. Smooth down her khaki shorts. Tighten the straps on her sandals so they wouldn't slap on her grandmother's floor. Then the face. Fortunately, a summer tan hid the shadows under her eyes that came from a restless night. But her hair! Sarah scowled at the mirror. What had started the summer as a close-clipped cap of hair had now deteriorated into dark brown overgrown spikes. She was going to have it done before her teaching classes started, but not today. And she'd come without a comb. She ran cold water over her hands and smoothed them over her head, creating the unhappy effect of wet fleece. Lipstick? No, but cleanliness was all. She grabbed a paper towel and washed around her neck and face, then studied the effect. She saw a thin-faced woman with angular cheekbones, a wide mouth, and a stubborn chin. Large eyes of that indeterminate color Alex called tweed, but others named hazel. She knew that a grown woman, almost thirty, should not be worried about trying to please an elderly and hypercritical relative. But today, with Julia fragile and her grandmother anxious, it was all in the interest of family peace—as long as the visit was a short one.

Ten o'clock. She would arrive before her grandmother's lunch and deliver word of Julia's condition. And would not mention the matter of the nighttime attack—or nonattack. As a dutiful grand-daughter she would meekly receive advice about her spiritual shortcomings and perhaps join with her grandmother in a short reading from Scripture. Probably a cautionary selection from one of the more rigorous psalms.

Sarah sighed deeply, left the ladies' room, found her Subaru, climbed in, started the engine, and on a sudden impulse turned the car toward home. She would pick up Patsy, her beloved Irish wolfhound, as a contribution to the visit. Grandmother Douglas had a very soft spot for animals and had a statue of Saint Francis in her back garden, where were buried long-gone family pets— cats, dogs, a parrot named Martin, and a rabbit called Betty. This aspect of her grandmother, not often in evidence when she inter-acted with humans, did a lot to reconcile Sarah to visits that were laden with biblical advice.

Perhaps what Grandma needed was a new dog. It had been several years since the last dog, a springer called Pouncer, had been buried. A dog from the shelter, perhaps. Not a huge beast like Patsy, but something on the elderly side. Sedate and affec-tionate. She would make a mental note to visit the shelter in the near future.

With Patsy established in the front seat, his head almost touching the roof, Sarah drove slowly toward Camden, toward Bay View Street and the tall, dark Queen Anne–style house that her grandmother had lived in for over seventy years. Grandfather Anthony Douglas had departed this earth one Sunday morning on a cold January twenty years ago, an event that caused his wife to miss Sunday services for the first time in memory. Since then, Grandmother Douglas had been alone except for her faithful and long-suffering housekeeper, Hopkins. No one knew if Hopkins had another name; if she had, it was lost in the mists of the past.

Sarah, holding Patsy on a short leash, walked slowly up the stone stairs and was welcomed by Hopkins, an angular woman well into her eighties, someone who dressed always in black except for a lace collar pinned around her neck. Sarah, who thought she closely resembled the female who snatches Toto away from Judy Garland in *The Wizard of Oz* movie, always made an extra effort when greeting Hopkins and especially to ask about her teeth. Hopkins always seemed to suffer from some dental misery—from broken bridges to a number of root canals.

Fortunately, Hopkins adored Patsy, so that, after she had told Sarah of a broken crown on an upper left molar and reported that her grandmother was resting in the conservatory and "was as well as could be expected for an elderly person," she led Patsy off to the kitchen for a taste of boiled chicken.

Sarah, feeling the usual sense of oppression that the ill-lighted house with heavy furniture, ancient dark velvet curtains, oils of dismal moors and raging seas usually gave, walked cautiously toward the side of the house, trying not to trip over threadbare oriental rugs or knock over an umbrella stand or one of the bronze vases that balanced on tiny mahogany tables. How her grandmother and Hopkins had survived the place without breaking their hips, their legs, their necks was a genuine mystery.

She found her grandmother recumbent on a rattan sofa, wrapped in a number of tartan shawls, with the leaves of a sickly-looking rubber tree hanging over her head. What had once been an arena of shining glass and green and flowering plants was now down to a few straggling geraniums, a dusty ficus, and an enormous potted avocado surrounded by windows speckled with dust, a condition that probably bothered neither her grandmother nor Hopkins, since both were afflicted with failing sight.

Her grandmother sat up alertly. Pale blue eyes, a cloud of

white hair, spectacles with a gold rim, legs and arms of the thinness of an insect, her grandmother despite her age was still a powerful presence.

Sarah bent to kiss her on her tissue-like cheek, answered that yes, she knew she needed a haircut; yes, Alex was just fine; and that yes, Julia, although weak, was doing very well.

"That," said Mrs. Douglas in the high register of the very old, "is unlikely. Heart surgery won't let Julia do very well for quite a while. Now sit down, don't fidget, and tell me everything. I spoke to your Alex on the telephone, but I can't get anything out of him except soothing remarks as if I were a child, but I expect the truth from you. And I intend to find out for myself in two more days."

Sarah, who had been wondering how to begin the story without introducing the matter of a dead body, a police investigation, and Aunt Julia as a witness, was given a reprieve. The invaluable Hopkins entered with Patsy. Hopkins knew from long years of service that the entrance of a grandchild, that is, Sarah, from the disturbed outer world would send her prickly employer's blood pressure high and let her temper loose. Patsy was the mediator. The soother. A true and tried anodyne to the elderly nerves of a woman who happily was an animal lover.

And Patsy did his job. Trotting over to Mrs. Douglas, he laid his large gray head on her knee.

Who could resist? thought Sarah, always oblivious of a very real collection of dog haters beyond her grandmother's gates. Sarah certainly hadn't resisted. When found abandoned at a Texas wildlife refuge, it had been love at first sight, and Sarah and Patsy had been a duo now for over six years.

Sarah relaxed in her chair, barely listening as her grandmother, after running her fingers through Patsy's rough wiry coat, began a lecture on coat condition, a regular exercise regime, and the absolute necessity of giving certain vitamin- and mineral supplements, plus the vast superiority of home-cooked dog food. Ground beef, chicken, lamb, a broth, and whole-grain rice.

Having no intention of preparing Patsy's dinner from scratch, and since he was perfectly contented with commercial kibbles, Sarah, keeping an accepting smile on her face, began to compare her Aunt Julia Douglas Clancy and her grandmother, Lavinia Douglas. Mother and daughter. They had always seemed like opposites. Frail, severe grandmother, rarely leaving home except for church, her doctor, or her dentist. And feisty Aunt Julia, the outdoor tomboy, horse lover, fearless competitive rider (in her youth), and now the determined teacher of young riders and (to Sarah's mind) the breeder of large dangerous hoofed animals.

But mother and daughter, they really *were* alike. Contentious. Stubborn. Minds of their own. Demanding. And, if you could dig deep enough, loving—even if the loving was most evident in their relation to animals. But, Sarah reflected, it was often the way with stern rocklike characters. Only softness with domestic animals could properly be shown; demonstrations of affection to humans were a sign of weakness.

". . . and so, Sarah, do you understand what I mean by keeping me properly informed?"

Sarah came to attention. Was her grandmother still going on about proper dog diets?

"Yes, Grandma," she said, "I'll certainly try. But Patsy loves his kibbles."

"Which means you haven't been listening. I'm talking about Julia. She pretends she's strong-minded, that nothing upsets her except a sick horse. But that's not true. When she was growing up, she used to have terrible nightmares. Woke up screaming. Thought someone was climbing in her window. Or a bear was coming down the hall. I thought letting her have her own pony would calm her down because she would be fully tired out at the end of the day. Perhaps I was wrong. I'm not sure what life with horses has done for her."

"Made her very happy," suggested Sarah. "And she and Uncle Tom had a fine life as long as it lasted."

Grandmother Douglas dismissed Tom Clancy with a wave of the hand. "It made Julia center on things of the world and did nothing for her inner life."

Sarah gave up. She rose from her chair, leaned over and kissed her grandmother. "I'll tell her you're sending your love and will visit in a few days."

"There's something you're not telling me," said Mrs. Douglas. "I do read the newspapers, you know. I saw that Dr. Henry Philips was killed. He was running the hospital when your grandfather was on the hospital board. Dr. Philips was much younger, of course, but acted as if he were king and emperor rolled into one. A disagreeable person. A busybody, beside which there were rumors of incompetence. Mistakes. Medical mistakes. But please don't tell me that Julia had anything to do with this murder. Or that she was there. Or near the place it happened."

"Wouldn't that be a coincidence," said Sarah smoothly.

"Knowing Julia," said Lavinia Douglas, "I'd say that she probably found the body."

Here Sarah could tell the truth. "She did not, Grandma. She was in the middle of a heart attack and not looking for dead bodies."

"One more thing," said her grandmother. "Tell Julia's nurses that when she was little she was prone to nightmares. And I suppose that having major surgery and a heavy dose of anesthetic might have started them up again."

And Sarah, her head buzzing with this bit of news, departed shaking her head. She had been more than half-inclined to believe in Julia's story, but now the idea of someone who had suffered childish nightmares shed a small amount of doubt on her tale of a nighttime strangler. Once outside, Sarah found much relief in kicking a large stone out of the driveway and then in racing Patsy up and down the sloping street. A visit to her grandmother often prompted violent action, and by the time she returned to her car, breathing hard from exertion, she felt that she had a least expelled some built-up toxic substances from her body and was ready for the journey back to the hospital.

Oddly enough, just as Sarah began to question her aunt's encounter with an attacker, Alex really began to believe in it. If she had indeed been some sort of target, perhaps for the peace of all concerned, Julia should be shifted to another ICU bed. But how?

He couldn't upset the nursing staff by asking for such a move without a solid reason (and Julia's story hardly qualified), and, moreover, he was not the surgeon or the cardiologist on the case and so couldn't toss his weight around. For the time being he would wait. It was daytime, security was in place with nurses and interns lurking in every corner. He'd talk it over with Mike, then with Sarah, and see if she thought a second appearance of the "strangler" possible. And if she had intimations of future disaster—as she often did, to everyone's great annoyance. Especially the local police.

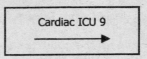

Cardiac ICU 9

High Hope Farm

Training-Boarding
Equitation

9

JULIA Clancy had had a Wednesday morning of great discomfort. Discomfort physical and discomfort psychological. The physical was to be expected. Everything hurt. Her back, her shoulders, her incision that gave her the sense of having spent too much time on a butcher's block. But all this was to be expected. Surgery—or the "cardiac procedure"—guaranteed it. One must bite one's lip and humbly accept offered medication.

But the psychological aggravation was something else. The decor of the Cardiac ICU, with its smooth beige walls, was dispiriting enough. But add to that the array of lines and tubes leading in and out of her body, everything gave Julia a strong sense of being trapped in a windowless cell for the deranged.

And there seemed to be a conspiracy underway. The health care attendants, from surgeon down to the lowest aide, now acted as if she had gone completely around the bend, and to alleviate this sad condition they put themselves out to soothe her, to console, constantly to express the idea that it was perfectly natural after surgery for the post-surgical mind to be out of the loop. But, they said—patting her shoulder, stroking her hand, attempting to brush her hair, straightening her pillow, checking her IV, her heart rate—usually, all in good time, the brain probably would wobble back to center after a certain healing period had passed.

"Just relax, take it easy, breathe deeply; how about a nice glass of juice, a little sherbet, a back rub, something more for pain? said nurses Donna, Linda, Tanya, Amanda, Joe, Martha, Arnold, Hannah.

"You're doing a great job," said physicians' assistants Ted, Rick, Nick, Millie, Molly, Aaron, and Jason when they checked Julia's overhead monitors.

"Keep up the good work," said cardiologist Dr. Eugene Santoro and his cohorts. "Your vitals are good. Confusion is perfectly natural. Happens all the time."

But Julia, having heard the strange expression "pump head" spoken outside her ICU space, demanded an explanation from one of the interns, a Dr. Jason Hickson. Dr. Hickson was less than two months into his first year of internship and very wet behind the ears and so an easy prey. Fair-haired, blue-eyed, with the face of a spaniel puppy, he turned from a faint pink to a deep red as Julia bore in. The more he tried to escape from explaining the term "pump head"—it was a sort of joke, nothing to do with a patient, just part of a surgical procedure, belonged to a piece of equipment—the more entangled he became, until he finally crumpled and told her that, yes, in some cases, particularly with older patients—here Julia glowered—there had sometimes been problems of memory loss and lack of concentration after a "cabbage."

"Cabbage!" demanded Julia. "What in God's name are you talking about? A vegetable? Are you saying that I'm a vegetable?"

"Oh, no," said Dr. Hickson, now wriggling like a worm on a hook, "it's just a word. A term. For 'coronary artery bypass graft.' CABG. It sort of looks like cabbage when you write it out. And not that many people have serious effects or anything, and I'm sure, Mrs. Clancy, that you, even if you're having a little trouble getting your head clear . . . but in a few days . . . or weeks . . ."

At which Julia rang her bell and pulled her pillow over her head.

Sometime later that afternoon, when Sarah made it back to

the Cardiac ICU after dropping Patsy off at the house, she was informed by two nurses, one aide, and a resident that Mrs. Clancy was doing just fine, but that her mental confusion, the upsetting dreams of last night had distressed her, and that Sarah might find her aunt having periods of agitation.

"We've given her something to calm her but it doesn't seem to last," offered Nurse Hannah—or was it Nurse Tanya—Sarah was losing her grip on which nurse was which; they had all begun to merge into a mass of helpful but similar persons. Sarah tried to take a quick squint at the ID tag around the nurse's neck, but the print was small and it didn't seem proper to be bending over someone's bosom on the odd chance that she could see the name clearly. So Sarah simply nodded, noted that this one had dark hair, looked very familiar, and had flights of geese on her jacket.

"I'm Hannah Finch," said the nurse, realizing that Sarah was staring at her tag. "I have birds on my jackets because 'finch' is a bird. That's how the patients can remember me."

Sarah said, yes, the birds were a clever idea, but to get back to Aunt Julia . . .

"She just can't get over the idea that someone went after her last night," said Hannah. "And of course people *did* come into her unit because all the patients have their monitors checked constantly."

"I'll do what I can," said Sarah. But she told herself, as she walked slowly down the hall to Julia's ICU, that probably all she was good for was a listening ear.

The listening ear got a workout.

Julia was now sitting up. Or propped up in the green vinyl armchair surrounded by her IV stand, attached to a number of leads and what must have been a catheter emerging from under her clothing and leading to a plastic container of urine. Her hair was rumpled and her bathrobe looked as if it had been made out of a horse blanket—and an old one, at that.

Julia jerked her head up and greeted her niece with almost a show of enthusiasm.

"Sarah, thank heavens you're here. You're my last hope. Everyone thinks I'm crazy as a bedbug. Though I've been bitten by bedbugs and they seemed to know exactly what they were doing. I heard someone outside my door calling me a 'pump head,' which is a lovely term for people whose brains have been deprived of oxygen or something. But you believe me, Sarah, don't you? Someone tried to throttle me last night. I don't know why unless they, he, she think I know something. Which I don't. Not really."

Sarah hesitated the smallest fraction of a second.

And Julia flung up her free arm in despair. Then grimaced at the pain that radiated from neck to chest to back. "Even you. I thought I could trust you to believe me. To listen."

Sarah recovered. "Aunt Julia, I never said I didn't believe you."

"But you thought it."

"It's just that . . . well, you've been through an awful lot lately and everyone says the anesthetic, the whole surgery business, is very upsetting. And grandma—I've just come from a visit—grandma says you used to have nightmares."

"Oh, Lord, now the fact that when I was five years old and dreamed of a bear in the cupboard is going to be held against me. I suppose she's praying for me."

"She could be doing worse," said Sarah, perching on the end of Julia's bed.

Julia pressed her lips together, tightened her jaw, and then sighed mightily. "Maybe, maybe not. But now I'm tired of this chair. Of sitting up. I need to lie down again, but before I call the nurse, just do me one favor. See if you can change my room. Or my cell. Whatever they call this space. Just to humor me, and I'll admit to anything. Being psychotic, seeing pink elephants, whatever it takes to move me out of here."

"You mean, send you to the psychiatric unit?"

"No. Just down the hall, nearer to the center of things. There must be an empty bed somewhere. Nearer to the nurses' station, perhaps. This room is at the end of the hall and I asked what was across the way. Only a supply closet. It's like being on a peninsula and no one would notice who came sneaking into the room. It gives me the creeps."

Sarah got up. "I'll see what I can do. But I've brought you something to cheer you up. I stopped at the farm and everything's okay there, but I found these." Sarah produced two small framed photographs, the first of the late Thomas Clancy on his favorite gray hunter, Finnian, and the other of Duffie looking over the pasture gate. These she arranged on Julia's bedside table, and was pleased to see Julia brighten at the sight of the pictures.

"There," Sarah said. "And I don't think you're psychotic. If switching rooms will make you feel safer, maybe they can do something."

A short conference at the nurses' station produced a sympathetic listening and the assurances that Mrs. Clancy's present situation was as comfortable as any in the whole Cardiac ICU floor. In fact, more so, since her unit, number 9, at the end of the hall, was a quiet one—less foot traffic, fewer carts jangling back and forth. Besides, it had one of the newer hospital wonder beds, the sort that could weigh a patient without the patient's getting out of bed, whose side rails floated up and down with the touch of a nurse's finger, a mattress that could recontour itself with the flip of a switch, furnish heat in crucial places—in fact, do everything but read bedtime stories aloud.

"So you see," said Nurse Hannah, "your aunt couldn't be in a better spot."

Sarah gave it up and started back to Julia's room. And was caught by Alex, who planned a quick look-in on Julia while making his patient rounds. He was still wearing, now in a rumpled condition, what Julia called his "doctor coat," one with a ripped pocket, and Sarah, while deploring his appearance, hoped his patients could chalk it up to some form of endearing casualness.

"Alex," she said, "Aunt Julia wants a new room. Not one at the end of the hall. She thinks the middle-of-the-night attack was the real thing. Can you pull some strings?"

"I'm willing to believe she saw someone in the middle of the night. Maybe some sleep-deprived intern wandered in and out of her room because he was mixed up about what room he was going in. But I can't wave a wand and get her a new room."

"Well, try," Sarah urged. "And how about getting Mike Laaka to put a guard by her door."

"I've talked to Mike. He said he can't get authorization for anything like that without real evidence. And George doesn't want to step on hospital toes."

"Damnation. Look, Alex, that was a real body they found in the john. Very dead Dr. Henry Philips. Not just a stuffed pillowcase. And Julia was somewhere around. Seeing things. So how about believing her just because?"

They had reached the door to Julia's cardiac unit, and both paused. "Okay, okay, I'll try again," Alex said.

But on entering the room they found Julia in bed, eyes half-closed but with her free hand she was drumming her fingers on the blanket.

"Something on your mind?" said Alex, leaning over to kiss the top of her head.

"No one thinks I have a mind," said Julia, opening her eyes and then closing them. "I've just been told that this room is fine, the quietest on the floor, and that the care I'm receiving is top-notch, tip-top, state-of-the-art, and the cat's pajamas. So I have a plan. Which I will reveal to no one."

"Oh, God," said Alex. "Spare us. Forget about a plan. Look Julia, we'll do what we can. About moving you. Keeping an eye on you."

"It's just a matter of finding someone who will really listen to you," explained Sarah. "Perhaps from the psychiatric unit. To swear—"

"That I know a hawk from a handsaw?" said Julia. "Please keep the shrinks away. Forget about moving. Now, I want you both to go on about your business. Leave, get out. Sarah, if you could check at the farm again . . . See if the hay's been stored and that the farrier came. Ask if the grain order went in. Alex, you probably have some poor sick souls sitting there in your waiting room. Both of you come back tonight after my supper or dinner or whatever they call it in the hospital. Broth, Jell-O, and Wheat Thins. And then we'll see what's what."

Further arguments were stifled by Julia's turning away slightly to lie on one side and pulling a black sleeping mask over her face, and Alex and Sarah, dismissed from attendance, thankfully departed.

And Julia, pulling the shade off one eye, watched their disappearing backs with satisfaction and then reached for her bedside table, fumbled about and came up with a booklet entitled: *Welcome to the Mary Starbox Hospital.* She pawed about for her glasses, found them, opened the booklet to the section labeled: "The Hospital Staff," and skipping the section about how the staff was "here to make your visit a pleasant and comfortable one," ran her finger down a paragraph on the importance of a patient's tranquil mind, paused, and bent back the page top. Then, putting the booklet carefully aside, she reached with her free hand for the telephone, dialed, waited, and then spoke clearly and firmly. "Patrick, is that you? No, never mind how I am. I'm better than I look. But I need to see you. About a plan. Yes, right now. Don't argue. Good-bye." And Julia, smiling the smile of someone about to take charge of her own destiny, sank back on her pillow.

Sarah and Alex paused at the side door of the hospital before separating to go to their respective spheres.

"Damn," said Sarah. "I don't know whether to believe her or not. If the police can't come up with a guard, maybe I should sit outside her door tonight with an Uzi. The trouble is, I've never thought of Julia as old and helpless."

"Nor with her wits scattered," put in Alex.

"Well, she *is* mortal," said Sarah. "But she's always been so self-reliant. Even when Uncle Tom died, she pulled herself together and worked out her feelings by riding large horses over large fences and scaring us all to death."

"Don't count her out just yet," said Alex. "But the idea of Julia with a secret plan in her head scares the hell out of me." He looked at Sarah. "If you're going to Julia's farm to deal with stables and hay, watch out for those feet in sandals. Have you any idea what a well-shod hoof can do to a bare instep?"

"For Julia, a hoofprint on my bare foot would be a badge of honor. Now listen, I'll meet you later at the hospital and check out the scene. But you know it strikes me as absolutely stupid for anyone to try a personal attack on someone in their own hospital room. Aren't there more subtle ways to do someone in? I mean, there's a whole pharmacy available here."

Alex shook his head. "You're assuming that if Julia really was attacked, it was by a medical person. Someone who could get his hands on serious stuff."

"Like cyanide?"

"Or something similar. But the nonmedical type might go for tubing. I can tell you now that Dr. Philips was strangled that way. Every supply closet is stuffed with tubing. All sizes and lengths."

"For every need?"

"Right. But now I've got to sneak past a waiting room filled with patients who have been waiting much too long. See you later."

Sarah walked slowly to her car, finding as she went that the idea of a nonmedical person using crude strangling methods was no more comforting than the idea of some doctor or PA or nurse deciding on cyanide. But I should look into lethal drugs, she told herself. After all, the aborted attempt to throttle her aunt—if it had really happened—didn't work out, so maybe next time a drug . . .

With these not very comforting thoughts running through her head, Sarah reached her Subaru, climbed in and took off for Julia's High Hope Farm.

She met farm manager Patrick O'Reilly just as he was climbing into the front seat of the farm pickup truck. Waving, she jumped out and hailed him.

"Patrick, listen. It's important. Aunt Julia has a plan and—

Patrick leaned out from the truck and cut in. "She just called for me. And sure, she has a plan. That lady always has something up her sleeve. By now she'll be having some daft idea of escaping the hospital even if she has to blow the place to bits."

"Patrick," said Sarah with great urgency, "whatever it is, don't let her do it. If you're part of some crazy scheme, try and derail it."

"Ah, now, Sarah. Leave the lady to me. We've known each other a long time, and if I agree with her in the beginning, well, it's often I get my own way in the end." With which Patrick turned the ignition on and wheeled out toward the main road.

Sarah, finding some satisfaction in this exchange and partly soothed by Patrick's soft confident Irish voice, walked slowly toward the lower barn, trying to bring her thoughts back to the matter of grain to be ordered and the possible nonappearance of the farrier.

Patrick appeared at Julia's bedside bringing with him, Julia decided, the only healthy air she'd breathed in days. Straight from the farm, he carried healing odors of straw, hay, oats, sweet meal, scents from the variety of supplements that kept the horses sleek and happy, and all tinged with the faintest hint of good hearty manure.

Now he hung over her, standing awkwardly, aware that his farm boots had brought in chunks of clay and that his clothing was strictly of the work variety. His thin black hair had apparently been given a quick wipe-down and lay flat on his sunburned skull. His expression was worried, his wide mouth clenched closed, and his hands deep in his old brown riding breeches.

"For heaven's sake, Patrick, sit down," said Julia, indicating the green chair. "You're making me nervous hovering there. And don't look as if I'm about to pass out on you. I have a plan to explain."

Patrick, long used to the ways of his employer, sat gingerly on the extreme edge of the chair and nodded. "If you have the idea of leaving this place," he said, "you'd best be clearing it with Sarah and Alex. They'd have my hide, and yours, too, Mrs. Thomas Clancy, if they thought for a minute . . ."

Julia waved Patrick to silence. "Just listen. I'm not trying to leave the hospital, not yet, anyway. I just want to leave this room.

I think it's . . ." Julia searched for a description that would not suggest lunacy. "I think it's contaminated, but the hospital people won't admit it."

"Then I'll just go and get some of those nurses to clean the whole place while I stand over them," said Patrick, rising from the chair.

"Stop," said Julia. "Forget what I said. This room is too isolated, so I just want to move. I have good reasons that no one believes. Just take my word."

Patrick subsided and remembered his promise to Sarah to listen first and overcome afterward. "All right, I suppose now you should be starting at the beginning. Tell me and I'll try and keep my mouth shut, hard as it may be."

And Julia told in detail her memory of her night's encounter, and when it came to an end, Patrick shook his head.

"Holy Mary, Mother of God, and you're telling me they thought it was all part of some kind of dream you were having?" He paused, studied Julia, and finding her eye sharp and her chin firm, added, "I think I'll go along with believing you. I've never known Julia Clancy to go off the deep end with wild fancies and ghosts under the bed."

"But," concluded Julia, "even if I'm addled out of my skull, there's no harm done in taking precautions. No one's going to get me a new room. Even Alex can't seem to manage it. If I'm lucky, Mike Laaka will be around some of the time, but he can't live outside my door. First, I want you to take a good look at this bed of mine. See if it can be fixed, or unfixed, so that they'd be forced to move me somewhere else."

Patrick rose and walked slowly around the bed. Bent over and examined its lower machinery, its buttons and levers, the side-rail release, the head- and foot-raising system. Then ran his hands over the headboard and finally knelt down and put his head directly underneath the bed.

"You could disable it by undoing a few nuts and bolts, couldn't you?" suggested Julia.

"This bed," said Patrick, almost in admiration, "it's a fair marvel. We should all have one."

"Help get me out of this room," said Julia, "and I'll buy you one."

"No, thank you. The missus and I are happy as we are in our old double with the four posts. We'd both be likely to be killed in a thing like this."

"Well, can you do something to it? Make it seem like its machinery is out of whack?"

Patrick scratched his head and then slowly shook it. "No way. It can't be put out of order with a screwdriver or a hammer. I'd need a crowbar and an ax, and you don't want vandalism added to your bill. And wouldn't the nurses just be bringing in another one? So what about pulling the plug on all those recording boxes hanging over your head? Cut the wires?"

"No," said Julia. "If you fool with those, the whole hospital comes in at a run yelling about Code Blue or Code Red or something like that."

Patrick shook his head. "What else do you have up your sleeve?"

"Plan Two," said Julia firmly. "See this picture?" She reached over for the small framed photograph of Tom Clancy sitting on his big gray gelding. "Who's this?"

"Lord, I think you do have a loose marble in your head. That's Tom Clancy, God rest his soul. On Finnian. Your own husband and a finer man never took a ditch or cleared a five-foot fence."

"Yes," said Julia crossly. "I know it's Tom. But here's what you don't know. Tom Clancy, my husband, died in this very room. What do you think of that!"

Patrick opened his eyes wide. "I think that's a bottle of hogwash. Tom Clancy died in Vermont at the hunter trials south of Middlebury after Finnian balked at the in-and-out. Some damn fool on the course raising an umbrella. Tom went over and down and that was that. 'Twas nothing to do with the Mary Starbox Memorial Hospital."

"You're not paying attention," said Julia. "Since we can't take the bed apart and we can't destroy these monitors, we'll go the psychological route. I'm going to be very upset by the unhappy coincidence that I'm in the very room my beloved husband died in. I'm depressed by surgery—which is perfectly true—and here I am in this room . . . what's the number, anyway?"

Patrick rose stiffly—his arthritis was keeping pace with Julia's—went to the door, returned, sat down. "You're in number 9."

"That's it," said Julia. "Now, I'll need you, and later Sarah and Alex, to be around, after I've discovered I'm in a room which because of its tragic memories will be a continual setback to my recovery, and we don't want that. I'm going to get hold of that Father Stevenson from my mother's church. I've just met him and I think he's just right for the job. He can speak for me."

"And why would he do that?" Patrick demanded. "Seeing as how you don't go to church and every Sunday I have to pray for your everlasting soul."

"I have a sense about these things. Now go to the farm and come back here when you and Rafe have got the horses settled. After supper. We'll take it from there. You're my backup because Sarah and Alex weren't around in Maine when Tom died."

"Nor were any of us in Maine," said Patrick stubbornly. "We were in Vermont."

"You're not listening," said Julia. "I'm putting together a script. Like a play. You've got a starring role. I'm trying to save my life so that I can keep the farm going and keep paying you a decent salary. It's all for a good cause."

"I've never been one for the theater," said Patrick. "And besides, do you know if this part of the hospital was standing when Tom Clancy was supposed to have died in it?"

"It doesn't matter. No one is going to look up his obituary to see when he died. Or where. And I will be too upset to recall times and dates. And when you're here supporting me in my distress, I want you to be heavy-duty Irish. Thicken up your accent. An Irish accent always melts people down, and I've noticed that bit by bit you've been losing yours."

"God and the saints in heaven preserve you," said Patrick with feeling and sounding entirely too Irish. "And myself, too, since I'm going to be part of this unholy business. Good-bye, Julia

Clancy. I'd like to say 'Rest in peace,' but with you I'm not thinking it's possible."

After Patrick's departure, Julia rested for a moment, took a long drink of grape juice, and then, invigorated, rang her bell. There followed a satisfactory chat with her nurse, a new entry to the parade of attendants. This one was Debbie, in a navy-and-green-striped tunic. Julia had lowered her eyes, looked alternately teary-eyed and pensive, kept her voice low and choked—a difficult achievement for one with the personality of a terrier—and said that she thought she needed counseling, pastoral counseling. Father Stevenson. Such a kind man.

Debbie, a faithful churchgoer of the Baptist persuasion, agreed with great enthusiasm to the idea and inwardly sighed with relief. She had been briefed on Mrs. Clancy. What this patient needs, she was told, was calm reassurance. Family and medical staff had not been able to manage the job. But a minister, someone who dealt in the matters of the spirit, unnatural worries and apprehensions, well, let him give it a try. The minister chosen by Mrs. Clancy had already met the patient—that was a plus—and was a man who could be pictured assisting Moses cross over the Red Sea or helping Paul to his feet on the Road to Damascus.

Debbie patted Julia (who made an effort not to recoil because she had just about reached her limit in comforting pats) and said she would send out a call to Father Joshua Stevenson, who was, she hoped, still in the hospital making the rounds of St. Paul's-by-the-Sea parishioners.

"I just know he can help me," said Julia in a thick voice. She reached for a Kleenex in the box on her table and closed her eyes. And Debbie tiptoed from the room.

10

SARAH'S visit to High Hope Farm proved a blessed relief from the hospital atmosphere. She found Rafe Posner in the lower barn, saddling a sturdy black pony named Magic Duncan.

"Everything's under control," he said. "The lessons are going along. We've picked up two more beginners, and we're using Duncan, along with Conkey, for the dressage demo." He grinned at Sarah, a glint in his eye. "Don't repeat what I say, but things are going more smoothly with Mrs. Clancy away for a while. Some of the students are frightened out of their wits when she barks at them."

Sarah nodded with understanding. She knew that her aunt had no time for soft words when a rider did something unbelievably stupid—and dangerous—when mounted on one of her horses.

"Not that I blame her," explained Rafe. "We don't want kids pasted against the arena wall because they didn't pay attention. I keep telling 'em horses aren't toys. But the last few days have been pretty peaceful. But don't get me wrong. Julia Clancy's a great lady if you don't mind sharp edges. So how's she doing?"

On this point Sarah assured Rafe. And then, for no reason

that she could explain, found herself asking if he knew anything about the late Dr. Henry Philips, since Rafe and his family had lived in and around Knox County all his life.

"I guess I'm just curious," she said, "because I hear different opinions of the man."

Rafe did know something. To Sarah's surprise, he opened up and let out a flood.

"A real asshole," he said. "I knew him back when. I delivered the *Courier-Gazette* to the old guy when I was maybe twelve, thirteen years old. On foot, anyway. He yelled at me to get the hell off his porch because my boots were filthy. Which, to be fair, I suppose they were."

"A lot of people are grouches when it comes to their property," Sarah said.

"Not just that. Once I fell skiing, and when I went to the ER with a broken ankle, there he was—even though he was supposed to be almost retired and only doing management stuff—throwing his weight around, bossing the emergency room staff. Moved the intern aside who was checking me, took a look at my ankle and my X-ray and said I was trying to get out of school; that I was one of those goddamned teenagers polluting the country, so to get off the table and go on home. I got up, hopped off on one foot to get my coat. But then he went to harangue someone else, and another doc stopped me and called in an orthopedic guy and I was fixed up with a cast."

Here Rafe paused, took a soft brush, and with angry energy began sweeping it across Duncan's black coat. "And listen to this. My Aunt Gussie went into the hospital with what she thought was indigestion. Dr. Philips was around as usual, poking his nose where he shouldn't, and he countered the diagnosis of a cardiac problem, said he knew a gastric upset when he saw it, and gave her something like Pepto-Bismol and sent her home. She died that night. Family thought about suing, but my uncle worked for the hospital in maintenance, so they dropped the idea. To repeat, this Henry Philips was an interfering bastard. The hospital is lucky to be rid of him for good."

"Well, I did hear," said Sarah, cautiously because she didn't want to stir up any more smoldering fires, "that after he retired he kept coming to the hospital."

"Oh, sure," said Rafe, whose over-vigorous polishing of Duncan's quarters had resulted in a gleaming black surface, "you can't keep a bad thing down, is what I say. But people tell me that in the last few years, old age kicked in and he was pretty harmless. And his wife, she died a little while back, kept an eye on the old geezer. Anyway, you tell Mrs. Clancy everything's okay here and she's to get well. I kind of miss her charging around, blistering everyone's butt."

· And Sarah, feeling all at once a great need for open-air exercise, even with a hot sun beating down on her head, made for the dog run attached to the back of the farmhouse and released the two English setters. Here was one service she could perform with pleasure. With two leashes in her pocket in case of trouble, with Tucker and Belle loping in front, she headed for a distant pasture, a long sloping hill watched over by two sleepy Welsh ponies standing in the shade of a tree swishing their tails against the flies.

But even as she trotted along behind the dogs through tufts of dry August grass, the thought of a dictatorial Dr. Henry Philips kept reinserting itself. How could this picture of an interfering CEO and later nosy retiree relate to the picture of a submissive, bruised Henry Philips waiting patiently for his turn to be examined by the ER staff? It wasn't in character, even as an old man. Unless he had had some sort of accident which altered his personality; made the lion into a lamb . . . well, not a lamb exactly, but a ragmop of a man.

Sarah slowed down to a walk. Tucker and Belle, panting, had now stopped by a mound of weeds and were snuffing and pawing at it. Sarah, hoping they had not found the residence of a sleeping skunk, walked slowly toward them, the two leashes in hand. The digging became more excited, and Sarah, grabbing the two collars, snapped on the leashes and began tugging the setters back in the direction of the farmhouse. She had better things to do than deodorizing two long-haired dogs. She needed to unearth some facts about Dr. Henry Dent Philips. If she could find out that he was one of those thought of as "he got what was coming," wouldn't that point in the direction of someone he had outraged? Betrayed? Malpracticed on—was that a verb?—like Rafe Posner's Aunt Gussie? Perhaps like those three volunteers? And wouldn't the discovery of such a person—or persons—go a long way to establish motive?

Simple, Sarah told herself. The police, of course, were working from the crime scene and then backward toward possible suspects. Why shouldn't someone—not necessarily, of course she herself, but someone not yet identified—work from some past outrage toward the present scene? Revenge at last; a long-hoped-for event. The police, she had often thought, were not very sensitive to the emotional aspects of a case. State Police Sergeant George Fitts was a facts-first man, and Mike Laaka tended to go for action, not brood over complicated and often contradictory personal issues.

Why not a little detour from her day's plan? Hit the Rockland Library newspaper archives because wouldn't this Dr. Henry Philips be the kind of man who attracted public attention, had his finger in the civic pie? This would be research that would not include Alex, who waxed angry over his wife-the-snoop persona. And not Aunt Julia with her mysterious and probably risky plan. A plan that must be derailed tonight when they met at her bedside.

Two hours spent going over the microfilms of old newspapers revealed what Sarah had suspected. From the sixties on, Dr. Henry Philips was everywhere. He practiced medicine, he ran the hospital, chaired committees; he headed fund-raisers, played in charity golf tournaments, and spoke to auxiliary health groups. He trotted off to medical conventions, he received awards, plaques, and a variety of testimonials.

But more to the point, Dr. Philips was mentioned in two lawsuits that had resulted in charges being dropped. But, Sarah told herself, trying to keep an open mind, in a litigious society this had probably happened to many physicians. For Dr. Philips these two affairs—a charge of wrongful diagnosis and one of sexual harassment—were both settled out of court and vanished from the pages of the subsequent issues.

The archive room was stifling, something wrong with the air-conditioning, or the fans, perhaps, but as a final effort, Sarah reread the notices of the murder, the body finding, the paragraph about the police continuing the investigation. Of an obituary there was none, only a short note to the effect that the man was dead, had been eighty-six years old, a widower survived by his grandson, Dr. Jonathan Philips, and various other distant family members; that a more complete notice would follow.

Sarah, now overheated, cramped from bending over the microfilm screen, left the building feeling that it would take an army of detectives to unravel the life and times of Dr. Philips, what with his tail of critics, enemies, and, it must be admitted, probably a troop of loyal followers. The man was not, she was sorry to discover, a complete monster, although some, like Rafe Posner, might think the world well rid of him. And if she had to guess, she'd say the alienated outnumbered the faithful. But why would any of these alienated ones choose to throttle the man in a most public place? And more to the point for Sarah, would he—or she—want then to knock off a witness, an elderly lady in the throes of a heart attack, who might just have seen even more than she had so far revealed?

A little maggot in the back of Sarah's brain began to squirm about. Why try to track all the citizens who had held a grudge against the doctor? What about an in-hospital employee with a motive? Someone in hospital garb who knew his or her way around the hospital by day or night? Someone, like one of those volunteers, whose family member had died under a cloud at the Mary Starbox? Undoubtedly there must be other hospital employees who harbored anti–Dr. Philips sentiments; judging from the newspaper stories. The man, through the years, had certainly cut a wide swath through many departments.

For now Sarah would have to let these thoughts simmer on low heat. It was time to focus on her proper job: protecting and soothing Aunt Julia. Protecting her from a frightening nocturnal attack or helping her recover from a series of unnerving hallucinations so common after open-heart surgery. Whatever the cause, Sarah had now definitely decided to spend the night in the hospital, even under Julia's bed, if that's what it would take to calm her aunt's anxieties.

Sarah shook herself, climbed into a car whose interior almost sizzled from the built-up heat. She would keep her ears open, engage in casual conversation—maybe with these same volunteers—and if something sounded a loud bell, gave the sense of revenge accomplished, she'd tell Mike. And then, duty done, she'd shut up.

She swung out of her parking space, turned toward the center of Rockland, and as she paused for the turn onto the main street, gasped, and twisted her wheel right. A sleek silver automobile shot around Sarah's Subaru, accelerated, took the left curve at speed and sped on down the street. And Sarah, suddenly furious, steaming not only with the heat and general frustration, but with a rush of anger, gunned her Subaru, rammed herself into the one-way traffic in front of a slow-moving SUV, and put herself on the tail of the silver car, now caught in the summer tourist traffic.

Male or female driver? Medium for a woman, shortish for a man. Light-colored shirt or jacket. License plate? But a space opened up ahead, the silver car suddenly accelerated, zoomed past, accelerated past the Reading Corner bookshop, the Amalfi Restaurant, zipped past an appliance store, a clutch of antique dealers, a travel outfit, and roared ahead, then slowed as the traffic thickened. But Sarah, too, was caught in traffic and had just time to see the silver car make a hard left just before McDonald's, whiz off toward Route 17. Stamping on the accelerator, Sarah, three cars behind, desperately tried to keep the car in sight. But even as she crossed the Old County Road and went down Route 17, she asked herself why, why was she going through her own fit of road rage just to tail an anonymous car, one of the many speed demons who used the roads as their personal raceway? Her anger was absolutely senseless; however, this conclusion didn't make her slow her car. Instead, she leaned forward and inched up on a blue pickup directly in front.

By the time the silver car roared down Route 17, cut onto and out of Route 90 and made the turn for Bowmouth College campus and skidded through the stone pillars of the hospital entrance, Sarah had been forced to pull over to allow an ambulance to wheel by, its lights flashing. Then, reaching the hospital grounds, she just caught a distant sight of a silver car twisting into the lines of cars in the employees' parking lot.

What now? She had no identification sticker allowing her to use the employees' lot. But the physicians' lot, yes. She and Alex sometimes traded cars, and the Mary Starbox sticker was in place. Sarah pulled past the employees' lot, wheeled into the physicians' lot, crammed her car between an MG and a dust-covered Bronco and hit the ground running. Around the emergency entrance, around the side of the building and in time to see the double doors of the side hospital swing closed behind a distant disappearing figure.

Sarah stopped dead. What in hell did she have in mind? A citizen's arrest for reckless driving? She was crazy with the heat. Aunt Julia was her job, not the pursuit of someone with a heavy foot and an attitude. And yet. And yet there couldn't be any harm in looking around to see if she could spot the guilty car. Note the license plate in case they ever met again.

But the employees' parking lot yielded one undeniable fact. Silver-gray cars were a dime a dozen. The flavor of the year, or the last four years. If only Sarah had been like her car-mad brother, Tony, she would have been able to identify the make, the year, and the model of the speeder with a glance. But no, Sarah had wasted her adolescent years with dogs, cats, poetry, and field hockey, and now she was served right. For a minute she played with the idea that she could identify the car by laying a hand on its hood to see if it was hot with engine activity, but a trial on a nearby Volvo on that sultry day in August only proved that all car hoods could probably fry an egg.

Okay. That was that. She would probably not see the woman again. A woman? For what it was worth, which wasn't much, there had been something about the set of the head that suggested female. So, incident over. On to Aunt Julia. Buy her a magazine. Some periodical that featured nothing close to the bone, nothing to push up her blood pressure. But the gift shop only featured a selection of sports and women's magazines mixed in with depressing paperback titles like *You and Your Health.*

Sarah settled for a copy of the *Bangor Daily News* and headed for Julia's room. The door was open and she was halfway into the room when she saw that Julia had another visitor. The god from the Sandwich Islands, the Reverend Joshua Stevenson. The man was dressed in what might be termed Maine casual. The round collar around a well-worn short-sleeve summer shirt, tan khakis, tan leather walking shoes showing much wear.

Father Stevenson—did he use the title "Father"? Sarah wondered—was standing by the head of Julia's bed, in his hands the photograph of Tom Clancy astride Finnian, his big gray gelding. Julia was sunk back on her pillow, a wadded-up tissue in her fist, making low murmuring noises.

The sight of Sarah roused her to hesitant speech. "Oh, Sarah. I'm so glad. Father Stevenson here is looking at Tom's picture. The one you brought in this morning. I've been telling him all about Tom. How he died in this very room. ICU Number Nine. After that dreadful accident."

Sarah looked confused. "But Uncle Tom died in Vermont, didn't he? At that horse show."

"Hunter trials," corrected Julia, a stickler for equestrian correctness.

"Yes," said Sarah. "I heard about it when I was in Boston. The beginning of the fall semester. It was so awful."

"Twelve years ago," said Julia plaintively. "We brought him back to Maine and he died here. In this room."

Sarah frowned. "He wasn't taken to the nearest hospital in Vermont?"

"Sarah, you're upsetting me with that kind of question. Tom wanted to die in Maine. If he couldn't do it in Ireland. It was . . ." Julia faltered, perhaps for dramatic effect—it was hard to tell, Sarah decided, because after all, Tom Clancy had been the light of her life—"It was," Julia repeated, "his last wish. So we honored it."

Father Stevenson said nothing, simply inclined his head as if in sympathetic understanding. Then Sarah, feeling as if she had suddenly become part of a badly written soap opera, reached down and kissed Julia lightly on the cheek, and as she did saw her aunt's left eye close and open. It was such a quick movement, the merest blink, that for a second Sarah wasn't sure she'd even seen it. But if it meant what she thought it did, her aunt was up to no good. This idea was immediately confirmed when Julia reached over with her non-IV hand and squeezed Sarah's arm. Hard. It was a squeeze that featured a stabbing fingernail so that Sarah had all she could do to keep from shouting "Ouch."

Standing up straight, Sarah shot a quick look at their visitor. Had he caught the action? No, because he had moved silently to the window and was studying the photograph of Tom Clancy. Well, forget about derailing Julia's plan; it was already an object in motion. And it seemed, although built on a palpable lie, to be workable and relatively harmless. And so, Sarah thought, for now I'd better play along, assume the role in which her beloved aunt had cast her: that of the comforting niece who would move heaven and earth to get her aunt out of this room of tragic memory.

"Poor Aunt Julia," Sarah began. "I don't think anyone would want you to stay here. Not after what you've told us." She turned to Joshua Stevenson, who had now turned and was giving Julia a speculative look. "Don't you agree?" said Sarah. If this was Julia's plan to move to another room, the force of Father Stevenson would be needed, and Sarah must give him a push.

"I certainly think," said Joshua Stevenson, "that Mrs. Clancy should be listened to."

This was ambiguous and not satisfactory.

"Yes," said Sarah. "And I'm sure you can manage it. The doctors are really focused on her physical problems. I'm worried about Aunt Julia's being so unhappy in this room that it's going to interfere with her getting better."

"Exactly," said Julia weakly. "I'm so upset that I'm not drinking all the fluids I need."

Father Stevenson again inclined his head. "I don't suppose

the consolation of the church is what you had in mind when you called for me," he said.

"What I have in mind," said Julia more briskly—it was hard to keep an old warhorse like herself in a low-key mode—"is more the power of the church to move an old lady from one room to another. So the old lady doesn't lose her mind for good."

"The nurse at the desk said you might have had a bad dream last night. Or some sort of encounter. An attack, perhaps," said Father Stevenson.

"Oh, that," said Julia, dismissing last night. "I've gotten past that. It's being in this room. Tom dying. So what can you do? And don't tell me that the church has limitations. My mother goes on about faith moving mountains. But I only want to move down the hall."

Sarah, watching, saw Joshua Stevenson's face give a sudden twitch and then quickly settle back into a half-smile, but what his answer would be she would never know. Alex came into the room, shook hands with the visitor, kissed Julia, and asked cheerfully how things were going.

At which point Patrick arrived.

Sarah would remember the next half hour as something like a quartet of badly matched instruments, each playing its own tune without regard for the others. Julia did a reprise of her dismay of finding herself in the equivalent of Tom's deathbed, Patrick went into a strong Irish recital of Tom's handling of horses and how Mrs. Clancy here would sure be after living with a ghost if she stayed where she was. Alex, uninstructed in the matter of Julia's plan, or "act," played the heavy, pointing out that this part of the cardiac wing was a recent addition to the hospital, and if Tom Clancy had died twelve years ago, well then . . .

Sarah cut him off at the pass. In this she was joined, to her surprise, by Father Stevenson, who now replaced the picture of Tom Clancy and Finnian on Julia's bedside table. "It's a wonderful picture," he said. "A handsome man. And a handsome horse." He turned to the visitors. "What do you say we give this good lady a rest time, and then we'll come back and see if we can settle the matter to her satisfaction?"

Alex nodded and then added, a puzzled expression on his face, "Julia, you told me Tom died in Vermont. It happened right after his fall at the jump. That you were glad he didn't suffer."

Sarah, reaching over to punch Alex, was saved, literally, by the bell: Alex was being paged on the hospital loudspeaker. He called in, listened, gave a sigh, and turned to the group. "The ER. Emma Littlefield. The woman who won't come to my office. Only now it's her sister. I'll have to go. Julia, we love you and whatever you all decide is fine with me."

Julia watched him go and then turned to Sarah, Patrick, and Joshua Stevenson. "Thank heaven. Alex is really mixed up and making mountains out of molehills. I'm glad he won't be around for a little while. And now, I do need a rest. Patrick, thank you, and please go back to the farm. You need to be there for night check. And look at Duffie, see if he should stay on Bute. That's Butazolidin to you laymen. It's for horses, but I sometimes take it for my arthritis. Sarah, you should go home. Father Stevenson, could you come back in half an hour?"

"I'm spending the night," said Sarah firmly. "Even if you don't want me."

"We'll see, but thank you," said Julia. "Now be off. Go get yourself something to eat. Or take Patsy for a walk. And please not a word of this to anyone. I mean it. Not the doctors, not the staff. The nurses think I'm an old pest. Well, I am old, and"—here her voice sank—"and I am very much distressed."

The three met in the hall. Then Patrick, shaking his head over the whole affair, said something about hospitals being places of the devil, and took his leave. And Sarah turned to Father Stevenson. "What do you think?"

"I think," he said carefully, "that Mrs. Clancy may not make it to Broadway, but it won't be for lack of trying. But I'm in her camp and I'll throw my weight around and see if I can set up a move to another room later this evening. I have friends in high places."

"You mean God?" said Sarah.

"The superintendent of nurses," said Joshua Stevenson. He lifted a hand in farewell and vanished down the hall.

Mary Starbox
Memorial Hospital
Emergency ⟶

11

SARAH drove home to Sawmill Road in order to make domestic arrangements for Patsy, who by now would be thinking himself a neglected and starving Irish wolfhound. After attending to his kibbles, filling his water dish, and cleaning the dog run, she assembled the necessaries for spending the night at the hospital curled up in Aunt Julia's armchair. A small pillow, a toothbrush, toothpaste, underwear, and clean socks fitted into a canvas bag took care of necessities; for sleepless moments, she had *Northanger Abbey* (almost finished), with *Jane Eyre* on deck.

Arriving back at the hospital without encountering any speeding silver cars, she went directly to Julia's room. Only the soft overhead light by the bathroom was on, and Julia was reclining on two pillows, her IV-attached arm extended, her eyes closed. Sarah, about to tiptoe out, was recalled.

"Don't you go sneaking around," said her aunt. "I have ears in the back of my head."

"You mean eyes?" said Sarah, halting.

"Eyes, ears, it's all the same. It comes from sleeping in the barn waiting for one of my mares to foal. The least sound . . ."

"No matter what room you end up in, I'm spending the night," Sarah announced firmly. "I've fed Patsy and I have my things. I'll use your chair and I won't make a sound."

"No such thing," said Julia. "I don't know yet about any room change, but I don't want you sleepless and cross tomorrow when it isn't necessary. Everything's under control. Father Stevenson is wheeling and dealing. Have you had dinner yet? Go have it, go home, and I'll see you in the morning."

Sarah gave up on arguing. She would go to the cafeteria, have a leisurely meal, read for a while in the waiting room, and then, when Julia would surely be asleep, she would sneak back to room 9 and check to see if her aunt was still a resident. If this was so, she'd settle down in the chair and be the watchdog. If Julia had been moved—her bed empty or a stranger in place— Sarah would hunt her down in her new quarters. A simple plan, which had the great advantage of not allowing for a showdown with the patient.

Once in place at a table in a far corner of the cafeteria, a slice of turkey and a salad in front of her, Sarah, looking around, saw that the evening cafeteria population differed noticeably from earlier regulars. Those that came by day had been a mix of the usual hospital staff, volunteers, and visitors—anxious visitors, the profoundly depressed visitors, the happy upbeat visitors. But at night the happy families had left, the volunteers had gone home, the residents and interns showed clear signs of fatigue, and the visitors now in place, having coffee and a snack at a late hour, all seemed low-key and somber, obviously persons remaining in the hospital for the long haul.

Then, as a small group (nurses? aides? lab workers? cleaning persons? surgeons? technicians?) came through the double cafeteria doors, Sarah was reminded again of the absolute impossibility of telling people apart unless someone wore a bone through the nose or had two heads. And then there were those androgynous creatures in scrubs and caps, masks hanging down, some shuffling around in their OR booties. Only the people perhaps coming from the outside world in street clothes seemed to have separate identities. Otherwise, it was a masked ball. Sarah began to imagine having to pick one of them out in a police lineup and found herself grinning.

"What's so damn funny?" A familiar voice. Mike Laaka, a tray of food held in front of him.

"Hi, Mike. Sit down and eat something. I just thought about the police or a witness trying to recognize hospital suspects."

Mike settled two cheeseburgers and a bag of chips next to Sarah's place and pulled up a chair. "Glad you think that's so funny. For us it's a class-A headache." He looked around the cafeteria. "Hey, where's the mister? Not joining you?"

"Called to the ER. A sister of Emma Littlefield was brought in."

"Poor guy. That Emma is something else. And, jeez, do I hate that place. The day that old Doc Philips got his, what a goddamn rodeo. We've filtered out a few people who were known to be somewhere else, but we've still got about twenty or so hospital personnel to place, plus all the incoming and outgoing patients and their families."

"Not to mention the volunteer squad," said Sarah.

Mike nodded. "Listen, we're having more trouble pinning down those guys than the hospital staff. Most of the staff stick to one or two areas, are assigned to a floor or a department. Those volunteers are like lice. They go everywhere."

"They do have a uniform," Sarah pointed out. "Doesn't that help?"

"A different uniform every few years or so. Blue now, green before; faded, new. And a few of the old-timers seem to wear what they damn please."

Sarah was silent for a minute, took a small bite from her slice of turkey, drank a few inches of iced tea, and then made a decision. "You know, don't you, that some of the volunteers lost family members here. Maybe a mistake was made, or something peculiar happened. I had lunch with three of them and they talked about it."

Mike considered, then nodded. "I'd guess half the people

whose family members died in the hospital think things could have been managed better. And doctors, nurses—anyone—can and do make mistakes. Yeah, I know there've been some rotten apples. A couple of docs have lost admitting privileges. Did something they shouldn't have. Wrote a wrong prescription, wrong dose. Sex with a patient. Once a pedophile was loose in the pediatric section. You name it. Happens in hospitals all over the country."

"But as a motive for throttling Dr. Philips?"

"Hell, Sarah, there were probably people standing in line for the job. Except," Mike added, "whoever did it had to be right there when Philips came into the ER. Ready to grab the chance. It couldn't have been a planned event. No one knew the guy was going to fall down his cellar stairs."

"How about sifting through hospital records and see who might have been really traumatized because Dr. Philips screwed up with a family member."

"God-a-mighty, Sarah. What a pain in the tail that'd be. Maybe we'll have to, sometime, but right now we're trying to find out who was where and when. Total nightmare."

"Speaking of which—"

"You mean Julia? Yeah, I'm going to have someone check at odd times all night. Keep an eye on her room."

"And if she moves to another place?"

"I'll keep an eye on that room. But Alex didn't think she could pull the move off."

"Aunt Julia's working from her own script," said Sarah. "Tragic memories. Uncle Tom Clancy died in that very room. In that very bed, maybe."

"My God," said Mike, staring. "But I thought . . ."

"Vermont. Right. His horse shied. He died instantly. Julia's pulling out all stops to get herself moved. Calls her room at the end of the corridor an accident waiting to happen. But no matter where she ends up, I'm spending the night. The family guard dog. Or maybe I should have smuggled Patsy in. The Hound from Hell."

Mike took an enormous bite out of his cheeseburger,

munched, and nodded. "Not a bad idea. Patsy'd be a lot more use than you would. Skinny Sarah facing the strangler—if there was a strangler—doesn't make me happy."

"Shut up, Mike. No strangler would go to work with a witness sitting there. And I've brought a flashlight and a whistle. What more could Aunt Julia want?"

"Someone with a semiautomatic weapon," said Mike. "Now, take care. I've got to go back to work. And don't let your Aunt Julia pull a fast one. We'll be watching her, so don't you go and try to play cops and robbers, you hear?"

"As I said before, shut up, Mike." Sarah waved her napkin at Mike and returned to contemplate a dish featuring blueberries sinking into a limp piece of sponge cake.

Alex had his hands full. In the ER examining bay he not only had Emma Littlefield to cope with, to listen to, but her obviously ill sister to check over. Emma, pushing eighty, sharp as a fox and twice as clever, he knew. He could cope with her ups and downs, her ever-changing collections of aches, pains, palpitations, and imaginary symptoms, as well as some perfectly legitimate health problems. Her sister Florence was something else.

Florence Littlefield was a fierce scrap of a woman; someone who, from the first word she uttered on seeing Alex approach, made it clear that, unlike Emma, she didn't have any use for hospitals, doctors, examining tables, medications, and treatments of any sort. A small gray-haired woman with a determined face and alert pale blue eyes, she faced Alex from her propped-up position on the examining bed. Altogether she closely resembled Emma, although the fact that she had not dyed her hair black, as had Emma, gave her the appearance of being the older of the two. However, she was, Alex noted, flipping through the resident's scribbled notes, only seventy-one.

"I'm not here because I want to," Florence said. "I was dragged. By her." She pointed at Emma, who stood frowning at the foot of the bed. "Emma almost lives here. It's her recreation. Her social club for hypochondriacs. Me, I'm independent. It's just that I had this pain. And I was a little breathless, but what can you expect."

"Let me explain," said Emma. "I know all these symptoms. In my opinion, what Florence has and won't admit is a perfectly clear sign of a sort of cardiac condition. I think—"

At which Alex, who had been briefed by the ER resident as he walked toward the examining bay, thanked Emma and went to work on Florence. A few questions later, a look at Florence's EKG, noting the fact of her elevated blood pressure, listening to a description of her anginalike symptoms—given grudgingly with fill-ins by Emma—was all it took for Alex to summon cardiologist Eugene Santaro.

Gene Santaro had often pitied Alex McKenzie for his involvement with Emma Littlefield and had sincerely hoped never to have her under his care. Now he and Alex had a double dose: a possibly ill but angry Florence Littlefield in tandem with her demanding and voluble sister Emma. And Emma was keeping up a nonstop commentary on Dr. Santaro's every move, every remark. The trouble was that all Emma's reading of Mayo Clinic and Harvard health letters and her visits to medical Web sites were paying off. As Dr. Santaro went over his patient, listened, thumped, and examined the monitors and made notes, Emma, sitting on a stool at the edge of the alcove, rattled on about systolic hypertension, aortic valve disorders, rhythm abnormalities, the possible need for an ACE inhibitor, a beta blocker, a calcium channel blocker, a pacemaker, an angiogram.

At last, even mild-tempered Gene Santaro had reached his limit. "Alex, will you take Miss Emma Littlefield *now* to the waiting room and discuss the possibility that we may be admitting her sister to the hospital."

Alex took hold of Emma's elbow and propelled her in the direction of the waiting room. "Miss Littlefield," he said between his teeth as he moved her toward an empty chair in the crowded waiting room, "sit down, please, and think about the fact that your sister may need you to be a very calm and supportive person through the next few days."

At which Emma hesitated. "You think it's something serious?"

she asked. "Because maybe it's nothing to do with her heart, though all the symptoms seem to be . . ." Here Emma trailed off and then shook her head. "Of course, it might be something gastric or a form of arthritis. Florence is a difficult person to live with. I stay only with her out of a sense of duty. She hasn't a positive sort of personality. And she's very stubborn."

"Wait and see," said Alex. "But it won't help if you go frightening her with every cardiac symptom in the book. So I want you to sit quietly, look at a magazine, and I'll be back as soon as I find out what Dr. Santaro has to say."

"I'd rather know what you have to say," snapped Emma. "You're my doctor, whether you like it or not. I chose you particularly. You remind me of my Uncle Jacob, who was something else."

Alex couldn't help himself. "Something else what?"

"Everything. Looked like a real gentleman and fooled everyone. Forgery, embezzling. Did it for years and finally got caught in the act. Served time. Now what about this Dr. Santaro?"

Alex with an effort rose above his apparent resemblance to Uncle Jacob and returned to topic A. "I am not a cardiologist," he said firmly, "but Dr. Santaro is. I trust him. He has had a great deal of experience." At which Alex turned and left Emma glaring at him, clutching her handbag in two tight claws. But then, as he reached the door, he saw her sitting rigidly at the edge of her chair staring into space.

And suddenly Alex saw her in a new way, her black-dyed hair incongruous against her white and lined old face, not only as a trouble and a nuisance, but as an old woman who was trying with all her might to keep a grip on her world. Just as her sister Florence wanted to refuse medical help and so remain her own boss, Emma, by mastering the lingo and symptoms of a hundred different pathologies and by making the doctor see her on her own terms, could respect her aging self. Alex returned to the waiting room, tapped Emma on the shoulder, leaned toward her hearing aid, and whispered that everyone would do their best and Florence would be taken care of.

And so it was that after another series of diagnostic tests and at the urgent request of Drs. Santaro and McKenzie, Florence Littlefield was placed on the short waiting list for a room and given the promise of an angiogram the next morning. And Emma was told to go say good night to her sister, then go home and have a good night's sleep, as she would need to be ready for the morning. Florence was now in a stable condition and would be given something to help her sleep.

Alex looked at his watch. Getting late. Almost midnight. And since he had to make rounds early the next morning, it was perhaps time to pack it in. But not until he'd checked on that other difficult patient, Julia Clancy, who was bound to him by affection and family tethers. She would, he hoped, be resting quietly, sleeping or lying calmly in her room in an accepting frame of mind. And, if she had prevailed, resting in a new room.

He caught up with Sarah as she was coming around the bend in the Cardiac ICU complex, a small duffel bag over her shoulder. She pointed to the end of the hall at Julia's unit, number 9, its glass partitions now covered by the pale blue curtains, which had been pulled across their width.

"Don't go in because she's really out," said Sarah. "I took a look just now and she didn't move a muscle. I'm going to spend the night in the chair. I think it goes back into sort of a recliner."

"Guardian angel against the dangerous intruder?"

"Guardian niece armed with a ballpoint pen and a whistle. Mike Laaka's deputy, Katie Waters—you know, from the sheriff's department—stopped by and said she'd check on Julia every now and then."

"So I gather Julia's room-switching idea didn't work out."

"Well, she's still in there, unless that's a stuffed scarecrow in her bed. But it's funny. She really had a plan. Aided and abetted by Father Stevenson. They were pulling out all the stops because of Uncle Tom dying in room nine."

"Which he didn't, of course."

"As Julia might say, why fuss over details. Anyway, maybe they'll move her later on tonight."

Alex nodded. "I've used up whatever clout I had in the matter. Listen, I'll go along now and see you in the morning. Early.

Rounds and a new patient. Florence Littlefield. Emma Littlefield's sister. She's being admitted and probably already has a bed. She'll be having an angiogram in the A.M."

"You mean there are *two* Littlefield ladies?"

"Opposites. Emma loves medicine and ailments, but I think Florence would burn down the hospital if she had a chance. Fought the whole examining scene. Another tough lady, short and scrappy."

"What you needed. Two Littlefields."

"You know even my stone heart melted. Two old gals at the end of the road. Emma's beginning to have some of the ailments she only pretended to have last year. And Florence may be facing a stent. Or cardiac surgery. Nothing fun, anyway."

"And so good night," said Sarah. She reached up and planted a kiss on the side of Alex's chin. "You need a shave and I need a shower."

Alex reached over and ruffled her already disordered hair. "And peace be with us all," he said. "At least until six o'clock tomorrow morning."

"That remark," said Sarah firmly, "is just asking for trouble."

"Peace," Sarah muttered to herself as she tried to settle into a comfortable slumping position in the partially expanded green chair. Peace in a hospital setting was nothing but a bad joke.

And this damn chair. The vinyl surface of the thing was no doubt great for its easy-to-clean properties, but it didn't do much about holding the human body securely on its glassy surface. And the angle, half up and half down, made Sarah feel like an oyster slipping out of its shell. Moreover, the cotton blanket, borrowed from Julia's cupboard supply, kept sliding to the floor. She had nudged the chair away from the bed and over to an alcove so that it was half-hidden behind alcove curtains. Now if Julia woke she wouldn't see her niece hovering, and yet Sarah would be close enough to comfort and listen to any complaints that Julia might want to make.

Julia Clancy. Indomitable, cactus-like, dear Aunt Julia. In the short time since she had been admitted, her aunt seemed to have been shrinking a little each day. Sarah remembered how small she'd looked when she first saw her in that giant hospital bed with its side rails and overhanging monitors. Now, tonight, she seemed to have lost even a few more inches, her body making an even smaller lump under its cover than it had yesterday.

Oh dear, Sarah thought. We can't let her shrink into nothing. She needs something to light a spark, give her a jolt of energy. Maybe Patrick could bring Duffie over in the trailer and walk him around in the parking lot. Or the two setters, Tucker and Belle, could be slipped into her room. After all, the hospital used those so-called therapy dogs to brighten up the patients' dreary days. She remembered a sheltie being trotted down the hall the other day, and earlier this very evening a white standard poodle in a show cut with its nails painted red had appeared in the patients' sitting room. Or, she thought sleepily, maybe we could smuggle in the pony, Gingersnap. And with the picture of the little pony being worked through the automatic sliding doors of the hospital lobby, Sarah drifted into sleep.

And woke with a sense of sledding down a slope into some-thing hard. The floor. The blasted chair. She cautiously rolled over, stood, and peeked over at the recumbent form of her aunt. Not awake. Not fussing. Good. Sarah sat back in the chair, re-adjusted the reclining angle, stuffed her handbag into the hollow of her back, and drew the cotton blanket over her shoulders. Then, just as she was sliding back into sleep when, wouldn't you know it, in came another nurse. Or aide. Or physician's assistant. Some hospital health-care creature. One of that endless troupe of sleep destroyers.

But this person was at least making an effort at being quiet. Sarah half-opened her eyes and saw a blurred image in white while being only aware of the slightest rustling, the nick of a hand bumping into the IV pole, a shuffling of feet on the linoleum floor, a pause. Several small movements. A quiet departure.

Silence. Blessed silence. Sarah closed her eyes.

And suddenly was jarred awake. All hell was breaking loose.

The door banging open. People on the run. The light full on. Someone in scrubs pushing a cart. Another cart. Attachments, tubes, orders of "Stand back," orders in a tense voice. A man in navy scrubs close to Sarah saying, "Shit, oh shit," over and over. More arrivals. A loudspeaker barking about a code. Someone saying "Flatline." Another going on about no pressure. Responses, no responses. Another shouting, "Get the blood down to the lab. Stat!"

And then the man who had said "Shit" backed into Sarah, who was now standing, clutching the cotton blanket to her chest, a look of absolute horror in her staring eyes.

"Who in hell . . ." said the man.

Sarah clutched at his sleeve. "What's wrong? I can't see."

The man moved himself between Sarah and the bed and the frantic activity there, and so blocked her view. "Who," he said, more gently, "are you? And why—"

Sarah interrupted. "It's my aunt. I was spending the night. She was nervous. And what—"

At which the man took Sarah firmly by the shoulders and, still shielding her view of the bed, began to turn her toward the door. "You don't want to see all this," he said. "I'll come and get you in few minutes."

Sarah pushed herself free of his grip. "I'm not going anywhere. That's my aunt over there. I'm staying."

"Look," said the man, "help us here. You'll be in the way. You don't want that, do you? We'll do our best for your aunt. I'll get back to you as soon as I can. I promise."

At which Sarah gave in and let herself be escorted to the door of number 9. Turned over to a hovering nurse. Escorted to the small waiting room in the end of the corridor. "Please stay right here," said the nurse. A familiar voice and face, Sarah thought dumbly. One of the hundreds of voices and faces she'd met over the past few days. She tried to pull herself together. "My aunt," she repeated. "I'm one of her closest relatives. I was spending the night. Please let me—"

But the nurse—it was that motherly one who had called Julia "dear"—Clare Somebody, tonight in a bright pink flowered number, an incongruous outfit considering what had just gone on in room 9, put her hand on Sarah's shoulder. "You don't want to stop what they're trying to do. Save your aunt. Now can I get you something? The whole team is in there, so I'm free just now. Let me get you something to drink. Water. Some tea." And she was gone.

And Sarah fumbled her way to a chair, folded herself into it, and tried to think about losing Aunt Julia Clancy. Being without the piss and vinegar that Julia brought into the world with her. And Julia's mother? Sarah's Grandmother Douglas. Ninety and frail, a mere splinter of a woman. How awful to be ninety and survive your seventy-one-year-old daughter. Would her grandmother go on about it being. "God's will" and that we must accept what He brought her? Sarah didn't think she could stand it.

"Oh, goddamn," she said aloud.

"I agree," said a voice.

Alex. Rumpled. Plainly roused from bed and called to the scene.

"Alex!" Sarah yelled and hurled herself at him. Clutched his neck and sobbed into his neck.

"Hey," said Alex, putting his arm around her. "How did you know? And how did you get here? This waiting room. I thought . . ." He stopped, his expression puzzled.

Sarah lifted her head. "Okay, tell me. No one else will. Is she gone? I mean, dead? Was it another heart attack?"

Alex nodded, his expression sober. "Yes, she's gone. No one's sure yet why. We'll have to wait. Lab tests, all that. It was sudden. Went just like that, judging from the monitors."

"Oh my God, my God," said Sarah.

"I know you're sympathetic," began Alex.

"Sympathetic, hell!" Sarah shouted it. "Sympathetic! Is that how you describe it? Is that how you feel? A little sympathy. It's Aunt Julia? Remember Aunt Julia? I love her. I thought you did. She's family. I'm not just sympathetic, I'm about wiped out. You should be, too. Not just Goddamn Doctor Cold Fish standing there like some block of ice."

"Wait up. Wait up." Alex pushed Sarah away and held her arms in a tight grip. "Listen. Hear me. Not Aunt Julia. Repeat: not

137

Aunt Julia. Julia's fine. Cardiac ICU Three. Her room was changed after all. Apparently sometime just before midnight. I found out when they called me to come into the hospital."

"What!" Sarah found her voice, now hoarse from emotion. "Not Julia. But I was there. Next to her bed. Right there. With Julia. Spending the night in the chair. Keeping her company. I was there when everyone came pounding in. Hooking her up, started the resuscitation business, if that's what it was. But you're saying she's alive? I don't get it."

"Listen. Please. Julia is okay. Alive. Trust me. But I have to ask: Did you talk to Julia before you settled down for the night?"

"No, she was asleep. Remember, when we met in the hall, I told you I'd looked in and she was quiet. Asleep, I thought. And then you went home."

"And when you went back into the room?"

"Still quiet. Sleeping. I thought she'd had a good sedative. Anyway, I tiptoed around and pushed the chair out of her sight and tried to sleep."

"Did you look at her?"

"Of course. I thought she looked even smaller, as if she were shrinking each day."

"You could see her face?"

"She was half on her side. But it was her shape. Her head. Gray fuzzy hair."

"What you saw," said Alex slowly, "and who you spent part of the night with, was Florence Littlefield. My patient and Gene Santoro's patient. She was admitted this evening and taken up to a bed. Cardiac ICU nine because Julia had somehow finally managed the switch. I don't know exactly how, but she did it. There was a discharge in room three, Julia was moved in there, room nine was cleaned up, and Florence was put there. Florence had had some sort of cardiac event yesterday and Gene Santoro had arranged for her to have an angiogram in the A.M."

"And I," said Sarah in an unbelieving voice, "was with Florence Littlefield when she died. Not Aunt Julia."

"Not Aunt Julia."

"And this Florence, she died of a heart attack? Suddenly? No noise? She stopped breathing?"

"She certainly stopped breathing. The monitors went off and the troops came in. But we don't know if it's a heart attack. Time will tell. Lab tests. Autopsy. The works."

"You mean it might be . . ." Sarah couldn't finish the sentence.

"Florence was in a fragile condition. These things happen."

"Even after you guys had got her, what's the word, 'stabilized'?"

"Even so."

"And I was there. The whole time. And I didn't know."

"Apparently you didn't. But don't go jumping into space on this, wondering if you could have helped. People do die suddenly. Some die quietly, they just stop breathing. So don't blame yourself for not knowing who was in the bed. Two short older women with gray hair covered up would look pretty much alike. And now I've got to see Florence's sister, Emma, and break the news. We've sent a taxi for her."

"Oh God," said Sarah again, for lack of something more specific to say.

"That sums it up," said Alex. "Now go home, get some sleep, so you can cheer up Julia in the morning."

"And try to tell her that the patient in room nine was done in."

"No. No. Absolutely no. We don't know anything like that. You have homicide on the brain. Go breathe some fresh air. I said cheer Julia up, not scare her. Not feed her fright—or paranoia—about being attacked."

"I think that right now," said Sarah, "I'll sneak into room three and plant a kiss on her old gray head and she'll wake up and give me hell, but it will be worth it."

"Amen," said Alex, turning to leave.

12

SARAH, feeling as if her body had passed through an entire washing machine cycle—wash, tumble, rinse; and spin—walked unsteadily toward the middle section of the corridor and ICU number 3. If Julia happened to be awake, Sarah would try to be entirely calm. "Just looking in," she'd say. Then she'd settle into one of those awful vinyl chairs by Julia's bed and take a good grip on some reachable part of her aunt's anatomy. And not let go.

But instead of a sleeping Julia, she found the lights on, her aunt propped up on two pillows, and deputy sheriff's investigator Katie Walter sitting beside her. Julia was holding forth. Sarah, standing at the open door, heard the words "conditioning," "hoof care," "shoulder confirmation."

And Katie was bobbing her head. Yes, she saw what Mrs. Clancy meant. "But the asking price for an eighteen-year-old gelding, even if it was a thoroughbred . . ."

Sarah felt a sudden quiver. Not exactly distress. Nor anger. Some untoward emotion. The incongruity of it. At the end of the hall in ICU 9, chaos, emergency, sudden death. Here, in ICU 3, her aunt lecturing on horses.

Julia lifted her head and saw her niece. "Sarah. I thought you'd decided to go home. I couldn't sleep. Not with all the noise. People running races, shoving carts around, the loudspeaker blasting. But Katie Waters here was kind enough to come in and have a chat. She's looking at an eighteen-year-old gelding. If the price is right."

"Which now isn't even in reach," said Katie. "And I've been keeping an eye on Mrs. Clancy's room—first room nine, and then Mike Laaka let me know about the switch. Then, with the commotion, I thought I'd see if everything was all right, that Mrs. Clancy wasn't worried about the noise. So here we are having a nice horse talk. I grew up with standardbreds, but now I want a riding horse, not a trotter."

"Who could sleep?" said Julia. "But since I was awake and those vital-signs busybodies would be about to turn up anytime now, I thought I might as well stay alert because you have to watch them every minute. And Katie's on night duty, so I'm not keeping her up."

"I thought I'd just stick my head in, see if everything's okay," said Sarah in what she hoped was in a voice empty of any emotion.

Julia looked squarely at her niece. "Shouldn't it be? You know something? Is that why you're here in the middle of the night? But," she added, as if trying to understand a riddle, "this evening you were insisting on spending the night with me even after I said you didn't have to. You're as stubborn as I am, so I thought you'd do it. But then you didn't turn up after all. I was a little surprised you didn't stick to your plan."

"I meant to spend the night," said Sarah. "But I didn't know about the room change."

"Father Stevenson worked his magic. Because of Tom dying in nine."

Sarah ignored this. "Even Alex didn't know," she said.

"A last-minute victory. I got lucky because this room faces the nurses' station. Which is what I wanted. The whole point of moving was to beat the odds, be near the center of things, where no one would dare sneak in on me. Strangle me. Even if it was just my postoperative brain going over the edge, hallucinating, I wanted to move. To hell with privacy at the end of the hall. I've turned cowardly in my old age."

"And like I said," put in Katie, "Mike Laaka told me to keep an eye on Mrs. Clancy, wherever she ended up."

Julia twisted around and with her free right hand grabbed hold of the IV pole with its tubing, and being careful not to dislodge the needle implanted in her left hand, pulled it to her side and struggled to a sitting position. Her eyes were wide open, her expression intense. "I think I'm understanding something. Tell the truth, Sarah. Don't try and distract me. Something happened in room nine, didn't it? All that noise and rushing around. And that's why you're here because you found out I wasn't in that room. Right? And something happened. So, for God's sake, spit it out!"

But before Sarah could pull herself together, Julia turned on Katie. "Katie, did you know what was going on? What was all that noise about? People running?"

Katie shook her head. "Cross my heart. I only knew that there was a code—you know, an emergency call—on this floor. One of the Cardiac ICU units. It does happen. This is a hospital and the floor has some pretty sick people. But it wasn't my business. I just stayed out of the way and came in to make sure Mrs. Clancy didn't get all roiled up."

"I wasn't roiled," said Julia sharply. "But now I am. All right, Sarah. Give. What happened? And don't go sliding over the details because poor old Aunt Julia might faint with anxiety and give herself a setback. I can just hear Alex telling you to button your lip. Well, I will have a setback if I don't hear exactly what went on."

"Well," Sarah began, wondering how to thread her way through the events without suggesting that a homicidal masked person might have mistaken Florence Littlefield for Julia Clancy. "Well," she began again, "I came into your room, nine, just before midnight. Saw you were asleep—"

"Someone who wasn't me," corrected Julia. And then, eyebrows up: "Good heavens, can't you even tell me apart from someone else? I mean, there you were smack-dab right in the room."

"Yes, but the light was dim and I was trying to be quiet and not bump the bed," said Sarah, feeling that the explanation was going adrift, and she was showing up as an idiot who couldn't tell a close relative from a total stranger.

"And nothing seemed strange about the shape in the bed? I'm only five foot three."

"Nothing seemed wrong. You, or this Florence Littlefield—she's short, too, I guess—was lying partly on your—her—side. Away from me. Sheet pulled up, only fuzzy gray hair showing. Sleeping. So I tried to be very quiet, hunkered down in the chair, and all sorts of people came in and out checking monitors, heart rate, and so forth. Noisy bunch. But then a quiet person came in and did some things, I don't know what. I didn't really look. Just had an impression. But I thought, what a relief. Someone's trying to be considerate. And then I guess whoever it was left and the whole place burst apart. Apparently Florence Littlefield had an attack. Her heart stopped. Or something. Alex was called in—she's one of his patients—and the cardiologist on the case, Gene Santoro. And there'll be an autopsy, lab reports, and so forth."

"Because they suspect something?"

"No, I'm sure it's routine. When someone dies like that."

"A perfectly natural unexpected death?" said Julia, her voice sarcastic.

"I suppose so," said Sarah, trying to keep any doubt from her voice. "This is a cardiac unit and people are sick. As Katie said. I'm sorry it happened. And for at least ten minutes I thought it was you. I couldn't believe you'd died. Just like that. When I thought you were sleeping. I was so sad. I'd been right there and I couldn't help you. I couldn't even help this Florence Littlefield."

"That," said Julia, "shows you are a very kind person and have the right instincts. It's a Douglas family trait. Except for my mother. Her instincts have been swallowed up in the church. But I'm glad you missed me when I was gone. It's a little like being at your own funeral when someone thinks you're dead and you aren't. But who is this poor Florence woman who looks like me? A twin? A doppelgänger? Fate. It's quite spooky."

"I'll say it's spooky," said Katie, who had been listening to the explanations with deep interest. "But I suppose if the overhead light had been on, this woman wouldn't have looked a bit like Mrs. Clancy."

"Which brings us to what really happened," said Julia. "Someone in a dim light lying on her side who looks like me, someone who could even fool my own niece, and perhaps fooled the person who came in. Who may have killed her thinking it was me. All because I made such a fuss about moving, so this poor soul got what was meant for me? How awful. Tell me, was she strangled with tubing?"

"Aunt Julia," said Sarah in distress, "no one is saying Florence Littlefield was murdered. Strangled or anything else. It's just a . . ." Sarah fumbled for the words. "A weird coincidence. Very, very sad, but you didn't cause her to die. It's one of those things."

"Hearts are funny things," put in Katie.

"Thank you, Katie," said Julia. "I'm trying to forget that fact. But now if this death isn't a natural thing, I shall have to start feeling proper guilt. I put so much effort into being moved. I lied about Tom dying here; I bothered every nurse and doctor I could find. And that trusting Father Stevenson, I worked him over until he buckled under. Oh dear."

"Now, Aunt Julia . . ." Sarah began.

"Mrs. Clancy," said Katie. "Don't start that kind of thinking. Whatever happened, it doesn't have anything to do with you."

Julia shook her head. "I think it has a lot to do with me. If it turns out to be murder, it's just as if I presided at an execution. And I'm not going to let me off the hook."

"Damn it," said Sarah. "Stop that. Maybe this Florence died of cholera or a burst appendix or a stroke, for all we know. You are legally in room three."

"Which ignores how I got into room three. By putting on an act."

"Forget that. What you did wasn't a crime. You were really upset. Honestly upset, and that's as valid a reason as using Uncle

Tom to make the change. And I helped you out in that story. Now you're acting like you got out of bed and went creeping into room nine to kill another patient."

"I did it by proxy."

"Aunt Julia!" Sarah almost shouted it. "Cut it out. And don't try and turn into your mother right in front of my eyes. Before you know it, you'll be talking about sin and God's will, and that's just not you."

"Right," said Katie. "You're my role model, Mrs. Clancy. I want to turn into you when I'm seventy. So don't go all limp on me or I'll call for a psychiatrist. Or better"—here Katie grinned down on her—"I'll sic Sergeant George Fitts on you and he'll straighten you out."

"Well, well, here you are." A cheery voice. "All awake when you should be sleeping. What is this, a party?"

It was the nurse. The one who always patted Julia's hand. The one who a little while ago had taken Sarah to the waiting room. What was her name again? Hannah? Clare? Yes, Clare."

"It's Clare," said the nurse, moving forward to inspect Julia's monitor. "Time for vital signs, dear," she said. She bustled forward and eyed the monitor above Julia's head. "Your heart rate is up," she announced. "What have you been doing? Visitors in the middle of the night. That's a real no-no. You need your rest." She turned to Sarah and Katie. "If you two could just step outside. We need to settle our patient."

Sarah, trying not to catch Julia's eye, grabbed Katie by the arm and slipped out of the room. "I know she's trying for the maternal approach, but with Aunt Julia it doesn't go over."

"Julia needs a nurse like Sergeant Joe Friday or Clint Eastwood."

"I think that flowered costume makes it worse," said Sarah. "All those pink flowers down the breastworks."

"Like a kindergarten teacher for the socially challenged."

"Let's get back to Topic A," said Sarah. "Can you page Mike and find out what's what? I mean if he's on duty here in the hospital."

Katie sighed. "I don't know if he hung around. But I'll try his page. You can try and listen in, but don't tell anyone."

The result was a Mike Laaka sounding badgered, bothered, and generally wiped out. "Sorry, Katie," he told her. "I was going to catch up with you. But I've been trying to follow what the docs are doing about this Florence Littlefield thing. They've got the body down in the hospital morgue now and they'll be doing the post soon."

"Are they calling in Johnny Cuszak?" Katie asked—Johnny being one of the state forensic pathologists.

"Are you buying Julia Clancy's idea that someone was out to get her? And they got Florence instead? None of which anyone can prove."

"Answer my question? Has Johnny come in?"

Pause. Then, reluctantly, "Yeah, he might be here. Or he might not be. They don't tell me nothin'."

"Except?"

"Okay. Except you're to keep an eye on Julia. You'll be relieved in the A.M. George doesn't want any more trouble from this place. Especially with Julia. George hates hospitals. Think they couldn't run a convenience store if they tried. He'll be around later when the autopsy and lab people finish up. He'd like to treat the whole cardiac ICU floor as a scene of crime—hell, the whole hospital as a scene of lots of crimes, but the hospital staff is fighting the idea. They're having enough trouble with the police messing around in the ER after Old Man Philips was strangled in the john."

"And that's it? George acting like El Supremo, or just taking precautions?"

"Who knows. But tell Sarah—I know she's probably hanging over your shoulder—to go home, rest up. George wants to see her first thing in the morning. In that hospital meeting room we've taken over. I mean, after all, Sarah was there."

"There?"

"In at the time. Time of death. Florence Littlefield. She's what they call a witness."

"So it's not just an ordinary heart attack."

"Precautions. That's what we're taking."

"Okay, I'll tell her." And Katie snapped her phone closed. Turned to Sarah. "You heard that?"

"Not all of it. I get the gist. And I will go home. So I can come back. And Katie, I left my handbag, my little duffel in room nine. Can you collect them, you think?"

"Now you're talking evidence," said Katie. "No way you're going to get your hooks on that stuff. And if there's been a homicide, you are not only the star witness. You are the star suspect. Under the pretense you were watching Aunt Julia, you plotted her—what's the word? Her demise. You've always wanted a farm filled with horses."

"Oh, go to hell, I'm too tired for jokes," said Sarah, moving toward the waiting room door. She paused. "Go on back to Julia's room and save her from Nurse Clare. Because if you don't, there may really be a justified homicide before morning."

In the improvised police "situation" room, holding cooling cups of coffee, sat three weary discouraged medical types: Drs. Alex McKenzie, Eugene Santoro, and hospital pathologist Margie Soldier. It was almost three o'clock in the morning, and a preliminary autopsy had been finished. Some lab reports were in, most of them inconclusive. Cardiovascular disease was present, yes, but it was not apparently the villain. Florence Littlefield appeared to have simply stopped breathing. And Alex and Gene Santoro had for the umpteenth time gone over the symptoms presented by Florence Littlefield on her appearance in the ER; symptoms that led to her being admitted to room 9 on the Cardiac Intensive Care floor.

"Well," said Margie Soldier, who had chosen a straight chair in the belief that a more comfortable one would lead to instant sleep. "Her potassium level *was* elevated."

"Not that elevated," said Alex.

"Before she was admitted," said Dr. Santoro, "her potassium level was on the low side. Why was it up?"

"If either of you want me to say she appears to have had a fatal dose of potassium chloride slipped into her IV," said Margie, "forget it. Her potassium was up but it wasn't out of the ballpark."

"No sneaky resident on cardiac service came along last evening, looked at her chart, noted the low potassium and upped it, did he? Or she?" said Alex without much hope.

"No way," said Gene Santoro. "I think Florence Littlefield was just one of those cases. We think positively, but her body thinks negatively and out she goes."

"It was quick," said Alex. "Which suggests that—"

"That what?" interrupted Margie. "That some agent or person unknown came into her room and *did* something. You guys. Alex, you're to blame. I've heard that being one of the county medical examiners has gone to your head. Finding bodies all over the place. That one last spring on the golf course."

"So what do you suggest?" asked Gene Santoro.

"That we wait," said Margie. "Lab results. Tissue sections. Body fluids. You know the drill. And I've got to get back to the morgue. Dr. Fisher said he'd finish up, but I like to keep an eye on things."

"A proper attitude" came a man's voice from the door.

"Oh, hell," said Margie Soldier. "What are you doing here?"

"Prevailing wind," said the voice cheerfully. "That, and a request from the Criminal Investigation Department of the Maine State Police, aka Sergeant George Fitts."

"Hello, Johnny," said Alex. "You're all we need."

"Words I've been waiting to hear all my life. Okay, Margie baby, rise and shine."

"I'm not Margie baby, and I'm not shining at three in the morning,"

"Okay, okay, but time's a-wasting. Let's hit the lab. You can teach me a few things." Johnny Cuszak gestured to the half-open door. He looked remarkably bright-eyed for that time in the early morning. He had shaved, brushed his bristle-black hair, put on a crisp blue denim shirt, and somehow found time to pick up a cup of coffee which he carried in one hand.

Alex and Gene Santoro rose with one accord, both men heavy-eyed, moving slowly. "We're off," called Alex to the two pathologists.

Free of the room, Gene Santoro turned to Alex. "What about Florence Littlefield's sister? You've seen Emma?"

"Tried to explain to her what I didn't understand myself. She didn't seem exactly stricken with grief, so I'd say she has very mixed feelings about losing Florence. They weren't that close. But she's plenty mad at the hospital."

Gene Santoro lifted his eyebrows. "Trouble down the road?"

"She's convinced some god-awful mistake killed her sister. Which it may well have. You can't even begin to calm her down on that subject. She's a walking medical dictionary and knows all the buttons to push."

"So where is she now?"

"Father Stevenson is taking her home and we've arranged for a neighbor to stay with her. But I'd say Emma regards Florence's death as a challenge, and she intends to make the most of it."

"Christ," said Gene with feeling.

"Exactly," said Alex. "Good night. Tomorrow is almost at our throats."

The two men departed for their abbreviated night's rest and Margie Soldier, reluctantly, it must be admitted, led Johnny Cuszak in the direction of the stairs down to the bowels of the hospital and the morgue.

The next morning, Thursday, the twenty-third of August, Sarah woke with eyes feeling like sandpaper, her tongue dry, and her head pounding. She abandoned the idea of breakfast—she'd grab something at the hospital cafeteria later—and settled for a cup of tea and two Tylenols. Thus armed, she gave Patsy his kibbles and water, climbed into her car, and feeling that her reflexes were sluggish, drove more carefully than usual down the winding road and over the hills toward the Mary Starbox Hospital.

And because she was still forcing herself to pay more than the usual attention to the road and passing cars, she was just able to veer out of the way of an accelerating silver car that exploded from the hospital entrance, squealed on a tight turn, and screamed within inches of Sarah's rear bumper.

Sarah jammed on the brakes, brought the Subaru to a stop on the grass edge of the hospital entrance, and swiveled her head to try to catch a glimpse of the speeding car. No luck. Just a vanishing back window and gone. Sarah, shaking, her headache ratcheted to a higher level of pain, put her forehead down for a second on her steering wheel and gave in to an overwhelming sense of a world out of joint. People in cars who shouldn't drive them, people in hospital beds who shouldn't be dying. A former CEO throttled in the ER. Parts of this little hospital world were more than out of joint—they had gone completely wacko. Of course much of the greater world beyond the hospital gates, beyond the state of Maine, had been out of joint for so long that thinking about it only gave her a dull ache. Better to think about what went on in front of her own nose.

And Florence Littlefield had died—never mind how—in front of her nose, almost within reach. A happening, if she'd been slightly more alert, she might have prevented. It all went so smoothly. There was Florence, one minute being given some life-giving—or death-dealing—dose by that dim figure in the white coat. Did it wear a white coat? Yes, she thought so. She had opened her eyes briefly when the soft footsteps came in the room, and then thankfully closed them, grateful for the quiet entrance. Death on soft feet. Little cat feet. Who had said that? Carl Sandburg. Only it wasn't death but the fog creeping around. Somewhere in Chicago, was it? Well, the coast of Maine could beat Chicago on fog any day, fog real and fog metaphorical.

Sarah pushed herself away from the steering wheel. Time to start functioning. Cheer up Julia because her tough old aunt seemed to have started on a guilt trip just as if she'd arranged, through artful manipulation, to do in—by proxy—Florence Littlefield. That way of looking at things couldn't bring Florence back, but it might certainly push Julia into a setback. And setbacks are what seventy-one-year-old ladies who have just had bypass surgery shouldn't have.

First, she had to see Mike Laaka and hope to be told that the autopsy showed that Florence Littlefield had departed the natural way of someone with a severe heart condition. Then back to Julia with the good news. Or, if the news suggested that Florence had been put to death by intention, then she, Sarah, would be on hand to help Julia deal with it.

And, if necessary, add Patrick to the support team. He was someone who could tell Julia to shape up, could describe some horse problem to worry about, the lameness of her Duffie, perhaps, or talk about the mare Angelina, about to foal.

But what about that silver car? Was it driven by someone with a genuine death wish? Two encounters in a short space of time with a silver car? Was it a sign? A car driven by someone who hated Subarus? Who hated Sarah? Some student from her past who had been given an F in English and had had his or her college life blighted? But did each speeding incident involve the same car? As she'd noticed before, the parking lots and the roads were filled with silver-gray cars. And some of them, she had to admit, were probably driven at top speed by an overwrought, sleep-deprived nurse, doctor, aide, resident, or intern whose debilitated physical state had shifted into road rage.

Sarah braced her shoulders, put her car in gear, and moved slowly into the incoming hospital flow of traffic, comforted by the idea of a second cup of tea and perhaps even a warm muffin with a little jam on its top. It was witness time. Mike and/or George would do the talking and she would sit back in her chair and let them get on with it. But if either of them got uppity, well, she was in no state to be bullied—she'd let them have it. Aunt Julia was her concern and she didn't want to spend the whole day while the police nattered on about every minute of the past night. What she could tell them would take no more than ten or fifteen minutes. She was in no mood for endless repeated questions. Suggestions that she didn't know what she was talking about. Particularly when these came from Sergeant George Fitts, the man whose blood—make that lubricant—ran like a thick cold stream through his spare body. She tried to picture herself as New Hampshire's favorite animal: a coiled rattlesnake next to George's desk, twirling her tail and saying, "Don't tread on me." Yes, she was feeling remarkably like that snake.

Hell. Whom was she kidding? Sarah as a venomous snake was

about as convincing as Sergeant George Fitts as a ballet dancer. She, Sarah, was doomed as a snake or any other dangerous creature because slightly built women with unruly short black hair and large gray eyes and a soft low voice just do not command respect in the world of hard knocks—or hard punches. Taken all in all, her outward self was the sort that made others rush for a bowl of chicken soup and a blanket. Besides which she was an English teacher, a career choice that might cause irritation but hardly fear.

Sarah found a parking place in the visitors' parking lot, slammed her car door shut, and in reaching for her briefcase—a substitute for the handbag left in ICU number 9—she managed to entangle herself in the loose seat belt, stumble from the car and fall to her knees.

And as if to underline her recent self-appraisal, two hefty men from a pickup nearby scrambled out of their truck, raised Sarah to her feet, rescued her briefcase and dusted it off.

"Hey, gotta watch it, lady," said the first.

"So take it easy now," said the second.

And Sarah, feeling more like a clumsy rabbit than any rattlesnake, thanked them and, trying to keep her head high, walked toward the side hospital entrance.

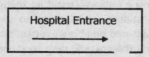

Hospital Entrance

13

SERGEANT George Fitts loved order, system, and the beauty of a methodical investigation that marched forward digesting facts, expelling useless material, and building up the muscle and bone of a well-shaped case. This being so, Sergeant Fitts hated hospitals. He hated them even more than he hated academic institutions—particularly high schools, which harbored that most unruly of creatures, the adolescent. In fact, George Fitts had found only one institution that approached perfection in organization and disciplined and decisive action: the Maine State Police. If only, George thought sometimes, the state government and its appendages, corporations, private businesses, and families could somehow run their affairs on the lines of the state police.

George had just delivered himself of what Deputy Katie Waters called his Hospital Hate Lecture. Katie was now off duty after a long night and had caught up with Mike Laaka on her way out. "George sees hospitals like that animal in biology, what is it, a hydra?" said Katie. "All the department heads chewing on each other."

"Yeah," Mike agreed wearily. "Plus all those rotating interns and residents, and fellows and med students wet behind the ears.

Plus staff physicians, attending physicians, and free-flying visiting physicians with admitting privileges."

"To which we add," said Katie, "everyone down to the cleaning teams and God knows who else is tucked away on the hospital grounds in a dark hole or hiding out in the maintenance buildings."

"Of course, George does like little community hospitals. He can get a grip on 'em. Tie 'em in knots, bring 'em to heel. But monster teaching hospitals like the Mary Starbox Memorial, hell, he might as well be fighting with the U.S. Congress."

"You and me," said Katie, "we don't have expectations."

"Good thing," said Mike. "But I get along with most of the folks at this place. It's not their fault they're operating in a cement mixer. Besides, half the staff at the Mary Starbox, they're as overworked and kicked around just like I am."

"Don't pull that sob stuff," said Katie. "You're made of India rubber; they could bounce you off the wall and you wouldn't feel a thing."

"Sympathy from a colleague?"

"All you're going to get," said Katie. "And now I'm off for home and bed. But has it struck you that if anyone had listened to Julia Clancy the night before last, well, maybe we'd have one less homicide on our plates."

"That's what I'm trying not to think about," said Mike, turning and heading for George's temporary office/meeting room.

George Fitts, after the murder of Dr. Henry Dent Philips, had spent time during a quick coffee break browsing through some of the hospital brochures and in particular a glossy number featuring photographs of the staff physicians. He had been particularly caught by the fact that each of the doctor's faces was curled open in a wide smile, toothy grin, or, in some cases, a hearty laugh. These he displayed to Mike, remarking that the state police would never have allowed such unnatural pictures of their people. "A bunch of clowns," he added.

"Just a happy band of healers," said Mike. "I suppose that's the photographer at work. Image is all." He flipped over several pages, skimming through Anesthesiology, Emergency Medicine, Family Practice, Internal Medicine, and through to Surgery. "Jesus," he said, "they look like they've all been dosed with laughing gas. Dr. Santa Claus. Pretty scary for patients."

Mike sagged in his chair. He was very much on the rumpled side, as befitted his all-nighter at the hospital. George, a man never known to sleep, was his usual tidy and brisk self—gray cotton trousers, pressed; lighter gray cotton shirt, pressed; shaved and alert. His mouth, as always, was held in a taut line, and his rimless glasses enlarged his pale steel-blue eyes. Mike sometimes thought that George fitted the image of a serial killer.

Mike now pointed to the photograph of the hospital CEO, Dr. Jonathan Philips, grandson of the late unlamented Dr. Henry Dent Philips. Jonathan was featured on the first page under the heading: "A Friendly Message from Our CEO." "There's an exception to the happy-face rule," he said. "What a mug. Looks like Dr. Jonathan might burst into tears. Reminds me of a dog, coonhound, maybe."

"But," said George, "from that picture he looks like the only member of the hospital staff who might take his job seriously."

Mike studied the photograph. It showed a long-faced man of middle age, with large ears, drooping mouth, and thinning hair, who had stared directly into the camera without apparently trying to alter his expression of doubt mixed with despair.

"At least he's off the list for his grandfather's death," said George. "He was having a meeting on the orthopedic floor. We might have him in later for another talk when we settle the matter of this second death.

"Hey," said Mike. "It wasn't the *second* death. This is a hospital, and if you're counting deaths, here's the list. Last night there were five deaths: a trauma coming in by ambulance died in the OR; two old guys from the pulmonary floor; a teenage boy who drove himself into a semi. And Florence Littlefield."

"Besides Florence, were any of the others unattended?"

"Nope. But Florence was attended. Sort of."

"If you mean Sarah Deane, that's what we don't need. A witness who was half-asleep under the delusion she was watching her aunt. Who claims nothing much went on except the usual parade of monitor people."

"Best we've got."

"I know, I know. She's coming in, right?" George looked at his watch. "In about fifteen minutes. Okay, I know the hospital staff is afraid of the police overreacting. But now I've ordered the Cardiac ICU corridor closed off as scene of crime. Until we get the report that this was a natural death. I want floors swept and bits and pieces bagged along with trash from wastebaskets. Get hold of the laundry, towels, bed linen still on the floor. Food trays, water bottles. Supplies of dressings. Patient's personal possessions, but have a nurse or the patient sign for anything you take. And get those boxes—Sharp Boxes, they call them—where used disposable equipment—syringes, needles—are dropped. Check the waiting room, the restroom toilets, locked medicine cabinets. And room nine. Lucky we've had a guard on it since they took the body away. Clear out the place before the cleaning staff beat us to it. Then we'll have the incinerators and basement laundry room to look over. Got it?"

"Yeah," said Mike. "I got it. But the staff will be steamed. And the other patients. There'll be hell and more to pay. Precious routine upset, patients' lives at risk, patients riled, medications maybe screwed up, not to mention scheduled lab tests and procedures. Patients coming in from the OR or transferred from another floor."

"I made a few calls before you came in," said George. "Warned Dr. Jonathan Philips, who will tell the department heads. Better safe than sorry. He's given us the green light as long as we back away fast if the autopsy shows nothing suggestive and we don't come up with . . ."

"Come up with what?" demanded Mike, "a scalpel with Florence's blood on it?"

"Our evidence team should be on that floor right now," said George, ignoring as usual Mike's sarcasm. "You," he went on, "get there and try and calm things down."

"I get the dirty jobs," complained Mike.

156

"You should have joined the state police, not the sheriff's department."

"Then I'd get respect?"

"You'd have a respectable job," said George, indicating the door.

Making it into the interior spaces of the hospital without further stumbling, Sarah's first concern was Aunt Julia. Was she still (figuratively speaking) pouring ashes on her head as the guilty party who engineered the fate of Florence Littlefield? Sarah couldn't believe that tough-as-leather Julia Clancy was going to be mired in a swamp of guilt and lose her notable ability to criticize, carp, and generally manage the people about her.

Arriving at room 3 Sarah found her aunt had a visitor.

Poking her head around the door, Sarah saw that Father Joshua Stevenson of St. Paul's-by-the-Sea, in jeans and a denim work shirt, was leaning over Julia and speaking in a low comforting voice.

Conclusion: Julia, still stricken by guilt, was receiving the consolation of the Church. Or at least from its representative. Unseen at the door, Sarah listened and found that this particular representative had chosen a subject less overwhelming than the Forgiveness of God. An equine subject. The horse as one of God's creatures. How one forgave a horse that threw you onto the hard ground. And how forgiveness, even of one's self . . . here Father Stevenson hesitated, no doubt struggling to make a convincing metaphor out of a very awkward trinity.

And then Julia raised her head from her pillow. "Sarah. It's you."

Sarah slid into the room and agreed that it was she, smiled at Father Stevenson who, like many of the past night's participants, seemed on the frazzled side.

"Father Stevenson," said Julia, "is being kind enough to talk to me."

"She's pouring a great deal of blame on her head," said Father Stevenson.

157

"Well-earned blame," said Julia. She raised herself on her pillow and indicated the door. "I'm trying to work out a penance. Come back in about an hour. And while out there, see if you can find Florence Littlefield's sister, so that I could begin to apologize."

Sarah frowned. "Why don't you wait a little on that. I've heard she wants to sue the hospital for what happened. I wouldn't go charging in—"

"I don't charge in," snapped Julia in something like her old voice. "But in this case I insist."

"Apologies are always good for what ails you," said Father Stevenson. "But I spent a great deal of time last night with Emma Littlefield, and she intends to call lawyers and set up for some sort of legal action."

"If you want me to wait, forget it," said Julia. "I plan to admit everything. I am entirely guilty. Not the hospital's fault. They did their best to make me stay where I was. So let them take me away. No lawyer. And I'll try and make it up to Florence Littlefield's family. And Sarah, you look as if you didn't approve, so go away. Leave me to work it out with Father Stevenson."

And Sarah took herself off. Julia had moved from feeling merely guilty to something like tying herself to the stake and asking for a match.

In the interest of a mild exercise that might help her wake up, she took the stairs down to the lobby floor, all the while trying to dredge up strategies for diverting her aunt. And from what she'd heard of sister Emma Littlefield, the woman would be only too glad to add Julia to the list of persons she wished to sue—if it appeared that Florence had left the world in an unnatural manner. Then Emma, as the bereaved sister, albeit with the personality of a piranha, could probably take Julia to the cleaner's—along with the greater part of the Mary Starbox Hospital.

These unsettling thoughts brought Sarah to the wide hallway just before the lobby and she hesitated, not ready in body, or in mind to face Sergeant George Fitts. She leaned against the lobby wall, feeling like something washed in on a high tide, a dead haddock, perhaps.

Here she was, a supposed witness to something she'd been too sleepy to focus on. She probably couldn't have identified Alex if he'd turned up in room 9. And if Florence Littlefield proved to be a homicide, well, the hospital staff and the police would be on edge and she would be on the police hot seat for days to come. It was like being part of one of those medical mysteries she'd read. Her brain in its tired and unruly state began to serve up titles for a murder mystery set in the confines of the Mary Starbox. *Homicide in Hematology? Death in Dermatology? Violence by Volunteers?*

Sarah opened her eyes. Volunteers? That crew of helpful people who went everywhere, knew the hospital as did almost no one else. And those three she had talked with, those three who had lost family members, well, why not? Dr. Henry Philips killed on purpose? Florence Littlefield, a Julia Clancy look-alike—at least in bed—a case of mistaken identity? She paused. She was running on empty. Nothing was making sense.

"Oh, shit," she said loudly to a framed oil painting of the Owls Head Lighthouse.

"Sarah Deane," said a voice. A uniformed deputy stood at her shoulder. "I've been sent to find you. Sergeant Fitts wants you right away. You had an appointment."

Sarah knew that George, when interrogating someone, was always at his peak and conducted the affair as if he were probing with pointed tools, snipping off bits of answers, putting them into some invisible category. It was, she thought, an almost surgical procedure that usually left the victim psychologically—if not naked—stripped to her underwear.

She decided to attack first.

She straightened herself, trying to appear wide-awake, and marched into the room where she found George bent over his long table covered with notebooks and folders. She hesitated only a second and then, without being offered one, took a nearby chair—an upholstered tapestry number dragged in no doubt from one of the waiting rooms in the interest of making the person being questioned feel at ease. Seated, she glared at George.

"I'm very very sorry about everything that's happened. But

159

where is my handbag? My duffel? They have my licenses and credit cards and college ID. I had those things with me the whole time. Next to my chair. No one touched them or dropped bits of DNA on them. You can't possibly think that I had anything to do with what went on in room nine. Anyway, I want my things back."

George bent his mouth into what Sarah supposed passed for a smile. But he said in an unexpectedly soft voice, "Settle down, make yourself comfortable. I've sent for tea and coffee, something to eat. I expect you haven't had much sleep."

Sarah eyed him suspiciously. What was this? Why was George acting like a pussycat? Watch out, she told herself. And returned to Topic A.

"My handbag," she repeated. "My things."

George nodded. "All in good time. They're perfectly safe. But we have to check everything in room nine. You know that. Now tell me, how is your aunt? She's someone I'm always very impressed by."

It takes one to know one, Sarah told herself, remembering a number of clashes between Aunt Julia and Sergeant Fitts during a nasty incident one summer at High Hope Farm. Julia, on the whole, had come out ahead.

"Aunt Julia," she said, "is doing pretty well. Considering."

"Considering what?" said George.

"That maybe someone tried to throttle her Tuesday night, only no one believed her."

"If I remember correctly," said George in the same low disarming voice, "her doctors didn't believe her, nor did the nurses, and I've heard that Alex, and you, too, had a few doubts—unless you were misquoted by Alex. Mrs. Clancy was considered to be suffering from post-surgical confusion. Possible hallucinations. The police went along with the medical opinion, in spite of which we had a sheriff's deputy check on room nine and transferred surveillance, as soon as we heard about the move, to room three."

Faced with what were undeniably true statements, Sarah subsided briefly and then returned to the attack. "Why not keep a guard on nine *after* Florence Littlefield was moved in? Half the hospital staff apparently thought that Aunt Julia was still there."

"Not half the staff. Perhaps some floor aides and a few nurses still thought that. Residents just arriving on the floor. Moving Mrs. Clancy was a last-minute thing. Even Mike didn't hear about the switch until very late. And of course we had no reason to think Miss Florence Littlefield was in danger."

The door opened behind Sarah and George lifted his head. "Ah," he said. "Here we are. Tea, Sarah? I seem to remember you're a tea drinker. And one of these corn muffins with a little jam?"

Sarah eyed him. "Do you keep records on everyone, George? Their little habits, tea or coffee, strawberry jam or honey, arsenic and old lace?"

George shook his head. "I've known you, Sarah, for quite a while now," he began.

"You mean I've sometimes gotten into your hair."

George passed one hand over his smooth skull. "Considering that I'm almost completely bald, that would be difficult."

Sarah, who knew George as someone who rarely indulged in even a droplet of humor, found herself off base. And now, like a helpful host, George passed her a mug of tea and indicated the sugar, the milk, and the plate of corn muffins. "Please drink, eat, while you let me say again that the police have to check everything. Particularly the things not being guarded by an innocent niece sleeping in a chair in the wrong room."

Although Sarah would have liked to continue on the offensive, somehow the steaming tea had more to offer. She mixed in a spoon of sugar, poured in some milk, took a long swallow, a second swallow. Closed her eyes and leaned back in her chair.

"Believe it or not," George was saying, "we really need your help. Anything you remember. Even if you were half-asleep. Different sounds, someone coming in who didn't fit the pattern of the others."

Sarah took another long drink. Reached for a muffin and a plastic knife and smeared it generously with apple jelly from a tiny package. Bit down, chewed, swallowed, and washed it down with another draft of tea. And decided to cooperate. The sergeant's mellow mood might not last much longer. And maybe, if she answered the questions quickly, she might get out of the room without being shredded.

"Sounds," she said. "There were certainly sounds. Beeps and that blood-pressure thing blowing up, and people going in and out. Someone always twiddling with dials or fumbling with the IV. I'd half wake up and then go to sleep again."

"And the patient, the person in the bed, didn't wake up. Didn't stir around?"

"Never. I just assumed Aunt Julia was completely zonked from sedatives."

"Any sounds different than the others?"

"The only thing different from the general comings and goings was the person who tried to be quiet. The last person in."

George lifted his hand, poised his pen over a pad of paper. "Quieter? How?"

Sarah considered. "Well, whoever it was didn't just walk in; almost tiptoed. That caught my attention. I was grateful. Someone who cared about a sleeping patient."

George made a note. "Then?"

"Then the person fiddled around—the IV pole, the tubing, I think—I only watched with half an eye. Then the person left. Very quietly."

"And?"

"Riot act. Codes and beeps and things going off. People running."

"The patient through all that? No reaction?"

"Not a sound. As far as I could tell. But with everyone running into the room, all the commotion, I couldn't say for sure. I got out of the way, Backed up to the wall while everyone was crowding around Aunt Julia. I mean, I thought it was Aunt Julia. It was horrible. She was going to die right in front of me and I couldn't do anything about it."

"Go back. Give me descriptions of anyone who came in right from the time you settled into the chair."

"Just quick glances. Some wore scrubs, some a shirt and light-colored pants, smocks with designs. The last one, the quiet one, I think, wore a white coat. A shirt underneath, maybe. But one of the early ones wore a white coat, too. You know, the kind all the doctors and lab people used to wear."

"Man or woman, the last one?"

"I couldn't tell. Anyone in scrubs or long lab coats and wearing those shower caps looks the same unless they're built like a truck or some old-fashioned sex goddess."

George lifted his head. "Sex goddess?"

"Oh, you know—Venus de Milo, Mae West, Elizabeth Taylor—one of those busty types." Maybe, thought Sarah, George wouldn't know a sex goddess even if she turned up in his bed.

"Okay," said George. "People in medical outfits are unisex. How about those in colored jackets and smocks?"

"Flowered are most likely female. Plain colors, and white jackets, male or female. I didn't examine anyone for breasts or ankles or neck size. I was trying to sleep."

George pushed a notebook aside. "Sarah, thanks for your help. Please get it out of your head that I'm about to put lighted matches under your fingernails. And as soon as forensics finishes with your things, I'll see that they're sent on to you."

Sarah nodded. George in a friendly mode was absolutely even more sinister. But the tea and the muffins had restored her to something like health. She smiled. "Thanks for the tea, George. I think it works better than lighted matches any day."

Maine State Police
No Admittance

163

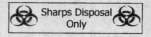
14

SARAH, released from the George Fitts presence, walked slowly into the main hospital lobby, which, as usual, teemed with arrivals, departures, families, and assorted waifs and strays, not to mention the grim-faced with small suitcases (admissions), and the pale-faced pushed via wheelchair and attendant toward the front doors (discharges). Skirting the traffic, Sarah headed for a lone chair behind an artificial ficus tree in a corner. She needed to regroup. Think about what she had told—or not told—Sergeant Fitts and then decide her next move.

First, why was George going all warm and fuzzy on her? In the past when she had turned up on the edge of his investigations, he had been less than welcoming. Now, he served tea and muffins. Why? Easy. George wanted something. He was softening her up. There would be more sessions and less comfort food. He was probably going to try and burrow into her unconscious and try the recovered-memory trick. What had she *really* seen; what had she *really* heard? Except, from her past experiences with him, George didn't monkey around with psychology. But he just might borrow a psychologist for his own purposes, so maybe there was a memory-recovery session in her future. Sarah sat up straight. Over her dead body.

Bad word choice.

She opted for fresh air. A bench under a tree. Alone. She had made it half across the tree-lined path toward a small fountain and single bench when she was hailed. Three people waving, indicating their picnic table.

Like Fates. Make that volunteers. The same three volunteers who had joined her, how long ago was it? It seemed like weeks, months. But, thinking back, Sarah realized it had only been days. She slowed her progress, knowing that she was damned if she did, damned if she didn't. To ignore them was to play the snob. But to join them might suck out whatever bodily juices had been stimulated by the tea and muffins. Already her headache seemed to be reasserting itself.

She turned and headed in their direction. There they were. David, who lifted people in and out of wheelchairs. And the woman with the hatchet face? The one who once kept a horse at Julia's farm and had tangled with Julia. Christie Rivers. And the third? Fuzzy red hair. On the plump side. Nervous but friendly. Stella Somebody. Sarah took a quick look at her watch. Ten minutes, fifteen max. Then she had to be at Julia's bedside. She lifted her hand in a returning wave.

As Sarah was about to sacrifice her fifteen minutes of peace, Alex McKenzie and Eugene Santoro, shadowed by Mike Laaka, found themselves following along on the Cardiac ICU corridor with the state police forensic evidence team while they burrowed into private units, equipment rooms, the waiting room, collecting, tagging, and bagging. Alex's and Gene Santoro's assigned roles were to reassure those patients who were conscious that all was well, just a little routine look-around. But even the most alert of these tended to slip down under their blankets and glower when the team in coveralls, latex gloves, and head coverings began their methodical sweep.

Julia did not glower, but Alex thought she seemed less assured than usual and did not snap at the intruders as she once might have. Instead she remained stony-faced and unresponsive as the forensic team did its work. To Alex, she only nodded and turned her face to the window.

Finally, at something like eleven forty-five that morning, the booty was gathered together, ready to be toted off to the police labs. One item of special interest to the watching physicians was the Sharp Box, the container for needles, syringes, and other contaminated hazardous items such as clamps, staples, and bits of tubing.

Alex, hunting up an aide, asked how often the boxes were emptied and the material disposed of and was told that this happened when the boxes were full.

"Not every day?" he asked.

"No," he was assured. "Not unless they were full. Sometimes some are full by noon. Depends on the procedures."

"Which means," said Gene Santoro, who stood next to Alex, "we've a pretty good chance of finding things that were in every ICU Sharp Box last night."

At which point Mike Laaka arrived in the hall outside room eighteen, now temporarily off limits by virtue of a locked door and yellow tape. He was accompanied by the forensic team leader, one Pete Long.

"Those boxes," said Mike. "Could we have a quick inventory of the contents of each one before you disappear?"

"Keep your pants on," said Pete. "Give us a chance to get the junk to the lab."

"You've got the room number marked on each box?" asked Mike.

"Jesus," said Pete, "what'd you think we're doing here? Playing marbles? We've got room number, time when the box was collected, patient's name, how long that patient's been in that room, what other patient's been in that room. What medications were prescribed. So cut the half-ass questions."

"George Fitts," said Mike, trying to sound exactly like George, "would like that inventory ASAP. They've cleaned up space next to the autopsy room for you to do that. Mask, gloves, gowns. Everything nice."

"Aw, Jesus," said Pete again. "We'll try and push it. But give us to one-thirty and then come on down. That'll give us a chance to spread the goodies out."

So, at one-thirty, Mike, Alex, Gene Santoro, under the watchful eyes of Pete Long and pathologist Johnny Cuszak, surveyed the unpleasing collection of used syringes, needles, small ampoules, vials, and other bottles of medication, each tagged with the room or area from which it was collected.

Like insulin.

"How many diabetics on the floor?" asked Alex.

Gene shook his head. "Just made rounds this morning. No new admissions with or without diabetes. We transferred one diabetic, an eighty-five-year-old man, three days ago to another floor."

"Come on," said Alex. "With that population, the over-sixty crowd, you've got to have at least three or more diabetics."

"Sorry to disappoint you," said Gene. "But cheer up. By tonight we'll probably have six."

"What," put in Johnny, "are you two suggesting? Death by insulin? Someone running in and zapping Florence Littlefield with insulin?"

"Something killed her," said Gene.

"Something? Like a thing? Like an outside agent?" Johnny gave the two physicians a disgusted look. "Alex, I know, from time to time has homicide on the brain. But you, Gene, you've been contaminated by him."

"You're betting on natural causes?" said Gene.

"I'm not betting. Wait until we put the whole show together. Go through this mess."

"We need the report fast. Like now," said Mike.

Johnny Cuszak shook his head. "I know George needs a homicide a week to keep his blood circulating. But that's no excuse for the rest of you buggers. Right now, looking at this stuff, I don't see anything that scares me. Just the usual meds. And I'm moving the stuff on; you've had your look. Here's a deal. If a syringe with a residue of hemlock or henbane or foxglove or jellyfish toxin or parts of a peach pit dripping with cyanide turns up, listen, I'll take you both out for dinner at a class-A restaurant. Okay?"

"Okay, okay," said Gene. "Sorry to waste your time."

But Alex persisted. "Humor me. Let's pretend for a minute that Florence was a victim of homicide. Person unknown comes into the room. Person either gunning for Florence Littlefield, which seems unlikely, or for Julia Clancy, Julia being a possible witness when she was in the ER. No one notices this person. Easy because ICU nine is away from the mainstream. So person does something. Injects the IV or directly into the patient."

"Listen," said Johnny, "I've already said—"

"Quiet," said Alex. "Let me finish. The patient stops breathing—as planned—the person beats it out of room nine. The code goes off, the place explodes."

"So then you're saying," said Johnny, "that this killer character got out of the room and dumped syringes or vials or something into another patient's Sharp Box."

"Right," agreed Alex. "I'd also guess the person shucked off his scrubs or jacket and dumped them in the outgoing laundry. And got the hell out."

"Why get the hell out?" said Gene, getting into the swing of things. "Why not, if you're a legit member of the hospital staff, maybe assigned to the floor, hang around, join the fun."

"Yeah," said Mike. "And maybe help with the resuscitation scene."

"You're saying nurse, doctor, aide, physician's assistant, aren't you," said Alex. "Not some evil visitor with a syringe hidden in a little get-well present? Because if medicine figures in the death, it would have to be someone with a little know-how."

"Hey, Johnny," said Mike Laaka impatiently. "Don't listen to these two. Get this crap out of here and call as soon as you can."

"Good-bye, Johnny," said Alex. "But Mike, what I'm saying is since you haven't ruled out murder, you'll still have to keep an eye on Julia Clancy. Not just for a day or so. Until you nail the murderer of Dr. Philips. Julia, through her own efforts, is known throughout the whole blessed hospital as someone who saw Dr. Philips still alive and might even have seen his murderer."

"And," added Mike, "your wife, Sarah, will soon be known throughout the whole blessed hospital as someone who was two feet away from Florence Littlefield's bed when she died. So we're going to ask her to report her comings and goings to our security people."

"Good. I was going to ask for that."

"Where is she now?"

For a minute Alex looked around as if expecting Sarah to appear from the utility room or from under a desk. She did things like that; never was where she should be. "I don't know," he said. "But I'll check in at Julia's room when I go."

"I'll get right on it," said Mike. "You probably have neglected patients to see."

"I'll hunt her down first," said Alex grimly.

"Don't scare the hell out of her. Saying she's next."

"You think I'm a total idiot? Besides, she wouldn't scare. She'd jump right into the part and start acting like some hotshot private eye."

"Which she's been known to do before," said Mike. "I'll be off and you page me or I'll page you when we get our mitts on Sarah. And at the risk of being boring, let's hope Florence Littlefield died from entirely natural causes."

This warm wish was not subscribed to by the volunteer trio Sarah joined. First, while listening to the chatter, she tried to reacquaint herself with them, go over their names. What Jane Austen would have called the "manner of their address." Particularly Stella— last name remembered as Dugan—the one with the nervous giggle. Fuzzy redhead, mousy, something out of a Beatrice Potter book. Or was she from *Alice-in-Wonderland?* Someone, anyway, ready to oblige, run, and get napkins, a box of doughnuts.

Gradually, as the level of noise rose, Sarah became aware that the talk had a single focus expressed with an increasing sense of excitement. The three were ignoring their lunch packages; there was better fodder in the conversation. One homicide followed (perhaps, likely, surely) by another possible homicide in the dark of night on the Cardiac ICU floor.

"It's all over the hospital," said Christie Rivers. "Even the *Courier-Gazette* sent a reporter to ask questions. And your Aunt Julia, on the same floor, was right there."

"What do you mean, 'right there'?" said Sarah, frowning. Did gossip really travel that fast in hospital circles? By laser or X-ray, perhaps.

"I heard," said Stella-the-Mouse, "that Mrs. Clancy wanted to be moved. From her room. That she'd had sort of a premonition. And then when she was moved, they put Emma Littlefield's sister in the room. And she died. The sister, I mean. There was a code but she couldn't be revived."

"I was there," said David. "On the Cardiac ICU floor."

His listeners stared at him.

"On the floor?" repeated Christie Rivers. "In the middle of the night?"

"My brother-in-law. Leon. Had an attack. Something blocked, I guess. He's in a sort of congestive-heart-failure condition anyway, and then this. I went in last night around eleven. Stayed until about three or three-thirty, until he was pretty stable and my sister was able to take over. ICU six."

Sarah swallowed hard. "You were there? I mean, inside one of the rooms? But you missed all the goings-on about Florence Littlefield?"

"I did stick my nose out of the door a couple of times, which wasn't very professional," said David. "I know better than to goggle at emergency scenes. But it's human nature. I even saw you, Sarah, looking like you'd been hit on the head with a brick or drowned in a farm pond. All stunned and wet-faced. You had Clare Mitchner—I guess she's on nights now—taking you somewhere. The waiting room, I'd guess. But I didn't want to bother you. I thought maybe your aunt was in trouble."

"I thought so, too," said Sarah shortly. She saw no need to explain her presence on the floor that night. It was a restraint she could have saved herself.

"You spent the night with Julia," said Christie. It wasn't a question.

"How on earth . . ." Sarah began.

"It's all right," said Christie. "I'm not spying. I had to come back to the hospital last evening. I'd left my handbag. And I ran into your husband. Dr. McKenzie. I asked about you, thought I'd suggest you and I have tea or coffee in the cafeteria if you were staying late, and he said you were going to spend the night with your aunt."

Sarah nodded helplessly. It was obvious not a step could be taken anywhere in the whole hospital complex without details being spread far and wide. David and Christie ought to offer their services to George Fitts. She turned to Stella Dugan. "Were you at the hospital last night, too?"

Stella looked surprised. "Why, no. Well, not exactly. But I live just down that road, Oak Street, right across from the side of the hospital. When I walk the dog I go past the psychiatric section." Here she gave her little giggle. "I can't get away from the place."

"And you walk your dog at night?" persisted Sarah.

"Well, I give him a quickie before bed," said Stella. "Just so he won't pee on the rug in the night. Last evening I was watching a late rerun of *West Wing*, so I took him out afterward."

Sarah stood up, smiled in a general way at the three, and said she hoped they'd see each other again. Sometime. But not soon, she told herself.

On the winding tree-shaded path, Sarah walked slowly toward the hospital entrance, her mind busy with the recent scene. The conversation with the volunteers had driven out her headache, but this had been replaced with a buzz of possibilities. Here were at least two people—she wasn't counting Stella and her dog—who had grudges against Dr. Henry Philips, and who had been, for one reason or another, unexpectedly at the hospital last night. David Bergman on the very floor when Florence Littlefield died, and who even noticed a disheveled Sarah being led away from the scene. And then there was Christie Rivers floating about somewhere, presumably looking for her handbag, and then bumping into Alex. Who told her where Sarah was spending the night.

Did any of this mean anything? Sarah sighed heavily. Probably not. As for entrances to the Mary Starbox, the hospital grounds, the surrounding Bowmouth College campus, the woods, paths, and scattered houses and cottages, not to mention Bowmouth Pond, all offered easy access. Stranglers, poisoners, murderers of all persuasions could come and go at will. Day and night. Doors always open. With these healthy thoughts moving around in her head, Sarah arrived at Aunt Julia's new quarters, room 3.

Julia was sitting up, hands folded in her lap, staring into middle distance. Scowling.

Sarah started with sympathy and ended in exasperation. To guilt Julia had added a crabbed view of the entire world: condemnation of the comings and goings of her entire family and indifference over the state of her farm, her horses, her dogs, her staff, and her loyal riding customers. Even Patrick came in for a humph and a sour word.

Sarah left her to the ministrations of a nurse's aide bearing a glass of juice.

Back home, with Patsy lying across her bed, Sarah crashed. Crashed until six that evening, when she was roused by a repeated telephone ring. Scowling—she thought she had put the phone on hold—she lifted the receiver.

"Hello, Miss Deane?" said a vaguely familiar voice.

Sarah, her voice foggy from sleep, said, "Yes." And added that she didn't want any. And not to call again.

"Miss Deane," said the voice more urgently. "It's Clare. Clare Mitchner. You know, I've been one of the nurses taking care of your Aunt Julia. I was with you last night."

Sarah shook herself awake. Clare's voice had an urgency to it.

"What is it?" she said, visions of Aunt Julia having another attack, or at the least drowning in guilt and sinking permanently into a black funk.

"It's Mrs. Clancy. I am worried."

"What's going on?" Sarah almost shouted it. "Has she had another . . ."

"No, no," Clare's voice reassured her. "Nothing physical. As far as we all can tell, she's doing beautifully. It's psychological. And you know I'm going to be one of her nurses and I just can't get through to her. Everything I say is wrong. And it's so important for cardiac patients, especially after surgery to . . . well, be easy in their minds."

Sarah relaxed. Good. Nothing physical. But there was Julia's depression. The guilt. It needed to be worked on. And Clare Mitchner also needed to be worked on because she was perhaps *the* nurse of all the troops of nurses and aides who most irritated Julia.

"We've all been worried," said Sarah. "Her state of mind. And that business the other night. When she thought she was being attacked." Or was actually attacked, Sarah said to herself.

"I know, I know," said Clare, sounding genuinely sympathetic. "And I want your help. You know her, what bothers her, how to, well . . ."

"Handle her?" suggested Sarah.

"Just get along with her. For her own comfort," said Clare. "I've always found that a warm caring approach works with older women. But not with Mrs. Clancy."

"No," agreed Sarah. "Julia wants it short and straight from the shoulder. No frills."

"So, I was wondering," said Clare, "if we could meet. For lunch sometime. I'm doing split shifts. How about tomorrow? There's a nice little place near the hospital, the Spring Chicken. I'd like to talk over strategies. Until your aunt's discharged. And the longer I annoy her and the longer she's depressed, the more she'll be set back."

Sarah thought for a minute and then decided that there could be no secrets from a nurse actually on the floor when room 9 exploded.

"It's a sort of guilt thing working now," Sarah told her. "Before, Aunt Julia was being a little unfriendly with anyone who tried to be too buddy-buddy, but now she feels that by moving out of room nine she made someone else die."

"Which," said Clare, "is totally irrational. I'm sure they'll find that Miss Littlefield died from understandable causes. Anyway, I'd be most grateful if you'd meet me and talk about how I can contribute to Mrs. Clancy's recovery because right now I'm apparently causing friction, even something like a good case of hate."

Intelligent woman, thought Sarah, and she agreed to meet Clare the coming Friday for lunch, at one o'clock at the nearby Spring Chicken Diner, just past the first hospital turnoff.

"Fine," said Clare. "They have good home-cooked food and I know you can help me with this problem. And please be perfectly frank."

Sarah assured Clare that frankness was her strong suit. And hung up. Okay, she told herself. She wants it straight, I'll give it straight. I'll say cut out this "dear" and "hon" business and stop treating her like an old woman with senile dementia. And if what I say makes her want to, well, not strangle me, but throw her dinner at my head, so be it.

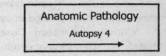
15

THE first lab tests were in, the collection from the Sharp Boxes had been sorted with the rooms of their origin noted, each patient's medication matched against items found in the box. To this inventory were added jetsam found in wastebaskets, patients' personal supplies, laundry clean and soiled, hairs, dust particles, threads, and fingerprints that represented more than half the persons officially connected with the hospital as well as a large segment of the visitor population from surrounding towns.

With all these data on hand, there remained the results of the postmortem examination of Florence Littlefield. The autopsy on her body from "stem to sternum," as Johnny Cuszak put it, had been finished by late afternoon of that Thursday, August the twenty-third. Conclusion: No evidence that Florence had been struck down by a major cardiac event nor by a previously existing but undetected respiratory or circulatory problem, nor any other discernible pathologies. General physical deterioration natural in one of Florence's age, yes; small blocked aging arteries, yes. But no "Wham, Bang, You're Out!" discoveries.

But add to these unremarkable findings the discovery of insulin vials in a nondiabetic patient's room, as well as an empty container of potassium chloride in yet another patient's room—a patient who had no orders for potassium of any sort—and the evidence of the lab tests taken on admission, and immediately after death—it all spelled in caps the word HOMICIDE.

"Cute," said Johnny Cuszak as he peeled off his gloves. "Sneak up, stick the potassium into the IV, wait a second, jab in the insulin to tamp down the potassium load, patient dies as you hotfoot it out of there and do what you have to do. Dispose of stuff. Change your clothes."

"Meaning that the murderer was part of the hospital scene," said Alex. "Insulin is easy to find, but you'd need access to medical supplies to grab the potassium."

"So the killer could go sliding into a patient's room without anyone taking notice. Middle of the night, half the patients are asleep or in a coma. Out of it. Besides, every patient is so used to being disturbed at two-minute intervals the whole goddamn night that they wouldn't blink if Dracula turned up and began biting their neck." Here Johnny bared his teeth and inhaled noisily.

Alex gave Johnny a sardonic grin, shrugged out of his gown and headed for the door, Johnny behind him. At the stairs, he turned back to the pathologist. "As we both suggested, the first job after finishing off Florence would be to ditch your clothes."

"Yeah," said Johnny, "the guy could have worn something different under the top layer. Scrubs are baggy and they'd hide anything. Same with a lab coat. Hell, you could hide a machine gun under one of those things. Big pockets. A large size."

"What about the laundry?"

"George lost that one," said Johnny. "Dirty laundry was taken to the basement sometime that night, probably shortly after the commotion. By now it's washed, sanitized, or disposed of. Listen, I'll call George Fitts, okay? He'll be expecting bad news. He always does. You call Mike and rattle his cage."

"Aw, shit," said Mike Laaka, hearing the news. "I need to catch up on my sleep. Why does life have to be so complicated? Old Henry Philips, I can deal with that asshole being knocked off and we've got to dig around and find out what went on in the

ER. But the Littlefield woman, what's she got to do with anything?"

"Probably nothing," said Alex. "Just substitute Julia Clancy for Florence and you'll get the picture. You'll still be keeping a sharp eye on Julia and Sarah, won't you?"

"We are and we'll go on doing it," grumbled Mike. "But at least Sarah won't go yakking about someone in a white coat up and down the hospital like Julia did."

"You hope," said Alex without conviction.

"So the fun and games go on," said Mike. "Christ, will the hospital people be ticked. Two homicides. Bad man Henry Philips, harmless old lady Littlefield, and their nice little hospital health world turned into a manure pile."

Jonathan Philips, MD, FACP, CEO of the Mary Starbox Memorial Hospital, and grandson to the late Henry Philips, had often thought that some of the goings-on at the hospital bore a close resemblance to life on a manure pile. But then Jonathan had never enjoyed the medical ambience. In fact, from an early age Jonathan, unable to see into the future, had never much cared for being in close proximity to the sick.

As a boy of seven he remembered all too clearly his mother, after eating a bad lobster roll, throwing up all over the kitchen table. He remembered, too, how, on her request for a towel, he had fled the room and hidden out in the garden until it seemed that either she had recovered or died, and so it would be safe to go back in. But somehow Jonathan, described accurately by Mike Laaka as having the general appearance of a hound dog, never seemed as a growing boy to have any particular adult goal in mind. But when he was sixteen, his father died, and his grandfather Henry Philips began turning up in his life and giving his mother advice on setting goals for the boy. As an only child he was the object of his mother's focus, and since her son had scored well in studies dealing with science and math, he was nudged in the direction of a premedical major at Bowmouth College.

"After all," argued his mother, a practical woman, "you haven't too much else going for you, dear. You're not exactly the salesman type. Medicine is still fairly respectable and you can make a reasonable living as long as you behave yourself."

This unsentimental advice Jonathan heeded even if he still disliked sickness in all its varied forms. From Bowmouth College it did seem easier on the whole to go to medical school. There his low-key personality, his success in all subjects that didn't involve much direct confrontation with human anatomy suggested that a future in research, in X-ray, in any hands-off branch of medicine might be the route to take.

But life is strange. In his senior year on family-practice rotation, his quiet ways and direct short responses to patients' questions in a low voice (he wasn't interested enough to go into lengthy pros and cons) were interpreted by several instructing clinicians as having a soothing effect on those patients he examined. More important, Jonathan showed no interest in dramatic self-promotion. Somehow these qualities, plus the prodding of his grandfather, Dr. Henry, steered the unmotivated young man into the field of internal medicine.

And so it was that Jonathan, still doubting his profession, continued working for a period of twenty or so years. Not an inspired physician, but one who by caution and conservative approaches—he followed Alexander Pope's caution: "Be not the first by whom the new are tried/ Nor yet the last to lay the old aside." He never wrote prescriptions for the newest pharmaceutical products; nor did he keep patients indefinitely on the old ones. This middle-ground system on the whole did little harm and even from time to time had beneficial results. But perhaps the one thing that worked in Jonathan's favor was that, although he made few friends, he made fewer enemies. Grandfather Henry Philips, through his consistent meddling in matters beyond his expertise, increasingly took over the attraction of enemies. The result was that by comparison, grandson Jonathan was seen as a benign presence, and when Henry was pressured to step down as CEO, Jonathan, although young for the job, was considered a fair replacement, one who would do little that was innovative, but also would not rock too many boats. And Jonathan, relieved of close contact with sick persons and into management, felt himself, if not happy (he was too melancholic for that), but at least moderately contented.

But two homicides in less than a week was a bit much even for someone who by nature kept all emotion, except perhaps gloom, at bay. He had spent quite a few unhappy hours with Sergeant George Fitts and had had a skirmish or two with Deputy Mike Laaka, a person who seemed in Jonathan's mind too much of a lightweight to be seriously engaged in the investigation of a double homicide in a large teaching hospital. And so it was late Thursday, after the news of Florence Littlefield's death had been ruled a homicide, and after another sharp go-round with George Fitts, that Jonathan wrote a note to his secretary, Carmen Wilson, saying that he would be late the next day; some unavoidable business had come up and she was to hold down the fort. Then he slipped quietly out of his hospital office and headed for the physicians' parking lot and his car. He had decided not to go home, where he could be reached, phoned, beeped, and e-mailed, even confronted at his doorway; instead he intended to drive somewhere out of the area, perhaps to a country inn, there to eat and rest, spend the night away from anything resembling a health care facility, and so regain some degree of composure. Fortunately for this plan, Jonathan had no wife (a two-year marriage had ended in divorce fifteen years ago), and he had no children, grandchildren, dogs, or cats which needed attention.

The idea of leaving the hospital without detection might have worked had not his silver 2001 Saab's ignition system gone completely dead. Only a clicking resulted to repeated key turnings, and Jonathan, climbing out of the car, began to consider other options: Call Triple A or a taxi. Arrange for a rental. But as he pondered these, help came in a welcome form. A familiar hospital staff member turned up at his side and said cheerfully, "Need a ride?"

Jonathan did. And because the good Samaritan claimed to be at loose ends and was thinking of dinner, Jonathan, feeling a lift of his habitual depression, feeling almost human, agreed to a dinner for two. He returned to his office and called Triple A—which in that part of Maine was handled by Shorty's Towing Service— to deal with a dead car. He would dine locally at one of the better restaurants, ask his friendly companion to drop him back at his repaired car, and then go in search of a distant hostelry in which to hide out—at least for twelve hours. Then, with an almost spry step, Jonathan rejoined his rescuer, climbing into what he perceived to be one of those silver-gray Japanese cars—they all looked alike to him—and folding his long legs before him in the passenger seat.

"No hurry about getting me back to the hospital," Jonathan remarked to the driver. "The man at Shorty's said all the repair trucks are stacked up. Humid night, tourists, and so forth. I told them if it was serious to tow it to the Saab garage. I can always find a rental or a taxi."

"I can take you home if your car's not there."

"Don't worry. I can borrow one of the hospital cars if worse comes to worst," said Jonathan.

Jonathan's companion nodded agreeably and stepped on the accelerator.

And if Sarah Deane had been watching the whole scene, it would have convinced her that every other member of the hospital population drove a silver or light gray car.

As for Julia Clancy, the fates were kind. At least for that Thursday evening. The news of Florence Littlefield's murder did not reach her. Sarah stayed away from the subject on two short visits; Alex likewise. Julia had asked about Florence in a halfhearted way and been given vague answers centering on the idea of "We'll see, nothing's really definite." But fatigue had stifled some of her anxiety and muted her anxiety on the possibility of guilt. She had been helped into a chair three times during the day and now found herself exhausted by the effort of shuffling about attached to an IV pole and a catheter and trying to sit upright in a slippery chair. As for riding a horse, even a docile and aged pony, the idea brought perspiration to her brow.

In this subdued state she received Patrick, who came with an old photograph album under his arm, from the years 1970 to 1973, showing a series of pictures of Julia and husband Tom riding, jumping, receiving ribbons and cups at a number of equine events.

"Thought it'd cheer you up," said Patrick.

"It depresses the hell out of me," said Julia. "I'm not fit to walk across this room. I'll probably have to sell the farm, the horses, the dogs, the whole damn business, and put myself into one of those long-term-care facilities where I can take little walks hanging on to someone's arm. Unless I'm in prison for arranging a murder."

Patrick fortunately had been briefed by Sarah with a phone call bringing him up to speed on Julia's determination to pour ashes over her head. "If she's absolutely miserable, make her just a bit mad at you," Sarah instructed. "A little healthy fit of temper might be good for her."

"Are you out of your mind?" shouted Alex when he had been told of the plan. "Julia's recovering from cardiac surgery and you want to send her blood pressure through the roof?"

"You told me her blood pressure was quite low even without medication. And besides, what's worse, mild excitement or heavy-duty depression?"

"She'll be more depressed if your plan sends her back to the OR."

"Aunt Julia," insisted Sarah, "needs a little bit of needling. I've told Patrick to play it by ear. Get her to respond. But if she stays the way she is, even without knowing about Florence Littlefield being murdered, she'll just go under completely."

"I'll have to clear it with Gene Santoro because someone fooling around with his patients will send him through the roof along with Julia."

But Gene Santoro, worried about his patient's increasing lethargy and unresponsiveness, thought that a little prodding by Julia's faithful farm manager might just bring her around. "You're damned if you do and damned if you don't," he said. "Some of my patients lose interest in living and just sink. Better . . ."

"Not 'go gentle into that good night,'" Alex finished.

"I wouldn't put it quite that strongly," said Gene Santoro. "But that's the general idea."

So Patrick, with permission to strike a few sparks from the Clancy temper, was prepared.

"This talk about assisted living or you going to prison is daft," said Patrick, settling down next to Julia and keeping his voice calm, as Sarah had instructed. "You've got to get yourself well, so start thinking about your horses. I'll wager that Duffie's missing you."

"Not true," said Julia listlessly. "None of my horses cares who dishes out their grain as long as they get something to eat."

"That," said Patrick, fighting to keep his voice on an even keel, "is the worst blathering nonsense I've ever heard. Tom Clancy would be ashamed of you. He always said you had more guts than sixty men, but I'm beginning to doubt it."

"I've no guts left," said Julia, closing her eyes.

"You know," said Patrick thoughtfully, "I'm thinking a long-term facility isn't the place for you at all. Let's be calling the grave digger and ordering up a coffin and arranging the wake because what's the use of living like some sort of burden to the rest of the world."

"I didn't say I was a burden to the world," said Julia in a voice with a little more snap. "Just to certain people."

"Well, it's plain you're so low-down helpless that there's nothing I can say to you. And sure, I'll be looking about for a place at another farm where someone in charge has a backbone, not just jelly in their spine.

Julia struggled to a sitting position, her eyes wide open. "Patrick O'Reilly, you unfeeling monster. How dare you say I haven't a backbone."

So it went. Back and forth. Patrick by some miracle keeping his Irish self in hard check, so by the time he left, Julia had some color in her cheeks and had almost enjoyed having a moderate row with her old friend—twice firing him, twice rehiring him; and hearing Patrick resign, leave, and agree to come back, all in the space of about fifty minutes.

And so Julia Clancy, still unaware that Florence Littlefield's death had been ruled a homicide, had the first real sleep since her heart attack. A sleep that despite the usual interruptions was almost satisfying.

Emma Littlefield, by an odd coincidence, also enjoyed a comfortable night's sleep. As next of kin, she had been informed by the police that her sister had not died of natural causes, had been offered the deepest sympathy of the hospital (a letter signed by Jonathan Philips just before leaving the hospital), plus the assurance from the police that a thorough criminal investigation was underway.

But Emma had been preparing, ever since her sister's death, for action. She had spoken to the Littlefield family lawyer, an elderly curmudgeon perfectly suited to the needs of the two Littlefield sisters. No matter how Florence had died, by a sudden unexplained attack or by evil intent, Emma and her lawyer, a Mr. Otto Warner, were ready. In the first instance, Emma could charge gross negligence; in the second, murder made possible through gross negligence. Either way, the suit being put together would spell either a fine fat settlement or court-awarded damages. It might take a while, but Emma would bide her time, continue to guard her health through multiple visits in the ER with Dr. McKenzie, and stay in for the long haul—or the big haul, as her lawyer put it.

In her discussions with Sergeant Fitts and Deputy Detective Mike Laaka, Emma Littlefield had not been quite accurate in her description of her relationship with her only sister. The two ladies had had more than a strong dislike for each other; in truth, they despised each other. But they had lived under the same roof from the time of their parents' death more from habit and financial necessity than any degree of sisterly fondness. Emma had often had fantasies of living without Florence—as, to be honest, had Florence about Emma. Emma had pictured home decisions that didn't involve her sister: getting rid of the old blue Chrysler, choosing which TV reruns to watch in the summer months, and, most importantly, buying food based entirely on her own taste. Emma had sometimes pictured Florence being run over by an automobile—Florence rushing across streets—or being felled by a falling tree limb, but she had not in her wildest imaginings considered that Florence would depart this life by way of hospital carelessness, a carelessness that might provide Emma with an enlarged income and the possibility of moving from the small dark Victorian family homestead to something modern and convenient.

Therefore Emma, that night, slept the sleep of one whose visions of moneybags danced in her head.

Two other people had hopes of a peaceful night. Exhausted by his multiple duties—internal medicine, the checking of Aunt Julia, the interrogations of George Fitts and Mike, Alex was home at last, lying in bed, and catching the last of the eighth in a cliff-hanger between the despised Yankees and the beloved Red Sox. He reflected, wrongly, that nothing could possibly happen in the next twenty-four hours to complicate his life.

Sarah, propped up on the other side of the bed, her head heavy from tension, fatigue, and general worry, made a list of things for Clare Mitchner to consider in the coming days as they pertained to the care of Julia Clancy. It was hard to tell a nurse that "hands-off" was a wise policy—part of nursing involved hands-on—but extra pats, hand-holding, sympathetic squeezes, hugs, sentimental touching of any sort just didn't cut it with Aunt Julia. *Think of her as a cactus*, Sarah would tell her. *And stick to the "Mrs. Clancy" form of address unless specifically told to use "Julia." Avoid endearments such as sweetie, hon, dear, dearie, sweetheart. In fact, focus on simple medical care and forget the TLC approach. If conversation is initiated by the patient, follow along, make positive noises on the subject of horses, dogs, Irish men, and the piano music of Chopin and Beethoven. If Julia goes on about being guilty, nod with understanding but try to move the talk elsewhere.*

"That," said Sarah, "ought to do it." She showed the list to Alex.

He glanced at it, nodded, and returned to the screen. "Two outs," he said. "And a runner on third. I think they could tie it up."

"I hate the Red Sox," said Sarah loudly.

"Be quiet," said Alex. "I think Pedro will go for it."

"Possibly I hate *you*," said Sarah.

"Wow!" said Alex. "Right over center field. Going, going, gone. He really nailed it."

Sarah turned on her side and whistled for Patsy to jump on the bed and lie between them. A full-size Irish wolfhound sharing a pillow ought to make her point: At times, some animals were infinitely better companions than some husbands. "I hope they lose the next five games," she muttered, pulling the pillow over her head. And, as had Emma Littlefield and her Aunt Julia, she fell into a deep sleep.

Dr. Jonathan Philips loosened his tie, shrugged out of his linen jacket—always conservative, he had dressed for a late-afternoon staff meeting. Now he put his head back, enjoyed the breeze from the air-conditioning vents, and relaxed in the front seat of the car. His companion kept up a quiet run of chatter about nothing consequential and, thank heaven, stayed away from topics involving medicine, hospital management, and the second homicide. A decision had been made to try a newly established country restaurant, the Blue Boar. This involved leaving the Mary Starbox Hospital well behind and pushing on down the coast to northeast of Belfast. But Jonathan was in no hurry. The night was young, he told his companion, adding that in one way or another he would be spending the night at one of the country inns in the area and that he'd covered his bases by leaving a note to his secretary about being late tomorrow.

But plans are made to be broken. Beyond Lincolnville, the automobile made a sudden buck, bounced, shot forward, and stalled. Jonathan's companion let out a muffled oath, restarted the engine, and pulled to the side of the road.

"Can't stay here," said the driver. "But never mind, I've got all-wheel drive." With that, the driver turned the car into a sloping lane. Carefully working the vehicle down the narrow lane, the driver headed toward a cleared space which faced a small inlet that served as an outlet of Duck Trap River.

"Maybe the spark plugs again," said the driver, wheeling the car onto a flat area near the edge of the water and turning off the ignition.

"Spark plugs?" said Jonathan, puzzled.

"They get wet sometimes. The humidity. Let's get the hood up and take a look."

Jonathan shook his head. "I know zip about engines."

"You don't have to," said his companion. "I'll release the hood and if you'll hold it up—it doesn't stay up always by itself—I'll get a flashlight and poke around."

This action went as planned. Jonathan held the hood up and his companion hunted around for the flashlight in the back of the car.

But instead of a flashlight, the driver returned with a tire iron, held carefully behind the back. Which heavy metal rod was brought down with great effect on the back of Jonathan's neck exactly between the skull and the cervical vertebrae. Jonathan's hand released its grip on the edge of the hood and he pitched to the ground. A second blow to the back of the skull put an end to Jonathan's twitching. A third finished the job.

Disposal of the body went smoothly. Dr. Philips was relieved of his wallet, his watch, a small appointment book, a ballpoint pen, and some loose change. Fortunately, an offshore wind had come up and the tide was just turning and going out. After some hoisting and heaving—a lifeless body is always difficult to man- age—over the small rocky beach, Jonathan's companion was able to wade into the ocean pulling the body behind until it was caught in the strong ebb that bubbled past the shore and started ocean- ward.

For a moment the driver watched what was left of Dr. Philips disappear into the darkness. Then it was back to shore to begin the business of cleaning up. The tire iron was rinsed and bagged, but disposal of it, along with the contents of Jonathan's pockets, would take place at different sites. The incineration of the driver's bloody clothes could be put off until early morning. It would be enough for now to take off the outer garments before getting back in the car, stuff them in a waiting plastic bag, and drive home in underwear. The absence of Dr. Philips from the hospital would cause no immediate concern, since he had mentioned leaving a note about being late the next morning. In fact, with luck, there would be no hue and cry until well past noon. The presence of his empty Saab in the physicians' parking lot was no problem. Shorty's people would have left a slip describing what action had been taken. It would be thought by hospital personnel (if they thought about it at all) that Jonathan had been offered a ride by a friend to an unknown destination.

Which had indeed happened. All the way to the Duck Trap River outlet.

Better yet, perhaps Jonathan's car might have needed a tow and so wouldn't be in the parking lot at all. This would be fortunate, since many hours would wear away before someone would think to check with local auto-repair outfits.

Although future difficulties were always possible when one takes decisive action, all in all it had been, the driver decided, a job well done.

16

MS. Carmen Wilson, self-styled executive secretary to the CEO of the Mary Starbox Memorial Hospital, arrived as usual at eight-thirty at the small outer office of Dr. Jonathan Philips. Here she followed her unwavering routine. Hang up the light summer jacket—hardly needed, since the spell in the humid nineties was expected, at least by the people from *Maine Weather Radio*, to continue. With her jacket on its hanger, she stowed her straw handbag carefully in the desk drawer, and put a new box of tissues on a nearby table. Some of the visitors to the office found themselves in a state of great grief or great anger, and tissues were often needed.

Then, after checking Dr. Philips's office and finding the note which told that his arrival this Friday would be delayed, she slipped into the lavatory to check on what ravages the sticky day had already done to her eyeliner and her lip gloss. Then she fluffed her curly black hair into a neovariation of the Afro, patted her chin, and readjusted her white shell earrings, always an effective contrast to her dark skin. Satisfied once again that she was one of the better-looking females employed by the hospital, she yanked up the straps of her bra to achieve a better breast elevation, opened the third button on her sleeveless Berry Red (as the fashion catalog called it) T-shirt, then kicked off her sandals and examined her newly painted toenails. Crimson with little silver stars pasted on each nail. Eye-catching, she thought. Good thing Gloomy Gus was coming in late. She could greet those needing his attention and perhaps siphon off a little of the same for her own. Dr. Philips was surely, Ms. Wilson thought, one of the most boring individuals ever to surface in her life, and people visiting the office might like to chat with something spicy while waiting to see the boss.

But Carmen Wilson wanted to be fair. The man wasn't all bad. Sure, he treated her like a stick of furniture—never too friendly, but never too harsh. She was just a useful item that looked up files, changed the ink-jet on his printer—he was a computer/ printer idiot—answered annoying phone calls and put through only those clearly sounding like high priority. And let's face it, Carmen told herself, Jonathan was certainly an improvement over his grandfather, that creep Dr. Henry, who just got himself throttled in the ER. Carmen had had several encounters when old Henry came snooping around when least expected, barking orders he had no right to give, and pawing through the files and papers on Jonathan's desk. And talk about pawing—wouldn't you know, Henry couldn't keep his hands to himself, the miserable old goat. Reaching where he shouldn't, patting inappropriate (as the harassment guide put it) bodily surfaces—well, the old geezer was better off dead. As for the news from the underground that a patient, one Florence Littlefield, had expired unnaturally, well, too bad, but those things happened—especially in large hospitals.

So Carmen settled herself for a pleasant morning. No Dr. Jonathan with new problems, files, requests, invoices, and letters of complaint to be answered. She adjusted the air-conditioning to a constant flow of cool air, plugged in the coffee machine, removed a chocolate chip cookie from her lunch bag and relaxed.

But then there was the telephone. She couldn't let every message be recorded. Sometimes a human effort was needed. On the third call from Deputy Mike Laaka, she picked up the phone.

"Where," demanded Mike, without preliminary pleasantries,

"is everyone? Your office is deadbeat. Where's Dr. Philips? Jonathan, I mean, I've called in three times."

Carmen broke in smoothly. "I'm sorry, Deputy Laaka. But Dr. Philips will be late this morning. Why don't I have him call you—"

Mike broke in. "What's with this 'Deputy' stuff? We went to school together. Listen, Carmen, your boss had a meeting scheduled with Sergeant Fitts twenty minutes ago. Where in hell is he?"

"You listen, Mike," said Carmen briskly. "He isn't here. Left a note saying he'd be late."

"Late? How late?"

"Just late. I guess he wrote it last night before he left the hospital. But he's had a lot of stress lately."

"We've all had a lot of stress lately. George is going to be chewing the rug if he doesn't show up soon. Doesn't the guy know that we've now got two homicides to fool around with?"

"He knows all about Florence Littlefield," said Carmen. "Unless you've got another one no one's heard about."

"Don't scare me," said Mike, adding without much hope: "Could Philips be in the hospital somewhere but hasn't come into the office? Is his car in the parking lot?"

"How would I know? I don't look around for it."

"Be a good helpful executive secretary and go and take a look. Call me if the car's there. And call if it isn't."

"Shove it, Mike. And you know where."

But Mike had hung up. Carmen, sighing, took her way to the physicians' parking section, noted that Jonathan Philip's 2001 silver Saab was not in its usual slot, walked up and down the rows of physicians' automobiles and then returned to the office, called Mike in the police command room with the news, and settled back to enjoy her coffee.

Mike, however, on orders from George Fitts, put in a call to Jonathan's house, to his summer camp on Pleasant Point, Cushing, and to his cell phone. Nothing. Then one after another, he tried Surgery, X-Ray, Orthopedics, the Cardiac complex, the Psychiatric wing, the ER, and on through all the hospital departments, finally in desperation calling the various rehab centers, the cafeteria, the labs, the pathology department, the autopsy room, and ending with the gift shop.

No Jonathan Philips. At one o'clock he called back to Carmen Wilson. Had Dr. Philip's mentioned anything about a meeting out of the area?

"No," said Carmen firmly. "I don't know about any meetings somewhere else. Look, he said he'd be late. And he is. So give the guy a break. And me."

No sooner had Carmen put down her phone and picked up her coffee, she was bothered by another call from the doyenne of volunteers, Christie Rivers.

"Just a reminder," said Christie. "Dr. Philips is due at two. The award ceremony. We're having it in the auditorium. Pins and citations for volunteers. I've got the list and the awards. All he has to do is show up, read names, and shake hands."

Carmen took a deep breath. She'd almost forgotten the award ceremony. "He's not here right now," she told Christie, "but when he comes in I'll remind him." She paused. "Where can I call you if there's a hitch?"

"There can't be a hitch," said Christie crossly. "Why are you saying that? The thing was arranged six weeks ago."

"I'll get back to you," said Carmen, and put the phone down. Only to pick it up to be told that the finance department needed Dr. Philips's signature on some orders ASAP. Then Dr. Gene Santoro called saying it was imperative that Dr. Philips meet with the hospital lawyers over the Littlefield business. Emma Littlefield was preparing to bring suit, charging negligence leading to the death of her sister. He and Dr. McKenzie would be there as part of Florence Littlefield's medical team, but Dr. Philips had to be kept in the picture.

Carmen's dream of a restful office period had long since vanished and her luncheon sandwich, eaten hastily between phone calls, began rotating uneasily in her stomach, along with two cups of over-sweetened coffee.

* * *

Sarah met Clare Mitchner at one o'clock at the small diner the Spring Chicken, that sat about half a mile from the Bowmouth College campus. She had come from seeing Aunt Julia, who had been given by Alex the news that Florence Littlefield's death was now officially a homicide. Julia had met Sarah wearing what Sarah considered a Great Stone Face, all too representative of Sarah's Grandmother Douglas's habitual look of disapproval. Nothing Sarah could do could make her respond in a natural manner; Julia had added to her sackcloth a grim acceptance of the murder as her personal burden. Sarah gave up on the job of consolation or argument, said good-bye, vowing silently to enlist Patrick again, possibly with Alex as a backup. Perhaps it was time for one of those antidepressants used by at least three quarters of the American adult population—something, anyway, that might pull Julia out of her cloud.

The Spring Chicken had gone through a number of rebirths from the simple Spruce Tree Diner to the Maine Meal Diner to the College Café. Now featuring a chicken motif throughout its interior, it had added booths, a salad bar, and offered wine and beer.

Sarah snagged a booth in the corner, chosen because it was out of the range of the majority of the customers and the traffic to the restrooms. Picking up a menu shaped like an oversized egg, she began to consider the task of redirecting a professional nurse's approach to a difficult—make that now almost impossible—patient.

Clare Mitchner almost made it easy. She arrived, a little breathless, wearing jeans and a checked cotton shirt. Her usually smooth brown hair was on the frazzled side, and she looked genuinely worried.

"I'm sorry I'm late," she said, sliding into the booth opposite Sarah. "The hospital called. Wanted me to do three nights after it was all set I'd be on days or split shifts for a couple of weeks. I put up an argument and they weren't pleased."

"You're not late," said Sarah, "I just got here. Get your breath and then we'll eat."

"And talk," added Clare. "I'm going to take the cues from you.

You know Mrs. Clancy. As a person. As your aunt. You know the family scene. Me, I guess I'm guilty of treating her the way I treat other elderly patients. But did I ever bomb with Mrs. Clancy."

Sarah grimaced. "It's easy to do. She's always had a sharp edge but now she's sick, feeling threatened, feeling frightened."

"And she's always been in charge of her life?"

"Right. Along with my Uncle Tom, he and Julia were the lords of all they surveyed—which means their world of horses and horse people. After Uncle Tom died . . ."

"I heard he died right in this hospital. In the room she was in. Room nine."

Sarah looked up. "How did you hear that?"

"How could I have missed it? Everyone on the floor knew that she was upset after surgery. Thought someone had attacked her in the middle of the night. So she wanted to move and later it turned out that a lot of her reaction had to do with her husband dying in that room."

At which a tiny waitress in a frilled apron decorated with a chicken motif materialized before them, dealt out menus, poured water, and recited the day's specials: chicken galore in all its forms, from salad to fried; the usual Maine fare of clams, mussels, lobster- and crab rolls; and a long list of hamburger variants.

Both women settled for the special chicken pie with vegetables plus iced tea and then got down to the whole matter of Julia's moving to another room.

"Give me a blueprint," urged Clare. "She really believes in the attack?"

"Yes. Thought the room at the end of the hall made her easy to get at. So she pulls out all stops but can't convince the hospital people to make the switch. In the end I think Father Stevenson helped her out. But I certainly didn't know about the move."

"Well, I was on the floor and I didn't know about it. And neither did some of the other nurses." Clare poked a fork into her steaming chicken pie and produced a length of carrot. "It must have been pretty upsetting for you to be in what you thought was Mrs. Clancy's room and think she died just like that."

"Terrible," said Sarah. "It happened so fast and I was half-asleep. No one could have seen me because I was over by the window. Anyway, someone came in and fiddled with the machines—and everyone came charging in."

"I remember taking you to the waiting room, you were a wreck. Some of us didn't know about the bed change until the lights went on in the room and we tried to resuscitate the woman who turned out to be Florence Littlefield. And now it's a homicide case and maybe your aunt was right after all. About the attack on her the night before."

Sarah shrugged. "Who knows. That night she never got a good look at whoever it was—if it was real and not a bad dream. She said he or she was in a gown, mask, booties, the whole costume. And I certainly didn't get a real look at the last person who came into room nine."

"So you won't be any help to the police."

"Not yet, anyway. I keep trying to remember details, but nothing so far."

"Maybe something will come back to you later. Meantime, go back to your aunt. How do I go about being a useful and helpful nurse?"

So Sarah said her piece about the nonsentimental approach, and as they finished their lunch with a raspberry shortcake topped with a sinister glob of real whipped cream, she was interested to hear that Clare, as a child, had tried to ride a huge Belgian horse. He had belonged to an uncle and she had called him Popcorn. Also, Clare told her, she had once owned an Irish wolfhound and was grief-stricken when he died at fourteen. This information not only reassured Sarah that Clare would not only be an ally in halting Aunt Julia's determination to spend her life in a convent for the guilty, but could also actively bring her back onto the road to a normal recovery. Also, as a side benefit, Sarah felt that she, too, had found a friend, one who appreciated the virtues of Irish wolfhounds.

They parted on good terms, Clare saying that she would be back on daytime duty tomorrow, and Sarah suggesting that they try lunch again. Perhaps try the Poulet Perfecto, one of the main features of the Spring Chicken menu.

In the meantime, the police search machinery had not turned up Dr. Jonathan Philips. He was not at his house in Bowmouth Village, not at his summer camp in Cushing, nor were there signs that he had spent the night at either place. He had not called the hospital during the morning, had left no voice mail. A check of the registers of nearby hotels and inns had yielded no such person. Nothing matching the man had gotten on a bus, taken a taxi or a limo to the Portland Jetport, or flown from Owls Head airport to Logan Field in Boston. Nor, as far as the police could tell, had such a man bused south, west, or north or taken the ferry to Nova Scotia, nor crossed the border to Quebec. Checks with rental car agencies had come up empty.

But finally a little dribble of luck. Volunteer Christie Rivers, arriving at the temporary police room, claimed to have seen Dr. Philips leave the hospital and walk toward the physicians' parking lot at something like six-thirty the previous evening. No, she did not see him again; yes, he was alone; no, they didn't speak, she guessed he was on his way home. "Did anything about the man arouse your interest?" asked Sergeant George Fitts.

"Nothing," said Christie, "about Dr. Philips could arouse my interest unless he fell flat on his face. Or handed me a hundred-dollar bill. He was always the same. Low-key and boring. I never notice him usually, he comes and goes, but this time I was watching for a taxi coming into the rear entrance. My car's in the shop."

Which statement moved George Fitts into another area of activity. He ordered Mike Laaka and Katie Waters to check every repair garage in a fifteen-mile radius, then expand the inquiry if that didn't bring results.

It did.

Shorty's Towing Service reported that, yes, they had had a call from Dr. Philips about what he thought was a dead battery. They were to charge the battery in the hospital parking lot, if possible; if not, the car was to be towed and repaired at the Saab dealer's garage.

From the Saab garage it was a short jump to discovering that the car had an ignition problem, would take a few days to get parts for and fix, and that calls a few minutes ago this very afternoon to Dr. Philips for approval of the work had yielded zip. His secretary had reported he was away from the hospital.

"A blank," announced Mike, reporting to George, who was glaring at a notebook full of false leads and blind alleys. "He's off somewhere in the wild blue yonder."

"Not the type," said George. "From all I've heard, he's the sort that does it by the book. A to B to C to D."

"So what next?" asked Mike. "Missing Persons? Next of kin?"

"He hasn't any next of kin. We'll go the Missing Persons route and run interviews with the whole hospital staff. Plus ground workers. Then hit the visitors."

But unexpected help arrived in the person of Clare Mitchner, fresh from her chicken-pie lunch with Sarah. George looked up expectantly.

"I stopped in to leave a note for Carmen Wilson," she said. "You know, Dr. Philips's secretary. About the awards ceremony. While I was there I asked about his car because I knew he'd had trouble and Carmen said he hadn't turned up today. So I told her I'd seen him last night when his car wouldn't start."

"Just where did you see him?" demanded George.

"The physicians' parking lot. My car was parked pretty close in the regular staff lot across the way and I heard him trying to start the car. You know . . . that whiny-whiny noise and those clicks."

"And?" said George, poising his pen over his notepad.

"And so I walked over. To see if I could help. Of course I don't know beans about automobile motors. But it seemed a friendly thing to do."

"Are you friendly with Dr. Philips?"

Clare hesitated. "I don't know if any of us are exactly friendly with Dr. Philips. I mean, we say hello when we meet him in the hall, and he knows most of the nursing staff by name, but that's about it. He comes to hospital parties, but he's really not the party type."

So what else is new? thought Mike, listening. He admired Clare. Those soft dark eyes, wide smiling mouth. His type. Maybe when this mess got cleared up . . .

These hopeful thoughts were interrupted by George, speaking in a commanding voice. "Miss Mitchner, slow down. Tell us exactly what you saw. What you did. What Dr. Philips did. No matter how trivial it seems."

Clare Mitchner wrinkled her forehead as if trying to remember. Mike thought she looked most desirable with this puzzled expression on her face.

"Well," she began hesitantly, "I can't remember the exact sequence. But I think I walked over to Dr. Philips, who was still trying to start his car. Asked if he needed help or if he wanted a ride somewhere. Like to a garage."

"And," prompted George.

"He said he was going to call AAA in his office and see if they'd come over. I just waited there by his car door, hoping that if he needed a lift it would be just to a nearby garage. I certainly didn't want to drive him all the way to his summer place."

"Which is where?" put in Mike.

"In Cushing. His secretary, Carmen Wilson, told me because once before his car conked out and she did the honors. Drove him all the way down to Pleasant Point at the end of Cushing. I didn't want to be trapped like that, but well, I'd offered, so I was stuck."

"And he took you up on it?"

"I thought he had. He came back from calling the service people, I brought my car over, and he climbed in. Then told me he'd just need a ride into Bowmouth, Main Street. Which was a relief."

"And you drove off with Dr. Philips."

Clare shook her head. "That was the funny part. We'd almost got to the parking-lot gate when he asked me to stop. Said he'd changed his mind. He'd wait for the repair truck. They wouldn't be too long and if his car only needed a jump-start; he had some errands to do."

"So you took him back to the parking lot?"

"No, he got out right there. Thanked me, said he'd walk back to the car. And that was that."

"You drove off?"

"Yes, I drove off."

"Did you look back and see him?"

"No. I'd been thinking about catching that French movie in Camden, but then I changed my mind. The air had cooled down, it was nice out, so I walked around the campus, around the library and the arts buildings. And then drove home."

"You live alone?" said Mike. He wondered if she was already hooked up with a live-in companion of the male sex.

"Yes, but I don't see what that has to do with anything." Clare sounded defensive, a little annoyed.

"We like to cover the bases," said Mike.

"And I'm one of the bases?" said Clare, now clearly annoyed. "For your information, although it's none of your business, I'm not married and nobody lives with me."

Before Mike could recover, the telephone rang. George's hand hovered, waited for the second ring, picked it up, and said, "Sergeant Fitts."

George was gifted with facial features that remained undisturbed regardless of the message he was receiving. Mike often thought that George's voice and face would remain robotic if he were told that he'd won ten million dollars on Publisher's Clearing House, or that the decapitated body of his mother had been found in the next room.

"Hold a minute," George told the phone. He covered the receiver and thanked Miss Mitchner for her information and said he'd be in touch. Mike, getting the nod, escorted Clare to the door.

"He's a tough one," said Clare, still sounding annoyed.

"George," said Mike, "is all Maine State Police. He doesn't get sidetracked and he stays focused."

"Ugh," said Clare, and departed.

Mike returned to George, bent over the telephone, busy with the notebook.

Then: "We'll be along. Leave everything as is."

"What?" Mike almost shouted.

"Body," said George. "In the water. Fisherman, Pete Horner, was out in his lobster boat. Pulled the body in with a gaff. Tied it to the side of his boat. Dropped the anchor and called the Coast Guard. Who came out, took charge, and called the Lincolnville police. Who called us. No ID on the body. Wanted to know about anyone missing. Like a tall thin male of middle age, dead for sixteen or more hours, judging from the condition of the body."

"And I just bet we're going to take a look."

George stood up, put his notebook into his rear pocket, and picked up the olive baseball hat on the desk, a hat with absolutely no logo, not even the Red Sox, and headed for the door.

"Shall I guess?" said Mike, starting after him. "Dr. Jonathan Philips is no longer a missing person."

"Never guess," said George, without turning. "It isn't professional."

17

TO lobsterman Pete Horner, a body was just a body. And what was one more to a sixty-five-year-old fisherman who had seen bodies of all ages and species, from drowned fellow fishermen and sailors to the odd suicide or trauma victim; to lost, harpooned, or shotgun-blasted seals, sharks, porpoise, and other ocean inhabitants. So the body of the late Dr. Jonathan Philips, no matter how tattered and torn, was nothing to get worked up about. But what he didn't want was any hassle from the police about his discovery.

However, officers who toil in the criminal investigation branch of the law often have their preferences in the matter of bodies and scenes of violence. George Fitts, true to type, preferred a corpse to be discovered within minutes of death, clothing intact and dry, the cause of death evident: the bullet hole, the compressed neck, the knife still sticking in the wound. At the site he wished to find footsteps sharply pressed into the ground, clear fingerprints, plus wads of hair and shreds of flesh clenched in the stiffened hands of the deceased.

Deputy Mike Laaka, who often fought an unprofessional tendency to nausea on viewing a mutilated or several-days-old corpse, hoped also for the body to be found immediately after death, or, even better, found years later, so he would be able to view the bare bones without losing his lunch. As for Mike's cohort, Katie Waters, she tried always to be elsewhere during a viewing. If this was not possible, she worked hard on breathing through her mouth and distracting herself by thinking about the need for clear and concise note-taking. As for forensic pathologist Johnny Cuszak, he simply wanted the bumblers and fumblers to keep their mitts off the corpse, their feet away from the site, so he could give the whole scene his professional once-over and then make sure the body was safely moved into its body bag, into the ambulance, and onto the autopsy table.

In the present case, none of these postmortem preferences were honored. Dr. Philips, since the evening before, had been flushed out by the tide of the Duck Trap inlet, tumbled about in the ocean currents, and his body nibbled by sea carnivores. On his first two tries, Philip Horner's gaff had punctured the corpse, but not held until his third attempt, and the coast guard men, in hoisting the body, had bumped it along the flank of their ship and torn off bits of clothing when they had hoisted him aboard.

Johnny Cuszak, with the victim finally in place on the autopsy table, felt much misused. Not a simple wholesome corpse; not a simple easily detected cause of death. And once again he was going to miss his daughter Jennifer's early-evening appearance in the Bowmouth Bears Little League game. What kind of a father was he, anyway? And after pushing for girls' baseball all these past years, he was never there to cheer her on.

"Get over here," he growled at Mike Laaka, who stood far to the rear of the autopsy table. "I don't care if you've just finished your dinner. You guys chose your job. This scene is part of it."

"I'd never have chosen your job," said Mike, who had been ordered to the scene by George, who was busy dealing with the fallout of Dr. Philips's death back at the hospital. "In fact, if I'd known . . ." He sputtered to a stop and took a long deep breath and blew out through his nose.

"If you're going to toss your cookies, toss them away from the table," said Johnny. "But stay close enough so I don't have to shout."

"I can get it on tape," muttered Mike.

"You need the visual impact," said Johnny, showing no mercy.

Two hours later, the ritual of measuring, weighing, making the incisions, taking specimens, and separating organs for close lab examination was finished. With a heavy sigh—Jennifer's baseball game would be winding up unless it went extra innings—Johnny allowed himself the luxury of a brief announcement.

"Didn't drown," he said as he peeled off his surgical gloves. "Dead when he hit the water. Blunt head trauma. Multiple blows—three, I'd guess. Heavy instrument. Long, narrow thing— probably metal—with maybe a small knobby head."

"What kind of a 'long narrow thing'?" asked Mike, who now that the eviscerated body had been covered and wheeled away, felt that he could participate in the investigative process. "And from where?"

"Hell, I don't know. Microscopic will probably say something about any residue. The ocean did its best, but probably didn't wash everything away."

Mike closed his eyes for a second, trying to picture a long narrow object capable of death blows. "Like a golf club? A crowbar?"

"Let the labs do their stuff," said Johnny. "I'll call you when I know anything more, so go away."

"Gladly," said Mike, untying his gown and pulling off his mask.

Back at the hospital, Sarah, having reported her location as requested by the police security machine, was making ready for a last-minute evening visit to Aunt Julia. She paused at the closed gift-shop door, thinking that such a visit might do no good, might even sink her aunt deeper into self-recrimination. Patrick's visit had helped, but the result was temporary. A new approach was needed. Something unconventional. Something that would put her aunt into gear, get her participating in life, even in life as lived in a hospital bed.

At which point, a medical person (female, white jacket, stethoscope, breasts) stopped and asked, "Are you all right? How about sitting down. Shall I call someone for you?"

Sarah, trying to look alive, reassured her questioner, said she was fine, just thinking.

Thinking. Okay, think. Perhaps Aunt Julia might be roused out of her funk by the news that Dr. Jonathan Philips had become the third hospital victim and this terrible fact might perhaps let her aunt believe that the hospital was under attack by a serial killer. Such an idea ought to jolt anyone out of the doldrums and bring the larger picture into focus.

"Nothing anyone can do," Sarah would say to Julia, "will bring Florence Littlefield back. I aided and abetted you in the bed switch, and so, I think, did Father Stevenson. But now we have this killer loose in the hospital, so you've got to help the police because we're all up to our ears in the whole business."

This was certainly not the usual way to rally a depressed patient, but Julia might begin to think that her guilty moping was not useful, in fact was counterproductive of anything positive. She might see that the recent crime wave was bigger than she was, bigger than her crisis of conscience. Here she was, a woman who had cut her teeth on murder mysteries, a person designed by nature for meddling in other people's affairs, and since she was also a hospital patient, might be a valuable cog in the investigation.

The police, George Fitts and company, Sarah reminded herself, will have a major fit at any idea of encouraging Julia to stick her fingers into the investigation. But what the hell. Family came first. Anything to rouse Julia out of her slump. She and her aunt could work together. Or at least pretend to. First, divert Julia. Then, if something came of their guesswork, well, all to the good. And not a word to Alex. He would never go around speculating on the basis of muddled facts and confused evidence. Such forbearance was perhaps fine for a physician, but a handicap in unconventional investigations.

Sarah, newly invigorated, pushed herself away from the gift-shop door, started down the hall toward the stairs and began the climb to the Cardiac ICU floor. She would buy a notebook. She and Julia would make notes about impressions, persons who might have said or seen something useful. They would straighten out the cast of characters—all those mix-and-match nurses and aides and physicians' assistants. They would both try to remember more of their encounters with attack persons.

In this mood Sarah walked briskly toward room 3. And stopped cold. From the door of number 3 Cardiac ICU emerged a narrow female figure in black dress. She held the door ajar, and a second similar figure stepped out of the room, this last woman slightly bent, leaning on a cane, also in black but with the addition of a gray scarf.

Grandmother Douglas and housekeeper Hopkins, both of whom looking as if they had just stepped out of one of Jakob Grimm's more stringent fairy tales. For a second, Sarah froze and watched the two dark figures hesitating, as if gathering strength for the elevator descent. Their dark shapes against the bland beige hospital walls suggested nothing so much as a pair of death figures—all they needed were scythes over their shoulders—ready to cut down the next moving object: a sheet-covered patient on a gurney, a passing physician, or perhaps a lab technician with her little trolley of tubes and vials.

"Sarah, is that you?" Grandmother Douglas had suddenly turned her head, gifted, as Sarah had long suspected, with eyes at the back of her head.

Sarah jumped and pushed away the vision of a visiting death duo. The high voice of her grandmother always had the effect of bringing her back to the straight and narrow. In this case, to explain to her grandmother why she was arriving at the relatively late hour of nine forty-five in the evening. But surely the question was, why had her grandmother left home at such a time when she should have been tucked into her four-poster canopied monstrosity and sipping her Ovaltine?

"Grandma," said Sarah, beating Mrs. Douglas to the punch, "why on earth are you here so late? Isn't it past your bedtime?"

"Nonsense," said her grandmother in her high sharp voice. She moved closer to Sarah with a tap-tap of her cane. "It's an emergency. Father Stevenson called me because he couldn't seem to reach you. Apparently you don't stay put where you can be found. He said that Julia was very depressed. And that she considered herself responsible for this Florence Littlefield's death. So of course I had to do something. Hopkins and I drove straight over to the hospital and I've had a long talk with Julia."

"You have?" said Sarah weakly, trying to picture the scene. Julia alternately breaking down and then blustering, Grandmother Douglas lecturing on Christian responsibility.

"Yes, indeed. I checked with this Dr. Santoro, who is apparently in charge of the case. He said that she had seen her farm manager and the visit had done her good. He thought I might brace her up. His words, not mine. I believe I have accomplished this. Hopkins will bear this out, won't you, Hopkins?"

"Why, yes, Mrs. Douglas," said the faithful Hopkins. "You did speak your mind. Talked right to her face, you did. Did Mrs. Clancy a world of good, I'm sure. Made her sit up and take notice."

Sarah stared at the housekeeper. It was perhaps the longest string of sentences she'd ever heard her make. She turned to her grandmother. "What exactly did you say?"

"I told her about the murder of Dr. Jonathan Philips and pointed out that there have now been three unfortunate murders which occurred in this hospital, and that it was not her place to start blaming herself for what went on here. Those deaths are now in the hands of the Lord. And in the hands of the Maine State Police and the Knox County Sheriff's Department."

Sarah couldn't help it. "You're saying they work together?"

"Do not," said her grandmother, taking two unsteady steps closer, "be smart with me, young lady. But yes, I believe that the forces of goodwill overcome. And that Julia must remember that she is only a small cog in a very large wheel, and she must try to help the police and stop thinking of her own emotions. She can pray for forgiveness and then stop all the fussing."

This was close enough to Sarah's own opinion that she could

only nod her head. "Do you think I should go in and see her now?" she asked.

"Of course. Say good night and point out how useful she could be. Julia always loved to poke her nose where it didn't belong. Now she has a fine opportunity. The police need everyone's help."

"As well as God's?" said Sarah.

"That," said her grandmother, "goes without saying. And good night to you, Sarah. Hopkins, I am ready."

"Yes, Mrs. Douglas," said Hopkins, holding out a supporting arm. And the two black-clad ladies moved with slow steps and great care toward the elevator doors.

Sarah identified herself to the sheriff's deputy sitting next to Julia Clancy's door, saw him check her name against a string of approved names, then opened room 3. She found her aunt propped up on her pillow, the bedside lamp shining a circle of light on a yellow pad of paper.

"I'm making a list," she announced. "Things to do."

This sounded promising. Persons in the depths of depression do not make lists. They may make farewell declarations, but not lists of things to do.

"Yes," said Sarah encouragingly.

"My mother was here," announced Julia.

"I saw them outside, just leaving."

"She came in full battle dress. With Hopkins as aide-de-camp."

"As soldiers of the Lord?"

"Soldier-ettes. Mother believes in the feminine suffix. No chairpersons for her."

"And so?" prompted Sarah.

"I'm making a list of things to do. First I want to take care of my guilt in switching beds, so I'm making a hospital donation. This will be a specific gift. In memory of specific persons. Starting with Tom Clancy."

"In memory of his not dying here."

"In a way. And then I'll do something about Florence Littlefield."

"Her sister, Emma, is suing the hospital and the whole staff. There may be no hospital left to donate to."

Julia, moving her non-IV hand, raised the pad of paper. "Questions to ask," she said.

"Questions about what?" asked Sarah, although she already knew the answer. Julia was falling in with her grandmother's plan, which was also her own plan.

"You and I," said her aunt firmly, "are going to get a grip on what's going on here."

"The three murders?"

"Perhaps more to come. We will work undercover."

"Cover of a blanket?"

"Don't be sarcastic. It's not becoming."

"You're beginning to sound like Grandma."

"We will find out things that the police, not even George Fitts with his knife-at-your-throat approach, might not find out. The same with Mike Laaka. They both have two major disadvantages."

"Which are?"

"They're policemen, of course. No one tells a policeman everything. Or even half of everything. Policemen aren't the sort you let your hair down for or feel comfortable with. Even if you're only a witness, they'll watch for mistakes, wait for you to trip up, wait to—"

"Pounce and cuff you?"

"In a sense, yes. But sick old women and harmless-looking English teachers can accomplish wonders with normal women chitchat."

"How about Dr. Alex McKenzie, spouse of the harmless-looking English teacher?"

Julia frowned. "I thought of Alex. He's internal medicine and he probably listens to more troubles than we hear in a lifetime. But then I crossed him off."

"Too straight."

"Right. Eagle Scout. Camp Spirit."

"And what do you propose we start doing?"

"Make friends. I'll try to hold off barking at that Clare woman.

Nurse Honey-Dear. And get a line on all the others. And I'll work on my memory. I'm sure things are just under the surface of my brain. You can linger in the cafeteria, chat up the volunteers, the physicians' aides. Start working on motive. Who hated Old Man Dr. Philips so that they killed him and then got his grandson, who from all I've heard was as dull as dishwater but perfectly harmless? And who thought I might have heard or seen something, so I needed to be choked to death?"

"You mean, find out exactly what really terrible things Philips senior did?"

"Correct. And now it's past my bedtime. And yours. Is there still a deputy stuck outside my door?"

"There was when I came in."

"Tell him to go home, though I don't suppose he'll listen."

"I doubt it. I love you, Aunt Julia. Sleep well."

"No one in this pit sleeps well. But thank you."

And Sarah slipped out of the room.

By Saturday, August the twenty-fifth, the media were having a field day. The first murder, that of the retired, not-much loved Dr. Henry Philips, had achieved only two or three days' worth of front-page paragraphs, together with out-of-date photographs and biographical details dug up by local papers from their archives. The ruling that Florence Littlefield had been a second homicide victim increased the coverage tenfold: pictures, more photographs (Florence shown in 1989 dishing out strawberry shortcake at the Union Fair), statements from hospital personnel, a highly inaccurate drawing of an ICU unit, full front-page columns in the *Portland Press Herald* and the *Bangor Daily News*, three paragraphs in *The Boston Globe* and a two-column effort on page 3 in tall letters "SHOCKER!" in the *Boston Herald*.

But in the words of Mike Laaka, when the news of the death by violence of hospital CEO Dr. Jonathan Philips became generally known, the shit really hit the fan.

"Jesus God-a-mighty," said Mike to Katie Waters when they

met in the usual police situation room. "This is Maine, not Chicago. We don't have these things."

"It's a slow season on the news front," said Katie. Even on the hot August morning she was looking cool and collected in tan cotton trousers and a black T-shirt. A night's sleep had restored her usual humor and upbeat view of life—upbeat even in view of triple murders.

"I mean, look what they've got," said Mike.

"The vipers, you mean?"

"Who else. It'll be front page on the *National Enquirer* and the *Star, People*, and all those rags. They've hit gold."

"Nah," said Katie. "You can't beat out Britney Spears and Michael Jackson and Prince William and the Kennedys. Or sleazy corporate directors. This is small-town stuff."

"Hell, it is. Three hospital murders. The press loves weird hospital stuff. And look how Jonathan Phillip was found. Floating around off Lincolnville Beach. Head smashed. Body stuck with a gaff by a lobsterman. The coast guard to the rescue. Victim's car missing. Grandson of number-one victim. And that's just the beginning. By the time the news guys finish with the stories, they'll have old Doc Henry as a lush, Florence Littlefield as an addict who overdosed, Julia Clancy as a practicing witch, and Jonathan as an undercover FBI agent."

"Have you considered fiction as a career?" asked Katie.

"Who needs fiction?" said Mike. "Real life is so exciting."

At which point George Fitts arrived with a stack of notebooks, a sheaf of papers, and a laptop, and the area resumed the aspect of a serious workplace.

These items George placed carefully down on the long table set aside for his particular use. "Here's what we've got," he said, pulling up a wooden office chair and beginning to sort papers, books, and to open the laptop.

Katie and Mike remained silent. George as an officer in charge of dim-witted troops was playing a well-known role.

"Sit down," ordered George. "I've made copies."

"Of what?" ventured Katie.

"I'm about to tell you. The first set of lists is for Homicide One. We've broken down the lists of persons in or in easy reach of the ER on the morning and early afternoon of August seventeenth. Visitors, patients, hospital staff people, including the registrars, the secretarial personnel and maintenance people, and of course the physicians on duty or near the scene."

"And the ambulance drivers," put in Mike.

George frowned but continued his recitation. "Yes, the ambulance drivers. From four nearby towns. Then we have volunteers and fringe workers. Teenage candy stripers, two taxi drivers, a van from an assisted-living community, and a lost pharmaceutical-company representative."

"Lost?" queried Katie.

"He was looking for the doctors' office block. Then we have cars bringing potential patients coming to the ER for treatment."

"Wow," said Katie. "A gen-u-ine hornet's nest."

George gave what passed for a satisfied smile, a sort of glacial smirk. "We start on the premise that the three homicides are related. As is the failed attempt on Julia Clancy, which we are now taking seriously."

"A little late for that," remarked Mike.

"Mrs. Clancy," George continued, "was known to have been on the scene, or near the scene, of the first murder. The attack she described the night of August twenty-first, when she was in Cardiac ICU nine, even allowing for post-surgical nightmares, was most possibly a genuine murder attempt. We'll list those persons around that night under Attempted Homicide."

"Lists and labels drive me crazy," said Katie. "But what are you calling the Florence Littlefield death?"

"Florence Littlefield is the Second Homicide. But we have to consider that the victim was supposed to be Mrs. Clancy. The bed switch apparently wasn't known by the murderer."

"Julia Clancy will be glad to hear you've become a believer," said Mike.

"The third murder is that of Jonathan Philips. I actually call them H-1, HA, H-2, and H-3."

"Which makes them all sound like a kind of boat race or a

flight of spaceships," said Mike. "I suppose what you're going to tell us is it adds up to a plan to get rid of the Philips family because of some evil deed done by the old bird."

"And," added Katie, feeling that she was being remarkably sharp-witted for so early in the morning—it must have been the three mugs of coffee—"all you have to do is to see which of the same people turn up for the three murders and the failed attempt."

"Correct," said George, looking annoyed. He liked to spin out these details, make sure every nut and bolt was in place, before he flipped the scarf off the table, waved his wand, and said, "Presto!"

"Okay," said Mike. "Who gets credit for four appearances on four different scenes?"

Katie raised her hand. "Wait up, Mike. You've only got three different scenes. Room Nine Cardiac ICU had a double feature. Now all we have to do is find out who was lurking in the john, hiding under a gurney, crouching behind an oxygen tank."

"We begin," said George, unwilling to be rushed, "with the list of medical personnel on or about the ER when old Dr. Philips was strangled."

"How about motives?" put in Katie.

"Haven't you learned," said George crossly, "that it's facts first: time, place, opportunity. Motives later. Motives just confuse the initial investigation."

"That," Mike explained to Katie, "is because anything that smells of psychology or general nuttiness George can't handle."

"At the beginning of any case," George, finally goaded into response, replied, "I stay on hard ground. Later, if I have to, I'll go wading into the swamp. Motives live in the swampland."

"Me," said Katie in an aside to Mike, "I love swamps."

Thus it was that two teams prepared to advance the investigation into three murders and one possible attack. The legitimate team headed by the Maine State Police CID, the sheriff's department investigative division, and the state's forensic pathologists, were all professionals who hated interference by the laity. The second team—if two people could be called a team—was an amateur hit-or-miss duo made up of an elderly recovering cardiac patient and her niece. It goes without saying that two such groups attempting to unravel a triple murder could cause confusion, collision, and the possible destruction of evidence. However, with good luck, the two amateurs might just ferret out personal information, recover memories of relevant objects, and might have intimate encounters that would never be available to the official guardians of law and order.

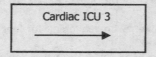

18

SUNDAY, August the twenty-sixth, dawned clear with washed blue skies. It was the sort of day—if one didn't happen to be a patient at the Mary Starbox Memorial Hospital—that sent the average Maine citizen into a state of rare optimism. Sent him outdoors to rejoice. The last few days of heat, humidity, and rumbling thunder had caused irascibility, sweating body parts, dried-out gardens, lowered well water, and a general question about whether August was worth it. But now anything seemed possible.

At least it seemed so to Sarah Deane, who lingered in bed for a few minutes savoring a dream in which she had been floating down a bubbling river supported by only a broken tree branch. Like Ophelia, she told herself, but without drowning. Now, seeing the bright scene outside the window, she climbed willingly out of bed. It was only 5:00 A.M. Time for many things. Alex had departed at four in the morning to see a patient who had overdosed with his prescribed medication. Poor patient. But also poor Alex. What a life. And here it was almost the end of summer and what he most wanted to do was to get away from

213

the hospital to check on returning shorebirds and departing migrants.

Oh, well, tonight looked hopeful. Alex wouldn't be on call and they could have an outdoor meal. Sit under the old oak tree, eat barbecued chicken. Or fish. Roast corn. Whatever. Maybe ask a couple of friends over, something they hadn't had time for lately. But this morning all was in order. A midnight shower had watered her small and largely untended vegetable garden, and the four peach trees were heavy with fruit. As for the future, the book order for her literature and writing classes had come in unexpectedly on time. Also, the meeting with her fifteen freshman advisees at Bowmouth College was still a week away and so could be shoved out of her mind. Perhaps she could take a hike with Patsy along the Appleton Ridge, followed by a swim in Fallen Tree Pond on a tiny strip of shoreline owned by Aunt Julia.

Aunt Julia!

Oh, God!

How had she spaced out like that? Acting as if life were just cresting along on a beautiful late-August day. A day in which she could walk her dog and swim in a pond. Instant amnesia. Sudden onset Alzheimer's. Sarah felt a chill and then a sudden bolt of anger. Focused anger. And hate. Hate for hospitals and Cardiac ICUs and that damn loudspeaker bleeping for doctor this or doctor that. And those claustrophobic beige walls and endless corridors hemming you in. Day after day she had been the good niece, the helpful useful niece, but she had other family people, didn't she? Her mother and father? Well, no, they were off in Colorado on an Elderhostel trip. Alex's family? In Norway for an ancient-language conference (Alex's father) and art-museum visiting (Alex's mother). Her younger brother Tony? Bopping around Santa Fe with his new band The Decomposers and snuggling with his criminally inclined girlfriend, Andrea. And Grandmother Douglas? All well on that front under the steady hand of Hopkins.

So who needed her?

Answer: Julia Clancy, still stuck in a cardiac ICU and probably completely stir-crazy by now. Aunt Julia, who had been deeply depressed, but last evening had been gung ho to be a private investigator. And who might herself be attacked if one of those guards from the sheriff's department spaced out or had to go to the men's room. I mean, he couldn't just sit there for hours on end holding a urinal, Sarah told herself. And besides, wasn't it high time they moved Julia to a genuine room? One with pictures and a view, not just designed as a glass fishbowl. Sarah would work on that. Father Stevenson might help; he seemed good at moving patients.

But what to do? No problem, have it both ways. Snatch a piece of the day and then hit the hospital. It was only six forty-five. Time to spare. Shower, grab breakfast, take a run with Patsy out into this splendid morning. Sit down for fifteen minutes and read the first pages of her new Robert B. Parker gripper—a writer who really understood dogs even if they weren't Irish wolfhounds. Books? Good idea. Pick up a couple of books for Aunt Julia. Books that would grab her attention or hit her funny bone. How about *Seabiscuit*, full of horses and action, and the new Janet Evanovich. Then to the hospital. Stay upbeat and get on with their private investigation. The personal touch. Be nosy. Encourage her aunt to make friends with anyone who came into room 3. This would be a big effort for Julia, particularly in the case of Nurse Clare Mitchner. But perhaps Clare had started on the path to friendship that Sarah had indicated. Sarah could only hope.

Arriving at the hospital, Sarah found that things were indeed looking up. Julia had been moved into a real—almost real—room. Skilled Nursing Unit (called SKU) number 25. Sarah retreated down the corridor and found her way to Unit 25, and just as she arrived the door opened and Clare Mitchner stepped out. To Sarah's surprise—and delight—she grinned, gave a thumbs-up and disappeared down the hall.

Sarah showed her ID and the two books she carried to the deputy on guard—a new man with a big stomach and as bald as a potato. Checked off his list, she pushed herself into the new room, a space complete with curtains, a lavatory, a window looking out on three birch trees, and a framed reproduction of Van Gogh's *Wheatfield with Blackbirds*—a disturbing choice perhaps, but better than a blank wall.

Julia was sitting up in the armchair, draped in a "new" light-weight dressing gown brought by Patrick from the farm, this one apparently fashioned from a discarded tablecloth. Her wire-gray hair had been pushed into something resembling order, her color was almost natural, and even with the protruding lines and tubes sticking out from hidden body parts, she looked almost healthy. Almost well. And, more amazingly, in good humor.

"Hey," said Sarah, pulling up a small metal chair and depositing Julia's new reading matter on the bedside table, "you're looking good."

"You mean slightly human? No, don't answer that. Are those new books for me?"

"*Seabiscuit* and a funny murder one. To keep you sane."

"I've read *Seabiscuit*, wonderful book. But thank you. And now I want you to know I've been wrong."

"About what?" Sarah had not gotten used to this new humble Julia. First the guilt and depression over her bed switch, and now an apology.

"That nurse. Clare What's-her-name. The one who used to slobber all over me and call me honey. Pat me. Call me Julia."

"And now?" Sarah prompted.

"Transformation. Stopped the sweet talk. Didn't treat me like a six-year-old. We had an adult conversation. Turns out she rode her uncle's big horse called Popcorn when she was little. Her family had English setters. We talked about field setters and show setters. She agreed that the field setters were the most sensible. Amazing." Here Julia paused, considered, and then eyed Sarah suspiciously.

"You put her up to this, didn't you?" she demanded. "Coached her how to treat the old bag, right? So it was all an act. I might have known."

Sarah defended herself. No, she hadn't coached Clare. Yes, she'd met her for a meal. Why? Because Clare was distraught. "Didn't know what she'd done wrong. Wanted to get along with her patients. The soft touch had worked with elderly patients but she'd bombed when she tried to be nice to you. I told her you didn't like soft soap and molasses. She shouldn't try so hard. And to call you Mrs. Clancy until further notice. You were another generation and you didn't like playing cozy."

"A Julia tutorial?"

Sarah lost it. "No, damn it. I just thought it might be a hell of a lot easier if nurse and patient got along with each other. Better for nurse. Better for patient. So do you prefer the soft-soap approach or the nurse who used to ride a big horse? Who likes English setters? A woman who, by the way, as a kid once had an Irish wolfhound. A woman you probably have a lot in common with if you weren't so goddamn touchy."

Julia smiled a crooked smile. "I think you're the one who's touchy. All worked up so early in the morning. I'm feeling pretty good, so I'll forgive you."

"How kind of you," Sarah snapped. This was the relative who needed her so badly that she couldn't take a whole day off and go hiking and swimming.

"I'm sorry," said Julia. "I know it's a pain to keep coming into this blasted hospital. But it's almost over. Good news. At last, I'm in a new room. And later today if all is well, they'll haul out my drains and catheter lines and I can go home tomorrow. So there. Alex and Dr. Gene Whoozit . . ."

"Santoro," put in Sarah.

"Both said it was okay. And I can start in cardiac rehab in about four or five weeks. You know, treadmills and weight lifting and rowing. And in eight weeks I can get on a horse, but I think I can cut some time off that one."

"Aunt Julia . . ." began Sarah.

"No. No lecture. Peace. I need to be on a horse. Better than any treadmill. I know I'm an old battle-ax and my tongue gets me in trouble. But this morning I'm in charity with all, including Nurse Clare, who has seen the light. At least in handling elderly curmudgeons. So now we only have a little time.

"A little time?" said Sarah, startled. "A little time for what?"

"Wake up. For our project. Our investigation. Our private personal investigation. The serial killer. You were all for it yesterday. I've been working on notes. Who and where. People I really remember seeing. I've already worked one of the lab females over.

Mary Vaughn, her name is. She goes everywhere on this floor and the one below, the long-term cardiac floor. And she hated Dr. Philips."

"Which one?"

"The old guy. Pinched her bottom. Upset her tray of equipment reaching around her shoulder to grab her breastworks. Interfered with her mother's hysterectomy by examining her when he shouldn't have gone near her. He wasn't an OB-GYN man. Except for feeling women. And then one of the volunteers I've known before at the farm, Christie Rivers, dropped in this morning. Says she's met you. Been working here forever. Says even young Dr. Philips wasn't much liked. That he didn't do much to stop his grandfather—who was supposed to have retired—from wandering around the hospital sticking his nose into everything. Trouble was that old Dr. Philips didn't give up his license to practice."

"So we have a day and a half to do what the police and an army of detectives and forensic people have had days to do."

"I'll be home after two days, but I can still work my end from the farm. Make notes, remember things. Now you get going. Go see the three senior volunteers, Christie and her buddies. They all seem to know you, and they go everywhere. Try to bump into the nurses I've had: Clare, that Tanya Someone, Hannah Finch. Here, I've got a list." Julia reached into the folds of her dressing gown and produced a small spiral notebook. "Some are only first names, but I've mentioned what they look like. Where they first turned up."

Sarah rose from her chair. "If you think there's really any point . . ."

"Don't go waffling on me," said Julia. "I'll bet right now you know something that the police don't.

Sarah hesitated. "Well, maybe one thing." "You see I ran into the volunteer trio the morning after Florence Littlefield died . . ."

"Was murdered."

"Okay, murdered. And it turned out that all three of them were in or around the hospital that night. Although I suppose the police know all this."

"Don't you believe it. Make notes. Time for you to hit the trail." Julia indicated the door with her free hand.

And Sarah hit the trail.

The trail led first to the cafeteria, where Sarah picked up a large selection of doughnuts and sticky buns. These she planned to carry out to the grounds of the Mary Starbox Hospital. But the entrance to the pathways was obscured by the police presence and what could only be called a media frenzy. The sharks were circling with a vengeance. Sarah returned to the hospital, slipped out a side driveway and saw that not only a CBS truck blocked the path but even a Maine Public Television Unit had set up shop. Shame on them. She doubled back, twisted around a planting of flowering hydrangea bushes, then suddenly, around a corner, she found a small black-headed microphone shoved in her face. A tiny woman in a summer navy business suit appeared from nowhere. Did she work in the hospital? asked the woman. How did she feel about the hospital being the center of a triple murder? Did going inside make her nervous? Did she know personally any of the victims?

Sarah shoved the microphone aside, said it was microphones that made her nervous and to go away. At which she left the scene on a run, the cardboard box of doughnuts bobbling dangerously in her arms.

Cutting around a small fountain and a circle of benches outside the psychiatric unit, she saw that the volunteers, on their morning break as she had hoped, were in place at a picnic table more distant than their usual choice. Probably also escaping the media. Joining them ought to be easy, Sarah thought. They had sought her presence before, now, laden with edibles, she might be doubly welcome.

But even as she thought this she felt a sense of shame. These people weren't friends, and she wasn't interested in their lives unless they pertained to an understanding of the murders, and in particular the two attacks on room 9. The truth was she was using these people. They had offered their *friendship* but she was now going to use them. And then move on. Despicable.

This deplorable fact established, Sarah paused at a slight rise of ground that overlooked the scattered group of picnic tables. If one ignored the hospital buildings rising behind them, the scene might be that of a park on a summer's day. Families having a bite to eat. Opening a thermos, unwrapping a brownie, an apple, a bunch of grapes. A small boy running down the incline, a springer spaniel bounding along ahead of him. A white-haired man with something that looked like an alpenstock picking his way slowly along a border of pansies, a young girl with long black hair, in jeans and T-shirt, by his side. A couple on a blanket reading a newspaper. Overhead, a small plane droned by. Two crows cawed from a nearby birch. A small yellow butterfly floated past. All so normal. Except . . .

Except this was not real time. It was time stolen away by all these apparently free people from a hospital world of blood, guts, and bones.

Sarah, her conscience temporarily shelved, advanced on the volunteers.

The picnic-table session, short as it was, proved interesting. Sarah was welcomed as an old friend, which provided her with another pang of shame. The trio, plus Nurse Hannah Finch from the ER (today in a smock featuring house wrens) were exclaiming over their experiences of being grilled by the likes of Sergeant George Fitts.

"They've got this list," explained Hannah. "Everyone in the ER when Dr. Phillips got throttled. That's me and all of us here."

"We just went in and out."

"The better to strangle," said Dave Bergman, reaching for and pushing half a doughnut into his mouth. "They're interested in how much I can haul, push, or carry. Like I've got the muscles to do the strangle job."

"I did a lot of wheelchair trips that day," said Christie. "It was in and out. Wheel to X-ray, the ER, wheel to the lab, wheel to the MRI unit. Pick up chairs, return the chairs.

"Plus the discharge jobs," put in Stella Dugan. "I don't usually do wheelchair trips, it's too much for me. But I did that day. Getting patients to the front door, helping them into their car." Stella-the-Mouse, as Sarah thought of her, looked tired and her usually immaculate blue smock was missing a button.

"How about you, Sarah?" Asked Christie Rivers. "Aren't you on the hot seat, too? You and your Aunt Julia."

Sarah admitted to repeated official conversations and then rolled the ball back to the group. "Did they ask you why you think someone killed the two Philips doctors? And, of course, Florence Littlefield?"

"Like one of us was working off a grudge," said Dave Berman, reaching for another doughnut.

"But we've told you, we all had reason to hate old Doc Philips," said Christie. "Because of neglect and making bad medical decisions. Stella even has more reasons to hate the Philipses. Not only her husband Terry, but her niece. Poor little Althea."

"Yes, Althea," said Stella. "But I'd rather not talk about her. It makes me too sad."

"Althea?" said Sarah, hoping to provoke more on the subject.

"We've all lost people here," said Stella. "It's what happens at hospitals. The police aren't interested in ancient history. They want to know where and when we were someplace in the last few days."

"And why," put in Christie, "did we pick up a wheelchair on the pediatric floor and take it to the ER? Why did we deliver a package to someone in the recovery area? What were we doing in Day Surgery? In Pediatrics? In the gift shop, for heaven's sake. As if we were carrying bombs in our pockets."

"Sergeant Fitts makes you feel like you should confess something," said Hannah Finch. She rose, looked at her watch. "Thanks for the feed, Sarah Deane," she said. "I'm due back on the floor in minus one minute."

"George Fitts is something else. He's got a grip on where we all were for all three murders, plus during the Mrs. Clancy business," said David. "Did I ever get a fishy eye when I said I was visiting my brother-in-law Leon on the cardiac ICU floor the night when Florence Littlefield died. And, you, Christie, coming back in for your handbag after hours. A likely story. And Stella, waltzing around with a dog that night."

Stella sat bolt upright. "I didn't get anywhere near the inside of the hospital that night. I was out on the paths in the gardens. It's a good place to walk a dog."

"So the police weren't interested in you being on the grounds that night?" asked Sarah, surprised. George always went for the no-stone-unturned in an investigation.

Stella gave a half-shrug and Christie broke in. "What's with Mrs. Clancy? There's a sheriff's deputy glued outside her door. And we're all being questioned about the night she thought she was being attacked."

Sarah tried again. Go back to Stella. "Did you think that Sergeant Fitts was asking questions that he shouldn't have? I mean about your night out with the dog?"

Again, Sarah was derailed. "No more speculations. It's time to go back to work," said Christie, taking command. "I'm sure Stella did everything proper. She always does. It's in her blood. Compliance is Stella's middle name."

"Only sometimes she has a little breakout, gets a little gung ho," grinned David. "But usually, she's Mrs. Helping Hand."

Sarah, watching Stella at David's remark, thought she saw a shadow pass over Stella's face. And then Stella smiled, but it was a small, tense smile.

"Hey, Stella, forget what I said about breakouts, I'm just teasing," said David, hoisting himself to his feet and gathering doughnut wrappers.

Stella looked at David, the small smile seemingly frozen on her face. "I usually do what people want me to do and I've found life has been a lot easier because of it."

"She won the Senior Social Honor Cup in high school," said Christie. "My parents held Stella up to me as some sort of flag. But never mind, Stella, I still love you."

"Yeah, so do we all," said David. "Our Stella is true-blue."

And Sarah saw that with this remark a steely look came into

Stella's normally bland eyes. And vanished almost before Sarah could fix on it.

Before Sarah could consider whether to wait and have a brief talk with Stella, all the volunteers, Stella included, took off down the path. Then, several steps away, Christie turned back to Sarah. "We'll have to keep meeting," she called. "Even after Julia goes home. You're in our club now."

"Yeah," shouted David. "It's been real fun. A new face with all us golden oldies."

Guilt, guilt, Sarah told herself. Okay, she'd join the club. But she could see herself forever locked into an eleven-o'clock doughnut-and-coffee orgy. Summer in the hospital grounds, winter in the cafeteria. The three senior volunteers would grow older and white-haired and totter toward their graves, and weekly, or even daily, Sarah would join them, would age with them, moving from her late twenties—actually she was on the cusp of thirty—into middle age. All to soothe her conscience and prove honest intentions and that her heart was pure. Damnation! This is what having a relative like Grandmother Douglas did to you. She paused by a planting of rugosa roses now well into the rose-hip stage. Okay, back from this guilt-trip business and ponder about what, if anything, she had learned from the meeting.

For instance: Stella was not entirely happy about being the "our Stella" who was "true-blue," in David Bergman's words. And what was this about a "breakout"? Being "gung ho"? And the dog walking. Why did she push the subject away? Dog walking was an acceptable activity day or night. And having the dog with you was almost proof that she didn't go *into* the hospital.

And who was this Althea? Not a common name these days. "Ancient history," Stella had said. So maybe long ago something had happened to this Althea, but it would take days of searching obituaries and hospital records to find anything about the girl. The woman? The baby? Althea was not the child of Stella Dugan's but her niece. But she could hardly turn George and Mike loose on this one. They would blister her tail and hang her from one of the hospital windows. Or better, how about the direct ap-

proach? Just ask. Stella Dugan, if found alone, away from her co-
workers, might be willing to talk about Althea. Unless, of course,
the information was dangerous. But to whom? Her family? The
other volunteers?

Leaving the problem of Althea on a back burner for now,
Sarah wound her way on a circuitous media-free route to the
delivery entrance into the basement, past the cardiac rehab center (soon to be the scene of Julia's exertions), past the pathology
department, to the stairs, and puffing up three flights (she was
certainly out of shape), to SKU 25. Checked off by the bald-
headed guard, she pushed into the room.

"I've got a possible something to look into," Sarah announced.

Julia looked up from her chair. Bright-eyed for a change. "And
I have one for you. My first contribution to our plan. Something
I've remembered. That night when someone got that plastic tube
around my neck, well, I saw—"

Sarah forgot about Althea. "What?" she almost shouted.

"A watch. A wristwatch."

"Oh," said Sarah blankly. Then: "Don't most people wear
watches?"

"Yes, but men wear large clunky things with alarm systems
and a hundred buttons for deep sea diving and running mara-
thons."

"So do women," said Sarah.

"But women's watches are smaller. Men's are larger. I've
never seen a man with a small watch. It's something that hasn't
gone unisex."

"Women wear sports watches. Big ones."

"This was a small one," said Julia in a triumphant voice.
"Smaller and not a sport type. Small as in female."

Sarah hesitated, not wanting to throw cold water on this
statement. This would mean a watch inventory. By her? Or, more
probably, the police. But there was another objection. "You said
there wasn't much light in your room at night. You said you
couldn't see that well. Just shapes. And you told us the person
was in a gown and wore surgical gloves."

"Yes, yes," said Julia impatiently. "But there was just a little glint of light that made me see a watch. I just pulled that out of my memory box. I saw it just before that plastic tube went all the away around my neck. Before I blacked out."

"Gold?" asked Sarah. Gold wasn't so common, would be easier to track. Most of the medical people she had seen wore utility watches. Chrome or steel or some black material.

"Silver. Or stainless steel," said Julia. "But what matters is that it was worn by a female. Listen, Sarah. You find me a male with a little watch on his wrist and I'll shut up."

"So you're thinking this was a female who got herself onto the Cardiac ICU floor wearing one of those surgical outfits, with an ID tag around her neck, and no one would question her?"

"You've got it," said Julia.

"And either she sneaked to the floor wearing medical attire and got hold of you or . . ."

"Or she was already working on the floor," finished Julia.

"So now we're talking about a female with a silver watch who had a grudge against Dr. Philips. And his grandson. Or both. And against you for seeing too much."

"Right," said Julia. "A female who's got strong hands and can move fast."

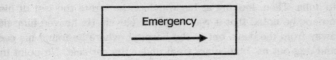

19

ALEX had spent the dawn hours of Sunday morning sleeping in one of the hospital "rest areas"—a euphemism for small, windowless slots with a cot on which exhausted residents and other staff physicians on call could crash. He had risen at six, showered, thrown on a fresh shirt, grabbed a hasty breakfast in the cafeteria, and made the rounds of his hospitalized patients, and said "hello" to Julia. Then, looking at his watch as he wrote the last of his orders, he noted that it was well past eleven. He heaved himself away from the desk, out of the hospital, where he found his car and dug out his binoculars from under the car seat. No point in losing the entire morning. He'd drive away from the hospital, leave the Bowmouth College campus behind, park somewhere and take a hike. Maybe climb into the Camden Hills, perhaps sighting a few warblers, a thrush or two, and, if lucky, see the northern hawk-owl reported on the radio's *Bird Alert*.

The only flaw in this scheme was the purposeful approach toward the physicians' parking lot of Mike Laaka. Mike looked like a fisherman who had just sighted a dorsal fin and was about to cast his harpoon. Alex slammed the door of the Jeep, ignored the beep that reminded him about his seat belt, turned on the ignition, and gunned the car forward.

Forward and directly at Mike Laaka who, having sighted his prey, had run between cars and now stood in his path, both arms outstretched.

Alex, furious, honked.

Mike leaped forward, seized the Jeep's door handle, opened it, and vaulted into the passenger seat.

"Sounding your horn in a hospital zone is disturbing the peace," he said. "Also, I could bring you in for threatening an officer of the law with a dangerous vehicle."

"Get out of my car," Alex snarled. "I'm leaving,"

"You're leaving in fifteen minutes. George's orders. A medical problem."

"That can't be answered by a hundred other doctors in the hospital? Come off it."

"You're one of the docs on the scene. Or some of the scenes. And you know too much to let you loose just now."

Alex heaved a sigh. Looked at his watch. It was already late and by midday any bird worth seeing would be in hiding.

Mike reached over and turned the ignition off. "I swear, just a few minutes. Strangulation has got George's interest."

And so it was that Alex found himself for the ninetieth time, he thought, confined in the first-floor dismal conference room that George Fitts and company now infested.

"Okay, George, why in hell are you ruining my morning?" said Alex, throwing himself into a chair.

George, at the table, looked up, nodded, waved Mike to another chair, and opened a file, produced a sheaf of papers which he passed over to Alex.

"Lists," George announced. "The people that we can verify who turned up near or at least two of the homicide scenes or the attempted homicide site—Mrs. Clancy's room. Not so many as you might think. The ER was packed with people the morning that Dr. Philips got his, but the attack on Mrs. Clancy and the murder of Florence Littlefield took place in a fairly restricted area—the Cardiac ICU corridor.

"What you mean is that the cast of characters who might have been in a killing mode isn't that big," said Mike. "But you're assuming it's the same guy all three times."

"Get to it, George," said Alex. "Let's go with one killer. For now, anyway. What do you want me to do?"

George pushed a sheet of paper at Alex. "Strangulation. What one of you doctors called blunt carotid artery injury. You've already told me that medical knowledge would be necessary to put together the potassium-chloride-and-insulin sequence. Now how about throttling?"

Alex scowled at the list, ran his finger down the paper and handed it back to George. "All of the above," he said. "Because anyone can strangle. A little muscle and a little know-how. A few paragraphs and illustrations in a crime encyclopedia can take care of it. With old Dr. Philips, the strangler wasn't dealing with a linebacker or a weight lifter. What he had was an almost ninety-year-old guy who had had a bad fall and was in no shape to resist."

"Summary," said George. "Strangling is simple."

"I didn't claim that," said Alex. "A knowledge of the human neck and the whereabouts of a carotid artery is useful. Let's say anyone over twelve who can find an anatomy book and has reasonable strength in his or her fingers and arms can pull it off. Question answered. So I'm off."

George ignored him. "Our list includes those who have enough medical background to handle the potassium-and-insulin sequence. And since you say almost anyone can strangle, here's what we've got: seven nurses, two physicians' assistants, four physicians—three residents—two attending, a respiratory technician, two lab people drawing blood, a technician fixing up the oxygen in one room."

"How about volunteer Stella Dugan? She was a nurse a long time ago," said Mike.

"She says she wasn't in the hospital that night," said George.

Claims she was walking a dog outside on the grounds. And so far, no one has said they saw her anywhere."

"How about Dave Bergman?" offered Mike. "He's been around the hospital so long, he probably has an MD. Says he was visiting his brother-in-law."

"I'm not forgetting him," said George. "He has an attitude problem, lost his temper here with me at least once."

"Okay," said Alex, rising. "That's it. I'm off. Start squeezing the medical folk."

At which the telephone rang.

Mike reached over and grabbed it, beating George's reaching hand by half a second. He listened. Then: "Holy shit."

Then: "Is she sure?"

George leaned forward and Alex sat down again.

"Hell," said Mike. "She may have been completely off the rails. Talk about hallucinations. Jesus Christ."

Another pause. Then: "Okay, okay. We'll look into it." Mike hung up and grinned. "Listen to this," he said, obviously enjoying beating George to a slice of news. "That was Sarah from Julia Clancy's room. Julia says she remembers seeing the watch on one of the hands that was trying to strangle her."

George frowned. "Not earth-shaking. Everyone wears a watch. And her vision was probably compromised by drugs."

"Maybe yes, maybe not," said Mike. "But Julia says it was small. Female-type watch. Silver metal, or stainless or chrome. That ought to clean a few suspects off the plate."

George's frown deepened into a scowl. "I'm not cleaning any-one off. Not yet. You, Alex, go with Mike and check this out with Mrs. Clancy. And find out if she's remembered anything else. Which I hope she hasn't."

"Hell, George," said Mike, "be grateful for once. It cuts your damn list in half. Or in thirds. I'm going to spend the day looking at ladies' wrists."

Julia, sitting in her chair, Sarah next to her, stuck to her story. Mike and Alex questioned her gently, both trying not to air the hallucination theory again. The light was adequate, she repeated, the size and the gleam of the silver watch was noticeable. She had been so frightened at the time that this detail had gotten shoved into the back of her mind. Now in tranquillity—semi-tranquillity—she remembered. "Like Wordsworth," she added. "The old goat held great store in remembering things in tranquillity. Yes, I know," she said, seeing Sarah, Mike, and Alex staring at her, "you all think I'm a horse-loving yahoo who can't read anything but a veterinary manual. But I read Wordsworth in school and if you want, I can recite that very boring poem about daffodils. The man bleating about wandering like a cloud. Pure mush. Wordsworth was always wallowing in the past."

Having disposed of one of Britain's major poets, Julia leaned back in her chair. "I'm going home soon, so I'll be rid of the lot of you. I'm ready for reentry. To the world. The farm. My job. But I am going to try and make peace with Florence Littlefield getting killed instead of me and the whole bed-switch affair."

"Don't worry about making peace," interrupted Alex, "You'll probably be named in sister Emma's lawsuit. Making peace may equal handing over cash."

Julia grimaced and then drew herself up as far as was possible for a short person encumbered with lines and tubes. "I'll be in touch. Sarah and I have a little program going. We'd decided that you police people were stumbling around and maybe we could help out with the personal touch. Have friendly talks. Ask questions. Be informal, not threatening. Your sergeant, George Fitts, would scare the tits off a cow. You know women are more sensitive in finding out things that aren't just black and white."

"Aunt Julia!" exclaimed Sarah, horrified. "You aren't going to tell them, are you? That was just between us. We weren't going to talk about it." She turned to the two men. "We were just going to look around. Without bothering George—or you, Mike. We'd get to know people, some of the volunteers, nurses, the aides. Even a stray doctor or two. Not to *do* anything."

"Right," said Alex, glaring at his wife.

"Well, since I'm telling you about the watch, it seems like a good idea to tell you about this little plan," said Julia. "Now don't start foaming at the mouth, you two. Sarah and I have people skills, so we'll be a real asset. I'm going home, so I'll have to work long distance. I may even remember something else, so I'm not turning in my badge."

Mike, who had been perching on the narrow windowsill of the room, stood up and leaned over Julia. "Hear this. And get it clear. We, the police, are going to have a deputy stationed at High Hope Farm until this case is settled. And we expect you to co-operate. You can spend the next weeks recovering your strength. And since we'll need to know who comes and goes to your farm, we'll need a list of the usual people who come for lessons and make deliveries. Horse owners, meter readers, the feed people, the blacksmith—"

"I won't have any spy or deputy hanging around my farm," said Julia. "And the word is farrier, not blacksmith."

"You will have," said Mike, glaring at her, "a deputy, like it or not, even if I have to chain him to your barn door. A policeman watching the place may help you and your blessed horses and Patrick and the other barn people, and the whole damn shooting match stay safe and sound. Now, second: No meddling at long distance. Keep your sticky fingers out of this investigation, behave yourself, get well, obey orders, or else. And, goddammit, that goes for you, Sarah. You snoozed seven feet away from a murder scene, so you're on the endangered list. Don't you go running off without letting our security people know where you're going. And when. I mean it, George means it, and if either of you get out of line, I'd be for locking you in some miserable little cell as a material and noncooperative witnesses."

"Amen and right on," said Alex, nodding approval.

"Well, now, Mike," said Julia, "you have quite frightened me. That was quite a speech."

"And a bloody insulting one," said Sarah. "The next time Aunt Julia remembers a watch on someone's wrist, I hope she'll keep that fact to herself. No more sharing. So you police types and you, too, Alex, can go fish. Or go to hell. Whichever. Aunt Julia, we will be in touch. But privately. No more chatting up these two creeps. Damn them both." And Sarah, glowering, jumped up from her chair and strode from the room.

"Hell," said Julia, again proving that she read more than equine manuals, "hath no fury like a woman scorned. You two were so patronizing that I'm surprised she didn't throw a bedpan at you."

Alex rose, leaned over and kissed Julia soundly on the cheek. "We always like to see our patients showing grit. It's a sign of recuperation. I'll drive you home tomorrow if you're really being discharged."

"Not if, when. And I'm having Patrick pick me up. A man I can rely on. An honest, straightforward man."

"But it won't be good-bye to the Mary Starbox Memorial," said Alex. "There's cardiac rehab in your future. We want Julia Clancy to be one hundred percent."

"I pity the nurses in the cardiac rehab room," muttered Mike.

"I heard that," said Julia. "And I agree. Let me at them."

"What's next for you, Mike?" said Alex, as the two men reached the front lobby. "An inventory of the wristwatches of every female in the hospital?"

"An inventory of the watches of the ladies who are on our list, anyway," said Mike. "Now I'm going to have to find a deputy—make that three deputies—who can manage Julia Clancy. Watching a facility like High Hope Farm will be a big job even with a cooperative owner. Which Julia ain't."

"Let's hope the murderer will stick to the hospital scene or just relax, since the two Philips men are dead and Julia will be out of the area."

"But Julia's still up for grabs—make that strangulation—whether she's out of the area or not. Particularly if she keeps remembering stuff like wristwatches. We'll have to stick to her like duct tape."

The two men parted and Alex headed for his car. He briefly considered finding Sarah and trying to make peace. But when

Sarah was good and mad—as she was now—she was likely to stay that way for a while. He would bide his time and opt for bird-watching. Woods, hills, quiet streams, peaceful ponds. Preferably with no humans in sight.

Sarah, having stormed out of Julia's room, found herself at something of a loss. She stuck her head in George's situation room and told a startled uniformed state policeman that she, Sarah Deane, complying with orders concerning her whereabouts, was going shopping. Which, she thought, was as good a cover as anything. But her planned morning occupation—sleuthing—had been disrupted, or put on temporary hold, her cover blown by Julia. So what now?

Well, she could take that swim. Get Patsy and take a drive. And think. There were a few uneasy fragments rattling around in her head. Stella-the-Mouse, for instance. Hadn't the mouse, despite being labeled Ms. Perfecta, seemed a nervous mouse? No real eye contact. Somewhat defensive about walking the dog. Moving away from the Althea story, whatever that was. A sad story, anyway. And when she was praised as being helpful, she turned frosty. Then there were what David Bergman called Stella's "breakouts." Did he mean psychotic fits or a case of hives? And then there was that unnerving little giggle.

What else didn't ring the right bell? How about that big horse of Clare Mitchner's uncle that she called Popcorn? A Belgian. Did Belgians come in all colors, including white? She'd have to ask Aunt Julia, but "Popcorn" suggested white. But then the name was probably a child's choice and so not necessarily logical. *I love popcorn. I love the horse. I will call the horse Popcorn.* After all, she, Sarah, had once had a male cat called Susie. Here Sarah found that without noticing it she had reached the edge of the visitors' parking lot. Where had she left her car, anyway? She walked a circle around a black Chevy pickup and a blue Dodge van, and two Explorer beasts while her mind kept busy trying to remember any oddities. How about that business of Christie Rivers taking her horse away from Julia's High Hope Farm? Did she leave in a real snit? Was there some unspoken grudge connected to Julia? Could it mean anything, or was it just another bit of flotsam? So what about . . .

Speculation stopped dead. A car, a sleek silver-gray car, peeled off around the lines of orange pylons separating the staff parking lot from the visitors' lot, and then squealed into a hard left, missing an entering blue sedan by inches, and whirled down the drive toward the outer gates.

And this time Sarah saw the driver. Knew her. Broke into a run, wrenched the door of her Subaru open, flung her waist pack on the seat, jammed the ignition key in place and gunned after the silver car. Out of the visitors' parking lot, past the ambulance entrances, narrowly missing the approaching Cushing Rescue Squad vehicle, and then braked at the hospital-gate entrance. Of course she braked. Who would be such a damn fool as to shoot out onto the main highway without a pause?

Answer: Only the driver of a silver car. The driver being that pillar of conformity, Stella-the-Mouse. Make that Stella-the-Maniac. Stella working off some inner rage? The silver car—Sarah couldn't identify the make—too many silver cars in the world—escaped between an oncoming nursing-home bus and a Federal Express truck and made tracks for Camden.

The town of Bowmouth, site of the Mary Starbox Memorial Hospital and Bowmouth College, lay between the small towns of Union and Appleton. The geography of this area was such that the route to Camden involved some serious down and up and hotdog driving. And Sarah, after finally ducking into traffic and following at a distance, began to have serious qualms. Obviously Stella was trying to kill herself or someone else in the bargain. But why should she, Sarah, make it a party? But just as she was about to ease her old Subaru into a more sensible speed, the silver car slowed and at the comparatively sedate pace of sixty miles an hour shot down Route 105, leaving small lakeside cottages and Lake Megunticook on her left. Then, slowing again to a modest fifty, it braked, took a hard left onto Molyneaux Road, and wiggled north onto Route 52, coming around the other side of Lake Megunticook and picked up speed.

Where were the police, Sarah wondered, when you needed them? Of course, she'd probably be the one nailed. And it was August, tourist time in Maine. So where were the tourists to slow up this mad woman? But then a tan pickup inserted itself in front of the silver car, the pace slowed—not even a raving maniac would try to speed or pass on such a curving road—and Sarah settled down to dogging a blue sedan that had slid immediately behind the silver car, and as they settled to a moderate pace, even had a spare moment to glance over at the bare cliffs and high rises of Mount Megunticook and Cameron Mountain.

And to take several spare moments to consider the object of her pursuit. Stella-the-Mouse. Was Stella perhaps the victim of some sort of apoplectic fit that caused her from time to time to charge about the county like a ballistic missile? Was this what David had meant by having "breakouts?" Perhaps she was one of those unfortunates with dual personalities or even with triple, quadruple personalities. "The Three Faces of Stella." Stella-the-Mouse, Stella the NASCAR Driver. Stella the Strangler, Stella the Syringe Killer? So how about Stella the Slugger—of Dr. Jonathan Philips? But somehow this last scenario didn't work. Hadn't Alex told her that he was knocked on the head by something heavy? But Stella didn't look athletic. Slugging a man twice her height seemed unlikely. And besides, was Stella even the driver of those earlier silver cars that had scared the daylights out of her? How many homicidal silver-car drivers were there around midcoast Maine, anyway? Maybe for Stella, today was a one-of-a-kind spasm of road rage.

From this speculation, Sarah's attention was diverted to the tan pickup keeping straight at the corner of the Youngstown Road while Stella, jerking her car right on Route 173, shot like an exploding firecracker toward Lincolnville Beach.

Sarah, now hungry, had a moment's pang at the sight of the Youngstown Inn "Fine Dining and Lodging," and then, her vision confused by the spots of sunlight and shadows cast by overhanging oaks and maples, concentrated on keeping sight of Stella as she wheeled and spun along the curving road, And then, suddenly, the road bent down, the Atlantic Ocean floated into sight.

Penobscot Bay, Route 1, the Isleboro Ferry, Lincolnville Beach.

Sarah saw Stella insert her car into a small gap of the north-bound Route 1 traffic, turn left, pass Chez Michel Restaurant on her left, the Lobster Pound Restaurant on her right, then take the next sharp right into a narrow parking lot by the Whales Tooth Pub, a small brick-sided building that bordered Lincolnville Beach.

Sarah followed and slipped her car into an open slot between a delivery truck and a bulky Chevy Tahoe—Sarah had belatedly started to pay attention to the makes of cars. But Stella had driven toward the back of the building; Sarah could see into an extended parking lot beyond the pub. Sarah's pursuit had never been part of a real plan; she had simply obeyed an overwhelming urge, one fueled by a mix of temper and curiosity, to follow the silver car wherever it went. But now that she had Stella more or less cornered, what next? Sarah stared at the expanse of placid ocean and tried to think. And then it hit her like the smack of a hand. Lincolnville! The body of Dr. Jonathan Philips had been pulled in from the water off the ferry pier. Just off Lincolnville Beach. Was this mad race a return to the scene? Scene of the crime? Something drawing the murderer? Something neglected? An object lost, left, then suddenly recalled?

Sarah's throat went suddenly dry.

WHALES TOOTH
PUB

20

JUDGING from the visible automobile tops in the back parking lot, the Whales Tooth Pub must be a popular restaurant. But Sarah couldn't just turn up at Stella's side and exclaim, "What a coincidence! Hey, how about lunch?" Instead, she lifted her head and studied the front entrance to the pub. No Stella. She waited. No Stella. Was there another back entrance to the place near the back parking lot?—this assuming that Stella had arrived with the idea of lunch.

Sarah fumbled about in the car and found a possible disguise: a navy-blue Red Sox baseball cap she had borrowed from Alex a few weeks ago when she was taking Patsy for a hike. Pulling this object well over her eyes—easy, it was too big—she climbed cautiously out of the Subaru, and keeping next to a line of bushes, walked to the end of the building and to the opening of the auxiliary parking lot. Yes, there was a back entrance, as well as several canvas-shaded eating decks partly hidden behind a neatly clipped evergreen hedge. And there was the silver car parked at the end of three cars. But no Stella sitting at a table. But maybe Stella liked to eat inside despite the beauty of the day. Maybe she had to go to the ladies' room. Make a telephone call. Then order lunch. Sarah, keeping her head down, the cap pulled forward, walked along the edge of the hedge. And waited. Nothing. Throwing caution aside, she walked up to the back door and peered inside the small dining room. No Stella. Then she walked back to the parking lot and saw the silver car was empty, and was, she noted, a Chevy Malibu of fairly recent vintage—Sarah was no better on the age of a car than she had been of the make.

Then up ahead, just past three visitors, there was Stella, still wearing her blue hospital smock. She was walking along on a narrow stony path that bordered the highest point of the beach—a beach made up of rounded rocks. Then Stella stopped for a second, looked around, appeared to notice that the three people trailing her had paused behind her and all were pointing across the bay at a schooner under full sail. Stella, now moving more energetically, stepped down the path toward a grove of alders, brush, and white pines and an enormous fallen tree trunk. More interesting than the scenery, to Sarah, was the fact that Stella carried what appeared to be an elongated bag, the sort that might include a folding beach umbrella. This item was a green affair with a barely visible motif of yellow and red fishes, or flowers.

Was Stella planning a quick dip before lunch, wearing her volunteer's uniform? Unlikely, unless she'd worn her bathing suit under it. And why Lincolnville, when there were ponds and lakes in great abundance near the hospital? In her fit of rage, had she needed salt water? And why wasn't she still on volunteer duty; it was only just past one-thirty and the three friends usually stayed past four. Sarah, involved in these questions, found that she herself had walked far enough along the path so that she had closed in on the three people watching the schooner. They, two women and a man in their retirement years, pointed, exclaimed, a camera was put forward, a pair of binoculars raised. And then they saw Sarah.

"Excuse me," said the first woman, a stout person in tight apricot-colored shorts and a T-shirt that stretched across a bosom the size of a watermelon. "Excuse me, but what kind of boat is that out there, do you know? The big one with all those sails.

We're just visitors. From Kentucky," she added, as if to explain the group's lack of nautical know-how.

Sarah, watching Stella moving away down the beach, put on a big smile, said that they were watching a schooner, and please excuse her but she thought she saw a friend up ahead.

"Wait, young lady," said the man. "Please, just a minute. Your friend won't go away, because it doesn't look like there's anyplace to go. Now just what *is* a schooner? Are schooners the ones with a lot of sails? Or is it the masts?"

Out of the corner of her eye Sarah saw Stella, now well down the beach, pause and seem to scan the beach ahead of her. Okay, maybe staying with these people was as good a way as any to remain hidden.

"A schooner," Sarah began, "has more than one mast." That seemed safe. Sarah was no student of ship classifications, but she thought she knew a schooner when she saw one.

"But not like one of those ships they showed in those old *Mutiny on the Bounty* movies?" said the lady in the shorts.

Sarah, watching Stella from the side of her eyes, who was now hovering at the water's edge, tried to remember Captain Bligh's vessel as shown on the silver screen. "That was a square-rigged ship, I think," she said. "You know, square sails. Other sails go sidewise—fore and aft, I mean." That, she thought, gave the right nautical flavor. "Marlon Brando was Fletcher Christian," she added. Sarah was a fan of classic movies and was up on the actors and the ships on which they sailed.

"That man!" said the woman with an expression of dislike.

"You're right about the sails," said the man. "And those old battleships had square sails like the ones at the Battle of Trafalgar Bay. Or the *Constitution*. Now are there any of those around Maine?"

But Sarah was gone. Stella had suddenly made a move and was now scuttling up the beach toward the rise of rocks. Ignoring the repeated calls from the Kentucky people, baseball cap pulled down, Sarah followed, making her way awkwardly now, the path having disappeared, so that walking was a matter of navigating over small loose boulders. But ahead Stella was having an even worse time. She tripped over the rocks, lost her balance, righted herself, and struggled forward. By now she was fairly past the first alder bushes and white pines, so Sarah, following, was able to slip into their shade. To keep watch.

Which she did. With amazement.

Because Stella *was* going swimming. Or anyway into the water. She had leaned against the trunk of the dead tree, pulled off her volunteer smock revealing a flowered blouse. The smock she now hung across one of the tree's limbs. Next, not a bathing suit coming out of hiding, merely a rolling up of the cotton trousers above plump knees. Then, after a quick look over her shoulder, Stella, her white pocketbook strap hanging around her neck, holding the beach-umbrella bag under one arm, still in her hospital white rubber-soled shoes, began picking her way across the stones to the water, a task impossible if she had tried to do it barefoot. Without hesitating, she waded into the water. Ankle, calf, knee, above the knee, the gray slacks turning dark with the water. Now she was waist-deep, small waves lapping almost under her arms. She looked around again. Paused. Then, reaching into the umbrella bag, fiddled with a fastening, turned her back, bent down, and did something. Sarah, squinting, couldn't see what. Perhaps she had emptied an unknown object into the water. Perhaps she hadn't. Or, since she had for the last hour been showing definite signs of insanity, perhaps she had merely wanted to cool off.

But now Stella straightened, turned, came stumbling out of the water and, dripping wet, climbed up to the beach top, over the scrubby ground to the dead tree. Paused, pulled on her smock, and with pocketbook and umbrella bag flapping behind, headed back for the parking lot.

Sarah, still in hiding, faced several choices. Go after the object—if there had been truly an object—that might have been slipped into the water? But could anything be found out in what was at least three feet of water? Sarah hadn't marked the exact place—an impossibility, really—and searching in armpit-deep murky seawater might take the rest of the afternoon, by which Stella would be long gone. Call Alex and tell him what she had just witnessed? But Alex was probably off bird-watching, and since not on call would have no cell phone. Or get hold of the police? Mike? No way. Not after that recent scene in Aunt Julia's room. Besides, what would she say? *I saw one of the hospital volunteers wade into the ocean and maybe dump something. Or maybe not.* A likely story. Maybe she should follow Stella or, to be sensible, she just go home and think it through.

You stupid fool, don't just stand there, she ordered herself. Of all the dubious options, the one suggesting to follow Stella seemed the most promising. Or the line of least resistance. She broke into a run, difficult on the narrow path, and by the time she reached the back parking lot she was just in time to see the silver Chevy slide out to the entrance and turn left toward Camden.

By sheer luck, a fender bender had occurred on the road opposite Chez Michel, all cars were being held up by a policeman, so that Sarah saw with relief that she was now only five cars behind Stella. She pulled the gear into neutral, and as she did, an abdominal spasm reminded her about her lack of lunch. For two cents she'd pull out of line and hit the Lobster Pound Restaurant for a quick sandwich. And to hell with Stella.

But now the police had opened a route for the stacked-up cars and they were off. Off at a peaceful, in fact, too slow a speed, the line of cars proceeded south on Route 1, Stella not trying to pass anyone, not revving her engine. Stella the Peaceful. Stella the Fulfilled One. But Stella was soaking wet, probably sticking to her seat cushion, would be going home to dry off, wouldn't she? Then back to the confines of the Mary Starbox Memorial to rejoin her volunteer fellows.

But no. Sarah couldn't believe it. Stella was going up Mount Battie. What the hell. If Stella had ever had a plan about today's exercise—which Sarah doubted—this turn onto the Mount Battie Auto Road defied reason. Stella, overcome by a sudden urge to view Camden Harbor from the top of Mount Battie, was going to spend $2.50 for the privilege of driving up the mountain road to view the distant harbor? All this while her clothes were soaked with sticky seawater.

Sarah, paying the entrance fee, muttering to herself, fell in line three cars behind Stella and proceeded at a snail's pace to drive up the curving mountain road.

Arriving at the top, she found a throng of visitors milling about, some heading for the round stone tower, some lining up to spend a quarter in the Tower Optical Company machines to bring the Camden Harbor view closer. And Stella? There she was, wet slacks clinging to her rump and thighs, clutching her white purse and the umbrella bag, following a foursome of visitors down a smooth series of undulating rocks to the lip of a serious drop into space.

No question, Sarah decided. Stella was insane. Mad as the March Hare. Call it what you liked—schizophrenia, multiple-personality disorder, bipolar something—she needed professional help. But then Sarah, who was sheltering behind one of the telescopes, had a horrible thought. Was Stella in some sort of suicidal depression? About to fling herself off into space, or at least down the mountainside in some final convulsion of despair? Wading into the water at Lincolnville Beach might have simply been a failed suicide attempt, so the mountain route—even on a small mountain like Mount Battie—might be easier. But the umbrella bag? Some sort of family relic, or a bag of evidence Stella would take with her? Because surely Stella might now fit the role of a killer on the loose, one ravaged by guilt and mental upheaval.

Sarah moved fast, pushing past a group of Cub Scouts, an Asian couple with binoculars, and began the descent down the rounded boulders. She had to be careful not to frighten Stella into jumping, so she must sneak up, appear silently behind her, grab her, and haul her away from the edge.

But Stella, instead of moving directly toward the lip of the last line of rocks, began a long sideways maneuver away from the visitor groups and toward a line of underbrush and evergreens. Then stopped, took hold of the umbrella bag with its red and yellow fish designs, turned it carefully inside-out, revealing a dull green interior, wadded it up, stepped gingerly down the rock edge and hurled it into space. Where it floated down, a thin green rag twisting in the slight breeze, and then vanishing into the tops of spruce trees. Stella turned, settled her purse back on her shoulder, and looking neither left nor right, strode back toward the two viewing telescopes and the parking area, her face lit with what Sarah could only say was an expression of happy fulfillment.

Mike Laaka hadn't really meant to spend the day making covert looks at the wrists of female staff members and miscellaneous employees of the hospital. But George Fitts, probably thinking this was a good way to advance the investigation a few millimeters and get the contentious deputy off his back for a short while, ordered him forth.

"Here's the list of the women who turned up or around at least two of the three murder sites or were on the floor when Mrs. Clancy was attacked. Not so many, as I keep hammering into your head, made every scene. Take the list of the men who turned up with you just to be safe and just glance at their watches. I agree that most men wouldn't be caught dead with a female wristwatch."

"The cross-dressers would."

"Don't annoy me. Cross-dressers go beyond wristwatches. Clothes, shoes, the works."

"So some male cross-dresser forgot to take off the watch. He stripped off the bra and the makeup but forgot the watch."

"Christ Almighty!" shouted George, who almost never swore or shouted. He had spent his career making himself into as low-key a presence as possible and still be alive. Today, as usual, he presented a completely blah look: trim and tidy wearing gray pants and gray cotton shirt that, while not exactly a uniform, ominously suggested it. Mike by contrast was Mr. Casual: jeans, black T-shirt with a Portland Sea Dogs logo splashed across his chest.

"Forget cross-dresser," said George, regaining his composure.

But Mike was off on another tack. "Okay, about this list you've given me. You can finger the hospital guys, okay. But what

243

about Lincolnville? Jonathan being slugged on the head some-where in Lincolnville. That didn't need medical expertise. Any goon can slam someone on the head with a piece of metal. Are you trying to tell me that you've got names of everyone who turned up at Lincolnville on the night he was killed? Come on, George. Hell, that's half the tourists coming to Maine. Not count-ing all the people working in the restaurants and offshore. Fish-ermen, pleasure boats. Passengers climbing back and forth off the Islesboro Ferry. Jeezus, you've got a mob there."

George pointed his ballpoint at Mike and from his expression Mike could tell that the sergeant very much wanted a small mis-sile to shoot out from it. Nail him right between the eyes. Splatter his brains on the floor.

"Listen for once in your life, Mike Laaka," said George in a voice that seemed to Mike to be emanating from a grinding ma-chine. "Simmer down. I'm not talking Lincolnville. That's another whole can of worms. Now we're looking at those people known to be around in the hospital and in the parking lot the night Jon-athan Philips disappeared. People like Clare Mitchner, who says he climbed in and then out of her car. And Carmen Wilson, who saw him walk out into the parking lot. So check out the watches and don't think that this is a great chance to go schmoozing with every female you run into. Just glance at her wrist or ask the time and move on."

"Like they're going to believe I want the time. Big clocks in every corridor. They'll probably think I'm checking their bustline by asking them to lift a hand. Though," Mike added thoughtfully, "if it's that Clare Mitchner, I don't mind. She's sort of my type. Cute, but not too cute. Tough, too, I'd say."

"Get out of here," said George, raising his pen again. "No funny stuff with the staff. We're under heavy pressure to clean the case up, nail someone, and clear out. I've heard that Emma Littlefield's lawyer is going to file suit. That's got the management pretty jumpy. And don't come back until about four. With some-thing useful to tell me."

As the first part of his research Mike decided to check out the general female population. The first three female hospital workers Mike met in the halls between Admitting and the pharmacy wore watches of modest dimensions: one gold, two silver or metal. Mike asked the time of each and each time a wrist was raised and the time given. Mike was a known quantity at the hospital, so few questions were raised at his inquiry, particularly as he had removed his own watch and flourished his bare wrist. The next woman, a five-foot respiratory therapist named Maud—an old acquaintance—wore a wristwatch the size of a manhole cover.

Maud, rather than hoisting her burdened wrist, cocked her head at the wall clock fixed above a sign pointing to the X-ray department. "You can read, can't you, Mike? Or are you picking me up?"

Mike, stepping aside this possibility, thanked Maud, dutifully looked at the wall clock, and then pointed to Maud's wrist. "My God, you'll end up with tendonitis or tennis elbow with that thing."

"No time for chat, I'm in a hurry," said Maud, "but that watch was my dad's. Marine Corps. Sentiment, and besides it works, every button and knob works. I suppose you're doing some hamhanded sleuthing about watches and mine doesn't fit the picture. Right?"

Mike began to explain that he was just curious, but Maud waved him away. "Go to it. But for the record, I'm the only woman in the whole damn place that wears a man's watch as far as I know. Put that in your little black book."

At which Maud departed down the hall and Mike, feeling that he had come out as low man in the encounter, pushed on. Enough random questioning, now to track down the females on George's list, some of whom, he supposed wearily, were off duty, on vacation, or otherwise out of reach. It was going to be a long day.

This proved an accurate guess, and Mike, feeling ill-used and hungry, reported to George at the required hour of four that of the ones on the list whose wristwatches he was able to get sight of, he could report that Carmen Wilson, secretary to the late Dr. Jonathan Philips (it had turned out that she had been delivering legal forms to the ER the day of old Dr. Philip's strangling), wore an expensive-looking silver watch with little diamonds. Christie Rivers, volunteer, and Clare Mitchner, RN, both wore cheaper stainless-steel models, one with a cloth band, the other with a chain link. And so did Dr. Margie Soldier, pathologist (she, too, like Carmen Wilson, apparently had been in the area during the ER strangling, besides reporting that six days later, she actually had talked in the hospital corridor with Dr. Jonathan Philips minutes before he headed out to the parking lot).

"We didn't have Dr. Soldier down for those two scenes," said George with irritation. "People just don't come forward. But you'd think a staff member would know better."

"You think she wants business, so she creates her own bodies," said Mike.

George returned to his notebook without rising to the bait. "As far as I can see among those around for at least two murder events, you've missed Nurse Hannah Finch.

"The one who wears those jackets with birds all over them?"

"I wouldn't know," said George. "Those details are for you to write up."

"Couldn't find her. She works per diem. All over the place. Wherever they need someone."

George underlined something in his notebook. Then: "How about Stella Dugan, the volunteer?"

"Left early. Before noon. But I'll check around again."

"And Christie Rivers? Where was she today?"

"Went home early with a headache."

"Make a call at her house."

"And ask her what time it is?"

"Think up an excuse. It's something you're good at. Get her into a little conversation and look at her wrist."

"Wrists are so sexy."

"Go away," said George.

"Then there's Sarah Deane. She'd hate to be left out," said Mike.

"Never mind Sarah. Although," he added grimly, "it would almost be a relief to find she'd gone homicidal and we could lock her up."

246

"George, I think this case is really getting to you," said Mike. "Sarah's been pretty harmless so far, but she and Julia have plans. I gave Julia and Sarah hell about sticking their snoots into the investigation, but who knows if it took. Made Sarah plenty mad, anyway. Alex backed me up and she went charging off in a real temper."

George rose from his desk, walked to the door, opened it, and pointed. "Find out where Stella Dugan is. And if Christie Rivers is really home with a headache. I'm sending for Dave Bergman to see if he knows why the two women didn't turn up today."

Sarah, trailing Stella Dugan down the winding road from Mount Battie, hung back at the entrance to let two more cars come between the Chevy Malibu and herself, and then followed her prey, who was now driving at an entirely legal speed limit. No more Stella the Speed Ball. It was back to Stella the Compliant, Stella Good Girl. And back to Bowmouth, Route 52, Lake Megunticook again, past the Youngstown Inn—again Sarah suffered a wave of hunger. And there was Stella turning down shady Oak Street in Bowmouth and pulling into a small cedar-shingled house that on its garden end faced the Mary Starbox Hospital grounds.

Sarah drove past. One block. Pulled over to the curb. Give up, go home, make a sandwich, and chalk it up to a different sort of afternoon? No, damn it. It was time for a face-to-face. Turn around, stop at the house, and tell Stella she had happened to see her turn in and thought it might be nice to say hello.

Yeah, sure.

Stella, if she had been at least half-awake, must have spotted her somewhere along the route.

Except hadn't Stella been so obviously a slave to her passionate driving and to her work—work that apparently involved wading into the ocean up to her armpits in Lincolnville and then tossing umbrella covers off Mount Battie—that any follower, even a familiar one, might have been missed?

Sarah could only hope.

She turned the Subaru around and pulled into Stella's driveway.

Stella, her wet clothes clinging to her body, stood beside the garage door reaching for the handle. She turned and without evidence of surprise waved. Then walked over to Sarah's car window.

"Sarah. I thought that was you. Back there a little ways."

Back where a little ways? thought Sarah. Lincolnville or Oak Street?

"Just as I drove into Bowmouth and turned and I said, 'Why, there's Sarah Deane.' Now why don't you come in. Iced tea. And I have brownies. I baked them last night."

And Sarah lost it. She had meant to say something like, "Brownies, iced tea? Great. I'd love something."

Instead she opened her mouth and blurted out a question that must have been seething somewhere in the murkiest corner of her brain.

"Stella. Who is Althea? The one you didn't want to talk about. Your niece."

Stella's mouth opened. And closed.

And Sarah, unable to stop herself. "You know. Back at the hospital. When we were at the picnic table."

Like a shade being pulled down a window, a shadow fell over Stella's face. Her eyes grew large and she stared at Sarah, as if suddenly presented with a ghost.

Camden Hills State Park

Mt Battie

Campers/Registration ⇨

⇦ Auto Road

21

NO one spoke. Clock time halted. Sarah, in horror at what had come out of her mouth, stared at Stella. And Stella stared at Sarah and then closed her eyes.

They both came to at the same second.

Sarah, shaking her head: "No, I didn't mean that. I meant to say . . ." What *had* she meant to say? That she'd love tea and a brownie?

Stella: "It's all right. I mean, most people know about Althea. It was just so sad."

And Sarah, sanity returning, shook her head. "Never mind about tea. Please. You're dripping wet. Your clothes are soaked. You'd better change."

Stella looked down at herself, as if surprised by the news. "Wet?" she said, puzzled. Then: "Oh, yes. I guess I am. I went swimming. It was so hot."

Sarah nodded understandingly, although the day, breezy and bright, had not been overly warm.

"At Lincolnville," said Stella. "You know, the beach."

"I never swim there," said Sarah, a true statement certainly.

"Lake Megunticook is so busy," persisted Stella. "Besides, I love the ocean. The salt water. It's so good for you."

"I suppose it is," said Sarah, thinking of the murky seaweed-covered cove.

"Then it was a beautiful day, so I just had to drive up Mount Battie."

"What a good idea," said Sarah, feeling that every response she made topped the previous one for sheer inanity.

"You know, Edna Saint Vincent Millay. 'All I could see from where I stood was three long mountains and a wood.' Then Edna turns around and sees islands and goes on about the sky. On and on."

"She certainly does go on," said Sarah. And to herself: *what a stupid conversation.* But of course it wasn't a conversation. The two were doing a slow verbal tap dance around a dangerous gaping hole. And it was time for Sarah to put up or shut up and go home. She hesitated, saw that Stella had finished talking. Stella, who now seemed calm and entirely rational, was waiting. She's expecting it, Sarah told herself.

"Althea?" said Sarah. "Tell me about Althea."

Stella's face began to crinkle, her mouth to pucker. "Come on in and have that tea and I'll tell you just a little about it. Though why do you want to know about another miserable thing that went on in the hospital?" She hesitated, her eyes narrowing. "You're not here because the police, that dreadful Sergeant Fitts, sent you?"

Here at least Sarah could tell the truth. "No way. The police didn't send me. No one from the hospital sent me. I'm just here because—" What Sarah wanted to say was *I followed you because you were driving like a lunatic and acting like a murderer*; instead she rummaged around and came up with something approaching accuracy. "Because I'm mixed up, along with Aunt Julia, with the attacks at the hospital, and we think we should try and find out everything we can about what awful things happened before."

Stella looked wary. Frowned. Shifted her feet in their wet squelching sneakers. She looked like nothing more than a plump rag doll that had been left out in a rainstorm.

For Sarah, revulsion hit home. Get out of here, she ordered herself. Stop playing games with this poor woman. Leave her to George Fitts. No, not George; Mike, he's kinder. Or leave her to a good psychiatrist, someone she probably needs badly. And go mind your own business.

But it was too late. Stella was pointing toward the house. Ready to usher her in. Ready perhaps to talk.

They went into the house; Stella changed into dry clothes. Brewed tea in a china pot shaped like a thatched cottage, cut brownies into small squares, each with a walnut imbedded on its top, and circled them neatly on a plate with a floral design.

During these domestic moments, Sarah found herself studying the kitchen. It was the sort of room she might have guessed Stella—in her mouse aspect—might have. A china clock with the cow jumping over the moon as part of its center hung on one wall. Flowered ruffled curtains framed the two windows, magnets in the shapes of fruit decorated the refrigerator, and along one wall by the little kitchen table hung a series of cut-out wooden objects that are routinely found in Maine houses: a lighthouse, a sailboat, a moose, a seagull. On the floor a braided rug. Not the kitchen of someone overcome at times with killer rage, periodically out of her mind.

But Stella had a dog.

Where was it? No barking had sounded when she had pulled into the drive. But Stella was walking—she claimed—her dog on the hospital grounds the night Florence Littlefield was killed. But, here in the kitchen at least, there was no sign of a dog. No water bowl with a rubber mat under it. No leash hanging by the back door, along with that raincoat and the camera case. But perhaps the dog was confined elsewhere—in the hall, down in the cellar, in a doghouse out in the fenced yard. Sarah, the dog lover, asked.

But Stella, now pouring out the tea, frowned. "Dog?" she said, puzzled. Then, as if recollecting something in the dim past, added, "Oh yes. The dog. At the vets'. An infection. His ear. All red and funny-looking."

Sarah made sympathetic noises, explained that she, Sarah,

had a wonderful stray Irish Wolfhound named Patsy, and asked what kind of dog was Stella's.

Stella hesitated. Then told Sarah that the dog was a no-breed. One of those mixed-up sorts. Not too large, a sort of a terrier. You know the kind.

Yes, Sarah knew the kind, but she wasn't sure that Stella did. But before she could probe further, Stella presented her with a steaming cup of tea and passed over a brownie on a small saucer. And said, "All right, I'll tell you about Althea. So much time has gone by that maybe it won't hurt so much. But when Dr. Philips was killed—the old one—it all came back. I've been a nervous wreck."

A condition, thought Sarah, taking her first sip of the scalding tea, which manifests itself in wild dangerous driving, wading on rocky beaches, and throwing umbrella covers off Mount Battie.

But now Stella was talking.

Althea. Her sister Joan's youngest child. Dead for almost twenty years. Premature baby. Convulsions, later diagnosed as a form of epilepsy. Cerebral palsy. And God only knew what else. From the moment she was born, the baby lived on the edge. In and out of the hospital. Crisis after crisis. Pneumonia twice in six months. Was probably retarded—yes, I know they don't use that word anymore and her mother never admitted it. Anyway, Althea lived to be almost three, but never said a word anyone could understand. A real pet, though. Everyone loved her, wheeled her around in a stroller, sang to her. Sometimes everyone in the family came for a picnic and Althea was passed around like a little doll. "For me, she was special. We didn't have any children. I used to baby-sit or help out because she needed a lot of care. Besides, I was her godmother. My middle name is Althea. Stella Althea."

Sarah nodded sympathetically. The story was coming out and must not be interrupted.

"When it happened," said Stella, her voice now hoarse, "we were all devastated. No one had expected anything bad. Althea was taken to the ER to be checked for bronchitis. Joan was afraid of pneumonia again, even though she'd been ever so much better the past few months. Hadn't had many seizures. Some new medication seemed to be working." Stella paused, stirred sugar into her tea, her hand shaking so that the spoon and the cup rattled together. And then, as she had in the driveway, she stared into space, perhaps again seeing a ghost. Of Althea? Of old Dr. Philips? Sarah wondered.

This time the pause was so long that Sarah spoke. "It happened in the ER?"

Stella nodded. "She'd just been examined by the resident on the emergency service and they were going to set up an X-ray and call in someone from respiratory. And find Dr. Glovering, who was Pediatrics chief in those days."

Again Stella paused, pushed away a tear from her left eye, and studied her teacup.

"Then it happened?" asked Sarah.

Stella nodded. And then suddenly she rose, almost ran from the room, and returned with two framed pictures. A little brown-haired girl with a round face and a crooked smile.

"I keep them in the living room," explained Stella. "Just look at Althea and you'll see how I feel. And you can't tell from the photograph that she was disabled."

Sarah took the first picture and studied the face. Somehow she'd seen that face before. Or was the child a sort of generic three-year-old and so looked familiar? And then Stella handed her the second picture. Althea sat on the lap of a girl Sarah knew quite well. And sitting next to the two was another recognizable girl. Two girls, perhaps twelve or thirteen years old, wearing jeans and T-shirts. The two grinning at the camera and both clutching Althea around the waist, Althea with the same crooked smile.

"That's Clare!" Sarah exclaimed. "Clare Mitchner. And Hannah, Hannah Finch."

"Yes, of course," said Stella calmly. "Clare was Althea's older sister, and Hannah is Clare's first cousin. And Althea's cousin. My sister Joan married a Mitchner, and my other sister, Polly, married a Finch. Hannah is their daughter."

"You mean," said Sarah slowly, trying to sort it out, "that you're all related?"

"Oh, yes. Bowmouth is a small town next to other small

towns like Appleton and Union and Liberty. People go to the same schools and end up marrying each other. And the Mary Starbox is one of the county's biggest employers. Half the people working there are cousins or stepchildren or uncles and aunts of someone else in the hospital."

Sarah suddenly saw the hospital harboring a huge complex of persons whose families had been "done wrong" by evil Dr. Henry Philips. Perhaps each death and the attack on Julia had been the work of one of the Stella Dugan/Clare Mitchner/Hannah Finch family members.

"How about Christie Rivers? And David Bergman?" asked Sarah.

"Christie's husband was the cousin of my sister Joan's husband," said Stella. "David Bergman is a second cousin to Christie. "It's like a network, everyone's connected somehow to someone else. Except," she added in the time-honored Mainer's voice of contempt, "those people who are from away. Like some of the faculty at the college, some of the doctors. Like your husband and you."

Which puts me in my place, Sarah told herself.

Suddenly Stella banged down her cup. "Let me get it over. Here's what happened. Althea was on an examining cart. Joan had called me to come in and give her family support. We were waiting for someone to take Althea to X-ray, when in comes Dr. Philips. He wasn't CEO anymore, but he had admitting privileges and did consulting. But everyone knew he stuck his nose in wherever he wanted and acted like God Almighty. Well, over he walked, making disgusting cooing noises, acting like Joan and I were his best friends and saying things like 'Isn't Althea the cutest little thing.' Then he pulled out his stethoscope, we tried to tell him she was going to X-ray, that she'd been examined. He said something like it doesn't hurt to have someone else take a look. He leaned over her, she started to yell—Althea's was usually pretty good about being examined, but he must have scared her, bending right over her face like that. Anyway, she yelled, Dr. Philips lost his balance, grabbed at the blanket that's wrapped around Althea, fell onto the gurney, over Althea, and they both go on the

254

floor. And Dr. Philips ends up on Althea. To make a long miserable story short, he crushed her chest, her aorta ruptured, and she died about an hour later."

"My God!" said Sarah.

"That's about it. Of course it was an accident. But the damn old fool never could keep his mitts away from anyone. This time he really did it. There was an investigation, but short of being cited for examining someone else's patient without permission, that was it. It was manslaughter, in my opinion. And in the family's opinion, too, but nothing much came of that idea. So you see, I don't like to think about Althea, but killing old Dr. Philips brought it right back. He deserved to be murdered."

"My God," said Sarah again.

A long silence. The clock with the cow jumping over the moon chimed six times and Sarah jumped up. "I'm so sorry I've stayed so long. Thank you for telling me. It's such an awful story. No wonder you hate the man."

"We all hate the man," said Stella firmly. "We hate the whole family."

"Dr. Jonathan Philips, too?"

"He should have seen that the old bastard was put out to pasture. But he didn't. Well, Sarah, thanks for listening. I'll see you around, won't I?" Stella began stacking the teacups and the plates.

"Aunt Julia's going home tomorrow if everything's in order," Sarah told her. "But she'll be coming back for cardiac rehab, and I'll probably be driving her some of the time, so I'll catch up with all of you volunteers out at the picnic table."

Sarah, her head buzzing with the grim tale of a family tragedy that touched, it seemed, half the population of the hospital, drove slowly away from the house. Drove a block and then stopped. There was little question that Stella was telling a true and terrible story about the child Althea. But, trivial as it might seem, there was the dog question. The dog that was walked on the hospital grounds. Sarah backed her car and slowed by Stella's garden. The rear was circled by a three-foot-high picket fence. But the view through the slats was clear. No dog kennel visible. No dog run.

No wire tether. No sign that a dog had ever been in that space; the garden was trim, the grass as smooth as a billiard table, the flower beds carefully edged and neatly planted. All in all, there was not the slightest sign that a dog had ever been put in what might be thought its exercise space. It was all very strange.

Alex came home from a day of hiking and bird-watching in and around the Camden Hills. This activity should have been the perfect antidote to workplace stress and the aggravation of the murder investigation. But somehow, even as he noted a peregrine falcon diving on an unlucky pigeon, even as later that day he saw not one but two blackburnian warblers and seconds later a scarlet tanager, he could not shake the hospital scene from his mind. In particular, Sarah's angry departure from Julia's room was weighing on him like a sack of potatoes. Finally, giving up the possibility of seeing the reported hawk-owl, he headed home. He hoped he would find Sarah in a better mood, that she had worked off her anger with some heavy-duty pruning of their overgrown garden or in a swim in Crawfish Pond. Swimming usually calmed Sarah down, and if this was so, they could both have a reasonable discussion about the perils of amateur sleuthing. And he could admit to the fact that he and Mike had been overbearing.

But their house on Sawmill Road was empty. Empty of Sarah, that was. Only Patsy, obviously stir-crazy from a day spent going in and out of his run was there to greet him. Alex filled the dog's dish with kibbles, noted that the clock now said six-thirty and marched out to the back porch; irritation, then something like alarm rising as he scanned the deserted curves of the road as it rose toward the house. Not a car in sight.

Cool it, he ordered himself. She's probably visiting Julia, a perfect time because Julia would have finished dinner and be ready for a visitor. Or, if not Julia, she might be at Julia's High Hope Farm picking up news from Patrick to take to Julia. Or, though this seemed unlikely if Sarah's frame of mind remained unchanged, she might have stopped over to say hello to her

Grandmother Douglas. The one place, he decided, she would not be, was with Mike Laaka or George Fitts. Not after her morning exit.

Alex, resisting the urge to get on his cell phone and begin tracking his wife, went back in the house, back to the kitchen, wrenched open the refrigerator door and helped himself to a bottle of Heineken's best. Distraction was in order. Well, forget the Red Sox. They were in the middle of their usual depressing August slide. Okay, try the bookcase—*not* a murder mystery—and thence to the front porch. There he settled himself on one of the creaking green rockers, family relics, and opened a recent biography of John Adams. A worthy choice and, Alex hoped, an absorbing one. He would read, drink his beer, and not spend a minute searching the road for Sarah's red Subaru.

But even the stirring events of revolutionary America cannot compete with a mind seething with a combination of worry and annoyance. Alex put down his book, marched around to the back of the house with the dim idea of distracting himself with physical labor. Weeds—burdocks, thistles, milkweed—all these and other undesirables had begun thrusting themselves from the field into the lawn and needed to have their heads chopped, their roots dug. Alex seized a hoe lying in a wheelbarrow, and began whacking.

Ten minutes into weed-killing and he knew it was no good. Where the hell had Sarah gone? Didn't she have any sense of self-preservation? She knew she was on George Fitts's endangered-species list? She was a witness—albeit one who had been half-asleep—to a homicide? And, goddammit, it was now going on past seven. He returned to the house and dialed Julia's room number. Changing his voice to one of nonconcern, he asked after Sarah. No, Sarah had not been in. Perhaps later in the evening. Was anything the matter?

"No," said Alex, keeping his voice level. "Nothing at all. I just wondered if she was delayed."

"Delayed doing what?" demanded Julia sharply.

"School research," lied Alex. "For her fall classes. She's probably over in the English department. Not to worry."

But Alex had stumbled on the truth. Sarah's mind had been much disturbed by the idea of a possibly vengeful extended family of Dr. Philips haters. To calm herself she had sought refuge in the one place where no one would disturb her: her small cupboard-like office in Bowmouth College's English Department. Sitting at her desk—dusty from two months' disuse—she considered her next move. Tell the police about Althea? But George Fitts wanted facts, proofs, not murky details about an injury done a child some twenty years ago. Well, how about describing the high-speed chase and Stella's wading into the ocean, maybe dumping some-thing, and then tossing an umbrella cover off the top of Mount Battie? Yes, that might rouse George into action, but she'd be given hell for tailing her in the first place. "That's police business," he'd tell her. Mike Laaka? Alex? That would be asking for more lectures and would end in more rows. Of course the Lincolnville scene was definitely police business. So who?

And it came to her. Of course. Deputy Katie Waters. Katie was human. Katie wouldn't wave handcuffs and arrest warrants in her face. So maybe she could use Katie as a conduit for the Stella-in-Lincolnville information. And, to keep the home fires burning, or at least warm, she'd call Alex and say she'd be late coming home.

But dialing her number three times brought only busy signals. So Sarah, not realizing that Alex was on the phone at the same time looking for her, finally made contact with Katie via a cir-cuitous route through the sheriff's department phone system. Ka-tie was at the hospital, had arrived early for her night shift, and would be able to speed over to the English Department, pull up a chair and listen.

Katie had no sooner settled in the one extra office chair when Sarah got down to it. She felt, as she spoke, that she was laying out one of the most improbable scenarios with an equally im-probable central character. But she began at the beginning, slogged through the speeding, the sightings, the final home visit, the Althea story, and the invisible dog. Then she leaned back in her chair waiting for Katie's reaction. A reaction that should be, she thought, one of total disbelief.

But Katie did not gasp or roll her eyes. She listened quietly and then shook her head. "Let me get this straight. Little Stella Dugan, everyone's favorite auntie, drove like a bomb all over creation, maybe dumped a weapon—"

"I didn't say weapon," said Sarah. "For all I know it could have been a bag of magic beans."

"Oh, let's say 'weapon.' For now, anyway," said Katie. "Anyway, then Stella tosses something off Mount Battie; you follow her home, nudge her into telling this story about her three-year-old niece that makes it perfectly clear that she and Clare and Christie Rivers and Hannah Finch and God knows who else had one hell of a motive for eliminating members of the Philips family."

"It's all yours," said Sarah. "Do what you want with it. I'm not up to George or Mike or Alex. That's why I called you. Did my duty and made a report."

"Your 'duty' was to stay in touch with the security people and let them know where you were going."

"Katie, forget the deputy-sheriff act. I called you because you are, or used to be, human. What was I to do? I've had three close calls with this silver car, the Chevy of Stella's . . ."

"Or Stella once and two other drivers. Hey, half the county drives over the speed limit. Yes, and they probably drive in a silver or gray car. Silver is in. They don't show the dust."

"Over the speed limit, yes. But not 'faster than a speeding bullet,' which was what Stella was doing. It was a scary performance."

"Okay, I'll take your word. Go home, stay home. I'll talk to George and company and see what's next."

"What puzzles me," said Sarah, "is that you've got this terrible accident that happened twenty years ago. No one harbors revenge ideas for twenty years. If someone wanted to kill old Philips, he's been available for a mighty long time."

"No," said Katie thoughtfully. "Not quite true. When we researched the old doctor, we came up with the fact that his wife died only three months ago. Everyone called her a dragon lady because she guarded Dr. Henry like a dragon. Knew his wandering ways with ladies. He'd lost his license for getting caught speeding once too often, so his wife drove him around. So he hasn't been all that available. Until lately sitting there all banged up in the ER."

Sarah nodded. "Okay, that does make sense. Anyway, if George wants the goods on Stella, he should send someone to Lincolnville Beach with a net. And to Mount Battie."

"He probably will. But tell me this. If you were trying to hide evidence, would you drive around like a maniac just asking to be arrested? And then choose Lincolnville Beach on a Sunday in August? Or Mount Battie? Wouldn't you sneak around in the middle of the night? But never mind, I'll go to bat for you. A proper report."

Sarah nodded. Stood up. Pushed her chair back against her desk. "Thanks, Katie."

"I'll walk you to your car," said Katie. "No, I'm not playing nursemaid. Them's orders."

After a multitude of phone calls, Alex had decided that since Sarah was not in the hospital, not visiting her grandmother, not calling on friends, it might just be possible that she *was* over in the English Department, doing something about her upcoming September classes. Though why she would choose Sunday night at eight o'clock, when the place was empty, was beyond him. Feeling that yes, he should apologize, he climbed into the elderly Jeep and drove down Sawmill Road and to the Bowmouth College Campus. To the parking lot that served the Political and Social Science buildings as well as the English Department. And yes, there was her Subaru. Alex was about to pull in next to it when he became aware of a figure—actually someone's head and shoulders—in the rear seat. Just a dark profile.

His first thought was that one of Sarah's friends was waiting for her out in the car, but out of some sort of undefined hunch he kept his foot on the accelerator, passed by the car, and circled around behind the Administration Building. Parked. And made his way quietly on foot around the north side of that building, and keeping away from the lamps that lined the college pathways, edged his way along behind a privet hedge.

The Subaru was still in place. And yes, the passenger was still in the backseat. He paused. Why in the back? Wouldn't a friend be in the front passenger seat? Well, there was one way to find out. A frontal approach. Quick. But not running. Not a rush that might frighten someone out of her skin.

Alex moved at a fast walk and headed for the front of Subaru. And then, when he was within some thirty or so yards, the back door was flung open, a figure hurled itself onto the pavement and began running, heading north, heading toward the Biology and Chemistry buildings. Keeping away from the walkways. Keeping away from the light.

And Alex, like a man set loose from the starting block, gave chase. But the figure was fast, staying ahead, a speeding shadow. Away it went, Alex pounding behind, past the Social and Political Science buildings, right turn around the Physics Department, a dodge behind the Nursing School, then behind the shrubbery of the Science Quad. Then out again, straight for the boathouse and Bowmouth Pond. And vanished.

Alex stopped dead at the boathouse, a low building surrounded by kayaks, shells, and small racing dinghies. Waited. A sound. A small rippling of water. A tiny splashing. He hurled himself around to the dock, down the ramp, just in time to see small ripples move against the side of the float. And to see the ripples disappear in the dark toward the north end of the pond. The north end, which ended in heavy reeds and marshland.

Cursing under his breath, he ran down the ramp to the float, pulled off his shoes, and dove in.

22

SARAH, with Katie close at her heels, emerged from the lower reaches of the English Department and headed for the parking area. Sunday night was hardly a popular time for office visits, so Sarah's Subaru stood almost alone in the middle of the lot. And it stood open, the back passenger door wide to the mild evening breeze.

Sarah skidded to a halt. "What the . . ." She paused. Yes, she was sometimes a little on the careless side. Didn't pay attention to details. But to leave the car like that?

Katie behind her exclaimed, "Good God, your car door is wide open. What'd you do, forget to close it? Talk about living dangerously."

Sarah shook her head slowly. "I didn't even go near the backseat. Well, I might have opened it automatically, but I would have closed it. And I didn't have a briefcase with me. Or a raincoat. Any of the stuff I usually throw in the backseat. So why would I open it?"

"I can't think of a single reason," said Katie. Then, with increased irritation. "I don't suppose you ever lock it."

"No. Not usually. Only if I go into town. Not in the faculty lot. Besides, I never keep valuables in the thing. Alex is paranoid about things like this and wants me to lock up at home, but I forget half the time."

"So tonight any old drunk or rapist or thug could have snuggled up in the backseat and waited for you to come back. Professor Sarah Dean. Hey, guys, easy meat."

Sarah, exasperated, swore softly. At herself. At Katie. "Look," she finally said, "this is a college campus. Not in session. Sunday night. The only ones around are probably the maintenance people, and I know them all. Plus old Professor McClure, who I think goes into his office to sleep and get away from his wife."

"Does the word 'naive' mean anything to you?" demanded Katie. "Or babe in the woods'? There are names for people like you. Like felony facilitator. Enabler. Has the fact that there have been three homicides and an attempt on the life of your aunt sunk more than two inches into your brain? If we find your body tomorrow in the garbage, I won't be surprised."

"Oh, Katie, lay off. I've had it. So I was careless. Maybe stupid. But now I'm going home and yes, I'll lock the front door, and forget I ever met you. And you can go to Sergeant Fitts and tell him to get his butt over to Lincolnville Beach and start wading in the ocean, and when he's good and wet he can take a running jump off Mount Battie and see if he can find a smoking gun. And for good measure he can send you to the hospital archives and see if you can find out if any legal action was taken when old Doc Philips killed little Althea Mitchner."

And Sarah brushed past Katie, took three strides, slammed the back door of her car shut, climbed into the front seat, and turned the key. And started up.

Katie ran after her, shouting. "Hey. Hey, wait up. You just loused up any fingerprints and now you're lousing up the car itself. Damn! You should be riding with me. I should impound your car. Hell, slow down. And don't touch anything in the backseat."

Sarah slowed imperceptibly, leaned out the window and called, "Follow me home if it makes you feel better."

"Don't," Katie yelled, "touch anything in the backseat." Then, as Sarah gunned her car ahead. "And don't try to outrun me. I have a hot rod."

The two women, Sarah in the now contaminated Subaru, Katie in a five-year-old blue Taurus from the sheriff's department—certainly no hot rod—proceeded at a brisk pace out of the campus exit north to Bowmouth Drive, past the hockey arena, and made the right turn onto Sawmill Road. There Katie saw Sarah safely into her house, heard the door lock click into place, turned around and pointed her car back in the direction of the Mary Starbox Memorial Hospital and Sergeant George Fitts in his cave. She had just walked through the hospital lobby and was turning over in her mind what to do about Sarah's car when she saw a familiar figure in front of her. Soaking wet, and, judging from his angry stride, mad as hell. Alex McKenzie.

Julia Clancy, relieved of a number of tubes, drips, drains, and other body intruders, had spent the early part of her last hospital evening—what she sincerely hoped would prove to be her last evening—walking slowly up and down the hall, cursing her feebleness, holding on to the wall rail from time to time, but rejoicing in at least making it to a sitting room equipped with easy chairs and tables of magazines. On this trip she was followed, as she knew she would be, by the ever-present watchdog, this time sheriff's deputy Arnold Dent. All the deputies she had had outside her door and on her trips in the hall had blended together into a balding middle-aged presence only differentiated by a mustache here, sideburns there, and, once only, a female who looked as if she could toss most males over her shoulder.

The sitting room, now almost vacant except for a visiting teenaged boy sprawled in a chair, offered a fine view of the visitors' three-story parking ramp as well as the roof of the psychiatric unit. But no matter. With a little bit of squinting from one window, she could almost see the shadowy rise of the Camden Hills and from the other, the contours of the rolling blueberry barrens of Appleton and Union.

For a few minutes Julia leaned against the glass and tried to imagine what it might be like to be out in the world again. Mistress of High Hope Farm. Owner of a number of horses, riding instructor, manager of a large farm, the employer of Patrick O'Reilly and his henchmen as well as a number of student workers of uncertain skill and commitment. The thought of all these, plus the approaching traditional High Hope Halloween Horse Show, brought a sudden weakness to her knees, and she sank down in the nearest chair. Leaned back and closed her eyes.

In which situation she was found by Father Joshua Stevenson.

"Well, look at you," he said, pulling up a chair. "Up and about. Ready to take off."

Julia opened her eyes and grimaced. "I just realized what I'm getting back to, the farm and all the work, but my legs are like rubber."

"You'll have someone to help you get around."

"Oh, yes. Patrick's wife, Mary—Patrick's my farm manager— is insisting on helping out. So now all I have to do is go home and be followed around by some policeman until they find out who's behind these murders. I told them it's got to be a woman. Because I saw the watch. A silver thing. Woman's watch. When I was being strangled. The light, what there was, caught the shine from the metal. That ought to narrow it down."

Joshua stared at her. "A woman. You mean you actually saw a woman's watch? In the middle of being throttled?"

"It's the only real detail I can remember, except for the mask and cap and booties. And a low, whispery sort of voice."

"Female voice?"

"Unisex, I think. But the police know this. I'm telling you because I owe you some information. But don't tell the police I told you. They don't like these details to get out."

"What do you mean, you 'owe' me?"

"I used you. Told you about my husband, Tom, dying in room nine."

"Which he didn't." It wasn't a question.

"How did you know?"

"That's part of my job. Besides, I think you overdid your part."

265

"Tom did die," said Julia defensively. "Suddenly. A horse accident. Awful."

"I'm sure it was, and I'm very sorry. But he didn't die in room nine."

"No. I needed you to vouch for my psychological distress."

"Which was real. You *were* almost strangled. And before you start in again on blaming yourself, you had nothing to do with the hospital putting Florence Littlefield in your room. They just didn't believe you were in danger."

"But I'm left with guilt, and sister Emma is left without a sister."

"Emma's lawsuit against the hospital has just been put on hold. I heard that someone has sent her a nice sum of money. More than enough to take care of her present needs and health care expenses. And I suppose I know who the someone is."

"My lips are sealed," said Julia. "But I've enjoyed getting to know you. Even if I never go to church and I lied to you about Tom. Now you might like to know that Sarah and I have been doing a little informal sleuthing. The personal touch. So how about you joining our team? Priests should be good at this. You go everywhere in the hospital. How about starting with silver watches on female wrists? Maybe God has a special mission for you."

Father Joshua rose, took her thin pale hand in his large brown one, held it for a moment, and then carefully replaced it on her lap. "Well, as you know, God moves in mysterious ways His wonders to perform, although as far as I know He hasn't yet revealed Himself as a private eye."

At which they were joined. Nurse Hannah Finch and Nurse Clare Mitchner. Both, now off duty, came over to congratulate Julia on her coming release. Hannah, today's shirt had hummingbirds, would stop by her farm to see how things were going, and Clare, in navy-blue scrubs, told her that she was thinking of taking riding lessons.

"But," added Clare, "both Hannah and I do per diem work and sometimes fill in at cardiac rehab, so we'll be seeing you there."

And Father Stevenson, as he was saying good-bye, found himself taking furtive looks at the two women's wrists. Both wore silver watches.

Back in George Fitts' hospital sanctuary, the subject of watches was being aired. Mike Laaka, having arrived with the news that as far as he could tell, at least three-quarters of the female population in the hospital wore silver or chrome or stainless-steel watches with assorted bands, stretch links, leather, colorful ribbons, now reported that when Christie Rivers was tracked down in her garden whacking at weeds, her hands were covered in gloves and what could be seen of her wrists appeared bare of watches.

"I asked her about her headache—she must have thought I was totally spaced—and she said she was better and what did I want. I told her you had a few more questions."

"Which I do," said George, "but not today."

"She asked did I have to drive all the way to her house when I was equipped with a telephone."

"And you didn't have any answer for that."

"Right, so I grinned like a goddamned fool, and asked her what time it was. And she told me to go into the kitchen and look at the clock."

"Which you did. And?"

"Clock right there on the wall. But next to the sink, along with a pair of glasses, one stainless-steel watch with a matching stretch band."

George scowled. "You waste my time with a shaggy-dog story before you come up with that?"

"I think you should suffer along with me. Besides, I got what you wanted. Christie probably thinks I was there to case the joint for a heist. Or blackmail her." Then, aware of a door being flung open, Mike swiveled around and saw Alex. An angry presence, his shirt and trousers dripping dirty pond water on the gray industrial-strength carpet.

"Cripes!" said Mike. "What in hell have you been into?"

"Where," said Alex between clenched teeth, "is my wife? Sarah."

"Jesus, how should I know?" said Mike. He looked at George, who sat pen poised over his notebook."

George shook his head. "We haven't seen her. She's supposed to check with security before she takes off."

"Fat chance," said Mike. "Lady Loose Foot."

Alex rotated to Mike, his face twisted with anger. And worry. "Sarah wasn't in the car but someone else was. Backseat. By the English Department. Faculty parking lot. Bolted when I came up to the car. I chased, the person, female maybe, maybe not, it was pretty dark, ran like a pro. Down to the boathouse. Dove in and headed for the marsh."

"And you followed. By water? Swimming?" said Mike.

"What in hell else was I to do? I thought maybe she—or he— had done something to Sarah. Had caught her coming out of the English offices. It was a knee-jerk reaction. Maybe I should have looked for Sarah first."

"To see," said George quietly, "if she was injured?"

"Or dead," said Alex, grimly.

"Sarah isn't dead," said a voice from the doorway. Standing behind Alex. Katie Waters.

During the next few minutes even the steel voice and iron hand of Sergeant Fitts couldn't contain the maelstrom of explanations, expletives not deleted, and generally tangled narrative webs.

Finally, after George had dispatched a police team to the Bowmouth boathouse and environs, they settled in chairs— George with notebook, Mike handling the tape recorder, and Alex in dry scrubs. Order thus established, Katie Waters kicked off.

She began with Sarah's call asking her to come to her English Department office and backtracked to the story of Stella Dugan the mad driver, the ocean wader, the Mount Battie visitor. She had just reached the point where Sarah had been thinking that Stella was about to hurl herself into space off Mount Battie when Mike raised his hand.

"Shouldn't we get Sarah down here? Hear it in her own words."

George checked the wall clock. "It's close on eleven. Yes, it might be more useful than hearsay."

Katie interrupted. "But Sarah told me to be the reporter."

"Alex?" said George.

"I will pull her out of her bath or bed with great pleasure," said Alex.

George considered. "No, let's hear Katie first. And see Sarah sometime tomorrow. Go ahead, Katie. Sarah went to Stella's house."

Katie nodded and tried to lay before them the tangled web of Stella Dugan's family connections. Stella's sister Joan Mitchner, mother of little Althea and Clare Mitchner. Stella's other niece, Hannah Finch, Christie Rivers some sort of cousin-in-law through her husband, and David Bergman, somehow a second cousin to the Rivers family. And Stella herself, godmother and aunt to Althea."

"It's more mixed up than a soap opera family," said Mike.

"The ones who were most hurt, were the Mitchners, Joan and her husband," said Katie. "But thank God, they haven't been anywhere around; they live in Vermont. Mike's right, it's like a bad soap opera."

"Lizzy Borden's happy family," said Mike with a grimace.

"To sum up," said George, "except for the Vermont Mitchners, all those people were around the ER or on the floor during the murders and the attack on Julia Clancy. So we'll be keeping a sharp eye on the whole bunch. Now, you, Mike, take a search team to Lincolnville and find out what Stella Dugan may or may not have dropped in the water. Then get over to Mount Battie. You'll need ropes and a park ranger to help you there."

"The assignment I was hoping for," said Mike under his breath.

"The whole thing may be a wild goose chase. Stella Dugan may be delusional and may have been so for quite a time. Driving like a fool is a clue to mental problems. And the Althea business is twenty years old. Even with Dr. Henry Philips's wife keeping tabs on him until lately, don't tell me the family has been sitting around for twenty years to kill the two Doctor Philipes. Motives only make real sense close to the event. When the facts support them. They fade as time goes by."

"I doubt that," said Katie. "Think of elephants. They never forget."

"Never mind elephants," said Alex. "What are you going to do about this backseat person?"

"We'll cover the campus," said George. "Even though it's likely too late. Plenty of time for the person to get loose. And town kids swim in the pond from time to time. Maybe one of them found Sarah's car door open. Maybe there were two of them. Or more."

"Like smoking, shooting up," said Alex. "Or drinking. Backseat sex. And one or more took off and this one stayed put. Until I turned up."

"Or," said Mike soberly, "someone was waiting for Sarah."

"A student," suggested George. "Wants to get in her class. Talk about a bad grade."

"Bullshit," said Mike.

"I'll make sure we keep closer tabs on Sarah's travels," said George. "No more tracking speeding cars."

"And I," said Alex, rising, "am going home and have a serious and productive chat with my wife."

"And," added George, "I'll have our guys pick up her car for a search. Early tomorrow A.M. We'll see to giving her a lift to the hospital in one of our vehicles."

"Hang on to her car," said Mike. "She can get to classes on a bicycle."

Sarah was almost of the same mind. Almost faint with hunger, she had wolfed down a peanut-butter-and-pickle sandwich (a guaranteed restorative) and drained two cups of tea plus a bowl of last night's vegetable soup. She had followed this with a call to Julia's hospital room to tell her she would help her settle in at the farm tomorrow. But then, during a long hot soak in the tub, up to her chin in bubbling green Vita Bath, she found herself in the grip of a delayed reaction to the day's happenings. Not from her at-home talk with Stella Dugan, nor from watching Stella drop unidentifiable objects in strange places, but from the chase. She remembered with a shiver the feeling of sheer terror when she pursued that silver Chevrolet as it rocketed over hill and dale, around narrow curving secondary roads at over sixty miles an hour. Somehow, lying safely in her bath, travel by automobile seemed suicidal. And travel by bicycle seemed an attractive option.

She toyed with the idea. A new Raleigh, perhaps. Never mind that it was no longer of British manufacture and came from somewhere in Asia. Who cared. She'd buy one of those splendid bikes with hundreds of gears and with shocks under the seat and wheels. A book-carrying attachment. She would roll every morning down Sawmill Road to the Bowmouth College campus. She would grow old on that bicycle and be known as that crazy Professor Sarah Dean, one of those eccentric white-haired academic figures who lectured on Jane Austen and George Eliot and who eschewed gas-guzzling conveniences. On her (by now ancient) bicycle she would careen from class to class on the college pathways and frighten faculty and students as they dodged out of her way.

These pleasant reveries didn't last. Sarah climbed out of the tub, wrapped herself in an oversize bathtowel, and faced an old truth: a bicycle that went down a hill had to come up. And after trudging from class to class, going to fractious faculty meetings and dealing with students who demanded higher grades, she was frequently as limp as a wet rag and needed automotive power to make it home.

Okay, keep the car. But was she going to drop the subject of a possibly revengeful Stella Dugan? Of course, because hadn't she turned the whole matter over to Katie Waters? Katie, who might at this very minute be retelling the story to George and company. The ball, to kick or toss away, was now in the police court. End of subject.

And yet, had she promised Katie *never* to engage in cozy family conversation with Stella again? *Never* to find out if Stella really had a dog that she walked at night on the hospital grounds? No, she hadn't promised. And what about Althea's sister, Clare Mitchner? Clare Mitchner, who in the past few days had become Aunt Julia's favorite nurse. Julia had reported that she and Clare had exchanged horse and pony stories. Julia's rocking horse, Brandy Boy; her first pony, Flossy, were compared with Clare's uncle's big horse, Popcorn. They had chatted about their dogs, Julia's English setters, Clare's family's setters, and her one wonderful Irish wolfhound. Sarah paused in her reflections. Something odd, something had once struck a wrong note. She couldn't remember. But one thing seemed sure. The police wouldn't bother researching the history of Clare's dogs. They might not even check up on Stella's dog to find out if she actually owned one. These were the trivia of the investigation and so suitable for the likes of amateurs like Sarah and Julia Clancy. Anything that turned up, well, naturally, she would report it, at once, to the police.

Feeling virtuous, Sarah went to the bedroom, opened the window wide to a cool summer's night breeze, pulled on a short cotton nightgown, and crept into bed. Patsy, who had guarded the bathroom door, joined her, his gray whiskery face settling onto Alex's pillow. For a minute Sarah considered unloading the details of her day's adventures on Alex when he came home. But then scrapped the idea. Because where in hell was he, anyway? Bird-watching after dark? Had he said anything about not coming home for dinner? But then she saw again his stormy face at their last encounter in Julia's room and the memory cemented her resolution. Forget Alex. She, Sarah, would do what she had to do. No more wild driving, certainly. But quiet research, sensible conversations with certain people, yes indeed.

The thought that Alex was at that very moment being briefed by Katie Waters, along with George Fitts and Mike, on the subject of strange persons in the back of her car did not occur to Sarah.

And certainly the idea that Sarah might be planning future investigatory efforts did not occur to Alex, so sure was he that the day's events as reported by Katie Waters, particularly the death-defying automobile pursuit, had for once taken the steam out of his wife. She would now be a more cautious and careful person. She would be aware of the need for personal security. She would stop worrying the police as well as her nearest and dearest to the point of exasperation.

Arriving home some fifty minutes later, Alex, mindful of fingerprints, with a handkerchief over his hand, tried Sarah's car door, found it, as often as he had before, unlocked. With his wrapped hand he removed the ignition key, pulled down the lock lever, closed the door, and in a state of great irritation walked to the house. And, as he inserted his house key into the front door keyhole, even the fact that Sarah had at least remembered to lock this one, did little to dispel his anger.

Maine State Police
Incident Conference Rm.

23

MIKE Laaka had only a few minutes on the road to Lincolnville Beach that night to think of bed and pillow. Then it was time for action. A police team had set up searchlights, stretched a yellow tape from the land surrounding the Whales Tooth Pub and on down the rocky beach to the water's edge. The tide was coming in and at eleven o'clock Sunday night stood slightly above mean low tide. The police search team, wet suits on, snorkels and masks at the ready, formed a line and began to wade into the water and slowly probing with nets, rakes, handheld metal detectors, and other miscellaneous search instruments.

Down the beach, down through the water moved the search team, walking awkwardly, slipping on the round rocks, sometimes floundering or thrown off balance by small incoming waves. The rain, promised for the evening, now made itself known and began to spatter off the shoulders of Mike's slicker. A long cold wet night lay ahead, and Mike tried to distract himself as, equipped with waist-high waders, he followed the team by picturing himself pushing George Fitts down into the water and holding him there, his foot on the sergeant's neck.

It was amazing, Mike thought, the amount of pure crud that

turns up in the water. Styrofoam cups, half-eaten lobster claws, rubber gloves, beer cans, condoms, single sneakers were hauled by the searchers onto the shore, including, as the chief item, a whole unopened carton of soggy Marlborough Lights—perhaps someone trying to quit had heaved it as a grand gesture of renunciation. But gradually the pile grew, was bagged, tagged, and lined up on the upper edge of the beach.

The night slipped by—midnight, one o'clock, two, and then, when any hope of finding an object of interest had pretty much vanished, a shout sounded from one of the searchers at the far end of the beach. A dark figure came striding from the water and in the artificial light he could be seen holding up a long thin object.

A tire iron. The man had stumbled right over the thing. Mike signaled the team members to keep moving and pushed in George's cell-phone number and explained the find to the sergeant.

"Tide's coming in," said Mike. "It's going to be harder and harder to work the same area of the water. We'll need a boat."

"Tire iron," repeated George. Silence. Then: "Okay, bag it and send it off to the lab."

"Should we stay here or—"

"Go on to Mount Battie. If this tire iron turns out to be a no-go, then you can go back in the morning at low tide. We'll get a boat later on if it's needed."

"You want me to take the tire iron to the lab? Myself?"

"No," said George. "I want you to direct the search on Mount Battie. Start with the observation place that Sarah described and work on down the rocks. Be sure you take ropes. Rock-climbing gear. I don't want any damn-fool accidents."

"I'll bet you don't, George," said Mike loud and clear.

There was almost the ghostly sound of a chuckle. "Hate to lose you that way, Mike," said the voice. "There are so many better ways to get rid of you." And the phone went dead.

"Blast him," said Mike aloud. George's humor, when it came out of hiding, was always the sort at which no one did much laughing. Particularly not the object of the "joke."

By the time Mike and the search team made it to the top of Mount Battie, the rain had cranked up another notch, to heavy unrelenting slashes of water blown sideways by winds straight out of the northeast. And these winds, by Mike's reckoning, had probably sent this umbrella cover that Sarah had described off into space. Anywhere on the mountain or beyond. Hung up on a tree limb, down under a bush, caught on a rock. Or worse, it was now in the hands of an adventurous tourist who had scrambled down the mountainside to grab a souvenir of his visit to the coast of Maine.

Sarah woke shortly before 7 A.M. Sitting up, she saw the indentation on the mattress where Alex must have spent the night. Okay, so much for discussion and possible reconciliation. But right now there was no time for nurturing or expunging a grudge against him. Or Mike. Or men in general. And speaking of men, she supposed she should check in with George Fitts early this A.M. Next, Aunt Julia was going home and Sarah should help settle her. Furthermore, it was the twenty-seventh of August, Labor Day loomed, and so did Bowmouth College's freshman class. There would be faculty meetings, class schedules, plus the general confusion always present the first few weeks in a new academic year.

She climbed out of bed, looked out the window and noted with interest, but not with surprise, that two men and a state police car were parked beside her Subaru, which was already being hoisted up on a tow vehicle. The evidence team would try to pick up any shreds left by last night's mystery passenger, and if she was lucky, her car would get a good vacuum job, which it badly needed. All right, just time for a quick cup of tea, hitch a ride into the hospital, try to reclaim her car, and then somehow try to engage Stella Dugan in warm friendly conversation. Perhaps after the usual eleven-o'clock break taken by the volunteers. Add to this a chat with Clare Mitchner. Ditto Christie Rivers. Ditto Hannah Finch.

* * *

George Fitts, at his desk in the hospital "situation room," had those same four females not only front and center in his notebook but very much on his mind. And where was Deputy Katie Waters? She was needed to fill Mike Laaka's place, since Mike was presumably still struggling with the winds and rain atop Mount Battie.

As if in response to this thought, Katie Waters, hair wet with the rain, walked into the room, hung up her slicker and reported.

"What I don't like," said George, getting right down to it, "is hanging everything on three, no, four women as suspects. It goes against all the statistics we have for linked murders. Usually it's the men who go in for multiple killings. And there are plenty of men around the hospital who hated the guts of the Philipses."

"Not so much the grandson," Katie pointed out.

"It's there. More low-key. Resentment more than hate."

"Resentment doesn't usually turn into hitting someone over the head with a tire iron—if that's what the thing was we sent to the lab."

"Prelim report," said George with satisfaction. "A few hairs, some blood cells. Enough for a blood type and a DNA match. Lucky there wasn't a storm to clean the thing or roll it farther out to sea. But do you see what I mean about the women as suspects?"

"Are you saying that no healthy female can swing a tire iron and nail a mere man?"

"I'm saying that Jonathan Philips was over six feet tall and not exactly helpless."

"Actually," said Katie, "if it weren't for the put-down aspect of you suggesting women aren't able to hoist a tire jack, I'd say I was glad it wasn't a woman. I'd rather nail a man. How about your favorite volunteer? David Bergman?"

"Yes, he was around the ER when Dr. Philips got his, and on the Cardiac ICU corridor when Florence Littlefield was killed. Claimed he was visiting a relative, which checks out, but there's still some time unaccounted for. Said he went home that night, but so do they all. And Bergman wouldn't have trouble killing Jonathan Phillips with a tire jack. And"—here George looked pleased—"just found out. David Bergman is a diabetic. So he's familiar with syringes, would have a supply of insulin, and can find his way around the hospital blindfolded. Could probably pick up some potassium chloride with a little effort. And slipping a syringe into an IV line is simple."

"Bingo!" said Katie. "Go out and grab him."

"It's this watch business," said George crossly. "Small silver or stainless-steel watch."

"As worn by well-dressed medical ladies. And David Bergman, what does he wear?"

"No watch. He says. Has a pocket watch. He claims. But—"

"But you don't trust this watch sighting. Because Julia Clancy was in the middle of being strangled and how could she recall a detail like that? And she took her time about remembering it, didn't she?"

"Correct," said George, pleased with this remark. Sensible woman, Katie.

"What about the person hiding out in Sarah's Subaru? No way that was David Bergman, he's is built like an ox. But this person wasn't that big and outran Alex McKenzie."

"I go with the idea of kids hanging out in the car," said George. "Find an unlocked car and do some drugs. Sex. Sarah's lucky someone didn't take the thing for a joy ride. With her in it. You, Katie, should have had the car impounded on the site last night. Since you didn't, we've sent an evidence team to tow it in. We're giving her a ride to the hospital."

"Sorry about that," said Katie, not sounding sorry. "Things were on the hectic side last night. Sarah got into the car and steamed off. I was stuck with following. How about this Stella Dugan wading into the ocean and dropping something? Claiming she only wanted to cool off. Considering how nutty she seems, I almost believe it."

At which point Sarah stood in the door, paused, grimaced— this room was really getting to her. Her face was wet with the rain, her short hair was flattened into a skullcap, and her short cotton jacket—a poor choice for the morning—looked sodden.

She advanced and halted in front of George Fitts. And almost saluted, the aura of the military around the sergeant being thick enough to cut with a knife. "Thanks for getting me a ride," she said. "So I bet you want me to start answering questions?"

George got down to business. Sarah answered crisply and to the point, Katie nodding every so often as Sarah's words confirmed her own earlier report. Then, as Sarah wound up with her visit to Stella's house and hearing the tale of Althea's death, George interrupted.

"Back up. We'll have to look into Stella's medical records if things heat up. But from an amateur's point of view, would you say she's usually as unstable as she seems?"

"Until I followed her racing off to Lincolnville, and going wading, and up Mount Battie, she seemed pretty normal when I saw her with the other volunteers. Nervous, sometimes. But not off her head."

"But you're not really sure about Stella dropping something into the water," said Katie. "Maybe she was washing her hands. And for all anyone knows, she could have been flying a kite off Mount Battie."

"The thing looked like a cover for something like an umbrella. It had red and yellow fish on it," said Sarah.

"Sounds like a kite to me. Or a flag. A sort of symbolic thing," said Katie.

"Our search team is still at Mount Battie," said George. He pointed to the rain-streaked window, the wind-tossed treetops beyond the hospital. "Lousy weather for finding anything."

Sarah, who had not sat down for her recital, now leaned over George's desk. "I think Stella knows a lot more than she's saying. About Althea. About the whole mess. About walking her dog if she really has one. And yes, I think her brain is muddled. Sometimes she's calm as a mouse, then next thing, she's blasting around at top speed and doing weird things."

George studied his notebook and carefully drew a series of linked circles. Then he looked up. "Does Stella Dugan know David Bergman?"

"Duh," said Katie. "They work together. Old-time volunteers."

"I mean, after hours? Have they a relationship? Really know each other?"

Sarah couldn't help it. "You mean a biblical relationship?

"What?" said Katie.

"Do they sleep together?" said Sarah, now heartily tired of the conversation. "Have sex? Fornicate? Make the beast with two backs? Screw each other?"

"You mean," said Katie slowly, "David Bergman could be the agent, killer guy and Stella the revenging auntie, they're lovers making plans and throwing evidence off cliffs and into the ocean."

"Well, why not?" said Sarah. "And now, since you security types want me to report on my travels, I'm going to see Aunt Julia and then see about reclaiming my car. And yes, I'll tell someone where I'm going." She turned, and without pausing departed, closing the door with a smart click behind her.

George turned to Katie. "Put together a file on Althea Mitchner. And dig around into Stella Dugan's background. We may not have four female suspects but a matched pair."

"The odd couple?" said Katie, reaching for her briefcase.

Julia Clancy's last day in the hospital had begun early. All at once, just after a nurse had finished with her vital signs at six o'clock, a sense of doubt crept over her. The more she thought about going back to her farm, the more she worried about dealing with the everyday minutiae of horse and stable care. Had she turned into a feeble creature who couldn't reach the top of a sixteen-hand horse to slide a saddle on its back and pull the girth tight, a doddering woman who crept around with a cane—one of those collapsible numbers with a rubber tip? Even the effort of packing up the get-well cards pinned to the bulletin board, the gathering of the odd books and magazines bestowed by friendly visitors had brought perspiration to her brow and a trembling to her knees.

Also on her bedside table sat a supply of dismal pamphlets presented to her by the health establishment: *Going Home After Cardiac Surgery. You, Your Heart, and Your Diet.* And, most unappealing, *Cholesterol and the Killer Foods*. And then there were a number of tracts brought in by her mother, Mrs. Anthony Douglas, and Hopkins at visiting intervals. These dealt mostly with afflictions of body and mind having to do with lack of Faith, a variety of sins and other forms of evil that man is heir to. For a moment Julia hesitated over the collection. Then, with a sudden spurt of energy, Julia ruffled brochures, pamphlets, and readings from Scripture together, wrapped the stack in a damp towel, and stuffed the whole into a plastic bedpan. And felt much better.

At which point Alex, Gene Santoro, and several members of Julia's surgical team came in for last-minute evaluations. Then the deputy on duty for watching Julia stuck his head in the room, announced that he was Bert and he'd be keeping an eye out. Bert was then followed by appearances of nurses and volunteers—or, as Mike Laaka, a racing fan, might have put it, visits from the current favorites among the suspect entries.

Clare Mitchner came, hugged Julia, said good-bye, and spoke of riding lessons. Hannah Finch followed Clare and helped Julia into the linen slacks and cotton shirt which Sarah had provided, Julia's heart-attack costume of jeans and farm boots having been returned to the farm. Then came Christie Rivers, who also promised a farm visit. And last, David Bergman arrived with a wheelchair for the departure.

"Hail and farewell," he said. "I'll leave your chariot by your room for when you're discharged. Then we'll wheel you out in style."

Julia, her brief burst of energy behind her, thanked them weakly for coming, waved a languid hand in farewell. And then leaned back in her chair and wondered if she could sustain any more casual callers. And now, when she least wanted it, one tiny unbidden memory poked its insistent head up into her consciousness. Dragged her back to the night of being almost strangled. She tried to shove it away. Coax it back where it belonged, the region of dream and confusion. Let me get out of here, she said to herself. All I want now is Patrick to come and get me. Patrick, who doesn't care what I remember as long as I don't neglect the horses. Good down-to-earth, feet-on-the-ground Patrick. He would never go on about whether she was going crazy, following her medication routine, or eating properly. Even Sarah, had started to behave like a mother hen—when she was not busy playing sleuth games. Of course, the two of them were supposed to be sleuthing together, although right now Julia wondered if she even had the strength to think about such activity. And then there was this sharp new shard of memory that refused to go underground.

Julia closed her eyes, slumped in her chair and waited for enlightenment. Nothing. Well, perhaps breakfast would help. Where was it anyway? And if it turned up could she eat the stuff: all those salt-free, butter-free, meat substitute items. Eggs from sawdust, meat from pine needles, oleo from motor oil. Maybe Tom Clancy had been lucky. He wouldn't have put up with food that didn't come directly from a pig, a chicken, a sheep, or a cow. Better to have been killed quickly riding his favorite horse.

On this dismal note, the door opened and Sarah stuck her head in. "All set?" she asked.

Julia opened her eyes. "Everything in order. Patrick's wife, Mary, is in charge of the house. I'll see you at the farm. You don't have to do anything but be cheerful, bring the dogs in for me to pat, and help me walk down to the stable. And, did you know, I'm going to have this new deputy, or maybe two of them, shadowing me."

"I've just said hello to one," said Sarah. "His name is Bert. And no murder talk right now. Just get home, stay alert, and get lots of rest."

"Isn't that a sort of oxymoron? I've just had the whole gang of nurses and aides and volunteers—or should I say suspects— in here. They were all kind and said good-bye. But I've just remembered something. Seeing the group must have brought it up and now it's getting a little clearer."

"Go on," said Sarah.

"I may not mean anything at all.

"I said, go on," ordered Sarah.

"I noticed that they all wore their ID tags around their neck. Or pinned to their jackets."

"Everyone who works here does. You're going to say that the ID photos don't sometimes look like the people wearing them. Men who had beards when their picture was taken have shaved them off. Women cut their hair or dye it."

"And," added Julia, "I suppose that it would cost too much to keep the photos up to date. Well, do you suppose you or Alex or the damn police could stand one more piece of recovered memory?"

"You mean besides women's watches?"

"Yes."

"The answer is no. They're still trying to swallow the watch business."

"All right," said Julia and clamped her mouth shut.

"It doesn't mean," said Sarah, "that I couldn't stand a piece of recovered memory."

"It's not like the watch. It was this little moment. Like looking through the wrong end of a telescope."

"Just tell me and then we'll see."

"It seems so improbable."

"Aunt Julia, if you don't spit it out, I personally will strangle you with IV tubing."

"It's the ID tag. Which, as you said, doesn't identify the person wearing it. Sometimes doesn't even closely resemble the person wearing it."

"Right."

"I almost have a sense of seeing an ID tag falling out of that gown the person was wearing when it, she, he, came at me."

"And?"

"A woman's face. Frizzy hair. Reddish."

"That's it?"

"I didn't recognize the face. That's enough, and it's probably a genuine hallucination. That would please the police. I think they'd like me to have at least one hallucination. Now on your way because here comes breakfast."

This as a smiling aide pushed the door open and slid a tray across Julia's bed table.

"Looks good," said the aide, removing the cover from a

mound of overly yellow scrambled-egg substitute with two slices of limp unbuttered toast on the side.

"It," said Julia sharply, "looks like hell."

"You have a good day," said the aide uncertainly and scurried out.

Sarah rose, walked over, and looked into her aunt's eyes. "Whatever you say or think you saw, dear Auntie, I promise not to think it's the product of a hallucination. And since half the ID photos don't look like their owners, the police should look for a woman who does *not* have frizzy red hair because by now she will be a dyed blonde wearing braids or have jet-black hair with a butch cut."

"I'll see you at the farm," said Julia, stabbing her fork into the center of the substitute eggs. "Don't tell the police anything about what I've said until I'm safe at home. They might just keep me here and transfer me to the psychiatric unit."

Camden Hills State Park

Mt Battie

Campers/Registration ⇒

⇐ Auto Road

24

SARAH left Julia's room and was detained briefly by Julia's guard, who informed her that her "cleaned" Subaru had been left for her in the physicians' parking lot. And the security people would like to know her itinerary. Sarah informed him that she'd be getting breakfast at the Bowmouth Café and then be off to her aunt's High Hope Farm, and walked purposefully away from the man.

But now what? Did she want to follow her stated travel plans? To the letter? Julia's latest snippet of memory was sticking into her brain like a fish hook. The silver watch was one thing; Julia might well have seen the gleam on an arm reaching to strangle her. And probably George Fitts and company, despite their doubts, had narrowed the silver watch wearers to a small group of suspects. But the wearing of such a watch wasn't ipso facto a piece of evidence declaring the owner a murderer. It was just another, possibly dubious, piece of the puzzle.

But a red-haired—make that a fuzzy red-haired—person. An actual face! That description almost shouted Stella Dugan. But was Stella's ID tag photo as different from her actual features as those Julia and Sarah had just been talking about? For all Sarah knew, half the female hospital staff had at one time frizzed and dyed their hair red. Fuzzy red hair might have been a very "in" style at the hospital a few years back. But Stella, although plainly unbalanced at intervals, when in her "right" mind seemed a conservative person not given to sudden fads and style shifts. Just look at her kitchen, a room whose frills and general décor had most likely been the same for the past twenty-five years.

All right, first hit a public telephone—she didn't want to turn up in person and be interrogated—and call George about Julia's new entry to her "recovered" memory scenario and point out that as far as she, Sarah, knew Julia had never met Stella Dugan. Next, a late breakfast, then off to High Hope Farm to be there to help Aunt Julia settle in. And, while there, check out the security system that the police claimed to have in place at the farm. How, Sarah asked herself, was any guard going to stop one of these nurses and volunteers (make that suspects) from paying friendly calls? Follow them around, leave doors open, set up surveillance cameras? Put Julia in a bulletproof vest? A strangle-proof throat guard? But what about the approach of someone with a syringe up her sleeve? A skull-flattening instrument down their jeans leg?

Pulling her slicker tighter around her, Sarah left the hospital, and ducking her head—was still raining hard—ran for the physicians' parking lot. There was her car, cleaner than she could ever remember it. Inside and out. Now what she needed was a bowl of oatmeal. To help her think. The mere possibility that Stella Dugan was indeed Julia's attacker was making her head spin. She already knew that Stella was involved in something strange. So why not the next step, the step that moved Stella from simply being a wildly eccentric relative and the grieving aunt and godmother of a dead child to the status of revenge-obsessed killer?

Working her way through a steaming bowl of oatmeal laced with brown sugar, awash in real cream at Bowmouth Café, Sarah considered the question. It didn't feel right. Stella might be part of the business, but not the whole part. Not the mover and shaker, the prima mobile. Stella still seemed too much of a mouse. Like George Fitts before her, Sarah couldn't picture Stella attacking Jonathan Philips. Yes, she could probably manage the job if she'd gotten the job on the man, but would she? Yet what other member of the extended Althea family would really fit the bill? Mike's and George's candidate, David Bergman, as Stella's partner in crime didn't ring a real bell, and Sarah began running over other possibles. But all that came to mind was Stella's dog. Or pretend dog.

Sarah, filled with oatmeal and a mug of Twining's Irish Breakfast Tea, climbed into her Subaru, intending to head for High Hope Farm. But, as if the car had developed a strong mind of its own during the café stop, it turned at the first right, took a left, and drove right down Stella's street. Right by her house on Oak Street. And parked some three houses beyond. Of course there was the small matter of informing surveillance people that she would be deviating slightly from her travel plan, but surely the police didn't want to hear of every small detour. She was going to High Hope Farm; but not immediately. Once again, as had happened in the past, Sarah knew she was, like the Elephant's Child, in the grip of something beyond her control, some "insatiable curiosity."

It was past nine-thirty. Stella, unless she was on another automotive rampage, should now be at the hospital. But the dog, if it existed, might be back from the vet's. With luck it would be in the yard, loose or on a wire. Or barking from a window at the passersby.

It was.

The barking began as Sarah neared Stella's driveway. Two more steps and she could see through the wide cracks in the three-foot picket fence enclosure a small white-and-brown terrier hurling itself against the fence. Stella's dog.

Why had she doubted it? Just because of a lack of doggy items in the kitchen. Stella was a tidy creature, so she would have kept these objects out of sight. The water bowl was probably in some closet. The mudroom.

But still . . .

Sarah walked slowly up to the fence. The barking revved up, then, as she, rather nervously, extended a friendly hand to be smelled, the dog sniffed, wiggled in excitement, and then stuck its nose out between the fence boards and tried to lick Sarah's hand.

Feeling foolish, Sarah withdrew her hand and then saw that the dog had a red collar. And hanging from the collar was a red name tag, "Patches," plus the usual metal rabies tag. She knelt on the ground and inserted her hand again between the boards and scratched under the dog's ear, while trying to read the metal tag. It was a town license. Squinting, Sarah just made out the word "Rockland."

But this was the town of Bowmouth. Did residents here get their dog licenses in Rockland, just as they did their automobile licenses, their driver's licenses? Sarah withdrew her hand, now wet with Patches's saliva, and retreated. The presence of the dog should put Stella's claim to walking her pet on hospital grounds to rest. But surely it wouldn't hurt to find out where the towns-people of Bowmouth got their dog licenses. She reached her car, climbed in and plugged in the car phone. Three minutes later, a voice from the Bowmouth Town Office assured her that the town took care of its own dogs. Right there at the office. With proof of a rabies inoculation. Three dollars if neutered. Thank you for calling.

Sarah hit the road. So Stella got a dog from Rockland. Big deal. Probably from the animal shelter off Dexter Street. So cool it.

Yet on the Tri-County Road to High Hope Farm, doubt returned. Stella had claimed to have sent Patches to the vet's on Sunday. Something about a bad ear. Yet Patches, from her brief look at him, seemed healthy and vigorous. Would it hurt to call a number of vets to see if they had proscribed medication for Patches? She would be . . . who would she be? The dog-sitter, of course. She yanked the Subaru off the highway onto a dirt farm road, pulled to the side, reached for the telephone book she kept on the backseat, and began to punch in numbers.

Fifteen minutes later, seventeen veterinary hospitals in two counties had been reached and Sarah had been given seventeen negatives. The closest she came was discovering a beagle called Peaches who had tested positive for Lyme disease.

With this information nesting uneasily in her head, Sarah hit the road for High Hope Farm, turned in and found an impressively sized sheriff's deputy holding up his hand, asking for identification. Julia's security system had been activated, and Julia, judging from the presence of Patrick's wife, Mary, standing at a front window of the farm, was now home and, it was hoped, contented.

Well, almost contented. Five minutes with Mary O'Reilly confirmed certain instructions on the subject of making sure that Mrs. Clancy was never to be alone, not even with the most innocent-seeming visitors. "And," added Mary with disapproval, "there've been too many already. Those nosy women across the road, and one of the nurses from the hospital. Took her lunch hour to come and say hello. Hannah someone. A bird's name. Robin or Finch. Mrs. Clancy needs rest and quiet. And already"— here greater disapproval—"she's already asking me to walk with her down to the barn. I've said no and Patrick's said no and I hope you'll say the same."

"But maybe later," murmured Sarah, thinking that a good whiff of hay and manure and running her hand along a horse's neck was perhaps the best tonic possible for her aunt.

Julia was discovered sitting in an upholstered chair by the front window, gazing at a pasture of horses as they moved slowly about the field, grazing, tails swishing. At her feet lay her two English setters, Tucker and Belle. By her side on a small table sat a teapot and a plate holding several digestive biscuits. It was a scene that should have conveyed domestic tranquillity, but Julia's fingers drumming on the arm of the chair and her fretful face denied the idea. A large pot of yellow chrysanthemums and a number of flowering plants with cards attached had been placed here and there in the room so that what was usually a warmly disordered room full of saddle-soap tins, sponges, odd bits of bridles and other such items was now strangely neat. Somehow Julia gave the impression of a visitor who has landed unaccountably in the wrong room.

"There you are, Sarah," she said. "I've been trapped here. So many people. They all mean to be kind, sending these flowers, but I feel like I've ended up in a funeral parlor. And now you can take me down to the barn. I'm perfectly able to walk, but the path is a little rough and I promised Alex I'd behave."

Sarah promised assistance. "But later. First, I called the police about your seeing the ID tag. The fuzzy redhead. Katie took the call and didn't faint dead away. I don't think you'll be bothered about it. Later I think they'll show you some photos for an ID. But now, drink your tea, have a biscuit, put your feet up for an hour, and then I promise to walk you down to the barn and let you pat at least three horses. Bargain?"

Julia nodded reluctantly. Then: "All right, let the police consider me a nutcase on a par with that Stella Dugan you've told me about. Otherwise, how goes the investigation? I'll bet you didn't come right here from the hospital. You went looking. What have you found out?" Then, seeing Sarah hesitate: "Okay, get on with it. I can handle a little gossip. We're partners, aren't we? It's my knees that are weak, not my brain."

Sarah went directly to her subject. "Did you ever meet Stella Dugan? One of the senior volunteers. Did she ever come in to your room at the hospital to bring flowers, messages? This is important."

Julia took a sip of her tea, reached for a spoon and added a teaspoon of honey. Stirred, drank again. And then shook her head. "I don't think I remember her. Except from your talking about her. And the other volunteers. You said she was on the mousy side. Didn't really speak up. But was always a sort of Lady Helpful."

"You're sure she didn't poke her head in and say hello?" asked Sarah.

"Oh, God, she might have. Sometime when I was half-asleep. But I can't fix her face. Or her voice."

"Okay," said Sarah. "Here's a puzzle for you. Stella Dugan seems like a perfect Girl Scout. She helps, runs and fetches, is known as being useful, helpful. Conscientious. But not exactly a memorable person. Except she sometimes gives a sort of nervous giggle."

"But, all in all, a sort of nothing? No grit."

Sarah nodded. "Most of the time that's Stella. But then you

haven't seen her in a car. I did. She drives like a rocket."

"That's quite understandable," said Julia. "I mean, if you're a mouse type."

"What do you mean?"

"To compensate," suggested Julia.

"For what? Being mousy?"

"How do I know? But if I were a meek creature like that—"

"Which you aren't."

"I might like to let off steam. Drive like a rocket."

Sarah hadn't thought of Stella's behavior in that light. "You mean that being a mouse is a strain. So you have to let go."

"It's just a guess. Remember I don't know the woman. But I know that after I've been civil and forbearing and had a brutal day teaching rude children how to ride while their mothers complain about my program, there's nothing like getting on a horse and riding over the cross-country course a little faster than I should. Or, if I'm indoors, I hit the piano. Lots of Chopin. Bang, bang, crash, bang."

"But you've never been considered mouselike."

"Forbearance and civility take a great deal out of me. And if I didn't have a horse or a piano available I might like to hop into the farm truck and drive like hell. Now let me get this hour's rest done with and I'll be ready to go to the barn. See what Patrick's been up to when I was in the hospital."

"What Patrick's been up to," said Sarah, "is worrying himself sick about you."

"Patrick knows me. If I came all over with soft soap, he'd have a seizure. And mark my words about this Stella Dugan of yours. Being Lady Bountiful and Lady Helpful takes a serious toll on your nerves. It goes against nature."

Against Aunt Julia's nature, anyway, Sarah thought, as she softly closed the door and left her aunt to her rest. But a seed had been planted, and it added itself to other disturbing seeds already rotating in her head. For instance, the Hannah Finch seed. Why so quick a home visit to a person who must have been only one of many patients Hannah had taken care of in the past few weeks? Had she been casing the place? And then there was Clare

Mitchner. Former irritant, now best buddy. A woman who was thinking of riding lessons. Was that sinister, or just a normal development—a development born of Sarah's instructions on how to deal with Julia?

Sarah stepped out on the porch, raised her eyes to the clearing sky, and swore loudly. What was the matter with her that she suspected these three women—no, make that four, with Christie Rivers—all of who seemed, on the whole, fairly harmless. Even Stella's movements of yesterday, though weird in the extreme, were not in themselves threatening. And there was the dog Patches to vouch for her story of walking the dog. Except what about the vet? What about the Rockland rabies tag?

Sarah, shaking her head, planted herself on a porch step and tried to soothe her mind by watching two foals trotting long awkward legs after their dams in the nearby field.

But if Sarah found herself disturbed by these four females, George Fitts and Katie Waters were going at it hammer and tongs. George trying to keep the investigation free of contaminating guesswork; Katie arguing that he was ignoring what should have been plain as the nose on his face. After all she, Katie, had just received the grade of A-plus for her summer course "Introduction to Abnormal Psychology" at the local college and had signed up for a fall-semester advanced course dealing with more of the same. And here she had a perfect example of abnormal behavior. Mike Laaka, if he had not still been trapped on Mount Battie, might have sided with Katie. A real plus for Katie was that Mike always felt remarkably free to criticize George, whatever the consequences.

It was well past noon. The sun showed signs of becoming a permanent feature of the afternoon, and a small ray of light shone through the window, making the meeting room space less grim than usual. A large-scale map of the areas and routes running from the Mary Starbox Memorial Hospital to Camden, to Lincolnville, to Mount Battie hung on the wall opposite George's desk. On it George had traced a blue line marking Stella Dugan's drive to the beach, to the mountain, and home, with a blue X marking the spot where the tire iron had been recovered. Another line, a dotted red one, marked the possible route taken by the killer of Jonathan Philips from the hospital parking lot to Lincolnville, with an X marking the place in the ocean where his corpse had bobbed up. In a folder at George's elbow were listed the movements and times of appearances at various scenes of nurses Clare Mitchner and Hannah Finch, and volunteers Christie Rivers and Stella Dugan—these referred to by Katie Waters as the four witches. George's preferred suspect, David Bergman, had a following page, and Mike's favorite, mostly for her well-shaped bosom and her come-get-me smile, was the late Jonathan's secretary, Carmen Wilson.

In the interest of comfort, a deputy had been sent to the cafeteria and had delivered sandwiches, with fruit juice for George and iced tea for Katie. Attention to nourishment for a short while kept the sparks from flying. But then Katie, after three bites of her sandwich and a long drink from her iced tea, faced George.

"Okay, George. I know those women, particularly Stella Dugan, who you think is your average ding-dong mental case, represent a big fat waste of your valuable time. You're not happy about nailing them because of what Julia Clancy claims to remember."

"I still think she may be imagining the watch and the ID tag with a face like Stella's."

"But Sarah told me on the phone Mrs. Clancy didn't even know Stella," insisted Katie. "That means she couldn't be transposing a familiar face."

"We can't act on that sort of evidence given by a post-cardiac surgery patient."

"How about Mrs. Clancy having been in a state of heightened awareness? Saw things more clearly."

"A defense attorney would rip that idea into shreds," said George firmly.

"But then what have you got?"

"A tire iron. For what it's worth."

"Which Stella may have dropped in the ocean."

"Which we can't prove," said George. "Not unless we find Stella's hair or prints on it. Otherwise, Sarah's guess of what Stella might or might not have been doing is worth—"

"So much shit. But maybe," added Katie with hope in her voice, "you could try hypnosis. Find out what Sarah really saw. It's a valid way of recovering memory."

"I hope the sheriff's department isn't paying for your tuition for your next psychology course."

"No," said Katie sadly, "but I'm going ahead by myself. But you're the one who needs psychology courses."

George raised his eyebrows. "I have already taken more psychology courses than are good for me." There followed a long pause while George leafed through his notebook, so Katie moved on. "At least you're going to be seeing Stella?"

"And Sarah," said George. "Sarah at four and Stella at five this afternoon. Stella has explaining to do and she's obviously been off balance. I'd like to search her car, even her house, but that would need a search warrant."

"And we can't get one without some useful evidence."

"Correct," said George. "But the tire iron and this piece of cloth Mike is looking for are what we need. Solid evidence. Now it's up to the lab. But I have trouble thinking of this Stella Dugan as a murderer. The physical act. She doesn't fit."

George finished his last bit of a tuna-salad sandwich, took a last sip of his fruit juice, carefully wiped his lips with the paper napkin, folded the plastic sandwich wrap in a neat square, and placed it on his desk while Katie muttered, "Obsessive-compulsive" to herself.

"I heard that," said George. "Obsessive-compulsive goes a long way in police work. Now see if you can make a case for Stella Dugan as a murderer. Using your psychology course."

"At first I asked myself why would the murderer of Jonathan Philips return to the area of the crime and wade out into the water and drop the murder weapon? If it is the murder weapon. With people all around to watch. And then, in front of even more people, toss something off the top of Mount Battie."

Here Katie stood up, grabbed a ruler, and marched over to George's wall map. She ran the ruler up and down the network of roads and highways. "Look at all those routes, all those miles from the hospital to Lincolnville. A hundred places to dump a tire iron. Woods, trails, cliffs, ravines. Why on earth would Stella drive like a maniac to dump a weapon—"

"A possible weapon."

"A possible weapon almost where the body was found?"

"I'm sure you have an answer up your sleeve."

"I said at first it didn't make sense. But then I got it. Think guilt. Start with Stella's state of mind. Then it makes sense. She's a murderer who wants to get caught."

"Wanting to get caught because she's crazy."

"We don't say 'crazy' anymore. But okay, crazy like a fox, maybe."

"And driving over the speed limit?"

"See, she wants to get caught," repeated Katie.

"How about what it took to get Dr. Philips to Lincolnville. . . ."

"Or somewhere around there. Think about Stella Dugan."

"That's what I'm trying to do," said George with exasperation. "Is she the sort of woman to lure the CEO of the hospital into a car? For what, a date?"

"She's offering him a ride home. His car's broken."

"But he's already refused Clare Mitchner with the same offer. Let's get back to facts. Stella—if she does get him into her car—manages somehow to get him to a place where she can stop and bang him over the head. While he just stands there? Here's another fact for you. Jonathan was over six feet tall. Stella Dugan? Five feet four if she's an inch. Does she remind you of the Terminator or one of Charlie's Angels?"

"No," said Katie reluctantly. "But think about her motive. That's what's wrong with David. No real motive. Not like Stella's. As for physical strength, appearances can be—"

"Not in this case. I've asked around. Stella doesn't do much wheelchair pushing. Not the heavy jobs, anyway. Mostly she takes messages, delivers charts. Directs people where to go."

"So wangle a search warrant for Stella's car. Everyone's car.

Me, I think the case now is clear as crystal, but you, Sergeant Fitts, are impossible," said Katie with annoyance.

"Being impossible," said George, "often gets results." It was one of those remarks that made George's associates tear their hair out by the roots. Now he lifted his shoulders in exasperation. "If that tire iron comes up with something positive, we'll grab those five cars and go over them very carefully."

Katie tried again. "Well, if you won't buy Stella, with or without David Bergman's help, how about Clare Mitchner? Sister of little Althea."

"I've got people looking up the Althea case. See whether Dr. Philips got a whitewash. Whether Stella's or Althea's family—which included Clare Mitchner—filed charges. So, to answer your question: Yes, Clare's in the running."

"Don't forget," said Katie, "she actually had Jonathan in her car that evening."

"And he got out of the car. Changed his mind," George reminded her.

"She could be lying. A cover-up."

"Of course. But she reported the event as soon as it was known that Jonathan was missing."

"Preemptive move."

At which the telephone jangled. Katie subsided in her chair and began to picture Clare Mitchner hoisting a tire iron over the head of Jonathan Philips. Clare was certainly a lot stronger than Stella, but somehow Katie couldn't seem to work out the action required. In the car? Out of the car? A flat tire? Jonathan being helpful. Possible. But then why wasn't Clare the one wading into the water and (possibly) dumping the tire iron? Being the guilty one who wanted to be caught. Because, of course, Clare seemed, from what she'd seen of her, quite rational. Unlikely to be propelled by guilt to do wild and foolish things. Katie frowned, abandoned Clare, and turned her attention to whatever possibilities Hannah Finch might present as a killer. And became aware that George had put down the telephone receiver and was writing in his notebook.

"Two items," said George. "One negative and a big positive."

Katie looked up. "Stella Dugan's confessed. Or thrown herself off Mount Battie?"

"Sarah's car didn't show up anything useful. Junk. A lot of dog hair, peanut shells, pencil stubs, gas-charge slips with her signature. No decent prints but hers and her dog's nose. But the tire iron is positive. Even with the water immersion, a few hairs stuck. The hair belongs to Dr. Jonathan Philips. The shape of the iron conforms to the wound configurations found on the skull. Good solid evidence."

"And is the tire iron missing from the cars of any of our favorite suspects? And do modern passenger cars even have tire irons? Or tire jacks?"

"We're checking that one. And impounding the six cars."

"Let me guess. The four witches and David Bergman and that gorgeous Carmen Wilson because she saw Dr. Jonathan that evening."

"So, Katie, go and collect the car keys of any of those cars now in the hospital parking lot. Take another deputy with you. For backup. And don't say you don't need backup. Are you armed?"

"I have something useful stuck down my bra."

"Go!" said George in a loud voice.

Forty minutes later Katie returned, produced five small paper evidence bags, each jangling with the metal keys, and dropped them on George's desk.

"No, problem. No one really fussed. Only Hannah Finch's car missing. She's on a split shift today and drove over to visit Julia Clancy. Which ought to make you nervous."

"We've got Julia well covered. And now we've got five of the automobiles located. I'll send someone after Hannah Finch's car. We'll be going over them immediately. One piece of news: Three of the cars are missing a tire iron. Or a jack. Any sort of tire-fixing equipment."

"Let me guess," said Katie. "Stella Dugan's? And?"

"David Bergman's pickup. Claims his was stolen. And Clare Mitchner says her car, one of those Japanese all-wheel jobs, was bought used without one. But even if Stella's tire iron is missing,

I still don't think Stella Dugan is up to such an attack."

Katie shook her head. "I'm not sure if that's a sexist remark or you're doing illegal profiling, but I'd still zero in on Stella as your perp. Yes, okay, David might be a facilitator. But Stella's so great for the part. Having her tire gadget missing is just another example of her wanting to be caught. It's like she's laying a trail. A killer saying 'Catch me, catch me.'"

"And we will," said George grimly. "Whoever it is."

Maine State Police
Incident Conference Rm.

High Hope Farm

Training-Boarding
Equitation

25

SARAH put in a busy afternoon. First she held a chat with Patrick about not letting Julia even think about climbing on a horse—hide her saddle, if need be—and then she brought her aunt, walking in slow motion, down to the barn. Patrick had put Duffie on crossties so that Julia could stroke his neck and run her hand down his legs without having to chase him around his stall. Next, Julia was allowed to pat the pony, Gingersnap, and then, to top it all off, to admire and tender a small segment of an apple to the mare Angelina and admire her new foal, born the night before Julia left the hospital. Then Sarah, seeing her aunt looking pale, unsure on her feet, escorted her back to the house, saw her settled on the sofa with the new John Grisham, and departed to keep her next date with George Fitts.

After checking out with the guarding sheriff's deputy and noting with approval the presence of a state trooper in full uniform sitting in the regulation-blue car in front of the house, she headed for her car. Then, looking back at the farmhouse, she saw that one of the student workers, who had been enrolled to give the two setters, Tucker and Belle, a run, was trotting along the edge of the pasture, both dogs pulling hard on their leashes.

Dogs again. Well, forget dogs. Stella's dog, anyway. And Clare's dog, the one she'd felt so sad about when it died. Forget Clare's dog even if it had been an Irish wolfhound and one of the things that had brought Sarah and Clare together in an alliance in managing Aunt Julia. Anything else to forget? Forget that horse called Popcorn. A Belgian, wasn't it? One she could hardly get her legs around. Had belonged to an uncle. Not relevant, Sarah decided. Forget horses. She didn't want to catch Clare in any sort of animal-related falsehoods. But there was Christie Rivers, a horse owner who had taken her horse away from Julia's care. Hey, who cared? Dogs, horses, enough already. Thank heavens Hannah Finch had only mentioned a parakeet in her life and David Bergman, as far as Sarah knew, had no pets.

Leaving High Hope Farm, heading for the hospital, Sarah, hardly to her surprise, found that she had again turned down Oak Street. Stella's street. A street with few houses, widely separated. But hadn't she just told herself to forget dogs? Well, one last look at Stella's house wouldn't hurt. And then she would let it rest. So help her.

She drove slowly by Stella's house, reversed, and went by again. No residents around. Good. But also no sign of Patches in the yard. But at a side window a familiar figure passed by, pausing a moment to do something with a curtain. Stella. So Patches may have been taken inside. Anyway, now that she was here, it might be a good idea to put the matter of Patches to rest once and for all. With the street quiet, it seemed easy to slip around to the back of the house and make a minor disturbance—nothing Stella could hear—to see if she could provoke Patches, an animal that obviously loved to bark.

Sarah drove past the house again, parked, and returned on foot. Bending low, moving quietly, Sarah worked her way around the house and skirted the white picket fence. Not a single woof. She stamped her foot and coughed. Nothing. Then she cleared her throat and let out a short woof herself. Sarah was quite good at dog imitations. In grade school she had played the part of a dog more than once, and as a senior in high school she had starred offstage as the voice of the Hound of the Baskervilles. But the woof brought no response, so she raised her voice into a long melodious howl.

Nothing. No yapping little terrier hurling itself against the back door. It was a summer afternoon, the windows were open. Surely if the dog was anywhere inside, it would have reacted. She tried again. A sharp bark. Two barks. Nothing. Was the dog tied up in the cellar, duct tape over its mouth? She barked again. Sharp, highly authentic barks. Her very best effort.

Nothing happened. Except the back door. Which opened and Stella stood on the deck. "Who is it?" she called. She walked to the edge of the deck and peered toward the fence.

And Sarah, bending low behind a quince tree hoped she was invisible. But Stella was now gazing at the far end of the garden and waving her hand in the air. "Go home," she called. "Bad dog, go home."

With relief Sarah saw Stella make several more shooing motions, peer around, and then retreat into the house. Having been spared a scene of serious embarrassment, Sarah stood up. Or tried to stand up. But one of the thin cotton sleeves of her shirt caught on a thorn, and Sarah, in sudden panic, pulled loose, heard the shirt rip and at the same time felt the thorn run down her arm like an angry fingernail. Bending low, warm blood trickling past her left elbow and down toward her hand, she made it out of Stella's yard. Then, trying not to run, she walked quietly to her car, ducked into the driver's seat. And then looked back. No pursuit. No open door at Stella's house, no Stella staring down the street.

Thank God. That was it. No more dog patrol. Sarah would be turning up in George Fitt's den in the next five minutes; and she could turn over the matter of dog/no dog to him. Or better, to Mike Laaka. Mike was a dog lover, could talk dog, while George had never struck Sarah as a person who settled down at home with a faithful canine at his feet unless it was a Doberman with a studded spike collar. More likely he spent his free time cleaning firearms and reading police manuals.

* * *

Mike, if he had been assigned to check on the existence of Stella's dog, would have rejoiced. His night on Mount Battie, his morning efforts to claw his way with the search team up trees, through the underbrush, had come to nothing more than massive irritation, fatigue, hunger, and a thousand abrasions on all parts of his body from contact with sharp rocks.

But finally, triumph. To the collection of Styrofoam, candy wrappers, pop bottles, and other detritus, each collected in its own evidence bag, he added one soggy, ripped piece of green cotton-nylon cloth, pulled inside out, but with a number of fish designs showing through from its other side.

Mike turned this treasure over to one of the search team with instructions to get it pronto to the lab. Then, weary, muddy, he climbed back into his car and headed for home, for a shower, clean clothes, and food. An hour later, restored to something like humanity, he turned up at the hospital at the exact moment that Sarah was entering George's sanctum for her four-o'clock appointment.

"Mike," said Sarah, with relief. "Good. I have this dog thing for you to think about."

Mike grabbed her hand. "Hey, look at you. You're bleeding all over the hospital rug. What have you been up to you shouldn't?"

"I'm fine," said Sarah in a cross voice. "I just need a Band-Aid." She raised her dribbling arm and pressed the cotton shirt-sleeve material against the scratch. "I got caught on a quince tree," she explained. "All those thorns." Shaking her hand free, she pushed ahead of Mike into the room.

George took one look at Sarah, rose from his desk, moved Mike to one side, took hold of Sarah's shoulder and steered her to a chair and said firmly, "Sit. And stay there."

He can do dog talk, thought Sarah. Maybe George has one after all. But George had disappeared into the hall, returned almost immediately with a passing nurse. In something like ten minutes, the wound had been washed, Betadine had been applied, and a double-size Band-Aid was in place. A reappearance of the kinder, gentler George, thought Sarah, which means I'll be skewered later.

"There," said George with satisfaction. "We can't have our private investigators getting an infection. And I've ordered tea to come in. We need you as a helpful, not a hostile, witness." He paused for a moment, seemed to consider, and then: "Sarah, I'm trusting you to keep the lid on this information, but since you're our number-one expert on Stella Dugan's comings and goings and you've heard the Althea story firsthand, I'm going to—"

"Share with me," said Sarah. "An expression I really loathe."

"And we don't usually like to share. But we need your input. First, think back once more. Did the object you might have seen Stella Dugan drop in the ocean make a splash? Make waves?"

"I think whatever it was just sort of slid into the water."

"Well, a tire iron found off Lincolnville Beach came up with a few hairs that match Dr. Jonathan's. And we just have a prelim from the lab that the green beach-umbrella bag shows signs of having held the tire iron, plus a match with the hairs from the iron. But Stella Dugan's car upholstery is clear so far. That either means she didn't carry the tire iron, in or out of the bag, or that the bag, being nylon, didn't shed any evidence. But it might have worked like this. Stella puts the tire iron in the green bag to prevent any soiling to her car. Later the bag is useful to hide the iron when she walks into the water to dump it off Lincolnville Beach. Afterward, she probably washes the bag by turning it inside-out. The lab says there's evidence of saltwater immersion."

"While we're sitting here chatting," said Mike, "Stella is probably on her way to Portland International Airport."

"Actually," said Sarah incautiously, "she's at home."

"Because," said George, as if he'd already known this, "you've been visiting. Or looking in on her. Is that where you met the quince bush?"

"More like hiding out in it," put in Mike.

Sarah was saved by the arrival of tea, coffee, a plate of bagels and cranberry muffins.

"You do live well, George," she said, reaching for a steaming mug.

George helped himself to coffee and a bagel and Mike did the same. "So, Sarah, did you try a visit this afternoon to Stella? Shall I check on her planting of quince bushes?"

"Damn you, George Fitts," said Sarah. "It's about a dog. Which may be imaginary. Not about finding Stella carrying murder weapons around. The dog thing might be a sidelight. Nothing to do with Lincolnville Beach."

"But it might be something we could just be interested in?"

So Sarah told the story of the dog that might or might not be. "You know," she said, "walking her dog is Stella's cover story for the night that Florence Littlefield was killed."

"Of course we know," said Mike. "Sweet little Stella out with her doggy, walking around the hospital grounds waiting for him to piddle. Which means she couldn't have been slipping a syringe into Florence's Littlefield's IV."

"But if the dog doesn't exist . . ." began Sarah.

"Stella wears a mask, scrubs, a lab coat," said Mike. "Gets hold of the potassium, the insulin, follows simple directions, and good-bye, Julia Clancy. Only it was Florence Littlefield."

"She could manage the medical end," said George. "I checked out her records. She worked as a nurse, an office nurse, for old Dr. Trainbore years ago."

Sarah mulled this over a minute, and then, unbidden, the dog came scampering back. She turned on George. "Most dogs, especially terriers like this Patches, have amazing ears, and they bark their fool heads off when anyone walks by their house. Even across the street, they'll hear you and bark. I don't believe this dog is a real part of Stella's life. Not a sound tonight when I'm sneaking around. Not in the yard, not in the house. Windows were open, and even if Patches was stuck in the cellar, I think he'd have heard me."

"But if you were being quiet, perhaps not," George said.

Sarah felt her face redden. "Actually, I wasn't quiet. I barked."

"You what!" George and Mike together.

"It's something I'm good at. Barking. Or howling. I did it in school plays."

The Hound of the Baskervilles?" said Mike.

Sarah nodded. "You got it." She took a last sip of her tea and told herself that so far George had been remarkably easy. Now he was writing in his notebook, closed it, and gave her what could only be called the Basil Rathbone version of a smile.

"Sarah, no one is going to believe this barking business, so I think we'll keep your recent visit to Stella to ourselves. Otherwise we may have to have you committed to, well, shall we say, the animal shelter? Meanwhile, I'll work on the dog angle."

At which Mike's cell phone beeped. He snatched it up, listened, grinned, and snapped it closed. "Final from the lab. Tire iron and bag. Jonathan's blood and hair. A good match. Now should I go out and put cuffs on Miss Mouse?"

"We've got someone watching her house," said George. "Someone who probably saw Sarah in the bushes. If Stella leaves, we'll catch her before she moves ten feet in any direction. And since we've impounded those cars, she'll be walking over for our five-o'clock interview. About ten minutes from now. And though I'd like to take her down to headquarters, all we have is Sarah's look-see evidence."

"Yes," said Sarah with regret. "I should have taken a camera to Mount Battie."

"No charges we can put together yet," said George. "But it's time we thought about Stella concealing evidence in a homicide case. Being an adjunct, a facilitator, before or after the murders. But for now we want to keep her on a long line. See where she leads us. And at some point we'll think about having her talk to a psychiatrist. And at getting a search warrant for her house."

"I've always thought you didn't believe in psychology," said Sarah. "But maybe you'd like to hear my Aunt Julia's theory."

"I can hardly wait," said Mike.

"Very simple," said Sarah. "Stella has built up a well-deserved reputation for being helpful, kind, thoughtful, and accommodating. A little timid. The Miss Mouse persona. So Julia says she has to burst out somehow. Driving like crazy, doing provocative things."

George frowned. "And Katie Waters is telling me Stella's feeling guilty because she *is* guilty and is dropping evidence in public

305

trying to get caught. Me, I'll stick with evidence—and try to forget the guilt theory. And Julia's compensation theory. For now, anyway. Okay, Sarah. You can go. Stay out of quince bushes."

Sarah reached the door. Turned. "George, do you have a dog? Have you ever had a dog?"

George gave another of his minimal smiles. "You mean like a rottweiller? A Doberman?"

"Or a German shepherd," suggested Sarah.

"Actually," said George in an almost affectionate tone, "I have two West Highland terriers. Westies. Female. Mona and Olive."

"And they bark like hell when anyone goes near them," put in Mike, who had had close encounters with the two.

Sarah, chastened, departed.

Either George is becoming human, she thought, or he's always been human and I've missed it. No, she turned this idea away. At home, all warm and cozy with his two Westies. Out in the world, Mr. Flint. He's as schizoid as Stella Dugan. With which thought she smacked almost directly into Stella, who was advancing over the threshold of the lobby, to keep no doubt her five o'clock date with the police.

Sarah reared back and Stella stepped aside, both speechless for the slightest moment. Stella recovered first.

"Well, hello again, Sarah. I suppose you've been talking to the police. I have an appointment coming up. All this nonsense about Lincolnville and Mount Battie." And then, peering more closely at Sarah. "What on earth did you do to yourself? Your shirt is ripped and you've got blood all down the sleeve."

Sarah pulled herself together. "Oh, it's nothing. One of those bushes with thorns. I tripped."

"Don't I know," said Stella. "I have this evil quince tree by the side of the house and I'm a bloody mess whenever I try to trim it or pick the quinces. But take care. Infection is so easy with little scratches if you don't pay attention. I know. I used to be a nurse." And Stella gave Sarah a sympathetic look, a quick wave, and was gone with a firm step toward the police meeting room.

And Sarah, watching her go, could only pity the police. She

almost wished she could sit in on the interrogation. Stella in her current mode—the cheerful helper—ought to get them exactly nowhere.

Sarah was correct.

Mike, listening to Stella talk pleasantly about the need to go wading in Lincolnville, the fun of reciting Edna St. Vincent Millay at the top of Mount Battie, how she often acted just on a whim, a crazy whim, began to feel that his own brain was becoming increasingly unhinged. Then, as the questioning became more pointed, he saw the look of surprised wonder in Stella's eyes, the lifting of her plump hands as if in slight protest as George brought up the tire iron, the piece of cloth, the blood and hairs found in the green umbrella bag, the bag that witnesses had said she had tossed over the ledge at Mount Battie.

For Christ's sake, Mike told himself as Sarah had before him, we've got an honest-to-goodness multiple-personality thing going here. Stella the Volunteer. Stella the Stealthy sneaking about, throwing things. Now here in the office: Stella Stonewall. No, "stonewall" wasn't right. Talking to this woman was like bouncing a rubber ball. You tossed a question or a statement off her surface and it gently bounced back in your lap. Or George's lap. Or it dribbled onto the floor.

And as the hour dragged on, Stella kept it up. She smiled. Gave her little giggle. Batted her eyes. Shook her head. Wondered just why the sergeant thought that. Just imagine thinking such a thing. She did try her best to be helpful. Always. That's why she volunteered at the hospital.

Presented with the fact that she'd been seen driving dangerously over the speed limit, she shook her head regretfully and said, yes, sometimes she did such a thing, had picked up a few speeding tickets. So naughty of her, but didn't everyone need a little excitement in their life?

Mike grinned at George's expression of annoyance because this last statement fitted nicely in with Julia Clancy's explanation of Stella's behavior. But now George moved on to the matter of the dog. Patches was tossed at Stella. Who tossed him back. Yes, the dog belonged to her niece, Clare Mitchner, but every so often Stella dog-sat him. Very recently, in fact. "A sweetheart, but you know terriers. Bark, bark, bark."

George, his face set in granite, played his final card. Althea. And Stella became gently tearful. "Such a loss. Such a beautiful child. But accidents happen."

George pounced. "Accident?"

"Well, yes. It was. I mean," said Stella, "old Dr. Philips didn't *want* to kill Althea. He just tripped. Or fell. And it was ruled an accident."

"You . . . your family didn't take the matter to court?"

"Oh, everyone talked about it. But then the hospital gave my sister, Joan, and her husband a settlement and that was that. But of course it didn't bring Althea back."

Mike couldn't resist. "Were you glad when you heard Dr. Philips was killed?"

"Oh," said Stella, looking shocked. "That wouldn't have been very Christian, would it? Besides, some people liked him, some didn't."

"But in your family," said Mike, "no one burst into tears when he was killed?"

"Mike," said George sharply. "Be quiet."

"It's all right, Sergeant," said Stella. "I know Mike. He never means half of what he says. Though that is not an appropriate question."

George nodded as if in agreement. Then, seriously: "Have you an attorney, Mrs. Dugan?"

"Yes. Are you trying to say I should call him?"

"It might be helpful in the long run. There's a question about evidence you may—or may not—have been carrying. Evidence that may be part of a homicide case."

And, thought Mike, here we go again, and what I need is a good night's sleep. But since no confession appeared to be in the cards, the dreary and familiar scene would be played out into the late afternoon and on into the evening: The call to the lawyer, his arrival, the discussion of possible charges with the assistant district attorney. Continuing to keep a deputy by the front of her house. The visiting by distressed family members, including questionable persons like Clare Mitchner, Hannah Finch, and Christie Rivers. As for Deputy Detective Mike Laaka and Sergeant George Fitts, CID, they were each left with a strong sense that even though a certain amount of legal machinery would be cranked into motion, they were no closer to solving the murders than they had been at eight o'clock that morning. And somehow neither man really liked Stella Dugan as the agent of a triple murder—death by strangulation, poison, and trauma. Only Katie Waters, embracing the idea that Stella Dugan's movements amounted to a loud cry of guilt, was in a state of contentment.

In the three weeks that followed, the county witnessed a double memorial service for Drs. Henry and Jonathan Philips; this attended by a niece from Wisconsin and members of the Mary Starbox Hospital community. Florence Littlefield was put to rest at a graveside service conducted by Father Joshua Stevenson in the presence of her sister Emma, Dr. Alex McKenzie, his wife, Sarah, and cardiac physician Dr. Eugene Santoro, plus two nurses who had been on the floor the night of her death. Julia Clancy sent flowers.

Otherwise, the world moved on. Julia improved in health and was able to walk to the barn without assistance and, under Patrick's careful eye, was allowed to sit on Duffie and walk around the ring. Sarah, unable to keep her vow to forget animals, asked Julia about a Belgian horse. Julia said it was a foolish choice for a riding horse, but Belgians were on the whole agreeable beasts, but much too big for comfort. Are they any particular color? Sarah had asked. "Chestnut," said Julia, "and I hope to heaven you're not thinking of getting one."

"What if a Belgian was named Popcorn?" said Sarah, in a last attempt to pin this oddity down.

"Horse names make absolutely no sense," Julia reminded her. "My Duffie is named Plum Duff. That's a pudding. And he doesn't look in the least like a pudding. But he was out of a mare called

Christmas Past. And think of Man o' War. Seabiscuit."

"Gingersnap is gingery-colored," said Sarah stubbornly.

"But my school gelding, Scarlet, is a flea-bitten gray. And one of my students has a black mare called Pale Lady. And how about your Patsy? A male dog. And I know in Ireland it stands for Patrick, but in the U.S. it means a female. I say forget names."

So Sarah made a great effort to put the horse of a different color out of her mind, although the troublesome subject of dogs refused to leave her entirely in peace. However, classes at Bowmouth College had begun, she was behind in everything, and it was not until the passage of three weeks' time, just before Julia's first initiation into the cardiac rehab program, that she was able to connect the problem of a dog to the hospital murders.

It wasn't, she told herself later, after the hem of the fog had lifted, the matter of the dog who barked or didn't. It was something closer to the bone, a matter of living long or dying soon.

26

THE first three weeks of September, which saw Julia Clancy's return to High Hope Farm, saw little investigative progress into the ways and means of the hospital homicides. Mike Laaka spent several fruitless days going over and over the times and places of the one male and five female suspects on the days of the murders and the attack on Julia. Then he reread every report, from the hospital, the legal world, and the newspapers on the death of the child Althea. Nothing new emerged. It had been a week of several high school driving deaths, so the Althea incident, even with the prominence of the doctor involved, was given little space. No charges were filed and the case vanished from the papers in a week's time.

George himself revisited Johnny Cuszak, the state pathologist, and again went over the details of the fatal injury to Dr. Jonathan. The angle of the blow. The weight of the recovered tire iron. How far must it have been lifted. From what height. The degree of strength from a number of positions, standing, bending, recumbent, required for the victim to have received his fatal cranial injuries.

"Like you think the guy might have planted himself down on

the ground and said, 'Hit me, baby,'" said Johnny, annoyed at these repeated interviews on the same subject.

"If the attacker happened to be short and not athletic, then we'd need to have the victim in a vulnerable position," said George.

"You already said that. Listen, anything's possible. A flat tire, the killer gets out the tire iron, the doctor kneels down, and whambo! Or the car stalls. Up goes the hood, victim checks the engine. Whambo! If the doc is bending over, a ten-year-old could do the job. And probably has somewhere. But listen, George, what's the matter with you guys? Why haven't you found where the body was put into the water? Found the tire marks. Or drag marks, bits of cloth, blood. Found the car, for Christ's sake."

"In case you haven't noticed," said George with heavy sarcasm, "the tide comes in and the tide goes out on a regular basis. So on the shore, body drag marks wouldn't show. Away from the tide line, cars and pickups do use access points around Lincolnville Beach and the outlet of the Duck Trap River. And they usually leave overlapping treads. But with the heavy rain . . ."

"Say no more," said Johnny. "But don't call me until you've nailed the bastard."

"Right now," said George, "we're looking at a number of bastards."

"Then," said Johnny unsympathetically, "go and finish the job. For what it's worth, my guess is that any person short of being a double arm amputee could have cracked Dr. Jonathan over the head."

Alex McKenzie, as he had told Sarah, and as he had repeated to George Fitts, Mike Laaka, and Katie Waters when bumping into them in the hospital, felt that from his experience with a variety of eccentric or psychotic persons, Stella Dugan didn't fit his idea of a killer. And, he added one morning after an exceptionally irritating encounter in the emergency room, if they wanted to take Emma Littlefield into custody, that was fine with him. Emma, now bolstered by her financial settlement, not visibly mourning her sister, was back on schedule with her ER visits, demanding Alex's instant attendance. "She has everything on earth wrong with her, imaginary or real," he said. "She's a clever old bat and she'd probably make a successful murderer if she put her mind to it."

As for Sarah, she would later think of the first three weeks in September as uneasily combining peaceful times and edgy ones. Peaceful because Alex, who had vowed since their last scene in Julia's hospital room to keep hands off, was not following her about with warnings about her extracurricular activities. This he found easy, since flu had made an early appearance in midcoast Maine, and he was much occupied with those of the elderly who hadn't even begun to think of flu shots.

Edgy because Sarah, not matter how she tried, could not get rid of a number of inchoate ideas. Among them: Stella's disordered mind and unruly thoughts on the subject of animals. Also, adding to her worries, stirred up by a number of visits to High Hope Farm, was her awareness that Julia was having entirely too many familiar visitors.

True to their promises, the four "witches," Stella Dugan, Hannah Finch, Clare Mitchner, and Christie Rivers, had made several visits to High Hope Farm. Stella, who had not met Julia during her hospital stay, came, as she put it, "just to be with the others and offer any help I can." (Back to being "true-blue," Sarah thought.) Hannah came because she loved farms. Christie Rivers came to assure Julia that there were no hard feelings about past disagreements, and because she enjoyed being around horses. Even David Bergman stopped by one early September afternoon with a basket of cucumbers and carrots from his garden, and Clare Mitchner began riding lessons from Patrick, which after two sessions proved she had a natural seat and a good sense of balance.

"Everyone means well, but it's a little like being back in the hospital," Julia grumbled to Sarah, who dropped in after classes on Tuesday, the eighteenth of September, for a quick visit. Julia, standing on the farm porch, looked almost healthy, color back in her face, wearing her faded jeans and checked shirt, her mop of gray hair cut and shaped, courtesy of Patrick's wife, Mary.

"And," Julia added, "people arriving in bunches cause a lot of fuss. They have to be checked in by those sheriff's men. As if we were running a minimum-security prison."

"Well, you are," said Sarah. "But they're paying you a compliment by coming. They think you're an 'interesting character.' Anyway, I've got a break tomorrow after my morning class, so I'm going to visit the volunteer snack party for old times' sake."

Julia lifted an eyebrow. "For social reasons? Or as part of our sleuth scheme?"

"Mostly social. But something's nagging me. I thought I'd stay in touch."

"Well, this Stella Dugan is the one on the hot seat, isn't she? Evidence connected with objects she was toting around. Hannah and Clare were making a joke about the whole thing. They called her Stella the Felon."

"Oh, great," said Sarah.

"Stella doesn't seem to mind. She just laughs. Well, sort of laughs. And speaking of Stella, just before I met her for the first time, George Fitts came over with photos to identify. A batch of people with red fuzzy hair. I know he wanted me say that Stella's was the face I saw on the ID tag, but I couldn't swear to it. All twenty faces looked alike."

"Something's got to crack soon," observed Sarah. "If it isn't Stella, it will be someone else. Alex says George still has his "situation room" going in the hospital and people go and come, everyone acts busy, but nothing comes of it. The latest focus seems to be on Carmen Wilson, the CEO's secretary. A lively lady. She told Alex that George Fitts is sex-starved and needs to have her as a suspect."

"George needs something," said Julia. "More than those Westies you've told me about." Then her attention moved to one of her English setters. Limping up the walk from the barn. "Poor dear," said Julia, her face softening. "Belle is almost eleven. Arthritis. I suppose I'll have to face it that both dogs are getting old. Along with me."

On this note, Sarah departed, her focus now on the undeniable fact that the life span of certain animals—unless they were parrots or elephants—was not as long their human friends wished. She would go home and brush Patsy and tell him how beloved he was and that if he wished he could always spend the night on their bed—or in it—and pay no attention to Alex's complaints on the matter.

Wednesday, the nineteenth of September, brought a day of glorious autumn weather, but no new revelations in the "Case of the Hospital Homicides," as the *Courier Gazette* put it. As for the principal players in this drama, they rejoiced in the beautiful weather and were spared any troubling intimations of what was to come. The skies didn't grow dark and frown, the earth didn't tremble, and no sparks flew from the heavens.

Routine was the pattern for that Wednesday. Sarah was to go to her early-morning class and present the work of John Donne to eighteen freshmen who seemed supremely indifferent to poetry written before they were born. Alex made ready to head to the hospital for his usual rounds and to interview a new secretary for his office.

"Carmen Wilson might like a change," suggested Sarah. "She's out of her job."

"Carmen is too distracting," said Alex. "I'm an old man now. Forty is looming."

And Julia, after her introduction to the world of cardiac rehabilitation on Monday, began on that Wednesday what would become a series of regular exercises in a program called Phase II, a category for those who still needed serious monitoring. She was introduced by Hannah Finch, doing per diem work in that facility, to a number of machines involving walking, lifting legs, moving arms, rotating shoulders while hooked up to leads and wires, plus having her heart rate and blood pressure checked at what seemed like five-minute intervals. Wasting time, Julia told them, because riding a horse once a day might offer the same physical benefits. This idea, however, was overruled by friends, family, her physicians, and, more importantly, by Patrick, who said he would not only hide her saddle but send her boots and helmet to the Salvation Army.

315

Sarah had made good her promise to join the volunteers at their eleven-o'clock break. Several children ran about in the distance, two couples walked the path around the rear of the garden, and a catbird called melody from the branch of a birch tree. The picnic-area grounds had been replanted with dozens of fall asters—rust-colored, white, yellow, purple, the little rock fountain was trickling past late-blooming lilies, the scent of the border alyssum filled the air, and all in all it was a scene of pure refreshment.

Sarah was hailed with pleasure and applauded for the lemon-filled doughnuts and sticky buns she produced from a plastic sack. Julia's progress and her return to health were celebrated. "I think she's going to be a good friend," said Hannah Finch, who had joined the volunteers that morning. "I do so love to have a farm to visit."

This seemed a bit ominous, Sarah thought, but then the others chimed in. Christie spoke of a new spirit of comradeship between herself and Julia. The ax had at last been buried. Stella claimed to have found a kindred spirit, one who loved the outdoors and animals. (Like Patches? wondered Sarah.) "And my niece, Clare, she really liked her two riding lessons," said Stella.

Profoundly boring as the subject had become, Sarah tried again. Had Clare really ridden a big Belgian horse when she was a child? "Oh, maybe." said Hannah. "Our uncle had four or five huge beasts, but I don't honestly remember whether Clare rode any of them. She might have. They all looked alike. Sort of a chestnut color. Sometimes he used them for logging and sleigh rides for us kids."

"One named Popcorn?" asked Sarah.

Hannah thought that was one of the goats because he was white.

"No," contradicted Stella, "Popcorn was that white angora cat of Aunt Sue's." She hesitated, seemed to consider, then smiled, that same small smile Sarah had seen before. "Yes, maybe it was the horse. I think so. It's hard to remember. So long ago."

Sarah decided temporarily to leave the possibility that Clare had lied or had confused a large chestnut horse with an angora cat or a goat. Or that Stella was having deliberate memory lapses. Try dogs, she told herself. "You've all had dogs," she suggested.

"Yes," said Stella. "All sorts. Big and small. Are you making an inventory?"

"I like to talk about dogs," said Sarah. "Didn't someone have an Irish wolfhound?"

This time Stella answered promptly, just as if she had been waiting for just such a question. "Oh, yes, him," she said. "Clare says she was heartbroken when he died."

At which David Bergman broke in with a rambling story about a Saint Bernard he had owned and the trouble with mange. "A great fellow, even though the dog-food bills almost broke me," he said. "Then he died all too soon and it was like we'd lost one of the kids."

They all nodded sadly. Then the ladies' watches (small and silver metal) were consulted, cups and papers put away, napkins dabbed at sugary lips, and the volunteer corps, together with Hannah Finch, returned to their base of operations.

Leaving Sarah thinking, erroneously, that nothing she had heard had moved her understanding beyond what it had been forty minutes ago.

A search warrant having been approved, Sergeant George Fitts and company had the task that Wednesday afternoon of going through Stella Dugan's house on Oak Street. Unfortunately, the glad welcome Stella gave the team suggested that nothing of importance would be found on the premises. "Unless," as Mike suggested, "the place is filled up with dried blood and Dr. Philip's hair, and she thinks it's part of some new game."

Whatever her reasons, at the team's arrival Stella began acting the part of the happy hostess. She made tea, offered a plate of sugar cookies. Pointed out the features of various rooms: the green-and-yellow afghan made by her mother over the wing chair in the living room, the grandfather clock in the hall, the family photographs on the bookcase shelf—Baby Althea front and center in the display. Then there was the family Bible open to the

Book of Job—was that a message? Mike wondered—the powder horn carried by some colonial Dugan displayed on a side table, a tartan pillow bought in Nova Scotia. At which point George, arriving ten minutes late, took hold of Stella's arm and gently escorted her from the scene. "You can come back when we've finished," he said. "And we'll be very careful."

"I suppose," said Stella, still cheerful, "you'll be taking samples of things. From the rug, the upholstery, things from the bathroom. Just try and not make too much of a mess. Oh, and before I forget it, Sergeant, I've left a bag of clothes for you in the laundry room. The things I wore to Lincolnville and Mount Battie that day. I haven't washed them because I thought you might want to take them to your lab. Something might fit in with the things you've found somewhere else. And I must have my car back. I really need it."

Grudgingly Mike admitted that the car would be returned shortly—none of the police wanted Stella, the reported speed demon, back on the road. "We've taken a few samples," he told her. "Upholstery, from the floor mats, the ashtray, the glove compartment. All routine items."

"Good," said Stella. "I'd like to think you'd do a thorough job."

"That female," exploded Mike, when George returned, having given Stella into the care of a waiting deputy. "Talk about a screw loose. Has she got an urge to live behind bars?"

"No," said Katie Waters, who, bending over, was directing the collection of fiber and fluff samples from the living room carpet, "It's guilt. I keep telling you, but you won't listen, either of you. Stubborn male thickheadedness. Stella Dugan wants to be caught in the worst way and she's doing her very best to help you guys do it."

The search continued through the afternoon and into the evening. Stella had been allowed to return, pick up a jacket—a fog was moving in—and had been given a ticket for a dinner at the Bowmouth Café. Finally, at a little after eight o'clock, she was escorted back to her house, and the search team, having packed a large number of evidence bags with what appeared to be completely innocent bits and pieces, departed.

Sarah, having barely survived student impatience with John Donne, spent the remainder of the day at Bowmouth College's English Department teaching a class in eighteenth-century satire and meeting with four students who had decided they didn't really want such a class, but what could they take that would be, well, more on the cutting edge? Sarah was pleased to point out that the date for dropping and adding classes had passed and they were stuck with a semester of Swift and Pope. Closing her office, she remembered that Alex had yet another evening medical dinner meeting, and so headed home for a quick-fix supper and some paper-correcting. Then it was bath and bed and the latest Scott Turow legal opus. And then to sleep, with Patsy, as was usual in Alex's absence, resting his head on the second pillow.

Neither Sarah nor the slumbering Irish wolfhound heard even the smallest noise or sensed that a shadowy figure, dropped off by a car on Sawmill Road in front of their old former farmhouse, now moved forward on velvet feet, all the while keeping close to the miscellaneous growths of fir, alder, and locust that bordered the driveway. Reaching the small parking space by the old barn, the figure crept to the Subaru, opened the tailgate without a noise, and most carefully slid into the opening and covered itself with an old gray blanket kept for Patsy's comfort.

Arriving home shortly after ten-thirty, Alex, always alert for breaches of safety, tried Sarah's passenger car door, found it, once again, unlocked. He removed the ignition key, pushed down the lock lever, closed the door, and shaking his head in disbelief, walked into the house, his face a thunder cloud of disapproval.

It was time for another talk. Three murders stared them in the face—and Sarah a witness, albeit half-asleep, to one of these. Yet here was his wife acting as if she wore an invisible cloak and nothing could touch her. Leaving the car open like that. Why in God's name hadn't she developed an ounce of self-preservation, an ounce of working caution? She was one of those whom the law labeled an "attractive nuisance." She invited trouble. She and Stella Dugan would make a great pair.

But the sight of Sarah asleep, tangled into a sheet, her pillow pulled over her head, suddenly cooled Alex's interest in a good

fight. A sleeping opponent doesn't make for equal combat. F[ur]
thermore, people awakened abruptly from their slumbers are [n]
usually open to persuasive argument and logic. Besides, he w[as]
himself exhausted. It wouldn't be a good scene. Okay, can t[he]
idea for now. He'd talk to her in the morning. Alex reached ov[er]
and with difficulty dragged the sleeping Patsy to the foot of t[he]
bed, brushed his pillow free of gray fur, and settled down. A[nd]
with the physician's ability, born of hundreds of broken nigh[ts]
to fall asleep on a moment's notice, Alex did just that.

And at almost six o'clock Thursday morning he woke, reme[m]
bered an early meeting with the Department of Medicine regula[r]
quietly slid out of bed, dressed, and leaving a note beside Sara[h's]
car keys on the hall table suggesting that a locked car is hard[er]
to steal than an unlocked one, opened the door. Got as far as t[he]
driveway, reversed, tore up the note as inflammatory, left anoth[er]
under her keys suggesting lunch at the cafeteria if she had t[he]
time, and departed for the hospital, driving slowly, since a hea[vy]
early-morning fog had settled onto the landscape.

Sarah woke refreshed, noted that Alex's space beside her h[ad]
been retaken by Patsy, remembered that he had a meeting, ro[se]
and dressed. What was she supposed to be doing today? Mornin[g]
a familiar English Department brouhaha on the subject of Eur[o]
pean classics versus relevant ethnic literature. Then an afterno[on]
seminar, the novel, Jane Austen's *Persuasion* (a choice that st[u]
dents would think was neither relevant nor ethnically meanin[g]
ful). Later catch up on Julia, and perhaps, just perhaps, anoth[er]
chat with Stella Dugan. Stella who, regardless of her complici[ty]
or lack of it, in anything resembling violence, despite her uns[et]
tled mental state still seemed to hold the answer to riddles co[n]
founding the police. Having seen Stella in action, in her ma[ny]
moods, Sarah doubted very much if Sergeant Fitts and Mi[ke]
would be able to get a straight answer to any question put to h[er]

But as Julia Clancy had informed her nurse after surgery, t[he]
best-laid plans of mice and men "gang aft agley," so Sarah in o[ne]

twenty minutes' time would discover that none of her day's planned agenda would take place.

Noting the drop in temperature and the fog rolling over the hills and barrens of Appleton, the disappearance of even the nearest trees and bushes, Sarah chose a heavier pair of slacks, a long-sleeved shirt, and grabbed a rain jacket. She reached for her car keys on the hall table; Alex had apparently snatched them out of her car to make a point about security. How boring. But reading his note about a possible lunch meeting, she softened toward her husband. Then, grabbing her briefcase, her handbag (finally returned by the police), a bottle of spring water, she scuttled across the damp surface of the parking area, unlocked the door of the Subaru, shoved her equipment next to her onto the passenger seat, slammed the door, started the car, and drove cautiously down the sloping drive to Sawmill Road and turned right in the direction of the Bowmouth College campus.

And peering through the windshield, Sarah stared in disbelief.

Out of the gray mist, swinging around a curve, a silver-gray car. A too-familiar-silver-gray car. A Chevy Malibu. Coming right at the Subaru, right down the center of the road. Leaving no room to dodge to the side.

Sarah slammed on the brakes and swore at the same time. Damn, the police must have finished with Stella's car and given it back. Suspect number one was back on wheels.

The silver car skidded to a stop directly in front of her and Sarah saw Stella Dugan climb out of the Chevrolet and walk toward her, a welcoming smile on her round face.

Stella's smile would be the last thing Sarah would remember.

Except, coming from nowhere, a solid thump on the back of her skull. Dazed, she slumped forward in her seat, hardly feeling the prick on her upper right arm. Right through the cotton sleeve, right into the soft tissue below the shoulder.

That morning a message came through to the Bowmouth College English Department to the effect that due to a family emergency, Assistant Professor Sarah Deane would be unable to keep her day's class appointments or meet with her students. Shortly afterward a second message came in to Alex's office, purportedly from the secretary of the English Department, saying that Professor Sarah Deane's cousin in Bangor had made an urgent call for help, a family matter, and that Sarah might have to be away for the rest of the weekend. Please tell Dr. McKenzie.

As for the subject of these messages, she, out like a light, bound by wrist and ankle, was lying along the back passenger seat of her own car, and traveling in a northeast direction toward places unknown.

Saw Mill Road

27

THE absence of Assistant Professor Sarah Douglas Deane on Thursday, the twentieth of September, caused no particular stir in the world of Bowmouth College and its affiliate, the Mary Starbox Memorial Hospital. The English Department often received messages about absent instructors, and since the faculty of this department was considered by its clerical staff as infested at best by unreliable types, at worst by pure flakes, no one thought much about the message. Arlene, the English Department's long-suffering secretary, simply made a few calls, left several notes stuck to several office doors, and went about her business.

As for Alex's newly hired office secretary, a Ms. Fairfax, she was pleased with the news from a voice which purported to be calling from the English Department that Sarah Deane had to leave town on a family emergency. Alex was already overbooked for office hours, so it was lucky that there would be no lunch date with his wife. When a Julia Clancy called in the late afternoon asking if Sarah had turned up in Alex's office, Ms. Fairfax, not yet familiar with this particular person, said briskly that Dr. McKenzie was busy with a patient and, unless it was an emergency, she would tell him later about the call. And no, a Sarah

Deane had not turned up at the office. Did Mrs. Clancy have an appointment?

Julia hung up and told herself not to call again. After all, Sarah did have a life beyond the fences of High Hope Farm, and Julia really hadn't wanted anything except to suggest that a drive into the country might be enjoyable. The leaves were almost at their flaming best, and besides, there was a Hanoverian mare for sale at a stable north of Belfast.

As for the police, George had received word shortly past noon from the state forensic laboratory that the injuries on Dr. Jonathan's skull were compatible with several blows by the recovered tire iron, but that this object was not one normally included with a Chevrolet Malibu. That it was a generic tire iron often found at an auto-supply store. Or in trucks and some SUVs. Mike, reporting in after this call, told George that regarding Stella Dugan's walking her (or Clare Mitchner's) dog Patches on hospital grounds the night of Florence Littlefield's murder, not one of the persons interviewed claimed to have seen Stella inside or outside the hospital (with or without dog)—this despite the fact that both exteriors and interiors of the hospital were overseen by security personnel. Back to square one.

Both men were arguing about the necessity of bringing Stella in again and pressing more strongly for hard answers when Katie Waters blew into the meeting room. "I think it's starting to unravel," she announced.

"What is?" demanded George.

"This bloody case," said Katie. "Guess who isn't here today."

"I'll bite," said Mike. "Unless it's Sarah, who's gone off sleuthing without letting security know where she is."

"I don't know about Sarah," said Katie. "Haven't seen her. No, it's Stella Dugan. Our faithful volunteer. Didn't turn up for the volunteer shift. Didn't call. Her buddies haven't heard from her. And she doesn't answer her home phone."

"I told you," said Mike to George. "She'll be at Logan Airport by now."

George scowled, picked up the phone, punched in a number, waited. "Art, George here. What—"

Here George was obviously interrupted by a long crackling noise. Then his scowl deepened and he instructed "Art" to stay put at the house and not move.

"Goddamn," said George.

"Which means . . ." said Mike.

"Stella Dugan left very early A.M. After the evidence was collected, we gave her the car back. So out she goes. Must have slid the car down and out of her garage without turning on the motor. Art was down the street a ways watching the house, but the fog had come in like a blanket, and she was off before he could get going. I've told him to hang around the house because most likely she'll be back. I'll have to send out an all-points."

"Once again, I repeat," said Katie, "the woman is guilt-driven. She's probably going to turn herself in at the state police station or throw herself off something. Or go wading for good off Lincolnville Beach."

At which the phone rang. George picked up, listened, swore again, muttered instructions, hung up. And faced his assistants. "Stella's back. Went shopping. Low on groceries. Stopped for lunch. McDonald's. Art helped her carry in the grocery bags. Says she plans to put in a couple of volunteer hours at the hospital."

"Jesus," said Mike. "That female!"

"Only thing," said George. "Art said her car fenders, the hubcaps, looked muddy."

"Aah," said Mike. "So she drove through a puddle. That fog is so thick and wet, you could swim in it. Everything's muddy."

"She won't run away," said Katie vehemently. "She's working very very hard to get caught. And you guys had better be ready.

Alex McKenzie finished office hours late. Ms. Fairfax, only days on the job, was still in a somewhat confused state. Files had been misplaced, patients put into the wrong examining room, and all in all he thought that he might prefer someone like Carmen Wilson. If he had to have an inefficient secretary, one with bodily charms might be preferable. A call to Sarah to ask whether he should bring home something like a pizza or a cooked chicken brought no answer. She was off somewhere, probably at High Hope Farm. But a call to Julia told him that Sarah hadn't been seen that day. At which point Ms. Fairfax stuck her head into the door of his office and announced that his wife had left a message. She would be out of town, maybe for a few days."

"Out of town!" exclaimed Alex, staring at her. "Where out of town?"

"Let me think. Bangor? Or was it Brunswick? It began with a *B*, anyway. Maybe Boothbay. Somewhere in Maine, so it won't be too far away," said Ms. Fairfax brightly. "It's some family problem. Maybe an emergency, but I don't remember that part exactly."

Alex, vowing to fire Ms. Fairfax in the morning, picked up his phone. A family emergency within the state of Maine didn't make sense. Sarah's parents were in Colorado on an Elderhostel trip, and his own parents were in Norway at a conference. Sarah's brother, Tony, was in Santa Fe with his band; her Grandmother Douglas was in Camden, not Bangor or Brunswick or Boothbay. And Julia hadn't seen nor heard from her niece. A call to the English Department got him a graduate student holding down the department's desk, the secretary having gone home. No said the student, she hadn't run into Professor Deane that day.

Mike and George were next. They had not seen, nor had they looked for Sarah. Neither had Katie Waters. "Shall we get into gear?" asked Mike. "Put out a call?"

"Did she check with security before she left our house?" asked Alex. "Usually does it from her car phone. Says where she's headed. What route she's taking. Except," he added, "she sometimes puts it off until she gets to where she's going and then reports."

"Hold on," said Mike. "We'll check on it. Call you back."

Four minutes later Alex picked up his office phone and got the news. "No call into security people in the morning. None later. Shall we get on to it?"

Alex hesitated. "Wait. Let me go home. Right now. Call you from there. If she's still missing you can send out the bloodhounds. And I'll come right back."

She was still missing. No Sarah. No Subaru. Only a hungry

Patsy greeted him. Beyond a message on the answering machine from the town office reminding Sarah of a recycling committee meeting that night, there was nothing else. The fax machine was empty. Alex sat down at the home computer, logged on, hit the e-mail, but beyond the college and hospital announcements and the daily spam deliveries, there was nothing.

Throwing a handful of kibbles in Patsy's dish—something he could almost hear Sarah commanding to be done—Alex hit the road, dialed George as the Jeep slid down the wet drive, turned right back into the fog, and headed back to the hospital.

Her head felt as if someone had loaded it with hot metal pellets and then started a relentless shaking. Her tongue was cardboard, her mouth cotton. She was blind. At least her eyes were closed and felt as if they had been glued shut.

And her wrists. No, one wrist. Tied! Some sort of chain. Sarah raised her right arm a few inches in the air and heard the slight rattle of metal hitting metal. With great effort, trying not to move her thumping head by the slightest millimeter, she squeezed her eyes open. The merest slot. Then wider. A narrow band of light showed through a curtained window. Where in hell was she? Not in the Subaru driving to class, that was certain. On a bed. Yes, her loose arm fingered what felt like a cotton blanket, and below it, the yielding scrunch of what was undoubtedly an old-fashioned horsehair mattress. And her right arm was tied with something like a long scarf, which itself was fastened by what resembled a chain dog leash. And this chain was wound around what felt like the iron headboard of a bed. She tried to raise her shoulders and turn, but the room revolved, her head beat a tattoo, and she subsided.

She needed a rest. Close your eyes, she commanded herself. Because I'm having an awful dream about a car accident and that I'm in a hospital. But not a modern hospital. Perhaps some field-rescue unit had brought her here. Because what health care plan included chaining the patient to a bed?

Then, slowly, memory crept back, a memory blurred by

shapeless shadows. Then sharper. Vivid. Stella Dugan's silver car heading toward her out of the fog. Seeing it, she had jammed on the brakes. Or had she? Had Stella front-ended her, smashed straight into the Subaru? Attack driving was something for which Stella had shown great aptitude. But did she see Stella get out of her car? She couldn't remember, but there must have been an accident because her whole head felt as if it had gone through the windshield. The air bags must have failed.

But if there'd been an accident, maybe Stella had been badly injured, an ambulance had been called, and Stella had been rushed away to the hospital. And she, Sarah, not as injured, perhaps only bumped on the head, had she been taken by some neighbor to a bedroom? To rest? To recover? But why was she fastened down? Answer: to make sure that she didn't try to start walking after a head injury, perhaps to save her from falling in the event she had a concussion. But where was her rescuer? Her landlord? Her keeper? Or, as was seeming every second more likely, her guard?

Gingerly Sarah felt the back of her head with her free hand. Moving her fingers along to the back of her skull, she felt a tender and sticky lump. Matted hair.

But if she'd had a head-on smash, why was her injury at the back of her head? She should have had frontal injuries. A broken nose, at least. It didn't make sense.

And it was all too much. Sarah closed her eyes again and drifted back into the heavy pulsing cloud of her headache. But then thirst asserted itself. She wanted water. Opening her eyes again, she cautiously moved her head to take in her surroundings. To see if this room (hospital, first-aid room, prison) provided water for the patient (inmate, prisoner).

Yes. On a rickety bamboo table by the bed stood a small blue pitcher and a matching glass. Moving with great caution so that her head would not explode before she touched the table, she fastened her fingers around the glass, brought it to her mouth and dribbled some of the water into her mouth, down her chin, onto her neck, soaking her shirt.

Another rest period. A long one with more drifting here, there, above, below, floating over some dark chasm. Then back. Eyes wide open.

She was in a small room. Board walls. A wooden chair. A bureau. Beyond the foot of the iron bed, a picture hung crookedly. Cows near a stream, grazing in a meadow. Off to the left, an amateur oil painting—lighthouse and breaking waves. The windowpanes were almost completely covered with faded red-and-white cotton curtains so thin that squares of sunlight came through and lit the room.

Think, Sarah commanded herself. The fog. Sarah remembered turning her car lights on and being blanketed by a heavy pea-soup fog. Then the "accident." But now the fog seemed to have burned off, so it must be late. How late? She twisted around and raised her left hand. Gone. No watch. Her handbag? Her briefcase? Her car! In God's name, what had happened to her car? She just couldn't remember the crash, the sound of crumpling metal. But that happened in accidents, didn't it? You hit your head, you lost consciousness. You forgot. Sometimes you lost a few minutes, sometimes days. Well, she'd lost the crash, the trip to this place, the people who took her to the room, put her on the bed. Fastened her wrist to the headboard. So where were they?

It was so quiet. Not a sound. With a house like this, every creak and crack would be heard. Even if her jailers (Sarah had finally settled on this term) were sneaking around in bedroom slippers, the floorboards would give them away. And no sound of cars or trucks, so the place couldn't be near a main road. Nor on a popular part of the ocean: no motor sounds, lobster boats gunning their engines. But there were birds. Outside, a blue jay squawked. Two crows called. Conclusion: She was in a building set away from everyday traffic, everyday working people.

Okay, take stock. Start with this place. The house, or cottage, camp, was old. The woodwork dark with age. The mixed furnishings looked as if they came from an attic. To Sarah everything spoke of a vintage summer place. Alex's mother and father had just this sort of room in their summer cottage on Weymouth Island, right down to the iron bed with the metal knobs, the wicker storage trunk, the paint-chipped bureau, those old-fashioned prints and amateur efforts on the wall.

Probably a summer place that, because it was September, might be closed up, except perhaps for weekends. Further conclusion, and this required a real facing of facts: The automobile accident must have been staged. By Stella and her magic silver car—because who else was there? Stella must have been lingering out there in the fog, waiting for Sarah to head out, and then, bang! Haul Sarah, conveniently unconscious, into the Chevy, or, easier, drive off with Sarah in her own Subaru. And doing what with her own Chevy? Had there been two people involved? One riding shotgun in Stella's car, ready to assist. Sarah dismissed the idea that anyone could have been hiding out in the Subaru. It had been locked, hadn't it? Because Alex when he came home must have locked her car and brought her keys in, left them on the front hall table. And she had to unlock her car before driving away. But right now this was a puzzle that could wait.

What couldn't wait was she herself. She was certainly being held here for reasons connected with the murders. Okay, she might have been seen trailing Stella, discovered hiding by the quince tree, heard asking awkward questions. But all those things didn't seem quite serious enough to provoke someone into assault and kidnapping. But her role as a possible witness to the killing of Florence Littlefield, now that was more to the point.

This conclusion added up to a frightening feeling that her present situation might quickly take a downhill slide. Maybe she had been left tied to the bed as a temporary expedient until the kidnapper(s)/killer(s) could decide what to do with her. Odd, though, a certain humanity had asserted itself. Water by the bed. Only one arm immobilized. And over there, next to the other side of the bed—she hadn't seen it before—a potty chair. A genuine nineteenth-century black-painted Windsor chair with a hole cut in its seat, the potty below on a shelf. For now she was being kept alive and healthy. But wouldn't she eventually be seen as a threat that must be dealt with? Permanently.

What argued against her being killed? For one thing, there

would be the problem of what to do with her body. Except in wilderness places, bodies were a nuisance. Do you burn the body in the barbecue pit or dump it? Drive it to some remote cliff and toss it over at high tide? But that strategy had backfired with Dr. Jonathan in Lincolnville. He'd floated right back into police hands by way of a helpful fisherman. So her killer might think first before striking.

These thoughts did not bring comfort. All right, Sarah told herself. Priority one: Do not become a body. First, drink more water. Try to get her head to stop ringing by moving very, very slowly. Then think about getting loose. Next, get loose. Even if she had to take the iron bed with her. She twisted around and examined her chained wrist. A tight fit. The chain was threaded through the wrist binding and then ran around the iron bedpost (a pointed projection that looked like the top of a mosque) and ran back to her wrist. Jerking the wrist away from the bedpost brought on a stab of pain and a dangerous clanking noise.

All right. Muscle wasn't going to do it. Ignoring the thumping in her head, Sarah pushed herself cautiously into an upright position. Damn metal beds anyway. A wooden bed might have been chewed or worried or kicked apart. But not one of these old-time iron models. She wiggled herself up against the head of the bed until she felt the vertical spokes hard against her spine. Then she ran her fingers up and down the cold metal surface, up to the bed knobs with their decorative curlicues. How could anyone sleep safely in one of these buggers? she wondered. If you missed your pillow as you flopped down, you could end with a skull fracture.

But now her searching finger paused. A crack, a fissure in the metal. Right below the metal mosquelike post. Could the thing actually screw on—and off? She reached, twisted. Nothing. Try again. Nothing. Third time. Three times equals magic, right? Right. The metal post moved with a scratching noise, moved a fraction.

Ten minutes later, her arm and hand sore from twisting, she was free. Well, almost free. The chain had been looped through a decorative aperture below the mosque, and now was part of Sarah's wrist equipment: chain fastened into scarf wound around wrist through to metal bedpost part. And back to wrist. Ten minutes of working with her free hand, holding the scarf material in her teeth, she at last disentangled herself and pulled her now much-chafed wrist loose. Carefully she replaced the bedpost and stuffed the chain and scarf into a pocket. Now to get the hell out. Her headache was subsiding. Maybe the car collision hadn't done that much damage, just left her with a bloody scalp.

How to leave? She tiptoed to a window and saw below a dirt road winding toward what appeared to a grove of trees, another dirt track heading toward what appeared to be a small pond. But no cars. Not a red Subaru nor a silver-gray Malibu. Cautiously, she slid the door of the room open and found she was on a second floor with a staircase a short distance to her left. She returned to the room for a quick hunt. But no handbag or briefcase appeared. And no shoes.

Never mind, she had legs. Softly she moved to the top step, and remembering the possible creaks, put her weight almost entirely on the wooden railing. Stopped to listen. Quiet. Down at the bottom she peered around. No one. But beyond what must be a dining room—empty—a back door. And by the back door a selection of footgear. Clogs, an old navy pair of sneakers, a pair of black rubber boots.

Sarah tucked the sneakers, whose size appeared to be possible, under her arm and slid out the back door, out into what must have once been a vegetable garden, now gone to seed, and then behind a line of maple trees. Making it past the trees, keeping close to a tangle of alders, forgetting caution and noise, she ran as if a shotgun were aimed at the middle of her back. Which she thought, pausing for breath, it might well have been.

But now what? And where? She looked back to the little cottage/camp from which she'd escaped. Generic cottage. Dark shingles, window frames painted green. A single chimney. Porch. A shed big enough for a car. A tangled garden. Nothing in the least remarkable about the scene. The sun said she was heading west, which was not much help. West meant anything away from the ocean but was otherwise useless. Finding a telephone would mean going back to the house, so that was not an option. Funny that there were no other houses, cottages, or camps around. This must be a huge piece of property, a working farm once and still held by a family. Or an extended family.

She found a rotting log and pulled on the sneakers over her now scratched feet. Get going, she ordered herself. But whatever she did, she must avoid roads, avoid people, especially those driving a silver-gray car, and that meant skulking through woods and fields and drinking from streams and ponds until she got her bearings.

Moving on was harder than it sounded, what with fatigue and bouts of nausea—or was it hunger? Perhaps she'd find an apple, try one bite. Or a handful of blackberries. But it was late for blackberries and there didn't seem to be any apple trees planted in the route Sarah chose to take.

Well, not exactly "chose." Sarah, after several turns in and then out of a wooded area, a crossing over a small stream, and dodging what might have been a cornfield decided that she wasn't choosing, she was simply stumbling in a direction that seemed to turn away from the cottage. How she wished that her time as a child at summer camp had been spent on pathfinding or orienteering instead of basket making and archery. Then perhaps she could make sense of where she was heading. She knew that in strange places one was supposed to blaze a trail, but it was too late for that. But at least she was well away from the little cottage and that was a comfort.

What wasn't a comfort was the returning headache. In the excitement of escape the pain had seemed to be receding. But now it returned in full force, to which was added a sudden stronger wave of nausea. Sarah slowed her steps, found a rock, and sat down. Her wrist, her arm, her whole shoulder throbbed. The landscape heaved slightly. Never mind she told herself, keep walking. Now the sun was lower, the air carried a chill. Clenching her teeth through a second wave of nausea, she levered herself up and started marching. Minutes seemed to be taking hours, but now the ground by the edge of the trees seemed to be turning into a path. This was hopeful. Sarah bent her head and slogged on. Left, right.

Full circle. Back to where she had started. Right into a small gravel area. Right next to the small shingled outbuilding. Directly toward a parked silver-gray car.

Sarah could only stop, gape, and stare. Look wildly around. And then stare back at the car. A silver-gray Chevrolet. Stella Dugan's car.

But no Stella in the driver's seat.

The car was in perfect condition. Sleek and shining in the late-afternoon sun. Not a scratch, nor a dent. Not a sign of having been in a recent head-on crash. Oh, God, why couldn't she remember? Or was this some sort of phantom, hallucinatory vehicle brought on by her head injury? Or, from a rational point of view, could this car simply be yet another of the thousands of silver-gray Chevrolet Malibus that infested Knox and Waldo counties? A car that had nothing to do with Stella Dugan?

The answer walked into view.

Around the back of the shed came Stella Dugan, dressed in her volunteer smock, a grocery bag in her arms.

For a second she stared at Sarah and then recovered. "Sarah! Good heavens! What are you doing? Don't you know you're sick? Or injured. Such a bad fall. Right on the back of your head. I think you blacked out and went down just like that. It looked like some sort of seizure. I didn't want to take you to the hospital, so I thought the best thing to do was get you to our camp, let you rest, and when you woke up, tell me what you want to do."

"What!" exclaimed Sarah. Then, pulling herself together: "I don't have seizures. I thought I'd been in a car wreck."

"Poor dear," said Stella, walking over and taking Sarah by the arm. "You look as pale as a ghost. Sit down. I was driving on your road and there you were, climbing out of your car. And then you collapsed. Right on the road. Let me take you back into the house for a rest."

Sarah shook her off. "And chain me to that bed again. No."

Stella reattached herself to Sarah's arm and Sarah, overcome by a wave of dizziness and the heavy waft of Stella's lavender perfume, let her stay. For the moment. Until she'd worked out a plan. If, in her present condition, she could think of one.

"I think," said Stella softly, "we should have a talk. Come and sit down. The bench over by the back door. Now tell me, how long have you been having blackouts like that? Or should I call them psychic disturbances?"

Settling herself and an unprotesting Sarah on the indicated log bench, Stella shook her head at Sarah as to a naughty child. "Now," she said, "I know more than you can imagine. I'm not blind. You followed my car all the way from the hospital to Lincolnville Beach. Are you a secret traffic monitor and wanted to call me on speeding, tell your friends in the police? Yes, I know I drive too fast. It's such a relief. Then you watched me wade into the water. No, let me finish . . ."—as Sarah began to shake her aching head.

"You followed me to Mount Battie. And turned up at my house. But then when we had tea together, I thought, well, Sarah isn't such a problem. Not a real danger. Maybe I can tell her all about poor Althea and it'll stop her from sticking her nose where it has no business."

"Is that what you think?" said Sarah, trying to stall and at the same time trying to fight off another bout of dizziness.

"Exactly what I think. But the last straw, the thing that made me sure you weren't going to give up, was your hiding by the quince tree and barking. Like a dog. In fact, at first I thought it was a dog. I'm quite impressed. You could get a job doing dog commercials."

"How did you—" Sarah started and broke off.

"A piece of cloth on one of the quince thorns. Then, when I saw you coming out of the hospital with a torn shirt and a bandage on your arm, I was sure. And"—here Stella sighed deeply—"I suppose I have you to thank for all those police sessions I've been having. Have you ever thought that the police don't need your help? And that you look pretty silly running around like Angela Lansbury in *Murder She Wrote*? You're simply not the type."

Sarah, with an effort, kept her mouth shut and tried to focus on the distance between Stella's body and herself. Knock her back, give her one hefty push. And go.

"So," went on Stella, her face rosy in the late-afternoon sun, "I decided to have it out. Face-to-face. Tell you, please, in my kindest way, to leave me alone. Everyone says that your Aunt Julia was a tough nut, but you, dearie, are worse than she is."

"You drove to my house this morning? On purpose?" said Sarah, trying to get this part straight.

"To talk. To catch you before you went to your class. But there you were coming out of your drive. Stopping. Getting out of the car. Having that seizure, the blackout. So, let's say I was worried about you and brought you here where you'd be safe. Fastened you to the bed in the guest room—Aunt Letitia's old iron bed—until I could figure out what to do."

"And have you figured it out?" asked Sarah quietly.

"Well, I think so. Looking at the pluses and minuses of the case, I think you've turned into a minus. Someone who has seizures and interferes with other people's lives."

Sarah blinked, swallowed hard, and then saw that Stella had reached into her volunteer jacket and come up with a small syringe. Filled with some sort of liquid.

"You're feeling a little sick," said Stella in a soothing voice, reaching for Sarah's arm. "This will put you right. After all, as I told you, I was a nurse."

At which Sarah, dizziness suddenly gone, her vision clear, shot to her feet, shoved Stella back with her free hand, jerked away while at the same time her other hand, now a fist, went into orbit and slammed Stella sharply on the nose. Stella gave a yelp of pain and Sarah sprinted free and sped across the driveway. Where to? Of course, the car, the silver car. She wrenched the door open. Let the keys be there, she prayed as she threw herself into the driver's seat and pushed down the door lock in a single motion.

And yes! Yes! The keys dangled from the ignition.

She turned the key, and from the corner of her eye saw Stella staggering toward the car, blood trickling down her face. Sarah pushed the gear into drive—thank heaven the thing had automatic transmission—and gunned the engine, swerving past Stella, whose arms were out wide as if to embrace her escaping car.

336

Down the drive, left along a dirt road, past the field she had recently tramped in, down to a left turn onto Macadam, and off in some direction. Which direction, she didn't care. Not now, anyway. Just get loose, and if she ended up in Canada, so be it. Sarah brought the car back to a modest fifty miles an hour and then told herself that Canada might indeed be a good choice because she'd probably be arrested in Maine for assaulting a beloved volunteer hospital worker.

High Hope Farm

Training-Boarding
Equitation

28

JULIA had been left out of the loop. Alex and the police agreed that this must be so. Someone just home from major surgery should not be stressed.

"Let her think Sarah is off doing something but we don't know the details," said George.

"Which we certainly don't," said Alex. "What I do know is that when I went back to the house, her car wasn't there." Having made a record run from Sawmill Road back to the hospital, Alex now looked gray with worry. Sarah had finally done it. Taken off and left no notes, no indications of when or where she'd gone.

"Car stolen?" suggested Katie Waters.

"I locked it last night. But any idiot can break into a car and jump-start it."

"Or hang around, wait for Sarah to come out and nail her," said Mike.

"Thanks for that idea," said Alex angrily. "But let's hope Sarah and her car are together, wherever that is.

George nodded. "I'll alert Julia's farm security to keep an eye out for her."

"And," Alex added, "keep watching that place like a hawk."

"Of course," said George. "And we've sent out an all-points for Sarah's Subaru. Troopers working north of Camden on route one, on seventeen to Augusta, and south from Rockland on one."

"Southwest?" asked Mike.

"We've alerted the sheriff departments of Knox, Lincoln, and Sagadahoc counties. The Subaru with and without a Sarah or any other driver."

Alex nodded. "I'm off. I'll stay in touch. You have my cell phone number. I'm going to hunt down that Stella Dugan and take it from there."

"We're trying to watch Stella Dugan," George pointed out, "She got loose early this A.M., but came home with groceries and did her regular volunteering gig this afternoon. Except she left the hospital about half an hour earlier than usual and hit the mall."

"And?" said Alex.

"George doesn't like this part," said Mike. "The place was a mob scene and her tail, he lost her. Somewhere before checkout."

"The other volunteers, did you ask them where she was going?"

"I put them on the grill," said Mike. "Take your pick. She's home, which is around the corner on Oak Street. Or visiting family members—you have the list. At her summer camp in Cushing. Or checking on the cottage on the old family farmland—west of Lake Saint George. Clare Mitchner suggested that Cushing was the best bet. And Hannah Finch said Stella talked about taking in a movie. The others said any of these or none of the above."

"We'll be covering all family members, especially David Bergman," said George.

"I'll try the family-farm," said Alex. "You have a map?"

"Kate has," said Mike. "It's a police operation, so you'll go together. She knows the area. Her dad used to hunt around there."

"Come on then, Katie," said Alex, striding to the door of the meeting room. "I'm out of here." Then he paused. "Firearm?"

"As they say," answered Katie, "I'm ready and loaded. My car, it's that Ford Taurus over by the physicians' lot. I've got the police radio hookups."

Another traveler in the latter part of that Thursday afternoon was Julia Clancy. She'd given up the idea of dodging away from her surveillance deputy, but since she was going directly to the hospital for her hands-on cardiac rehab session, there would be no follower inside the hospital; the place was already crawling with police.

Driven by Patrick, she was escorted by him to the basement quarters that held the different exercise and rehabilitation units for hospital and outpatients. Arriving at the double doors to the Lois Mills and Joanna Jordon Cardiac Rehab Center, Julia dismissed Patrick. "I can't have you sitting around here when you could be at the farm. No, no objections. Please go back. Check on that grain order. And then pick me up in an hour. By then I'll be exhausted and very disagreeable."

At which Patrick gave her a knowing grin and went his way.

Julia hung up her denim jacket, pulled on her all-purpose sneakers—as required—in the locker room, and then made her way to the cardiac rehab office. There she was met by her old nurse friend, Hannah Finch—today's smock featured pheasants. Hannah explained that she worked wherever she was needed, she and Clare. Per Diem. Anywhere. Lots of the nurses did. This afternoon and for the present, they would be down here, but Clare was just finishing with three other patients and taking their blood pressures. She, Hannah, would check the paperwork, weigh Julia, remind her how to stick the monitor leads to three points on her body, hang the monitor around her neck and introduce her to the director. "Sometimes we run a session in the late afternoon like today," said Hannah, "I remember that's the time you wanted. Anyway," she added brightly, "now you're up and running. Well, not running. Moving forward."

Julia, feeling like some sort of prisoner in a movie about aliens, followed Hannah to the nurse's desk, saw her name, weight, blood pressure, and heart rate entered on a screen, and followed her to the first torture instrument: the treadmill.

Alex and Katie, the latter driving at a speed that would have left Stella Dugan in the dust, covered the distance from the hospital to Lake Saint George in what seemed to be seconds. Kate obviously knew her way around on obscure roads, but Alex, sitting beside her, wondered if they might end it all in a muddy ditch in one of the more godforsaken parts in the county. In fact, so swiftly did they travel, so confusing were Katie's shortcuts, that both missed the silver-gray Chevrolet that shot out of a crossroad and sped away past them.

"That was a close one," said Katie. "Some people just don't want to live until dinnertime. But it looked like Stella's car, though that sort are a dime a dozen. But it wasn't Stella. A dark-haired driver. What'd you think? Shall we chase it?" Katie slowed slightly and looked over at Alex. But before he could answer, she shook her head. "The car will be miles away by the time I turn around. I'll call in and alert George. He can put out a call."

"Right," said Alex. "Let's go where we're supposed to."

After two false turns—old tractor trails to the original farm— Katie and Alex arrived at the cottage. Forty minutes later they agreed that the score was close to zero. One iron bedstead with a rumpled cover and an empty water glass by the bed was the total. Katie, put on plastic gloves and dropped the glass into one of the paper evidence bags she had brought, bundled up the bed-spread into a waiting plastic bag, left a yellow Scene-of-Crime tape on the door, and then the two without much hope continued the search outside. There, the small shed door was open, a splotch of oil in the middle of the dirt floor as well as heavy tread marks suggesting that at some recent time, a car or truck had been sheltered there.

"Truck or SUV," said Katie, examining the tire patterns. She reached for her cell phone. "I'll let George know. He can send someone over to do the forensic stuff. Also, did you notice, there's been a car, a smaller one, in front of the cottage. Tire marks in and tire marks out. And it looks like the driver spun out in a hell of a hurry. Does that make you jump to any ideas about that Chevy we saw steaming across our bow back there?"

"I'm not jumping," said Alex. "Fool drivers are all over. But what really gets me is this whole place being empty. I'm kicking myself for not bringing Patsy."

At which Katie's cell phone went off. She listened briefly, then snapped it closed.

"Two great minds at work," said Katie. "Mike—he's covering Liberty, Washington, Appleton townships—stopped at your place and picked up Patsy. Said for us to stay put, he'll bring the dog over because after all he's supposed to be a hound. And that, for now, let the other K-9 units concentrate closer to the college area."

"He picked up Patsy?" said Alex. "How? Broke into the house?"

Katie grinned. "No problem. The front door was unlocked. So were the back door and the door out onto the porch. You must have left them open when you went home to check on Sarah. Great security you two guys have."

"Christ Almighty," said Alex with feeling. "The two of us need brain transplants."

Before Katie could agree, Mike in a sheriff's car, lights blinking, shot into sight, rounded into the driveway and squealed to a stop. And released Patsy who, after greeting, Alex, began a wild sniffing tour of the drive, the bench, and the back door. Then upstairs, into the bedroom and began a long sustained whining.

"This," said Alex grimly, "is it."

"Was it," said Katie. She turned to Mike. "The place is as empty as a drum. We've checked the basement, the attic crawl space, all the closets, cupboards. The outbuildings. Sarah is outta here. Gonzo."

But the place was not as "empty as a drum. In their haste to depart both searchers had missed a partly filled syringe that had rolled under an overgrown hydrangea by the back door.

* * *

Sarah was feeling more than a little "gonzo." For the past twenty minutes she had been circling around the countryside trying desperately to keep to speeds that would not attract the arm of the law. I can see why Stella speeds, Sarah told herself, as she pulled into a rough patch of gravel by an abandoned chicken house. Aunt Julia's right, it does wonders for the nerves. Maybe speeding is contagious. Or, more likely, I've gone over the edge.

She turned off the ignition and breathed hard. She had to take time to get a grip on what had happened. And what hadn't. What hadn't happened was a head-on crash with Stella's car back there on Sawmill Road. Her last memory was of Stella coming around the curve out of the fog and straight at her. But what then? Sarah squeezed her eyes shut and again tried to remember. There was at the back of her memory a dim image of Stella smiling. Walking toward her? Then a bang on the head and lights-out.

But having abandoned the idea of an automobile accident, Sarah was left with the possibility of a blackout or a seizure, as Stella had suggested. These she rejected. Had she fallen backward somehow or been clobbered? Whatever happened, the syringe in Stella's hand suggested it might have figured in the earlier scene. And what had been in the syringe? Some knock-out stuff, no doubt. But only in the movies, as Alex had often complained, does the victim become fully unconsciousness in the first second of an injection. More time, he claimed, is needed.

So okay, it went like this. Hit me on the head, stick me with a needle, take over my car when I'm unconscious, then get me to the Clare Mitchner/Stella Dugan/Hannah Finch family cottage and tie me up? Why? Because, as Stella pointed out, I've begun to annoy her. Them? Ruin plans, anyway. Whatever plans were in the works. Why not kill me? Because, as Sarah had decided before, killing presented problems that no one had quite figured out—problems of body moving. Body disposal.

Sarah shook her head, found that it revived her headache, and stopped. She needed a rational approach to her present dilemma. And about time, since neither logic, sense, nor reason had figured in much she'd done lately.

First, since she probably wasn't going to escape to Canada,

make some calls. Searching about in the car she found, as she'd hoped, that Stella had a car phone. Start with Alex. Judging from the waning light, it must be somewhere around five or even later. However, a call to Sawmill Road brought only the answering machine. She left a brief word and dialed Alex's office. And found herself talking to Ms. Fairfax. No, Dr. McKenzie had left for the day. Who was this, please, and did she have an appointment? If she didn't, perhaps she should call in the morning and set one up.

"Just say Sarah called and everything's all right"—an untruth if there ever was one.

"Could I have your last name, please," said the efficient Ms. Fairfax.

Sarah hung up, dialed George Fitts's hospital office, which gave her Deputy Art Jenkins, who took the message and said he'd pass it on. And where was she? And wherever that was, stay put. Next, she called High Hope Farm and was told by the student stable helper who answered that Mrs. Clancy had been taken to the hospital. By Patrick.

Oh, God, not again. Had Aunt Julia been readmitted with another heart attack, or was this just a routine checkup? Or had she just gone to her cardiac-rehab program? Sarah couldn't remember the exact schedule, except that Clare Mitchner and Hannah Finch had both been talking about it. Rehab was, Sarah thought, the least sinister of the possibilities, but she was taking no chances. Forget about Art Jenkins and the order to stay put. She didn't know where she was, but there must be a main road somewhere around. She turned the ignition key, cranked the wheel, and hit the gas. And God help any policeman who pulled her in for speeding.

Julia was escorted to meet the director of Cardiac Rehab, one Jeri Schmidt, a tall dark-haired woman with a firm manner that suggested there would be no nonsense in her domain. She was dressed, not in the popular flowered or patterned smock, but in a crisp white medical jacket complete with an up-to-date ID photograph and her RN pin on her collar. "I'm going off duty after I finish some paperwork," she said. "But you'll be in good hands with Hannah or Clare. We run a tight ship here, we have rules, good ones, for the safety of everyone. But I'm sure you'll be a compliant patient."

There followed the briefest pause, as if Jeri already knew that Julia would be anything but. Then, with a quick nod, the director was gone down the hall.

The rehab room had emptied out, and the machines—treadmill, bicycle, step-up machine, rowing machine—sat idle. Hannah directed Julia through a series of warm-up exercises, pointed out features of each apparatus, the measurement of speed, distance traveled, and degree of intensity. Then called Julia's attention to a guide taped to the wall. She was to indicate the difficulty of each exercise so that she neither overdid (maximum difficulty), nor failed to exert herself at all (minimum difficulty).

"We start slowly," said Hannah, "and work up."

"*We* don't," said Julia, unable to hold her tongue. "I start slowly. You're not on the machine with me."

"Now, Julia," said Hannah indulgently. "Let's not make this any harder than it's going to be. I know you, but some of the other nurses might be put off. Now I'll set the treadmill for ten minutes at a low speed with zero elevation and we'll see how you do."

Julia, as so often happened in a "health care setting," found herself reduced to the age of about seven years, and so vowed to keep her mouth shut for the rest of the period. She would concentrate. She would not look away from the dials and lights that recorded her progress or lack thereof; she would make eye contact with no one. She would listen only to her own breathing. She would be all business. And, goddammit, all compliance.

So intent was she on this disciplined approach that she failed to notice that Hannah had slipped from the room, the door had reopened and been snapped shut. And that Hannah's place at the desk had been taken by another figure.

On Julia went. Step, step, step. She tried singing under her voice: "Tramp, tramp, tramp, the boys are marching," and "When

Johnny comes marching home, hurrah, hurrah." This is so boring, she told herself. But now even this mild effort was taking its toll. She was getting tired after only six minutes. She reached over to the dial and brought the speed down from fifteen to twelve. Probably against the rules, she thought, making an executive decision like that.

"You're changing your speed," said a familiar voice. "I think you should ask first. Here, let me turn it off and you can start again after a little rest."

But Julia had no chance of replying to this kind suggestion. A firm hand grasped her arm, twisted it behind her back, and at the same time a second hand went around her mouth. Before she could protest or try to wriggle free, she was dragged backward. Off the treadmill with a painful thump. Onto the floor. Flat on her stomach, both arms now clasped behind her back in a tight grip and tied with what might have been a piece of surgical tape.

"Don't you make a sound," hissed a voice, cranking Julia's head to one side and stuffed a wad of face tissue in Julia's open mouth. Desperately Julia twisted, tried to flip her body over, and at the same time use a foot to kick.

The kick connected with something soft, and the other person gave a gasp. And hesitated. But then, kneeling on Julia's lower back, she leaned forward and with one hand slammed Julia's face down. But in the second before her head hit the carpet, Julia saw the determined face of her attacker. Saw the syringe in her right hand.

"It's you," she managed to gasp in a muffled voice through the tissue.

"Of course," said an entirely familiar voice.

Sarah, as she sped south, untroubled as yet by police, and trying to keep at bay her worry about Julia having had a second heart attack, forced herself to think about her lost day. Had anyone noticed she'd missed her classes, her faculty meeting, not met Alex for lunch, not checked on Aunt Julia? If Alex had made it home, had he noticed that Patsy needed food? Needed his water dish checked? Needed to be taken for a run? He was beginning to get a little stiff if he didn't have enough exercise.

And then it hit her. That little bit of information, that bothersome teasing thing she'd salted away in her brain and had been looking for. Dog.

Aunt Julia's setter, Belle, limping up the walk; David Bergman and the Saint Bernard that had died all too soon. And Patsy. An Irish wolfhound. Getting a little arthritic. A wolfhound is a wonderful animal. But he's big. Big dogs don't live as long as small ones. It's very sad, but if you have a big dog, you have to face up to this fact. Yes, that was it. And Sarah had finally caught it. Something she should have caught the minute the story was told.

And then, just as she finally turned on the main route to the hospital and thought she was home free, Sarah picked up a follower. The car, a blue Ford Taurus, stayed for the first few miles well behind her. Sarah thought she'd seen the car before somewhere, but now everything seemed familiar, had a sinister sheen on it. But then, when the two cars hit a straight stretch, the second car began to blink its lights as it picked up speed. But Sarah was ready for this. She stomped on the accelerator, swerved toward the rear of the hospital and into the side service entrance and had the satisfaction of seeing the blue car overshoot and jam on the brakes. Sarah wheeled around, ducked into the back part of the service parking, threw herself out and, running full speed, got to the ramp that led to the wide doors of the lower delivery (and undertaker's) entrance. Always open, thank God. Then down, past the morgue, the children's playroom, the orthopedic rehab. First check the cardiac rehab, she ordered herself. That's where Julia *should* be. Great if she's there. But if she isn't, I'll push the panic button. Push it hard.

But after flinging open the double doors to the rehab center and plunging in, Sarah saw she was not alone. Coming from the other end of the long corridor, feet pounding like a hammer, ran a tall dark-haired woman in a white jacket. The woman beat her to it, got to the doors to the exercise room and snatched them open. Sarah, putting on an extra burst of speed, followed close behind.

Together, as if they had planned it, both women skidded to a stop. Julia was on the floor. Face hard against the rug. And with one hand holding Julia's wrapped wrists together, the other raised, holding a syringe, kneeling on Julia's back, Clare Mitchner

And then, as if filmed in slow motion for a second-rate medical movie, slipping quietly in behind Sarah and the woman in the white jacket, came another principal actor for the wrap-up, the last scene: Stella Dugan.

In each of Stella's hands was a painted green dumbbell. Raising these twin objects high in front of her, as if she were presenting valuable gifts, Stella stepped forward, her face lighted with a pleased smile.

And in one swooping motion brought both dumbbells down hard on Clare Mitchner's back.

Sarah, if she had been asked later on the witness stand, could not, even if her life and liberty depended on it, have given a coherent account of what happened. It was a scattershot of moving images.

The dumbbells thudding to the floor, rolling crazily across the carpet and coming to a rest next to Julia's cheek. Clare Mitchner, with a scream falling forward on Julia, the syringe rolling out of her hand. Julia struggling and turning under Clare's weight. Jeri Schmidt whirling around, giving Stella Dugan an elbow to her throat, a fist to her stomach, and then taking her head into a hammerlock. Katie Waters bursting into the room, followed by Alex McKenzie. Alex grabbing Clare Mitchner and Katie putting a pistol to her left ear. At the same moment Sarah, in the only action she could clearly remember, reached down, pushing the dumbbells away from Julia's head, pulled her aunt free and clear of Clare's writhing body.

Then, in an anticlimactic entrance, George Fitts, Deputy Art Jenkins, and Mike Laaka charged into the room as a disembodied voice from a wall speaker intoned: "Code one-oh-one, Code one-oh-one Cardiac Rehabilitation Unit. Repeat Code one-oh-one Cardiac Rehabilitation Unit."

* * *

The immediate outcome of what became known in the following months as the Rehab Rumble was straightforward. enough. Julia Clancy was placed, gasping yet protesting, on a gurney to the emergency room to have a complete going-over for any injuries sustained during her recent ordeal, and following a favorable report was ordered to spend the night at the hospital "where a cardiologist can keep an eye on you."

Clare Mitchner, suffering from a smashed cervical vetebra and multiple contusions, was, after being stabilized, put on the orthopedic floor with a sheriff's deputy on guard. Stella Dugan, her nose still bleeding from Sarah's blow, but acting as if she had been the recipient of a "job well done" medal, was placed in the psychiatric section of the hospital and told that she could have her attorney present during the interrogations that would be forthcoming.

Alex McKenzie—it was, of course, he and Katie Waters in the blue Taurus that had pursued Sarah into the hospital parking lot—was left with such warring feelings that he could hardly speak. Relief, love, anger, all radiated from his face as he escorted Sarah from the latest "scene of the (attempted) crime," and from there to see a neurologist about a possible concussion and scalp lacerations.

As for Sarah, the whole day had almost been too much of a bad thing. It had been a day that began with a bang on the head, a dose of thiopental sodium, then with her being tied up in a strange cottage, followed by an attempt to escape. This was followed by an unplanned return and confrontation with Stella. Then a breakaway in Stella's silver car and the plunge into the cardiac rehab mayhem. Sarah, thinking back, almost wished she'd had that seizure, the one Stella had insisted on—and in a peaceful coma, perhaps on some South Sea island.

Katie Waters and Mike Laaka had been given the task of helping the state police CID and the state forensic labs assemble the incriminating evidence found in the cardiac rehabilitation center. Later, they would oversee the forensic team's reexamination of Stella Dugan's Chevy Malibu, which had been declared squeaky-clean on the first going-over. Without a tire tool of any sort—as

Stella had claimed. Next the team would go over Clare Mitchner's Mazda Tribute four-wheel-drive number, a vehicle usually equipped, because of its trucklike nature, with a tire iron. But this tool had been reported by its owner, truthfully or not, as missing at the time of purchase in a secondhand-car lot. What had really happened, George Fitts guessed, was that of these two missing tire irons—Stella's and Clare Mitchner's—one had been used to land the killing blows on the back of Dr. Jonathan Philip's skull. Then, as everyone knew, Stella had dropped the murder tool—hers or Clare's—at a later date into the waters off Lincolnville Beach. From where it had shortly become a "found" object, along with its green umbrella bag on Mount Battie—all due to the unauthorized detective efforts of Sarah Deane. But one recovered tire iron meant that two were still missing. Either Clare's or Stella's plus the one claimed stolen by David Bergman.

But Mike Laaka had exploded when a search through junkyards was suggested. "Holy shit, George, let go already. Never mind whose car had the damn thing originally. You've got your mitts on the murder weapon. Who in hell wants to find two extra tire irons we don't need? We have the real thing with lab-certified evidence stuck to it. So nail the lady, or two ladies, who used that tire iron to whack Jonathan."

Of other former suspects, Hannah Finch and Christie Rivers were absolved of all blame in the triple murders, although it was suggested to both that if they had had more suspicious natures, they might have found out what was going on in their family circle.

David Bergman was declared innocent either by knowledge of, or participation in, the three homicides. However, five days later, Sergeant George Fitts had the pleasure of learning that David had been stopped for speeding and an illegal U-turn in Rockland.

Carmen Wilson, former "executive" secretary to Dr. Jonathan Philips, gave the hospital two weeks notice. There were bigger fish in larger seas, she claimed. By which statement it was assumed that some big metropolitan hospital figured in her future plans.

Ms. Fairfax's short-lived secretarial job in Dr. McKenzie's office was terminated by her employer, whereupon she immediately filed a complaint with Human Services for harassment and inhuman treatment of a sexist nature.

Nurse Jeri Schmidt, for her swiftness in responding to the sound of thumps and bangs in the cardiac rehabilitation exercise room, received a well-deserved commendation as Employee of the Month. This honor brought Jeri not only a certificate with a gold seal but a framed enlargement of her photograph set on an easel in the lobby of the hospital.

29

TO the great relief of the acting CEO of the Mary Starbox H[ospital], a Dr. Moses Williams, the "state police command cent[er]" was being dismantled and would soon be resuming its everyd[ay] identity as an all-purpose meeting room. Even better, by the e[ve]ning of Saturday, the twenty-second of September, the hosp[ital] would be free of the noxious presence of the police, leaving o[nly] its own security team and those deputies guarding the rooms [of] Clare Mitchner and Stella Dugan. George Fitts had spent lo[ng] hours overseeing the removal of computers, printers, teleph[one] cables, the fax machine, tape recorders, and other such impe[di]menta that are part of an on-site homicide investigation. Now [it] was time, much as he regretted sharing any information, to ha[ve] a conference with some of the leading players—not includi[ng,] George told himself thankfully, Mrs. Thomas Clancy.

The meeting for this affair was to be held at 11 A.M. a[nd] maintained only a few vestiges of its former investigatory atm[o]sphere. There was now only a tape recorder sitting on George['s] makeshift table/desk, which had been cleared of all extras exce[pt] the sergeant's notebook and a pad of yellow lined paper. A nu[m]ber of office chairs, plus the comfortable wing chair, had not [

been returned to their places of origin and these were arranged in a semicircle. George in his hospitality persona had arranged for coffee, juice, and a variety of sweet rolls to be sent in. Outside, a steady rain was sliding down the windows.

Alex and Mike Laaka arrived first, Mike looking rested, Alex with circles under his eyes and a frown fixed like a permanent mark over his eyes.

"George must be on medication," observed Mike, looking over the spread of food and drink. "He used to like to starve us."

"George," said Alex, "is this an apology in case you screwed up somewhere?"

George hoisted a coffee cup in greeting and then asked whether Sarah was coming.

"I assume so," said Alex in a restrained voice, his frown deepening.

"Hey," said Mike. "Are you guys on the outs? Because of Sarah's open-door policy? Make that open car-door policy."

"We've had a discussion," said Alex. "I was so relieved that she didn't have a concussion, that she was actually still alive, not lying in a ditch or thrown into a ravine, that I went overboard. Started arguing. Shouting. I lost it. And she lost it. And now, just because she won't take a reasonable view of self-protection, she thinks—"

"Thinks you're a self-satisfied, overbearing bastard," said Sarah, walking into the room. "But," she added, looking brightly at George, "don't let what I think change your opinion of the man."

George raised his eyebrows slightly and then picked up his notebook. "Sarah, satisfy an old friend's curiosity . . ."

"Friend?" said Sarah.

"Of long-standing," said George. "But you won't admit it. Now, you've told us, more or less, about your abduction. Your escape and driving off in Stella Dugan's car. But what made you suddenly head for the hospital?"

"We picked her up speeding and tailed her to the hospital," said Mike. "Driving like a madwoman."

"Or like Stella," put in Alex.

Sarah gave him a hard look and then turned back to Georg[e]. "Two things. I'd called the farm and heard that Julia was at t[he] hospital. I thought she might have had another heart attack, s[o] got going. And something else finally hit me. Something I shou[ld] have gotten at once. I've had animals on the brain, but nothi[ng] seemed to make sense. There was Clare Mitchner calling the b[ig] Belgian horse she sometimes rode Popcorn. Popcorn said 'whit[e]' to me, and Belgians are chestnut. But Aunt Julia talked me o[ut] of that. Said animal names never made sense. Which they don['t]. And then there was Stella's dog. Which turned out not to be h[er] dog at all. Probably borrowed for the occasion to prove to t[he] police that she had a legitimate alibi for Florence Littlefield's mu[r]-der. But also, there was Clare's other animal, her Irish wolfhoun[d]. She said she'd been heartbroken when he died at fourteen. [I] should have asked someone besides Stella if he existed. Me thin[k]-ing Stella could be a reliable informant was crazy. Stupid. I ju[st] thought how nice that Clare and I shared a love of Irish wo[lf]-hounds. I didn't catch her lie until I saw one of Aunt Julia's sette[rs] limping and heard David Bergman lamenting his Saint Bernar[d] who died, as he said, 'all too soon.' And I thought about Pats[y] and it hit me. Big dogs don't live long. Lucky if they make it t[o] ten. Maybe eleven. But not to fourteen, which is when Clare sai[d] her dog died."

"Except inventing a wolfhound was dumb," said Mike. "I sup[-] pose she made up the dog so you two would have something i[n] common."

Sarah nodded. "It worked. I was distracted by the fact sh[e] was so friendly, wanting advice on handling Aunt Julia. I real[ly] liked her. But all the time she's been lying right to my face."

"Clare is a clever lady," said George almost with regret. "Tha[t] business of coming to us to say she'd tried to help Dr. Jonatha[n] when his car wouldn't start. Saying she'd had him in her car unt[il] he changed his mind and got out. That would take care of la[te] evidence that would show he'd been sitting on the seat. Nic[e] work. Only Katie was on to it when she said it was a preemptiv[e] strike. Then we've got Stella as Clare's co-worker." Here h[e] looked over at Sarah. "We've all made mistakes. Missed things.["]

"I don't believe I've heard that remark," said Mike, grinning.

"For instance," said George, "we should probably have paid more attention to what Julia Clancy had to say about her night-time attack. Not listened to the medical babble about post-surgical hallucinations. And we have her to thank for remembering the watches. The small silver metal watch narrowed the suspect list down to women. And the ID with a fuzzy-haired redhead, I didn't put that one together. Stella, as a volunteer, wasn't on the floor that night; she'd gone home. So Clare must have used Stella's ID tag."

"My God," said Mike. "We're getting confessions from the great one. Sergeant Fitts, we'll have to arrange absolution and have you do penance."

George raised a clenched fist at Mike and then picked up his notebook. "Time to get back to the first murder," he announced. "See how much of it falls into place."

"Meaning facts?" asked Mike. "Or are we allowing a small breathing space for people's motives, wild stuff like that?"

"Start at the beginning," said George, "take it where it goes, but not too far into space. I don't think Stella Dugan's mental state is at the bottom of the business."

"But the three murders couldn't have come off without her," objected Sarah.

"Perhaps we'll find out," said George. "She wants to talk to us. In fact, she threw a temper tantrum down in the psychiatric section when they suggested that, in her psychologist's words, it would be "counterproductive to her sense of well-being.""

"We need Katie Waters here because she's really into the stuff," said Mike. "Katie'd make sure we don't upset Stella's sense of well-being."

"And Stella's lawyer is very unhappy. She won't let him sit in on the meeting."

"But you'll read her rights to her, have her agree to being taped," said Mike.

"Correct," said George. "But back to Friday, August seven-teenth. Mike, you like to talk, so you kick off. Alex, Sarah, speak up when you need to. But only if you need to."

"He's saying," put in Mike, "that he wishes you were some where else. Like on Mars. But, okay. Here's how it went. The night before the seventeenth, Dr. Henry Philips falls downstairs, gets a neighbor to take him to the hospital. Walks into the ER under his own steam. Even all bruised up, he must have been recognized— at least by the older medical people, because he'd been a big cheese once. Anyway, he waits his turn in the ER madhouse. Not the way the guy usually behaved, but he's old, not up to par. Obviously, Clare Mitchner saw him. Or Stella Dugan. Someone from that family group, anyway. Told each other. It's a chance Clare's been waiting for. But why after all these years? That really bugged me until I was put straight about his wife acting as body guard and driver."

"And maybe," put in Sarah, unable to stay quiet, "this was the first and best opportunity Clare's had. The man who killed her little sister. Something may have finally boiled over in her brain and she can't resist. He's available, he's battered, so he won't put up a fight, and the ER is wild. So get him alone and just do it."

"Let's stick to what we know," said George. "Speculate later on why."

"The 'why' part is easy when you think about Althea," Sarah retorted.

"Wait on that," said Mike. "Take Julia next. She has a heart attack, is brought into the ER, is stashed in an examining alcove next to Dr. Philips, who's sitting on a stool in there. He's wearing street clothes and must have been wheeled in by persons un known."

"Or people known," said Sarah. "Clare or Stella. The murder team."

"Let Mike go on," said Alex, and received a glare from Sarah.

Mike nodded. "There's a gap in the curtains between exam ining bays and Julia sees him, enough of him to describe though she never knew him personally. And she saw a wheelchair. Then the curtains are pulled, Philips is led out or wheeled out to the john. And is strangled. Julia later saw a gurney go by that might have had a body on it. There you have it. Murder numero uno."

"All the usual suspects were in and around the ER that day," Alex reminded them.

"Claude Raines," said Sarah. *"Casablanca."*

"Whoever," said Mike. "But it was hell to sort out."

"Fortunately," said George, "we next had the attack on Julia."

"I don't think Aunt Julia would have said 'fortunately,' " said Sarah.

"From an investigative point of view," responded George.

"Is there any other view for you, George?" asked Alex.

"Touché on you, George," said Mike. "Okay, the Monday when Julia's being wheeled to surgery, she blabs about someone she's seen in the ER. People passing by hear her. The news gets spread around."

"Like anthrax," said Sarah.

"Right," said Alex. He turned to Sarah. "Sometimes we agree, you know."

Sarah gave Alex a small acknowledging nod. "Julia practically arranged the attack on herself. Then afterward she couldn't convince the hospital people she hadn't had a post-surgical nightmare, so she pulled out all stops to be moved. Pretended that Uncle Tom died in room nine and she was being haunted."

"And Clare Mitchner was on that floor. Ever helpful. And had easy access to the surgical look," said Alex. "Mask, cap, gown, and paper booties."

"And a strong right arm," added Mike.

"My new best friend. And Julia's buddy," said Sarah regretfully.

"And I was going to ask her out," said Mike. "She looked like my type."

"I might have enjoyed arresting you for collusion," said George dryly.

"But where was Stella during the two attacks on room nine?" asked Sarah.

"Stella may answer that," said George. "Now get some more coffee, eat up, and I'll put a call into psychiatry for her. She's apparently dying to talk."

"Nice remark," said Alex. He stood up, walked over to the food table and poured himself a fresh cup of coffee. Where he was joined by Sarah. Under the cover of a Danish held near her face, Sarah whispered, "All right. Okay. Peace?"

"Peace is good," said Alex. "I'd like to give it a try."

"Peace is a two-way business. With no lectures included," said Sarah. "So it's a truce? Covenant, treaty?"

"You want my signature on that?"

"Buying me dinner at some classy joint might take care of it."

"Sold," said Alex. He turned to Mike, who arrived with an empty cup. "We've decided to remain a duo."

"For the time being," said Sarah.

"An investigative duo?" asked Mike, filling his cup.

Sarah grinned. "Don't ask, don't tell."

George came over, chose a small cracker, placed it neatly into his mouth and snapped down. And then waved the others to their seats. "Stella will be along in about five minutes. I have a report from the psychiatrist who's been assigned to her. Dr. Chen. First, you should know she's on medication. Not too strong, more in the nature of an antidepressive. It won't interfere with our talk."

"What do you mean by 'talk?'" asked Mike. "Are you going to crunch her?"

"I don't crunch. And it's Stella Dugan's moment. Which she wants to handle in her own way."

She certainly did, thought Sarah, watching Stella Dugan's entrance. The pleased half-smile Sarah had seen so often now seemed fixed on her face like a mask.

Stella had had her hair newly shaped, the frizz colored a deeper red, wore eye shadow, lip gloss, the whole face a tribute to the cosmetic industry. Certainly she, and possibly one of the aides in the psychiatry department, had taken great pains with her appearance. It was just as if she'd been made up for a talk show, Sarah decided. The famous person putting the awed interviewers at ease.

"Well, hello," said Stella, walking into the room. And then, seeing the coffee jug, the cups, the sweet rolls, widened her smile.

"Look there. All that's fit to eat. Do you mind?" And without waiting for an answer, walked over to the table, helped herself to a cup of coffee, a cinnamon roll, and a napkin.

"Sit here, Mrs. Dugan," said George, rising and moving the wing chair into front and center and shoving a small table next to it.

"Oh, call me Stella," said the guest of honor, taking her place and placing the coffee and the roll beside her on the table. "For when the going gets rough," she explained. "Then I need food."

"I hope," said George soberly, "we won't make things that uncomfortable."

Stella rewarded him with a broadened smile. "Oh, Sergeant Fitts, you are *so* tense. I think a little yoga might do wonders for your type of person. Okay, gang." Here Stella looked around at the group and acknowledged Sarah with a brief salute.

"My late hostage," she explained. "Clare's, too. But I put Clare out of the picture, didn't I, so I'll accept the honor."

"Mrs. Dugan . . . Stella," said George. "I am going to read you your rights and have you sign this paper acknowledging that you waive the right to have your attorney present. And that you agree to having your statements tape-recorded."

"Oh, sure, why not, let's make a day of it," said Stella with that familiar wavering giggle, a giggle that now seemed to Sarah to be teetering at the edge of hysteria."

George proceeded to wind up the legal duties involved with Stella's appearance. Then he leaned back, lowered his voice into an almost kindly tone. "Why," he said, "don't you start with a little of your background. Then fill us in on some of the events that took place in the last five or six weeks in the hospital. Your part in them. Or ones you had knowledge of."

"Events? You mean murder and gore and things that went bump in the night?" said Stella.

Good Lord, thought Sarah, she's even funny. I never saw it before.

"Anything you want to say," encouraged Mike.

Stella reached over, took a long sip of coffee, bit down on her roll, and washed it down with another drink of coffee. Replaced the cup on the table and leaned back in her chair, her hands folded on her lap.

"At the beginning," said Stella, "I was always Miss Good Girl. Goody Two-Shoes, if you're old enough to know who she was. "Never mind"—seeing George and Mike go blank—"It means I did what I was told. Always. You name it, I did it."

And so the story rolled. Honor Girl Scout, Perfect Ten at camp inspection for five weeks at Camp Merrilark. Class Secretary, Social Honor Cup. As a childless wife, then widow, the always available baby-sitter. Godmother to Althea.

"Make that fairy godmother to the whole Mitchner family," said Stella, her voice turning harsh. "Couldn't live without me, they always said. Auntie Stella who knitted such wonderful sweaters and mittens and made Christmas stockings. Auntie Stella who took the children to the mall. To the movies. Who held Althea and fed Althea and medicated Althea, and changed Althea's diapers while they all went off for a day skiing or camping. Got dinner for everyone when they came back too tired to cook themselves."

"And you resented this?" asked George, who liked to come to the point and summarize the obvious.

"No," said Stella, surprisingly. "It was the way it was. From the beginning. I liked being liked. I loved Althea. My baby, I called her. Which she was part of the time. So I didn't mind being part of a family who needed me. Not until . . ." Stella hesitated. The listeners waited. And waited.

"Not until?" Sarah prompted.

"You ought to know," said Stella. "You and your Aunt Julia. I had signed up. For the duration."

"Signed up?" said Alex, puzzled. He rose from his chair, restless as usual, and walked to the window, stared at the streaks of rain and turned back. "What do you mean?"

"Like the army," suggested Mike. "You were recruited and you 'signed up.'"

"I was the enlisted person. And my boss had an action plan. Which I didn't have anything to do with. At least in the very beginning. Clare, the whole family, had always talked about how they'd love to see the end of old Dr. Philips. I don't know if they meant murder or just hoped he'd die. Nothing came of it, of course. Just talk, I thought. And what with his wife always around, no real opportunity. Until that day when the ER was boiling over. And old Philips just sitting there."

"Waiting to be choked," put in Mike again.

"I guess so. He was a real mess, all bruised black and blue. Clare pointed him out and told me to get him into an examining bay and tell him to wait. I had my smock, I was known by him to be a volunteer, everyone was used to me coming and going. So I did it. Easy. Even though I don't do the heavy pushing, I could have wheeled a gorilla through the crowd that day and no one would have noticed. And he wasn't heavy. I left him in the bay, got him to sit on a stool. But I didn't notice there was a gap in the curtains. Pulled them closed as soon as I saw. But later, through the hospital gossip, I hear about Julia Clancy getting a peek. But it all went as if Clare had been planning it for days. She wheeled him into the men's john and did the job. And was back on the floor in a few minutes. She's speedy and she's got strong arms, good thumbs."

"The better to strangle," murmured Sarah.

"Yes," said Stella. "But when Clare found out about Julia sounding off, it worried her. Time to shut her up. It was supposed to be easy, Julia being in the Cardiac ICU where Clare was working. She wore my ID card which was okay because Julia didn't know me. The face wouldn't mean anything."

Sarah shook her head. "Aunt Julia remembered enough about the ID. She said she got a glimpse of it when she was attacked."

"We hadn't figured on that. Anyway, Clare botched the job and a code went off."

"So she tried again," prompted Mike.

"Yes, it worked the second time. Only on the wrong woman. Clare told me later that Florence Littlefield could have been Mrs. Clancy's twin. She didn't know about the bed switch because she'd been on break when it happened. You see Clare wanted me to hang around the hospital and come up before midnight and be a lookout on the floor. Wear a scrub shirt or my regular jacket, and if anyone asks what I'm doing say I'm delivering a message, checking on a friend. Whatever."

"So you kept an eye on room nine?" asked Sarah.

"To give Clare an all-clear when visitors had gone and the staff was busy or working with charts. I never thought about Julia being moved because everyone said she'd tried and been refused. Besides, I saw Sarah go into room nine to spend the night, and that was proof enough that her aunt was in there."

"I certainly thought she was," said Sarah.

"Which made you the second witness we had to deal with," said Stella resentfully. "First Julia, then you. But we didn't know if you'd really seen anything. Clare tried to quiz you on it, but you weren't sure about what you saw. Or didn't see."

Sarah looked regretful. "I never was sure. But how did walking a dog fit in?"

"Sometimes I dog-sit Patches. Clare thought he'd be useful as a cover story for where I was that night. Then I had to go and borrow Patches again in case you came back to nose around my house. But I gave him back too soon, so he wasn't there when you were hiding behind the quince tree. And Sarah, you really bugged me, coming around like that."

Sarah nodded in acknowledgment. "I gathered that," she said. "But things weren't making sense. I was eaten up with curiosity."

"You can say that again," remarked Alex softly.

"Watch it, you," said Sarah to him. Then to Stella: "The driving. Like a wild woman. Lincolnville Beach. Mount Battie. What was going on?"

In a moment Stella became absolutely still. As if she'd drunk some kind of evil potion. Her face changed. Under its immaculate makeup it began to redden. Her lips moved. Her body tensed. Her hands turned into fists.

"I was sick. Sick right to the bottom of my gut of being used. Like I was someone's maid. Good old Stella who's always willing. The family nana. The little engine that could." Now her voice turned harsh, a higher pitch. "Clare was always at me. 'Do this. Do that. Don't do this. Don't do that.' I asked her to quit when she was ahead. But she's a sort of, what do they call it, an over-achiever. So I got roped into doing more stuff. Helping with old Dr. Philips was one thing. He deserved his. But then she has to attack Julia Clancy, screws that up, then she kills the wrong woman because . . . and this I absolutely love . . . because Clare said I hadn't bothered to check new Cardiac ICU room assignments, so I didn't tell her about the room switch."

"Well, I certainly didn't know." put in Sarah.

"I've been Clare's Girl Friday, but she went too far. Killing Jonathan Philips wasn't part of any plan. He wasn't a threat. He was no prize, and he didn't ground his grandfather when he should have. But he wasn't the one who killed Althea. I've been so stressed out. I'd always taken my car out to work off how I felt, and this business of being a sort of a murder aide was really getting to me. I had to back up anything Clare had said. Like the color of the horse she used to ride. Saying she had an Irish wolf-hound when what she actually had was a little mixed-breed thing. Next, you know what?"

"No," said Sarah, to whom the question seemed to be addressed. "What?"

"I was told to dispose of the tire iron. It was from Clare's car, for that four-wheel drive of hers. I was supposed to help get rid of the evidence, wrap it in a beach-umbrella bag. No one would notice. Clare'd already dumped Dr. Jonathan's briefcase and wallet and other stuff into Lake Megunticook, but wanted me to finish the job. It wouldn't be safe for dear niece Clare. But who would suspect sweet old Auntie Stella dropping it off somewhere in the Camden Hills, into some old marsh or pond."

"But you chose Lincolnville Beach. And Mount Battie," said Sarah.

Stella raised her fists and pounded them on the arms of her chair. "You bet your goddamn boots I did. I wanted a public scene. I didn't care anymore about me. I wanted Clare to be caught. I'd drop the evidence where anyone could find it. And if I got caught, well, she would be, too. I even hoped I'd get nailed speeding with the tire iron sitting on the front seat next to me and I'd say it was Clare's. But all I got was you following me around. But that was okay, I knew you'd tell the police about it."

"Which is what happened," put in Alex.

"For all the good it did," said Stella bitterly. "Now I was number-one suspect. Thanks to Sarah. And no one was thinking about Clare Mitchner. Then Clare dreams up a new one. Sarah might start remembering about the Florence Littlefield scene, and besides, she was becoming a pest. Clare would hide out in the back of her car, pull a blanket over herself. Knock her out, stick a needle in her. Drive her off somewhere."

"So Clare was the person in the back of Sarah's car at the English office parking lot," said Alex. "She ran like a track star."

Stella sighed. "But botched it again. You almost caught her. It seemed easy because Sarah leaves her car open. Clare didn't even have to break in."

Alex opened his mouth, looked over at Sarah. And closed his mouth.

Stella took a deep breath. Now her voice was steadier, her face harder. "I was part of the last act. Clare wanted to try the car thing again. After dark she hid in the back of Sarah's Subaru parked at the Sawmill Road house. She was lucky Alex just locked the thing and didn't do a real search when he came home. He left early in the A.M., and then Sarah came out in the morning to drive to work. There was a heavy fog and she couldn't see that I was down the road waiting. I'd slipped out very early and that security guard didn't catch me. Anyway, when Sarah started off, I got going and drove at her as if we're going to crash. She stopped. I stopped. Got out, trying to look friendly. Sarah looked at me."

"That's all I remember," murmured Sarah.

"Clare hoped you wouldn't remember much. Anyway, Clare, from the back of the car, reaches over, bangs you on the head, knocks you out with a big paperweight, gets the thiopental into your arm. Then Clare drives you to the old family cottage, which is miles off the beaten track. Makes me warden while Her Majesty Clare goes off to work and tries to figure out a way of getting rid of you. Probably I'd be the lucky one to deal with your dead body."

"So you tied me up on the bed until Clare came back?" asked Sarah.

"I was going to feed you and I did leave water for you."

"For which I thank you," said Sarah.

"Clare drove your Subaru to a cabin owned by some friend who's back in New Jersey. On Lermond Pond in Hope. We'd left her own car there for her to pick up before I dropped her off to hide in Sarah's car. For all I know, it might still be there."

Again Sarah nodded, although she almost hoped the Subaru would stay missing; it had more than a hundred and ninety thousand miles on it. Perhaps a new Subaru Outback . . .

"I thought I'd done a good job tying you up with that dog leash and toweling," Stella's voice, still agitated, had begun to sound shaky. Her reddened face had faded into pallor.

"You did," said Sarah. "It took real work to get loose."

"After I finished with that, I turned up at the hospital for a few volunteer hours, then lost my security tail at the mall. Which was easy. Next I headed back to the cottage with a filled syringe Clare had given me in case of trouble. More thiopental. But while I was gone, Sarah, you got loose. I got a bloody nose and you went off in my car. That's it. But now I've had it. Period. It's over. I'm thinking after Sarah drove off, that Clare is—what do the children say? Clare is toast. Dead meat."

Again a pause, Stella's eyes now fixed at a distant point on the wall, as if Clare actually stood in the room. Then she almost whispered. "Clare won't be able to go on because I can't go on. This worm turned. You know what happened. Julia Clancy has a late date in the cardiac rehab room. And Clare's working there on an afternoon–early evening shift. She'd told me once that the rehab scene would give her another chance at taking care of Julia. Clare was really over the edge by now."

Both of them over the edge, Sarah told herself.

Stella turned angrily to George, then to Mike. "Even though Sarah grabbed my car, there was the old Ford old pickup in the shed. It started up and I just made it. There they were. Clare on top of Julia Clancy."

Here Stella's voice rose again. "I didn't give a damn anymore

365

about killing Julia. But Clare? I just couldn't wait. I wasn't going to be tied anymore to her plans. She was going to get me killed. I just wanted to get her first. As fast as I could. I was—"

Stella stopped in midsentence. The room was absolutely quiet except for Stella's breathing, which had almost become a gasp. Her hands rolled back into fists. Mike half-rose in his chair, Alex took a step away from the window, both ready to act.

But Stella wasn't finished. She stood up. Swayed slightly, then planted her feet. Spoke again, rushing, almost garbling her words. "My life has turned into one big pile of shit. I've been used like a rug to walk on. Like someone's rotten no-good lousy old slime who's only good for hauling trash. But dear helpful sweet thoughtful Aunt Stella, winner of the High School Social Honor Cup, left her mark on Clare, and now she's going to leave her mark on all you rotten crawling police people. All you lousy sneaking—"

Stella stopped speaking and suddenly pushed herself out of the chair, walked unsteadily over to the table with the coffee, and before anyone could stop her, took hold of the tray with both hands, and hurled it directly at George Fitts, crockery spinning in all directions, muffins and rolls airborne, the coffee carafe smashing down, emptying a pool of coffee on the carpet.

George ducked, Mike leaped, grabbed at Stella, who whirled and slammed her fist in his face. Alex jumped forward from the window, one arm reaching for Stella. Stella dodged under, got past Sarah's outstretched hand, and stumbled to the door.

Where she grasped the door handle and burst into wild choking sobs. And where she was captured by George Fitts. Who, with one arm held her close against his chest, patted her back with his other hand, saying softly, "There, there, Stella. It's going to be all right. It's going to be all right."

Then George turned her gently around, and holding her arm in his, led her toward the door and out into the hospital corridor.

For a moment there was absolute silence in the meeting room. Then Mike Laaka wiped the trickle of blood coming from his mouth and shook his head slowly in amazement. "Well, I'll be goddamned. I'll be goddamned."

Alex walked over to Sarah, who was staring at the open door.

He took her hand in his, looked down into her face, and said softly, "Time to go."

"Where?" said Sarah, looking around.

"Home. Let's go home."

| Saw Mill Road |

Afterword

High Hope Farm

Training-Boarding
Equitation

JULIA Clancy was planning an event. Not, as she noted to the recipients of the invitation, an "event" as in heart attack, amputation, stroke, or automobile accident. This event would involve friends, food, and the bringing together of a few of those persons whose lives had been entangled in the recent goings-on at the Mary Starbox Memorial Hospital. And, she had added in her telephone message, there would be a surprise affair that involved certain members of the High Hope Farm community. To Sarah Julia said, be sure to bring Patsy. And his leash.

"What on earth is she up to?" demanded Alex, always suspicious of Julia's plans, especially those that involved a "surprise."

"It can't be all bad if it includes Patsy," said Sarah, ruffling the stiff gray hair of her large friend. "But why the leash? I always let him run loose at the farm."

It was the twenty-ninth of September, seven days after the autumnal equinox. The leaves flamed red and yellow along the roads and ridges of Union, Maine, and the air was clear with a slight chill suggesting that summer would soon become a distant memory.

Julia, with the help of Patrick, his wife Mary, and her assistant stable manager, Rafe Posner, had arranged for a picnic table and a number of chairs to be placed just above the lower stable on a patch of lawn. From there, guests had a fine view of two paddocks and a number of fenced pastures. Julia was looking fit, her color healthy, and for the day she had chosen her best dungarees, had polished her farm boots, and was sporting a new red fleece jacket. This last was a gift from the hospital management as an apology to a patient who had been violently attacked by a nurse in ICU Unit number 9 and later in the cardiac rehab facility, and who afterward had let it be known that she did not intend to file a lawsuit. Julia, however, did mention that a contribution from the hospital management to the local humane society might be a welcome gesture.

Sarah and Alex, arriving some few minutes past the appointed hour of four, discovered a number of familiar faces. Katie Waters and Mike Laaka sat together on a wooden bench enjoying drinks from a dark and evil-looking punch bowl that sat next to the tea and coffee urns on the food-laden picnic table. George Fitts had been invited, Mike told them, but a possible homicide had surfaced in Thomaston and he had been called out. Standing next to Julia were the veteran volunteers, Christie Rivers and David Bergman, busy explaining to each other the value of certain kinds of soil in nurturing potatoes, carrots, and beets. Alex joined them, since he had lately decided that growing root vegetables might be a worthwhile and distracting project—for one member of the family, anyway. Beyond these people, Sarah could see another arrival coming down the path: an innocent member of the Mitchner clan, Hannah Finch, dressed that afternoon in a blue knitted sweater with chickadees, the Maine state bird.

Sarah turned to her aunt. "How did you persuade Hannah Finch to come today? Her family is in shreds."

"I'm glad she came," said Julia. "Proves she's tough. Besides, I told her she was our friend, and I wouldn't cooperate with the cardiac rehab program if she wasn't around to keep me behaving myself. She's a good nurse and the hospital needs her. She didn't have anything to do with the Clare-Stella operation."

This said, Julia took Sarah by the arm and brought her over to Katie Waters and Mike Laaka. "Confession," she announced, "is good for the soul."

"Where'd you pick that one up?" said Mike. "Don't tell me, Julia, that you're about to go on another guilt trip.

"It's an old Scottish proverb," said Julia. "And I do have a genuine confession. Even if it's too late. I told Sarah we'd work together and I'd keep my ear open for anything that would help solve the case. And I did. Well, beside the watch-sighting and the ID tag, there's something else. Not good. One particular thing Sarah was interested in was why Clare Mitchner had called a chestnut-colored Belgian draft horse she used to ride Popcorn." I told Sarah to forget it, animal names often don't make sense. But one day—it just came out of my mouth—I asked Clare when she was finished with a riding lesson, 'Why did you choose that name?' And she said because he was white. I didn't say anything, but I checked around and found that her uncle had indeed kept Belgian draft horses and they were not a mixed breed and they were chestnut. She probably did ride some horse somewhere which was white. But not a Belgian."

"She lied," said Mike, summing it up.

"Through her teeth," said Sarah. "Just like her imaginary wolf-hound living to fourteen. But I might not have listened to you because when I last mentioned the horse and dog thing to the volunteer group, Stella spoke up and backed all Clare's stories. Not with any great enthusiasm, maybe, but I was convinced. Then the subject was changed and I let it go. But now, thinking back, it was as if Stella was waiting for the question, had been told to be ready for it. Which she admitted. But, of course, no one knew she was working as Clare's aide-de-camp."

"No details until her confession. Or breakdown," put in Mike.

"Well, I should have done something about it," said Julia. "But the story was so old, Clare had been just a child when she rode the horse. Some horse. Besides, she and I were getting along so well that I just put it off. You see, she was showing signs that she might turn into a remarkable horsewoman, which is very rare, believe me. The sort of student riding instructors dream of. End of my confession. Except maybe I'm responsible for getting Dr. Jonathan Philips killed. As well as Florence Littlefield."

"Listen, Julia," said Mike sternly. "No more of that. The hospital should have made an effort to move your bed much earlier. They, all of us, were too hung up on the idea of you being out of your head. And everyone's sorry as hell about the murders. Bad things just fell into place, one after the other. But it's over. Done with. And Clare will be facing murder charges, three counts, as soon as she's well enough to show up in court."

"I should probably apologize for lousing up the whole Stella scene. Following her around the way I did," said Sarah ruefully. "Tipping her over the edge."

Mike shook his head. "She was already on her way over that edge. You might have given her a nudge, but it was going to happen anyway. As it did when she blew up in front of us. Niece Clare was the mover and shaker-up. Of Stella, anyway. The catalyst."

"What *is* going to happen to Stella?" asked Sarah.

"She'll probably be admitted to some sort of institution, get a psychiatric evaluation, have a treatment program started. Later on, if she's judged fit, she'll stand trial. Probably as an accessory to murder. And for her attack on Clare. Intent to inflict bodily harm. Ironically, it's in her interest to stay wacko."

Katie Waters reached over and punched Mike, hard, on the arm. "If you go around saying things like 'wacko,' I'll see that you're committed to some awful place for really wacko people."

"You tell him, Katie," said Sarah.

And then: "Looks like there's going to be a parade." She pointed to the pasture above the stable. Down the grassy slope came Patrick, his hands holding the leads of the black mare, Pale Lady, and Julia's pride and joy, the big gelding Duffie. And following Patrick, a tall, familiar figure leading the pony Gingersnap."

Julia raised a hand and called her guests to attention. "You're here because lately we've had a lot in common. And many of you have put up with a great deal from me. As you've learned, I don't behave well in a hospital setting—or a police one—so this is a way of saying thanks for your patience. Don't worry, I'm not having a personality change, and if I'm sent back to the hospital again, I'll probably be twice as nasty. But first we have our event. Then it's food and drink."

She lifted her head as a dark old Buick sedan drove up toward the front of the farmhouse and two figures, one in navy blue, the other gray slowly emerged and began the cautious descent down the path. Her mother, Mrs. Anthony Douglas, and the faithful Hopkins.

And Sarah, following Julia's gaze, saw, trotting obediently along beside Hopkins, in a bright red collar, the terrier Patches an animal belonging to Clare Mitchner but last seen barking behind Stella Dugan's backyard fence.

"There they are," said Julia. "With their new dog. His name is Patches. His owner is no longer able to take care of him. I think he's part Jack Russell. Hopkins has been working on obedience and there is no dog born that would dare disobey Hopkins."

With which Mike and Alex went up the path to greet the two ladies, assisted them to settle in two Adirondack chairs, and spread tartan rugs over their knees. And then Hopkins raised a forefinger, pointed at the dog, and said firmly, "Down! No bark!" With which Patches collapsed on the ground and put his muzzle between his paws.

"Mother has needed a new dog for a long time," said Julia pleased. "Now, Sarah, bring Patsy down here. Mike, please you go and get Tucker and Belle. Their leashes are beside the door of their dog run."

Then, like someone conducting an unruly orchestra, Julia moved through her guests, urging them to settle down, sit. And listen. The event was about to begin.

Advancing on the guests led by Patrick, Rafe Posner, and a number of working students, came a procession of horses, each burnished, each mane combed and silky: Duffie; the pony Gingersnap; the black mare, Pale Lady; the school horses, Duncan Conkey, Leto, Scarlet (who was gray), Bongo, Cinnamon (who was not cinnamon-colored), and last, Angelina, her new foal beside her, and all the other residents of stable and pasture, including an ancient mule named Jimbo.

"Front and center, dogs." called Julia. And Sarah with Patsy Mike and Katie with the two English setters, and Hopkins with Patches came forward.

And then, from the door of the barn, in full ecclesiastical robes, strode the man who Sarah felt had sprung god-like from the islands of the South Pacific, but in fact had been born in Port Clyde, Maine. Father Joshua Stevenson.

"Father Stevenson," announced Julia, "will now conduct a blessing of the animals."

Sarah couldn't afterward remember much of the service. There were biblical references to animals, something from Genesis about the beasts of the earth and the fowls of the air, and bits from Job, including the part about the horse with his neck clothed with thunder, and then, after an anointing—or was it a sprinkling? Sarah couldn't see clearly—of the equine and canine participants, there was ragged but enthusiastic singing of "All Creatures Great and Small."

Julia, after shaking hands with Joshua Stevenson, brought him over to her mother, where Sarah and Patsy joined them.

"That was very nice, very nice indeed," said Mrs. Douglas. "I'm sure it did Patches good. He has not had a proper upbringing." She turned to Julia. "Does this mean . . ." She hesitated. "Does this ceremony mean . . ."

"No, Mother," said Julia. "It doesn't mean that I'm going to start going to church. But I think that animals need all the help they can get, and, as far as I can see, blessing them won't do a bit of harm."

Mrs. Douglas turned to Father Stevenson for help.

He nodded, grinned at Julia, reached over and rubbed Patches under his chin. "I've never known a blessing to injure an animal. Or," he added, "any of the humans involved."

Acknowledgments

Again, many thanks for my medical watchdogs, Mac and Rob who have tried to keep me from literary malpractice. Errors in dealing with hospital procedures and events are on my head, no theirs.